WALKING THROUGH FIRE

A Misbegotten Novel

SHERRI COOK WOOSLEY

Talos Press

First Edition

This is a work of fiction. Names, characters, places, and incidents are either the products of the author's imagination or used fictitiously.

Talos Press books may be purchased in bulk at special discounts for sales promotion, corporate gifts, fund-raising, or educational purposes. Special editions can also be created to specifications. For details, contact the Special Sales Department, Talos Press, 307 West 36th Street, 11th Floor, New York, NY 10018 or info@skyhorsepublishing.com.

Talos Press® is a registered trademark of Skyhorse Publishing, Inc.®, a Delaware corporation. Visit our website at www.talospress.com.

10 9 8 7 6 5 4 3 2 1

Names: Woosley, Sherri Cook, author.
Title: Walking through fire : a misbegotten novel / Sherri Cook Woosley.
Description: First edition. | New York, NY : Talos Press, 2018. |
Identifiers: LCCN 2018014029 (print) | LCCN 2018016654 (ebook) | ISBN 9781945863349
    (ebook) | ISBN 9781945863332 (hardcover : alk. paper)
Classification: LCC PS3623.O728 (ebook) | LCC PS3623.O728 W35 2018 (print) |
    DDC 813/.6—dc23
LC record available at https://lccn.loc.gov/2018014029

Cover design by Mona Lin
Cover illustration courtesy of Jeff Chapman

Printed in the United States of America

To my son, I didn't forget you for one moment.

And

To all the Mamas out there who have fought, are fighting, and will fight for the mental or physical health of your child. You are strong. You are fierce. You will break and want to quit, but I believe you can put one foot in front of the other.

PART I

FIRESTORM

*Then, a face appeared from inside the havoc
of the fire tornado, wavering with the flickering of flames,
but still recognizable: a dragon's head.*

ONE

Photos spread across the oaken dining room table, but Rachel Deneuve's focus was on the window overlooking the driveway. She knew her son Adam would be mortified if he saw her watching for his return. Worry, a mother's natural instinct, was magnified in Rachel by the cancer cells made deep in Adam's bone marrow and held in check only by thirty months of grueling chemo. She wanted Adam safe and she wanted him home. From outside, a sustained rumble of thunder sounded a warning, the heavens ripping open with an anguished groan like a woman with birthing pains.

With a determined air, Rachel turned away from the window and the sounds of the summer storm toward her project: coloring in the phoenix at the top of the scrapbook page. The firebird's long tail feathers flowed down the side, framing the photo of baby Adam first brought home from the hospital. Adam was eleven now, so she was years behind on this project, but this seemed the right time to create a graphic story of their family—before the details became muddled. In light of the separation, the responsibility to be fair was heavy across her shoulders. As if she should count each time she or Craig appeared in a photo and the tally should be exactly even. It complicated the job of chronicling from Adam's birth, through his cancer treatment, and into their new formation, whatever that would turn out to be.

The pencil's red tip broke with a snapping sound. She'd pushed too hard. Irritated, Rachel threw down the pencil and shoved a strand of thick hair back behind her ear. Her bangs were cut straight across to draw attention to her large eyes, but right now the sensation of hair touching forehead was annoying. Everything was annoying. She wanted to take a shower and go to bed, but didn't want to be in pajamas when Craig dropped off Adam.

Tires rolled over gravel. Finally, they were here. Rachel automatically checked her appearance. Peacock colored tank top under a sheer white shirt, dangling earrings, a flowing skirt and bare feet. Her features were sharp, her neck long, her collar bones jutting. All speaking to a flapper aesthetic from an earlier century in New York City rather than the suburbs of northern Maryland. Craig liked tidy. Rachel resisted the urge to smooth the auburn curls she'd piled into a loose bun and opened the door to her husband and son.

Craig stood with his hand raised as if to knock on the door. Her door? A moment of confusion. This was all new. He was tall, relaxed, wearing a collared shirt. A small scar stretched down the left side of his neck from a childhood accident. Gray-green eyes that seemed to hold so many emotions at once. Nearly just as he'd looked in college when they started dating. More lines on his face, though. Being the parent of a child with cancer had done that to both of them.

"Sorry we're late. Adam wanted to take a shower."

Adam's brown hair was wet. Pale and small for his age, he looked scrawny standing next to Craig. He clutched an overnight bag with both hands. A wet beach towel lay behind his neck, soaking the edges of his T-shirt.

"You took him to the pool?" Rachel tried to keep her tone even, but all she could think was: *You let our immunocompromised son swim in a cesspool of germs.*

Craig rocked back on the balls of his feet. "It's the first official day of summer. Thought it would be fun." He nudged Adam's shoulder. "We had fun, didn't we?"

Adam nodded. He yawned. His eyelids drooped, covering the irises. The color—a thin circle of brown around gray-green—always made Rachel think of Craig's genes and her genes battling it out for dominance. Businessman versus artist, extrovert versus introvert.

A gust of warm wind made Rachel cross her arms over her chest. Branches on the maple trees lining the driveway rubbed against each other with an unsettling creaking.

"I should get Adam in bed."

"Yeah." Craig took a step back. "I'm heading to Boston for work. I'll have my phone."

"This late at night?"

"Any reason not to?" His question was a challenge, both confrontational and hopeful.

Rachel swallowed. Her heart cramped. They needed this break, but it felt so wrong for him to leave. She made a small shaking motion with her head, but couldn't think of anything to say other than, "I can't—"

"We'll talk when I get back," he promised.

She licked dry lips and Craig seemed to take her silence as assent.

Adam brushed past her to get into the house, but Rachel stayed to watch the taillights fade as Craig drove away. The stars looked different tonight, closer to earth, as if blinking an urgent message to the planet below. Atmospheric winds blew away the clouds until a gravid red moon dominated the sky. Rachel shivered, the night sky's vivid colors making her feel unsettled. It was as if, she thought whimsically, the air was vibrating at a frequency beyond human range.

She felt both dizzy and nauseous at once. Rachel recognized the familiar symptoms of an oncoming panic attack. Whether from imagining something horrible happening that had made Adam late, or the conversation with Craig, or the strange moon, it didn't matter.

"Breathe," she coached herself. She leaned against the outside of the door and closed her eyes, counting until her heartbeat slowed and her shoulders relaxed. Taking one more breath, Rachel opened the door and went inside with a fake smile. She needed to be strong for her son.

"Alright, buddy. It's just you and me." Rachel called as she shut and locked the door.

The bright kitchen lights dispelled some of the negative feelings of watching Craig leave, of the strangeness from the outside sky.

Adam was slumped over the kitchen table.

"Come on, no sleeping down here." Rachel put her hand on Adam's back to get him out of the chair.

"I don't feel good."

Adam's forehead burned against the back of Rachel's hand.

"You've got a fever," Rachel said. "I'll call the hospital." She hit the preset on her phone and put it on speaker so she could keep moving. In an oncology patient anything over 101.4 degrees meant an immediate trip to the emergency room. Years of chemo battling his leukemia meant Adam had no immune system to fight bacteria or germs.

Rachel grabbed the overnight bag that stood ready and ripped it open to find a tube of ointment. She helped Adam lean back in the chair and lifted up his shirt to expose the quarter-sized bump under his skin that was a medical port. Rachel squeezed a glob of white onto his chest to numb the spot where the winged needle would go in, covered it with a clear adhesive, and then pulled his shirt down.

Her phone was still ringing; the hospital's service hadn't picked up. That had never happened before, but it didn't matter. She and Adam had been through this drill many times.

Rachel said, "This won't be a long visit." But she moved to the dining room, sweeping photos, the scrapbook, and colored pencils into the emergency bag for herself. Better to be prepared to stay and then sent home than the other way around.

Grabbing her phone and wallet with one hand, Rachel put her other around Adam's waist and helped him out to the car.

"Don't forget the charger. It's in my bookbag," Adam whispered.

"Okay." Rachel left him leaning against the car and rushed back inside. After she'd retrieved the charger and come back to the front door, Rachel's heart sputtered. Adam was gone. A smell was in the air, at once electrifying and strange. The hair on the back of her neck stood at attention. A force gathered, invisible but tangible, and, with a crack, lightning struck the nearby maple tree. The topmost branch burst into flame. In the sudden light, Rachel saw Adam crouched on the ground underneath.

Rushing forward, Rachel threw herself to her knees beside her son. Oblivious to her presence, Adam stared down at his cupped hands. "I caught it. I caught the falling star." Fire reflected from the branch above seemed to glow in Adam's cupped hands, bright as if someone shined a flashlight from beneath them or from within. A disconcerting illusion.

More brusquely than she intended, Rachel pulled Adam to his feet and away from the tree. The branch fell from the tree to the lawn, the flames dying out with rebellious snaps and hisses. Rachel looked up at the deformed tree and kicked at the blackened branch with her booted foot again and again, not wanting to return from the hospital to find her home burned down by a spark in the grass. Her foot tingled and she ground the boot heel to erase the sensation.

Using the wet towel from around Adam's neck, Rachel wadded it into a ball and put it against the window for him to use as a pillow. She started the Ford NewWave with voice recognition and then glanced in the rearview mirror. Adam's cheeks were pink and his lips were chapped. She remembered the countless other times he'd been in this same position from eight years old until now as they'd rushed to the emergency room. She knew Adam better than anyone else in the world because of what they'd experienced, the absolute raw moments that no one else would understand. Like when he was younger, on his monthly steroid protocol, how he'd be angry and sad, full of energy and then crashing. How she'd be so frustrated with his mood swings, and then he'd put his arms around her neck, hot moist breath on her skin as he buried his face into her shoulder. They'd cry together, sitting on the carpet, arms wrapped around each other.

A sudden gust of wind slammed against the car. The maple tree, stripped of its leaves by the unseasonable wind and now missing its top branch, stretched skeletal hands into the sky. Purple swirled like a bruise through the blackness overhead. It was so dark. Where was the moon?

Rachel told the navigation screen to pull up the parking garage at the hospital. Overhead, sudden lightning arced and danced. *Tornado? Hope it holds off until I get Adam into the hospital.* The car's navigation lit up a yellow path. Less than an hour to get there. Not that Rachel didn't know the way, but she liked to see the miles tick down as they got closer.

Adam slept in the back seat. Her leg jittered because of the coffee she'd gulped to stay alert. They were making good time to I-95. Rachel tapped on the screen to get the radio on, anything to distract her from Adam's soft moans of pain. No local channels would come in so she hit 'scan.' Up ahead, at the exit onto I-95, a police cruiser slanted across the way, the officer turning people away.

Rachel gritted her teeth. It would take another twenty minutes to backtrack to Route 1. She drove along the right shoulder of the road right up to the cruiser. The officer waved his arms, a silhouette with blue and red pulses behind him. She had to stop or hit him.

He rapped on her passenger window with knuckles, shined a flash-light into the interior. Rachel squinted against the light and rolled down the window. The smell of something burning wafted inside.

The officer sounded angry as he said, "What don't you understand, Miss, about a police blockade?!"

"This is a medical emergency. My son's life is in danger." Rachel grabbed at her bag and shoved papers at him. Papers that, in a few spare sentences, told their story. Two and a half years ago she'd taken Adam to the pediatrician for strange bruises, then to the local ER for a blood test, then to Johns Hopkins in Baltimore, all in the space of three hours. A scream that lodged in Rachel's throat and didn't release until she sobbed in the hospital shower that night. ALL. Acute Lymphoblastic Leukemia. She and Adam had been immediately admitted and then stayed for thirty-one days in the pediatric wing where the rooms have a hospital bed for the patient and a pull-out sofa for a parent.

The officer flicked his flashlight, read the diagnosis, saw the doctor's orders, and spotlighted his flashlight on Adam in the back seat. Rachel felt more than saw the officer's uncertainty.

"I've got to get him to Hopkins," she said again.

"There's a storm coming. Big one." He stepped back, "Turn around and take cover."

Rachel nodded. "I understand." She did, but the officer didn't. Without knowing what caused Adam's fever, every minute mattered. Rachel eased her foot off the brake and slammed the gas pedal. Tires squealed. The officer waved his arms in her rearview mirror.

Behind him she saw the sky rip open. A flaming meteor fell and an orange glow lit the horizon. The world was on fire.

TWO

The officer had said a storm, but this was a fireball plunging into the Atlantic, or maybe even hitting Delaware's coast. The horizon glowed like daybreak and in the brightness Rachel could see smoke rising high in the air from where the fireball landed. A sudden wave of vibration rocked the car. Rachel clutched the wheel and pumped the brakes. The car slid to a stop on the side of the interstate.

Adam sat up and rubbed his eyes in the back seat. "Why are you driving all crazy?"

What she thought was: *I will do anything to protect you.* What she said was: "Go back to sleep."

Rachel opened the car door and, hanging onto the car frame for support, looked up. If the night sky was a piece of dark fabric, someone had taken shears and sliced a gash in it. Red light poured from the hole. Overhead, tiny red sparks floated through the atmosphere like flecks of dried blood.

"Fire," Rachel said in disbelief. "It's raining fire."

Panicking, Rachel threw herself back into the car. The radio, still scanning through a sea of static, settled on a strange voice, scratchy as an old-fashioned record, that was somewhere between a sportscaster and a personality. "Hello? Hello? What is this thing? Anybody listening? Ha ha, sweet freedom. That was a rough ride. But seriously, folks, I'm getting too old for this."

Some kind of machinery clacked in the background. The voice faded as if the speaker had stepped away from the mike. "What does this do? Oh, and there's a paddle wheel. That's clever." His voice boomed through the car's speakers. "The chessboard is reset. My fellow Misbegotten, let the games begin."

What is this nonsense? Rachel touched the screen away from radio and back to navigation. A clap of thunder made her jump. The GPS went wild, the screen zooming in and out and their spot on the map disappearing. Rachel turned it off. Didn't matter now. Sirens. The rearview mirror showed three state troopers tearing down the interstate. *They're coming for me.* Fear made her swerve, but they went right past. The troopers were driving away from the fireball, too.

In the distance, the orange glow had settled to a thin line in her rearview mirror. Rachel grabbed her cell phone, but there was no signal. Either something was wrong with her phone or this "storm" had messed up the entire wireless network. She touched the gold chain around her neck, the three jewels representing Craig, Adam, and her. She'd been wearing it the night of Adam's diagnosis and worn it every day since. The necklace became a worry stone, a symbol of their family for Rachel to finger as she waited for test results, waited to be allowed into the OR recovery room, waited for Adam to be released so they could go home.

The next exit was Moravia Road, and then a quick right onto Orleans Street; a straight-shot through the Baltimore ghetto to get to a world-famous hospital. Westbound traffic passed the grilled windows of a pawn shop, fast food restaurants, and boarded-up row homes, evidence of urban blight and a tax code that made no sense.

Rachel followed a curve in the road. Beyond the residential area, she could see the squat shape of the SHOP'N'SAVE grocery store. One diagonal block down, the expensive architecture of the research hospital and university rose above the surrounding neighborhoods. Two bridgeways decorated with colored glass mosaics stretched between red brick buildings. Science housed within a work of art.

The street lamps flickered out as Rachel pulled up to the next traffic light. She glanced down the side street to check for oncoming traffic and then froze. City streets on summer nights should have been alive with people sitting on stoops, walking with baby carriages. Instead, a tank drove down the empty street toward the intersection. Rachel gasped. *We're under attack. From whom? Baltimore is close to D.C. Does that mean the meteors were bombs?*

A sudden rapping on her window made Rachel startle and cry out. A man in a green camouflage uniform and a beret stood there, an automatic weapon strapped across his chest.

"National Guard, Ma'am. You need to get off the street."

She swallowed. "I . . . my son. He has cancer. The hospital is waiting. Er . . . the doctors at the hospital are waiting." She gestured at the building.

"The Secretary of Defense has declared a state of emergency. Go straight there." He stepped back. "And Ma'am?"

Rachel met his gaze.

"I'd hurry if I were you."

Hands shaking, Rachel drove the last two blocks and turned into the Orleans Street garage. The gate stood open. Instead of regular security, two National Guardsmen stood on each side of the entrance. One of the men jumped forward and yelled at her, "All citizens have been commanded to take cover!"

Rachel's limbs shook, the car rolled forward. She jammed it into park and was sliding her arm through the hospital bag when her door was wrenched open. The soldier yanked her out of the car.

"Leave the car and get to the bomb shelter in the basement."

"What's going on?" Rachel asked.

"Mom," Adam called from the back seat.

Rachel's focus returned to her son. *One thing at a time. Get Adam into the hospital. Don't worry about anything else.*

"Come on, buddy. We've got to hurry. You can rest when we get there." His hand, hot, reached for hers. She slipped an arm around his waist and adjusted their bag on her shoulder.

"Ma'am, the front doors to the hospital are sealed. You're going to have to walk up the stairs to the fourth floor and cross over the glass bridge. From there head to the basement."

Rachel nodded. "Near the OR recovery room. I know how to get there."

Adrenaline pumping, Rachel half-carried her son up the stairs, counting them out loud, 1, 2, 3, 4, 5, 6 and turn, 1, 2, 3, 4, 5, 6 and turn, repeat until they reached the fourth floor. At the opposite end of the bridge, the entrance to the Children's Center, Rachel saw shadowy movements, a line of people in wheelchairs with attached IV poles moving toward the elevators. Hospital personnel stood there, keeping order, pushing the lines along.

Rachel stepped closer to the glass sides of the bridgeway to look out over the city. Her breath fogged the glass. Blackness overhead was broken up with patches of sickly greens and purples. Not a single star shone white. Instead, the red sparks had arrived, grown to the size of snowflakes as they pinwheeled down faster and larger, each flake glowing with terrible beauty. Craning her neck, Rachel could see the gash was still in the sky, opening to some other place. While Rachel stared, another fireball pushed through the gash, plummeting toward Baltimore.

The glass bridge's walls began to shake. Rachel watched in horror as the meteor came closer, elongating its shape until it resembled a descending tornado of orange, gold, and angry red. Banging on the glass, Rachel screamed. She thought of all the people of the city asleep, unaware of what was coming.

"Mom?" Adam shrugged away from the arm she'd been using to support him. He placed one hand over his heart and the other one against the glass. "I don't understand what's happening."

A sound like rushing water filled the glass bridge. The funnel shape descended on Baltimore at an uncanny rate, growing in height and breadth as it tracked closer and closer. Rachel could see rocks and flaming debris circling round and round the eye. The road underneath buckled from the heat. And then the tornado touched down mere blocks away, moving east toward the hospital and leaving disorder in its wake. Houses burst into flames, buildings imploded on one side of the street while the opposite side of the street remained intact. People appeared at their windows and doors, some ran for their cars. Air thrummed inside the glass walls of the bridge. The tornado was only two blocks away.

Rachel grabbed Adam and stared into his hazel eyes.

She had to yell over the noise outside. "I don't understand either, but we've got to run across now."

The eleven-year-old shook his head, unable or unwilling to tear his gaze from the nightmare outside.

A siren, air raid or fire department, wailed into the night from somewhere to the north.

Burning heat, smelling like sulfur, permeated the glass and singed Rachel's nose hairs. Chunks of burning rock flew off from the tornado, terrible harbingers of what was coming. The stench was so strong she coughed. Sweat broke out on her forehead and under her arms. Rachel imagined the glass of the bridge melting, oozing and crinkling like Styrofoam in a microwave. Below, running through melting manicured landscaping, a man in uniform was on fire.

"There's no choice, Adam." She didn't know if he could hear her over the sound of the firestorm. "Now!"

She shoved him off balance and they ran, hunched over inside the glass walls as if to make smaller targets. Outside, lamplights, neon signs, restaurants all went dark, as if a breaker had been thrown. The picture windows—intended to showcase a panorama of Baltimore's downtown—framed chaos. Debris fell and people crawled from the wreckage of houses, mouths open in screams as they tried to hide from the fire, covering their bodies with pieces of housing. Wind whipped the flames higher.

Coughing and choking, Rachel pulled Adam toward the hospital door. They were only halfway. Her throat was raw and her skin burned as if she were under a magnifying lens. The tornado passed the stop sign at the end of the block. *We aren't going to make it.* Smoke undulated toward the purple sky. Then, a face appeared from inside the havoc of the fire tornado, wavering with the flickering of flames, but still recognizable: a dragon's head. The body burned red, the tip of the tail thrashed. The dragon extended its neck until one great eye met Rachel's through the glass. Green iris with yellow striations around a vertical black pupil.

Sweat broke out on Rachel's forehead. *This can't be real.*

An awful weight crushed Rachel, the air pressed against her bones. She couldn't move out from under the gaze of the beast, and her vision was filled only with its terrible light.

Black spots dotted Rachel's vision as if she'd stared at the sun. "I won't let you hurt him."

The dragon retracted its head, raised fiery wings and brought them together. The force cracked the glass of the bridgeway. Rachel used her body to shield Adam, but they fell to the floor, tumbling head over heels.

THREE

Rachel was disoriented as they tumbled, but she kept herself wrapped around Adam until they rolled through the door and into the hospital. Turning around to look behind, Rachel saw the glass bridgeway melting from the middle as the tornado plowed through where they'd been only seconds before.

An Asian nurse saw them on the floor and waved at the stairs. "Move, move!" she shrieked.

Blinking away her blindness, Rachel grabbed Adam's arm and ran down the stairs and through the heavy door at the bottom that opened into the basement bomb shelter. Rachel knew this area as the waiting room for surgical recovery. No windows to see out, the paint a somber gray. Patients and their families—a hundred, maybe more—sat on the chairs or huddled against the walls. Down here, at least, the sounds from outside were muffled. Instead, there was the sound of children crying and a general whirring sound from air intakes on the ceiling. *Generator*, thought Rachel.

A father pushed a wheelchair holding a girl in a hospital gown guiding her IV pole around the corner from the elevator hallway.

Behind him was the nurse who'd shouted at Rachel to hurry. "That's the last of the patients we were able to move," she told a white-haired doctor wearing a hospital badge that read 'Dr. Abramson.'

The heavy door opened again and one of the guards from the parking garage came in escorting a group of teenagers: two boys and a girl holding a whimpering toddler. Pink beads tied at the end of each of the toddler's braids made a clicking sound whenever she moved her head. One of the boys, hair in rows and wearing a white T-shirt, tucked the loose corners of a blanket back around the little girl. All had cinder burns on their clothing and skin. They'd been out in the storm. Now they stood by the door, seemingly unsure where to go in this room of brisk hospital protocol when all the center seats overflowed with patients and admitted families.

"My arm's burned, *ben dan*." The teenager in the white shirt scowled at a nurse. "I need help."

Rachel recognized the slang insult from one of the vids that Adam sometimes played.

"We'll get to you. Take a seat, please." After the nurse turned away, the girl with the toddler, who looked no older than sixteen, moved to a section of wall near Rachel and Adam and the boys followed her.

Rachel mustered a smile of acknowledgement for the group. "I'm Rachel. Do you need me to scoot over?"

"Jackers." The teenager in the hoodie folded his arms across his chest.

"Did you see the tornado?" She wanted to ask if he'd seen the dragon.

"We were at my house around the corner and the lights went out. Happens sometimes when my old man doesn't pay the bill. We went outside and it was like something you'd see on a vidscreen." He shook his head. "Unbelievable. We covered our heads and ran, so we didn't see much of anything else. There was a soldier at the door of the hospital. He waved us in, so we came." Jackers leaned his back against the hospital wall and slid down.

An overweight woman in a wheelchair on the other side of the young group leaned into the conversation. "There was a tornado? Is that why we're down here?"

Rachel's stomach clenched. She realized that the people already in the hospital hadn't seen any of the firestorm and the people outside, like Jackers and his friends, had only seen the last part. She and Adam were the only ones to witness the full power of the meteors and the resulting tornado. Including the dragon. If she told what she'd seen everyone would think she was crazy. Maybe she'd imagined the whole incident.

"Yeah," said Rachel. "That's why we're down here."

The pungent smell of sweat hung in the air. Adrenaline was wearing off and Rachel began to feel numb instead. She looked at her watch. 12:20 am. An hour since she'd left the house. It felt like so much longer.

Adam put his head in her lap. Rachel patted his leg. Her mind spun with images from the picture window. Flaming rocks falling on Baltimore. People screaming for help. Where was Craig? Had he seen the firestorm coming and gone back to their house or had he driven north towards Boston? She tried to make sense of the past hour. The United States, maybe other countries too, were being attacked by powerful weapons all at the same time. But that didn't explain the dragon. Or, maybe she hadn't even seen that part, just imagined it in the stress of the moment. It was confusing, like putting together a jigsaw puzzle with half the pieces.

She'd just shut her eyes when she felt pressure and saw that a nurse had covered them with a blanket.

"My son has cancer," Rachel said. "We came because he has a fever. He needs antibiotics."

The nurse nodded. "We'll bring around juice in a moment. And cool washcloths. I know it's hot in here."

This isn't an airplane ride. Will you bring peanuts too? Rachel bunched her hands into the blanket, tried to calm her thoughts. *Don't lose it. Breathe. Like in yoga, in through your nose, out through your mouth.*

The nurse had already moved to the next group. Rachel pulled out her phone to call Craig's cell. Still no signal. Rachel shook her head, brushed her hair back.

Flickering from the corner on the right caught her attention. A television was on, tuned to a news channel. Smallish by modern standards, but the technology was working. White on black closed captioning lagged across the bottom of the screen. A blond-haired man sat at a desk talking to a reporter in some unnamed city.

"The first storm fell over Florida. Satellite pictures show more firestorms moving across North America. Loss of life is impossible to gauge at this moment."

Rachel wanted to scream. Why did they keep saying 'storm'? It was raining fire. This was an attack. Something was inside each meteor. Then the meteors turned into tornadoes.

A map of the United States filled the screen. Swirling firestorm clouds tracked south from Canada, the edges touching Montana through Michigan, and moved down to Oklahoma. Another storm swooped down the east coast. According to this satellite loop, Baltimore was on the edge of the firestorm. The main push was over New Jersey, Delaware, and eastern Pennsylvania moving south. This must be the meteor she'd seen falling in the background behind the police officer. Her whole body shook. The meteor that hit Baltimore was moving west. Her house was right in the middle. Maybe it could survive one firestorm, but not two.

The reporter came back on the screen. "We have images coming in now."

Grainy photos filled the screen from live satellite feeds, but Rachel's mind was able to fill in the gaps. Just like what she'd seen outside the glass: fiery tornadoes crashing into buildings and starting fires so hot they burned the roads, random in their violence.

"While the precise nature of this crisis is unclear, we do have some information coming in from geologist Evan Rouche." The camera moved out to show a thin man in a brown suit twitching in the station's guest chair.

One more fidget and then Rouche said, "Something is impacting at different sites, something so powerful that it spawns tornadoes of fire. For rocks to be on fire, to be flaming, they'd be close to 400 degrees Celsius. They'll be triggering forest fires all around. We're going to see irreversible changes."

"What kind of changes, Dr. Rouche?" The anchorman leaned forward.

Rachel leaned forward too, although the TV's volume was all the way up.

The geologist looked at the man and then the camera, shaking as if he couldn't stay in his seat. "400 Celsius is 752 Fahrenheit! The majority of plant life on land and sea is dying right now. There's too much kinetic energy looking for an outlet. No telling how it will alter any organism that survives the next twenty-four hours."

Dr. Rouche's voice went on, but Rachel found it difficult to follow the scientific jargon.

A voice off camera interrupted, "Looks like it's snowing outside. Little red flakes."

Rachel clenched her hands. That's how it had started before the gash opened and released a meteor.

Dr. Rouche had left his chair. The camera continued filming the empty seat. There came a short scream. Just one.

Rachel's stomach heaved. She stroked Adam's hair in a rhythmic pattern and tried not to think.

She didn't want to look again, but she couldn't help it. A new camera had taken over the broadcast. Flames around the Statue of Liberty. Central Park burning down. Gray ash piling up on the streets.

The screen went to electronic snow.

A man stood up and clicked the remote from channel to channel, but there were no more transmissions.

"Oh, God. Oh God in heaven," Rachel said, gasping as she swiped at her phone. Sunday school teachings from childhood came back as Rachel panicked, wishing there was a loving deity to save them all.

No signal.

Dr. Abramson stood in front of her, a black yarmulke on his head. He cleared his throat. "I understand your son is an oncology patient and is presenting with a fever?" His voice was deep, soothing, and his dark eyes were comforting.

The geologist's scream kept repeating in her mind.

"What's happening?" Rachel whispered. She heard the break in her voice. "Are we safe?"

"I'm a doctor, Mrs. Deneuve. I don't have answers to your questions, but we do have supplies down here. Please let me help your son."

Rachel looked around at the people huddled in fear, hiding in the basement of Baltimore's hospital. She nodded her head. "Yes. My son. Please help Adam."

The nurse from upstairs came forward as Dr. Abramson moved away. She pushed a rolling IV pole and the hanging bag of medicine. Adam pulled up his shirt so that the lump under his skin was exposed. His expression was composed, resigned to a familiar routine. The nurse snapped on purple gloves and began cleaning the site. Sometimes nurses not used to oncology patients weren't as thorough, but this one did fine.

"I'll push on three," the nurse said. The needle went in and produced a blood return. The nurse hummed as she attached the antibiotics to his tubing. "Do you want it to go in over thirty minutes? I can push it up to fifteen."

Rachel nodded. "Fifteen, please."

"Okay. I'll send over a nurse to flush it and then take his temperature in about twenty minutes. We won't be able to run labs, but we can use broad spectrum antibiotics and hope for the best." She placed a hand on Adam's head. "May I pray for him?"

Rachel cleared her throat. *It couldn't hurt and maybe it would help.* "We're not really religious, but yeah."

The nurse tilted her head to the side. "If there's a better time to get religious, I can't think of it." She placed her hand on Adam's head, closed her eyes, and mouthed words that Rachel couldn't hear.

Then she moved to the group of teenagers. "Those burns look painful. Who wants to go first?"

"It's getting worse." The young man in the sleeveless white shirt groaned. "Spreading." He held out his arm. Black skin puckered and split, revealing pink tissue and scabs along the edge.

"Me too. On my neck." The teenage girl whimpered. She pulled her hair to the side and exposed a small mark. "Like it's burning all the way through my body."

"Okay, we're going to take care of this." The nurse called out for someone to bring over a privacy screen.

The screen wheeled into position around the young man.

Adam's machine whirred as the plunger moved down the syringe. Dr. Abramson came by to check and nodded his head. "One step at a time, Mrs. Deneuve. Don't overthink it."

"Thank you," Rachel said. She leaned her head back against the wall, and listened to Dr. Abramson's voice as he spoke to the teenagers. Jackers said they'd gotten out of his house before it collapsed. Fire fell on them when they were a couple feet from the hospital door.

"Good fortune for you, young man."

"Man, did you look outside? The city's burning. How's that fortune?"

"You aren't dead." The physician's voice was full of compassion and the young man's mouth twisted as if he was trying to hold back emotions. The physician stepped behind the privacy screen.

A scream erupted from the boy in the sleeveless white shirt. "Is that my bone? Don't touch it. I can see my bone." Another nurse rushed over and disappeared behind the screen. Rachel heard a snapping sound. She pictured the purple gloves going onto the nurse's hands.

The woman in a wheelchair on the other side of the privacy curtain looked around it at Rachel and raised her eyebrows as if to say 'are you hearing this?'

"We're going to have to remove the arm." Dr. Abramson's voice was firm. A smell like rotting meat reached Rachel's nostrils.

"The OR isn't sterile," a nurse said.

"Necrosis," murmured Dr. Abramson. "I've never seen it happen so fast. We're losing him."

A nurse brought a wheelchair behind the curtain and then the team moved with the curtain, shielding the boy from the stares of those in the waiting room as they disappeared into the OR doors at the far end of the room.

The toddler in the arms of the teenage girl whimpered. The girl, wearing a magenta shirt and a wide headband in her short black hair, rocked the toddler. The whites of her eyes showed her fear. She rubbed at the burn mark that stood out pink against the dark brown skin of her neck. To Rachel, the wound looked larger.

Wanting to help, Rachel called over, "Is your baby okay?"

"She's just hungry. I don't think she's burned. She had a blanket around her. Those nurses said they were going to pass out snacks, but it's been a while." Rachel noticed that the girl changed her speaking pattern from when she'd been talking to her friends, as if she had to be bilingual to speak to someone from the suburbs.

"It's no problem. I'm sure I have something in my bag. I always overpack." Rachel dug around. "I have a peanut butter and strawberry jelly sandwich, a juice pouch, bag of ginger snaps, or carrots with ranch dip."

"You don't have to give me your food. I'm not a *qigai*." The teenage girl looked at Jackers as if she needed advice.

Unsure of the slang, Rachel pressed, wanting to make a connection. "It's for your little girl. Just until the hospital gives us something."

"Daisy's my cousin," the teenaged girl said. The toddler had stopped crying and was watching with wide eyes. "But I guess she don't have anyone else anymore."

"What's your name?" asked Rachel.

"Brie."

"You should take it." The overweight woman wheeled herself through the space left from the privacy screen. She winked behind her cat eye glasses. "Trust me, hon. I know all about blood sugar. A snack will do her good." She rubbed a hand across pimples on her forehead. "I'm Glenda, type II diabetic, hospital frequent flyer."

"I'm Rachel, this is Adam. Pediatric oncology." Rachel held out the sandwich. "Here, Brie. Take it for Daisy." Jackers took it and handed it to Daisy. The toddler clutched it and put her face against the girl's chest. Daisy's shoulders shook with sobs. The back of her pink jacket rose up and Rachel saw a weeping sore about five inches across her back. It had puckered and split open. She remembered the teenager in the white shirt adjusting the blanket when they walked through the door. The little girl's back must have been exposed to the firestorm.

Jackers shook his hand and then flexed his fingers. Sweat beads stood out on his temple. "These burns are killing me. When they bringing the pain meds?"

Rachel clasped her own sleeping son, only a few years younger than Jackers.

Soft footsteps. A nurse. "Hey, I need to check this guy's temperature. Holy crap! Rachel? What are you doing here?"

"Naomi." The name came out strangled from Rachel's tight throat.

A few years older than Rachel, Naomi was a brunette with professional blond streaks and a lingering New York City accent. Efficient and controlling, Naomi was perfect for her job as an oncology nurse. She'd been one of Adam's team members from the beginning, moving with him from in-patient to clinic as Adam's progress paralleled her divorce. The daytime hours better suited her single mother status.

"Adam's got a fever." Rachel pushed her bangs to the side. "Why are you here at night?"

"I got a phone call maybe two hours ago. State of emergency; all hospital staff to report. I was mad because deadbeat daddy wouldn't answer the phone and I had to bring the kids to work with me. They're over there against the other wall." Naomi shook her head. "Saved their lives."

The door to the basement flew open. An exhausted looking guard announced, "It's over. The firestorm is over."

Rachel struggled to slide out from under Adam without disturbing him and hugged Naomi hard. Other patients and families laughed and slapped each other on the back. They shared weary smiles and surged forward to ask questions. "Yes," Glenda raised her hands in a cheer and shook them.

The guard held up his arms in a signal for silence. He said, "I was at the door to the main entrance. By my count, the firestorm lasted nineteen minutes before traveling west. Roads are cracked from the heat, electricity is out, and the surrounding neighborhoods are flattened. Little fires are sparking all around. I saw one fire truck on its way." Rachel glanced at her watch. In a few hours it would be dawn. This would all be over.

She touched Adam's forehead. Blessedly cool. The antibiotics worked. It must have been a common germ. He'd be exhausted for the next twenty-four hours, but there shouldn't be any other side effects. Rachel turned to Brie to share her relief, but the young woman had opened the sandwich bag and was trying to wake up Daisy.

"It's over, baby. Wanna eat something?"

The little girl's neck slipped off Brie's shoulder, her body arcing toward the floor. The pink beads at the end of her braids clicked together as she hung upside down in Brie's arms. Brie gave her a shake as if to wake her up, to get her attention, to make Daisy stop messing around, but it was too late.

Brie let Daisy's lifeless body fall to the floor and then touched the wound on her own neck. Her eyes grew wide and unfocused. Her breath became audible. Dr. Abramson pushed through the horrified circle staring at little Daisy and gently picked up the body. He cradled the dead little girl to his chest and carried her back to the OR. The first visible casualty of the firestorm to those inside. The hospital was supposed to be a safe place. Understanding rippled through the crowd that the horror was not over. Whispers began with accusations like "they were outside" and "contaminated" and "too dangerous."

Nurses came forward with a privacy screen to surround Brie and Jackers.

Rachel pulled her knees up to her chest. Adam moaned in his sleep. "Shh," she said. "Morning's going to come soon."

FOUR

"I won't be gone long," Rachel said to Adam.

"I'll watch him for you," Glenda offered. "Will you get mine?" She held out her ticket.

"Of course."

Patients and families had to stay in the bomb shelter, but each person received a meal ticket and could go to the cafeteria on the second floor to bring food back.

"Mom, I'll be fine. I don't know why they're keeping us here anyway. The storm or whatever is over." Adam stretched. He'd already finished the book she'd packed for him to read and eaten the peanut butter crackers the nurses had passed out earlier. He'd also changed out of his pjs and into his typical outfit: athletic shorts and a soft T-shirt. "I want to go home. I want to see Dad. He's gotta be freaking out and worried about us."

Rachel was saved from answering by the guard opening the door. He still wore an automatic weapon across his chest and looked to Dr. Abramson before allowing the line to walk upstairs. With no word from the Maryland governor or federal government, and with the hospital the only building standing with a generator, top medical administrator Dr. Abramson and Major K. Griffin of the National Guard had formed an alliance.

Coming out into the corridor, Rachel got her first glance out of the glass walls and was struck by how much Baltimore looked like a Dali painting. Midmorning, but the sun was gone, drowned by the ash-colored atmosphere. A clocktower in the middle of the hospital's parking circle had melted, the edges of the brick softening and the mechanical part stretching down like a runny egg. Ragged, burned human beings wandered the streets and searched through the residential rubble. Others stood in a procession that snaked from the hospital entrance around the side of the building with guards maintaining the line.

The parking garage was intact; the SHOP'N'SAVE a block over was standing, although the back corner had collapsed. The rest of the area was a pile of singed matchsticks. Someone had set up wood to barricade the entrance from the hospital side of the melted glass bridge. Rachel shuddered. A few more minutes standing out there and they would have been burned alive.

Back in the basement, Rachel gave Glenda and Adam their food.

Brie and Jackers were back at their spot, both bandaged. Hours earlier, before taking them to the OR, a nurse had explained to them that their friend's firestorm injuries were too severe and he had passed away.

"Kevin," Brie had said. "His name was Kevin."

Now, IVs hanging morphine bags fed them both. They stared at nothing with glassy eyes. Brie's head leaned against the wall with her bandaged neck arched.

Rachel asked, "How ya feeling?"

"They cut out a chunk of my neck." Brie whispered. "And put in a thermometer." She gave a bitter laugh. "To see if I'm cooked yet. Guess I got hope 'cause they didn't put me in with the Screamers."

The burn victims from outside—quickly nicknamed Screamers—were taken into an interior room beyond the OR. No reason was given, but those who'd been touched by the mysterious flames came in delirious and moaning. Their groans seeped through the hospital, the crying permeated the walls. The families in the waiting room looked at each other with suppressed panic.

Jackers grimaced and shifted his arm across his middle. His arm that now ended in a bandaged stump. His pants had been rolled up on the right side and a bandage covered his ankle to his knee. "Too much, you know," he said. "A god's blood falling on a human body. Can't handle it."

"What god?" Rachel asked. She didn't know what else to say.

"The sun god, *ben dan*. Why else is the sun gone? He got burned up by the others. His family roasted him."

Poor kid doesn't know what he's saying. Rachel caught Adam's eye. Adam's face paled and he crossed his arms over his body. Yes, now her son realized how serious this was.

That night, Rachel stretched out next to Adam on their blanket. She closed her eyes, but her mind kept returning to Craig. Was he trying to get to them? Where had he gone? Brie and Jackers had stayed in the main waiting room, claiming they were different than the Screamers, not wanting to be grouped with those who only came into the hospital to die. Rachel sympathized, but Jackers' constant moaning made it hard to fall asleep. Rachel brought her hands over her ears. The basement's lights never went all the way off creating an eerie ambiance. It all caused nightmares sparked by Jackers' story of the sun dying, as if the sun were a person, a hero's body being ripped apart and falling as burning flakes through the night sky.

The next morning, soldiers walked into the bomb shelter ahead of Dr. Abramson and a compact woman in uniform. Major Griffin had dark skin and brown eyes that seemed haunted by what she'd seen. Shorter than Dr. Abramson, she was the obvious muscle to whatever he was about to say. Rachel hadn't seen Dr. Abramson since he'd taken little Daisy's body back to the OR. Rachel assumed he'd been working with the burn victims. He looked like he'd aged ten years in three days.

"If I call your name, I'd like you to come forward." Dr. Abramson gestured to his left. Rachel grabbed Adam's hand. The doctor went down a list. Dread soured her stomach. Brie and Jackers moved to the left. Glenda was called. She wheeled herself to the left.

"Thank you. Everyone who is standing will be escorted to the doors. No one is permitted to leave city limits. Instead, you will continue to the community center set up in the stadium over on Russell Street." Dr. Abramson exhaled. "The rest of you may form an orderly line in front of me."

Rachel covered her mouth. She'd been in the stadium for Ravens' games. It was open to wind and weather.

Adam gasped. "They have to leave? But, that's not fair."

No, Rachel thought. *It's the impossible task of doctors deciding who they can help and who they can't.*

"I won't go!" Glenda screamed. "I need insulin. This is a death sentence!" One of the guards pushed her wheelchair toward the doors. Glenda stood and tried to step back, but the guard slung his rifle towards her. Glenda swayed on her feet. "Don't let them do this," she begged the people still standing inside the basement. "It's me this time, but you're next."

Rachel swallowed and clutched Adam's shoulders.

Major Griffin made a gesture to the guard as if to say 'get her out of here.'

"We have limited resources of both food and medicine. Major roads are damaged; travel is shut down." Dr. Abramson's voice cracked. He covered his eyes with his hand and then recovered. "The other doctors and I have analyzed the situation and made a plan to optimize what is in our pharmacy and cafeteria." He cleared his throat. "Please step forward, one at a time."

Rachel pushed Adam forward and stood behind him. They held out their wrists to receive bracelets that would allow them to stay within the protective walls of the hospital. Naomi moved forward to escort them up to the pediatric oncology floor.

"Why did they send out the burn victims?" Rachel whispered to Naomi.

"None of them, not one exposed to the firestorm, is responding to treatment." Naomi glanced over her shoulder to make sure no one was listening. "Doctors figure that they're wasting the meds. Either the fire was too hot for human bodies, or this is some type of thermophile virus. Either way, hopeless cases. And, if it is a virus, it could spread to those who weren't exposed. Dr. Abramson had to make the choice to give Baltimore the best chance to recover."

"Thermophile?" Adam leaned in close as they rounded the last set of stairs. "'Therm' means heat and 'phile' means love. Germs that love heat?"

"You shouldn't eavesdrop," Rachel said. "Smarty pants."

Room 833. They went up eight sets of stairs to the familiar room. This was the same room they'd been assigned when Adam was first diagnosed. A privacy curtain separated Adam's patient bed from the pull out couch where Rachel slept. White sheets and white blankets. The better to bleach away the vomit, blood, and medications, that spilled on a daily basis. A window framed a view of Baltimore's streets. Twenty-six steps, foot to heel, for Rachel to walk from the desk by the window to the hallway door.

Rachel leaned on top of the desk to peer out the edges of the window towards the stadium. Too much time had passed for her to be able to see the line of people kicked out of the hospital, but she wanted to see some sign, some clue of their presence.

Adam opened and shut the closet door repeatedly. "What do you think those fire-flake-things were?"

"I don't think anyone knows." Rachel frowned in annoyance. "Could you stop making that noise?"

With an exaggerated sigh Adam threw himself across the bed. The connected IV pole scooted across the floor but didn't tip.

"Be careful," Rachel said. "You'll pull out the needle." He was still accessed because he had one more dose of antibiotics. But, Adam knew all this. "What's going on?"

"This." Adam held up his arm. "It's really small, but I can feel it."

Rachel swung herself away from the desk and grabbed his arm, turning the wrist up and locking his elbow into place underneath the overhead light. There, the size of a pencil tip, was a burn mark on the inside of his elbow.

"No," Rachel whispered. Blackness clouded the outer edges of her vision.

FIVE

"How long? When?" Rachel tried to keep calm. "You've been infected. The virus is spreading."

"I felt it burn when the glass bridge broke, but I didn't see any mark and everything felt all fuzzy from being sick. The medicine made the fuzziness go away, but the burn didn't. I only saw it today."

Rachel dropped his arm and grabbed Adam's shoulders instead. "You cannot tell anyone."

"What about Naomi?"

"Especially Naomi. We can't put her in that position." Rachel straightened. "Go into the bathroom and wait for me."

"Why?" Adam said. She understood he was confused, but she'd made a decision as soon as she saw the burn. They were not leaving this hospital. Rachel went to her bag of art supplies and pulled out a special case of tools she used for etching. Behind her, she heard the bathroom door open.

She found the tool and followed Adam inside. There was a plastic "hat" used for urine collection and the usual gloves and alcohol wipe inside. "Sit on the toilet and push the pole to the side so you can stretch your arm across the sink."

"What are you doing?" Adam's eyes widened when he saw the etching blade in her hand. "You're crazy," he yelped.

"Shhh. We don't have much time."

Adam stretched out his arm obediently, taking cues from her confidence. She adjusted his arm so that the burn mark was in clear sight. Rachel knew Craig would be screaming at her if he were here. What she was considering was unthinkable. She had no experience. She had no assurance this would stop the burn from spreading. And, one never intentionally broke the skin—first line of defense—of a chemo patient. Cuts opened the body to infection.

But, she answered the imaginary Craig in her mind. *I'll just pretend I'm etching and removing the speck of ink. He's due for his last dose of antibiotics tonight to kill any germs that get in and I'm going to use gloves and an alcohol wipe.* The imaginary Craig was not convinced. *Our son will die if I don't*, she pleaded. Imaginary Craig disappeared and she took that as his assent.

Rachel washed her hands, put on the gloves, and wiped the blade of the X-Acto knife. The point pressed against Adam's skin. "Don't try this at home, kiddos."

Adam's voice couldn't mask his fear. "Yeah. How about 'don't try this at home, parents.'"

Voices and a closing door in the hallway made Rachel inhale. "Crap."

She gave a slight twist as she pressed. A single dot of crimson bubbled out of his arm. Adam didn't make a sound. Rachel grabbed the alcohol wipe and cleaned the area. The speck was gone. The voices were outside of their door. Someone knocked.

"Press this to stop the bleeding," Rachel said. "Don't come out until its scabbed." She scoured the room for a Band-Aid, but didn't see one. "Of course, not like we're in a hospital or anything. Probably better to not draw attention to the spot anyway."

The groan of the vacuum-sealed door made Rachel jump. She

wadded up the trash and walked out of the bathroom as Naomi walked in from the hallway.

"Hey, I've got Adam's meds. Where is he?"

Rachel hid the knife and trash behind her back. "Using the bathroom. He'll be right out."

Rachel checked the spot on Adam's elbow every day of the next week, but the area remained clear. Adam reported that he didn't feel any burning sensation and he had no fever. During the day Rachel charged her phone when the outlets worked, but there was no service. Still, she touched the screen every few hours. Home. Craig's cell phone. Their neighbors'. Every number in her contacts list. Repeat. She watched their hospital room's door, waiting for someone she knew to burst through, for Craig to come in. He wasn't going to. She'd seen the satellite loop. No one could have survived the full force of the firestorm. Better that they never knew the horror was coming, that they died in their sleep. After a couple rounds of dialing, she scrolled through pictures and wondered why she hadn't loaded more. Thank God she'd brought the photos for the scrapbook.

The door clicked open. Rachel expected to see Naomi, but it was Dr. Abramson.

"Rachel, we're going to schedule Adam for surgery tomorrow. His port needs to come out."

"No, he's not ready." Rachel shook her head, ready to plead their case. Each day of the past week she'd dreaded this conversation, practiced what to say. "We need to stay here, inside the hospital. It takes at least a year after chemo for his immune system to recover and he's been taking 6-MP and Methotrexate every day."

"That's part of the problem. We don't have enough supplies for daily chemo." Dr. Abramson sighed. "Adam is in a better position than some because he's farther along in his treatment, but having a plastic port sitting in Adam's chest is a liability when he isn't receiving chemo. Germs are attracted to foreign objects in the body. An infection could kill him."

"Okay, I understand. No more chemo, but don't send us away. What about Bactrim? He's supposed to take that for a year after treatment ends to prevent pneumonia." Panic set in. Rachel moved to stand right in front of the doctor, blocking it as if she could convince him if only she had enough time. "Please, please, we have to stay."

"I'm sorry, Rachel." Dr. Abramson hung his head. "I wish everyone could stay, but we've cataloged our supplies of medicine, our fuel for the generator, our food. We're working from a budget. That means you and Adam will be released to the stadium with the next group."

Released. She thought of Glenda. *You mean, sentenced to die.*

Rachel looked at Adam, who was sitting in his bed with his finger in a book from the floor's play room. His face paled. He knew what this meant. Finishing chemo should have been a party. After the official last dose, the oncology staff brings in a cake and sings "For He's is a Jolly Good Fellow" and everyone on the floor gathers around and celebrates for a few moments before returning to the fight against cancer in other children. This wasn't completion, it was quitting.

"No dinner tonight." Dr. Abramson said. "He'll need to be ready for surgery when the OR is open."

Dr. Abramson gently moved Rachel to the side. The door closed with a soft 'snick' of vacuum sealing.

Rachel tried to smile at Adam before taking a seat in the window. "You're done, buddy. Kicked cancer's butt."

"Really, Mom?" He turned away.

The hospital's historic red brick cupola reached to the bitter sky. From the eighth floor Rachel should have been able to see Fort

McHenry, Bethlehem Steel, the neon Domino Sugars sign, even high-rises over in Towson. The landmarks, unlike the cupola, were gone.

"What do you think it was?" she asked Adam, not really expecting an answer. "The firestorm? If another country attacked us, why isn't someone invading or claiming credit?"

"It wasn't a bomb, Mom. It was a dragon. Middle Eastern, I'd say. Asian dragons have those long mustaches. Western dragons have wings." Adam grinned from ear to ear. "Coolest thing ever."

He'd seen that too? A shared hallucination? She wasn't sure what to think, having convinced herself it couldn't have happened.

Rachel shifted her position in the window seat and looked out past the cupola to the broken street below. A combination of dust and soot coated the window. Using her closed fist, Rachel rubbed at the inside of the window as if that would help her see. During the week she'd been in the room, the SHOP'N'SAVE had become a rough courtyard. Long lines formed to pick through anything salvaged. Gun shots rang out, but no answering police sirens.

"I don't think so, sweetie." She tried to laugh. "This isn't like one of your books." But the hairs on the back of her neck stood up in memory of the eyes looking at her for a never-ending moment.

"When I had that burn—"

"Don't say it." Rachel looked around as if someone might overhear them.

Adam rolled his eyes. "I had the same dream that Jackers did. About falling through the sky, my body exploding into fire."

"That's your imagination's attempt to explain your fever."

Adam stared at her in disbelief, calling her out for lying, and then pointedly went back to his book.

SIX

The next morning Adam ran from one wall to the other, jumping at the last moment. Swishing imaginary baskets with an imaginary ball.

"I think you've won the game by now," Rachel said.

"I'm bored." The eleven-year-old shrugged as he pantomimed dribbling. "Being NPO stinks."

Nil per os. Latin. Not by mouth.

"I know."

He didn't answer so Rachel went back to staring out the window, the way she'd done all night. "If it makes you feel better, I won't eat today either."

Adam stopped shooting baskets. "You never eat when I'm going to have surgery."

"It's my show of solidarity. I can't take chemo for you, but I can not eat."

"If you really wanted to suffer, Mom, you'd give up the coffee."

Rachel looked down at her cup and made a face. "Rationing means I'm cut down to one cup a day. Don't take that away from me."

"Whatever. Can I walk around the unit now? I'm tired of being cooped up in here. At least you get to leave to go to the cafeteria with our meal tickets."

"Naomi said everyone should stay quarantined to control contagion."

"That's dumb. We can wear masks like during flu season or when we're neutropenic."

Rachel stared at her son, equal parts annoyed at his inclination to argue about anything and sympathetic to his restlessness.

"You need a haircut." His hair was thick, had the 'chemo-curl' that many patients experienced when their hair grew back. The color was different too. Lighter, less red than Rachel's own auburn color, but shaggy, falling into his eyes.

Rachel hugged her stomach. It hurt all the time now, anxiety making her muscles cramp. As a distraction, she swung off the desk and went past Adam's bed into the bathroom to run her wrists under cold water and pat her cheeks. She looked down at the golden bands on her finger. *Wedding band goes on first, closest to the heart. The diamond engagement ring holds it on.* Such trivial details. If she forgot it would the human race forget? Should someone be writing this crap down?

Her left index finger reached up to touch its reflection in the mirror. Wide eyes over purple circles stared back. *I should put ChapStick on, my lip is bleeding.* But Rachel found it difficult to move. It was easier to stand here and not think. She groaned. This waiting—for today's surgery, to leave the hospital, to see the damage to the city firsthand—made it hard not to slip into depression.

Perched back on the desk, Rachel could smell smoke through the window, though it was locked; sealed to prevent jumping from this height. Below, two black teenagers sat huddled in the street with no need to worry about cars now, picking at scabs on their legs. A plastic grocery basket sat beside them, fruit stacked inside. Every once in a while one of the boys would lean forward and wave his hand. Rachel imagined a single buzzing fly inspecting the rotten produce.

"I have to walk," Rachel said and escaped into the hallway. Walking the rectangle of the pediatric oncology unit wasn't exciting, but it gave the impression of doing something and she needed that illusion. Too soon she was back at the door to room 833. Pushing the door open with a practiced movement of her elbow, Rachel shoved her hands under the Purell dispenser on the wall. It was a moment before she realized there was a third person in the room.

A nurse, one Rachel wasn't familiar with, leaned over Adam from the far side of the bed, her face inches away from his.

Adam whimpered. "Stop."

"What's going on here?" In two steps, Rachel was at the near side of the bed.

Adam let his hand fall away from his chest. "My heart was thumping, like really hard, and burning, but I wasn't doing anything."

"Are you okay now?" Rachel asked, worried that this would affect his surgery.

He nodded, seeming to relax now that she was present.

The nurse pressed back against the hospital wall. She was petite, but her beautiful box braids were piled into a topknot and added to her height. Her skin was brown with a smattering of dark freckles. Her most startling feature, however, were eyes the green of an unfurled spring leaf.

Rachel found herself mesmerized, her artist's imagination working to bring the living sense of dappled light to paper.

"The boy has something that doesn't belong to him and I want it back."

"I don't know what she's talking about." Adam held his hands palms facing up as if to show he wasn't hiding anything.

"It has to be here," the nurse insisted, "but I've looked all through this place."

Rachel narrowed her eyes. There was something odd about the nurse. Not only did she appear to be a teenager, but there was something else about the scrubs and the facial mask hanging around her neck that didn't seem quite right. "Well, I don't think Adam has anything of yours. What do you mean 'this place?' Do you mean oncology? Are you on the wrong floor?"

"This whole place is wrong for me. The glass and bricks make me feel sick." The nurse gestured out the window. "I need my woods."

Rachel struggled to understand. Maybe the pressure of working in the hospital with little sleep and too many patients had triggered this odd behavior. She said. "You mean you're homesick? Where are you from?"

"The land between two rivers."

The land between two rivers? If that was a nickname for a place, Rachel wasn't aware of it.

The nurse continued, "But I'm lost and my husband is dead."

A wave of sympathy swept Rachel. She must be a recent nursing school graduate or maybe even still a student. "That, I understand." Rachel grabbed a bottle of water from the desk and held it out. "Have a drink."

The nurse looked up with tears shimmering in her green eyes. "You offer me libation?"

"Um, I'm offering you a drink." Rachel wondered at the nurse's word choices, as if English were a foreign language. Maybe it was.

The nurse straightened, although she only reached about five feet. "Your gift is accepted. You may both come with me."

Rachel tilted her head. "Where is it that you want us to go?" There was no way she was taking Adam to an operating room or even to have his vitals checked with this strange young woman.

"I will find a place where it is green and hilly." The nurse placed her arms akimbo. "I am strong enough to set up my own territory. You will be my first worshippers. This is an honor for you."

"Uh-huh." Rachel blinked her eyes. The nurse wasn't moving, yet her outline kept shifting, the edges of her body somehow blurring so that from one angle she was a human teenager and from another she was a fawn standing on hind legs, brown nose scenting the air for danger. It made Rachel think of the Guennol Lioness, a famous Mesopotamian statue of a lioness-woman. She shook her head to clear the strange impression and bring her focus back to the conversation.

"Well, thank you. But, we're going to stay here." Rachel glanced at Adam for his reaction to the nurse's bizarre invitation. "And, I think you should leave our room. Now."

"You would have been better off with me." The nurse tilted her head. "Still, you made an offering to me and my gift to you is this warning." Her hand dropped from her waist to point at Adam. "I know you have Shamash's heart, wherever you have hidden it so cleverly. I hope you are brave enough to protect it. Because the others will come for you." Her mouth twisted. "They will feel the heart and be drawn like wasps to honey."

"That's enough!" Rachel shouted, moving around the bed toward the nurse. "Get out of our room."

Adam pulled his knees up to his chest, eyes wide.

Rachel reached out a hand to yank the nurse from the corner where she stood between hospital bed and wall, but somehow the teenager ducked around Rachel and moved toward the door. As she did, the thing that had bothered Rachel became clear. The scrubs were a different design than all the other nurses, as if this young woman wore something from a television series or a Halloween costume.

"Mom? What was she talking about?" Adam had come out of his defensive position, but still looked unsure. "Who is going to come for me? Why?"

Rachel shook her head, trying to organize her thoughts. "I'm sorry, Adam. That woman was not a nurse. She was very confused and should not have been in our room." She cupped Adam's chin so he had to look at her. "But no one is after you. If they were, they'd have to come through me first. Got it?"

Adam nodded, his shoulders relaxing.

"Why don't you finish reading that chapter," she pointed toward the book on the bed, "so you aren't at a cliffhanger when you go to the OR?"

"I'm at the end of the book, not the chapter."

"Even better." Rachel tried to keep up the banter, but reaction was setting in, the crazy accusation and the young woman's fascination with Adam. Increasingly angry, Rachel yanked the door open to confront the young woman and instead met Naomi's startled eyes over a facemask.

Naomi rubbed her hands with sanitizer and stepped into the room. "Sorry for the wait, guys. Everything's in order but because Adam isn't an emergency his time slot keeps getting bumped."

Rachel peered in both directions down the hospital corridor as Naomi took Adam's vitals. "What if I keep getting bumped past when the generator is scheduled?"

"The surgeons won't start if they don't have time to finish."

"Naomi, what has four eyes, but can't see?"

"A potato?" Naomi pulled the blood pressure cuff tight.

"Mississippi."

"That's a good one, Adam." She jotted the numbers in his paper chart.

Unsettled by the fake nurse's disappearance, Rachel let the door to the hospital close and focused on Naomi and Adam. "Maybe we'll have to stay an extra day."

Naomi made a face to express that Rachel was being delusional and swung her hair back. It was French braided, greasy at the top in a way that never would have happened before the firestorm. She checked her watch and leaned against the wall. "He'll get Vincristine before they take the port out. I think the pharmacy downstairs still has a decent supply."

Adam said, "I hate Vincristine. Makes my hands and feet hurt."

"It's a neurotoxin. That's how you know it's working." But Naomi tempered her sharpness with a tired smile.

Rachel said, "And that's it. He comes out of recovery tonight and tomorrow he's discharged."

Naomi adjusted the stethoscope around her neck and faced Rachel. "I'm sorry, Rachel."

Rachel looked over at Adam and tripped over her words, "We're going to be exposed to everything when we leave here."

On the bed, Adam openly listened to the two women.

Naomi pushed off from the wall and nodded towards the door. "Walk with me."

Understanding that this wasn't an acceptable conversation for Adam to overhear, Rachel followed into the hallway.

The moment they were out of earshot, Rachel started, "I've spent the past two years learning the dangers of being immunocompromised and now you're telling me it doesn't matter."

Naomi closed her eyes. "What do you want me to say?"

"Tell me what's going on. For real. I've heard rumors the burn virus is a mutation caused by radiation from a broken nuclear power station. Or it's chemical warfare—created by nanotechnology to attack America." Rachel tried to laugh. "I've even heard that ancient demigods have come back to earth."

Naomi rubbed a hand across her forehead. "You really want to know?"

"Yes."

"No one knows."

A familiar oncology nurse walked toward them. "They're ready for Adam downstairs."

Rachel opened the door and waved Adam into the hallway. "By the way, a young woman walked right into our room. She was in there with Adam when I got back from a quick walk."

Naomi frowned. "No one should be in your room. The front desk stops anyone right at the entrance to peds oncology. What did she look like?"

"Young-looking, short with the green eyes? She's wearing khaki scrubs."

"I have no idea who you're talking about."

"She was in our room right before you came in," Rachel insisted. "You must have walked past her."

"There was no one in the hallway when I came to your room. I would have seen them." Naomi held out her hand for Adam to shake. "Mazel tov."

"Is that a new kind of chemo I have to get?"

"No, smart alec." Naomi, a mother of teenagers, rolled her eyes before Adam could. "It means 'congratulations.' Today you finish chemo and that's a big deal."

Rachel wanted to bring the conversation back to the fake nurse; she couldn't believe that no one else seemed bothered by the mystery.

Adam tried to grin at Naomi, but Rachel saw the corners of his mouth tremble with effort. "See you in recovery, Mom?"

Rachel nodded. He was so brave. "You know it, bud." When Adam and the nurse had disappeared down the hallway, Naomi tapped her finger against Adam's paper chart. "I hate to ask again, but we desperately need blood. I can make sure you get an extra meal ticket in exchange. That'll be good for Adam, coming out of surgery."

Rachel snorted. "The problems of being a universal donor. Can you take it from the other arm? I'm still sore on my right."

"Sure. I'll go get the phlebotomy kit. You'll be done and in the recovery room before Adam even wakes up."

"Right." Rachel went back into room 833. She reached for her coffee cup while she waited for Naomi to come back, but the Styrofoam was empty.

Naomi was quick, sitting Rachel on the hospital bed, pulling the cuff tight.

Rachel fidgeted. "I'm so glad that you and all your children survived." She looked away when the needle went in, gritting her teeth. "Are they safe here?"

"Yeah, they repurposed the Throckmorton building into residential suites." She touched Rachel's arm, "You can look now. Slow down how quickly you squeeze. I don't want you to pass out."

Rachel nodded, breathing in through her nose and out through the mouth. "I'll just pretend I'm in yoga class."

"You used to go all the time." Naomi spoke with an easy bedside manner as she used a roller on the tubes connected to the collection bag.

"Yup. A way to control my stress over Adam." Rachel forced a short laugh. "I'll have to go every hour now that I'm a single mom."

Naomi stopped writing on the label. "Single mom?"

"It's been ten days. If Craig could have gotten here, don't you think he would have?" Rachel bounced a curled knuckle against her mouth. "What father would stay away from his son?"

"There's something you aren't telling me." Naomi raised her eyebrows.

"We separated. Right before the firestorm." Rachel dropped her hand from her mouth. "And I don't miss him. I mean, I miss having a partner, someone who is as invested in Adam as I am. Someone I can trust. But, I don't miss the fighting, I don't miss Craig's sarcasm and his telling me what to do and then telling me I'm doing it wrong. So maybe it's paranoid, but what if he is okay and doesn't want to find us?"

"That's ridiculous." Naomi's tone disallowed any further discussion. "Craig wouldn't abandon you guys. Even if you don't have a romantic relationship anymore, you're still partners."

"Then he's dead." Rachel shrugged one shoulder. "That's the only other option."

"Welcome to the club of single moms. You get a temporary pass. Just until Craig gets here." Naomi adjusted the tubing. "Then I'm kicking you out to happy family club."

"I'm so scared of Adam asking again. He thinks that Craig somehow survived the firestorm.'" Rachel exhaled. "At least you had time to adjust to being in charge of every single decision." Her voice wobbled. "I look at pictures over and over and think I can't do this. I'm not enough. It's too hard."

"Hey! Look what I got for you. Don't tell anyone or I'll be in trouble." Naomi reached into her pocket and pulled out three single servings of peanut butter and a strawberry jelly packet. "Found this in the back of one of the file folder drawers. Have no idea how long they've been there, but they are all yours."

"Thanks." Rachel stayed down on the bed while the room started to spin. She opened the first pack and used her finger as a spoon.

Naomi leaned over her. "Hey, are you okay?"

Rachel felt the nurse's hand on her forehead.

"You're turning from green back to white."

"That's good," Rachel said.

"Yes, it is," Naomi said drily. "I'll tell you when I felt bad. Remember that day I had to tell you that Adam's neutrophil count was still zero after you guys had been here like eleven days?"

"I do remember that." Rachel sat up, bracing herself against the bed. "And you told me I'd be fine because I'd put on lip gloss that morning."

"It's true. If you've got enough life to put on lip gloss, you'll be fine."

"I have no other family. Where am I supposed to go?" Defeat swelled in Rachel's chest. "I've put my life on hold to take care of my son, done everything this hospital told me to, and now he's being discharged with no further care?"

Naomi's gaze dropped to Rachel's chapped lips.

"Please, can't you do something? Is there someone I can talk to?"

"Rachel, the policy is to fix up as many people as we can and send them on."

"I could teach art to the staff kids or help in the cafeteria. Don't let them send us out."

Naomi shook her head. "We're all going to be on the streets soon enough. How long do you think there'll be enough fuel for the generator? Clean water? Food?" Naomi ran her hand through her hair. "I've got to go to my next patient." At the door Naomi turned around, "Hey Rach, do me a favor."

"What?"

"Put some ChapStick on, sister. Let me know you're still fighting."

Rachel said, "Would you go to the stadium, if you were me? When your son has a weakened immune system?"

Naomi looked down at the hospital floor and then up to meet Rachel's eyes. "Not a shot in hell."

SEVEN

Rachel lay on Adam's hospital bed, still feeling hollow. She imagined an intricate map of blood racing around her body with a section missing. The section that had just been bled out of her. The packet was probably already being hooked up to a patient. Rachel swung her legs down and grabbed the three meal tickets, one for her, one for Adam, and one for payment for donating blood. She shoved the tickets into the tote bag she'd brought to the hospital what felt like forever ago.

Naomi's admission hadn't surprised her, but it still stung. The hospital was a fortress: safe, clean, had running water, lights. Everyone wanted in. It had become common for survivors outside the hospital to hurt themselves, cutting off a finger, slicing open their skin, drinking poison, to get in here. Maybe she could slice off her pinky as soon as they walked outside and then be re-admitted.

Down eight flights of stairs to the ground floor, the stairway door opened into an artery of the hospital. The hallway, like the rest of the building, was constructed to an impressive scale with artfully tiled floors and glass walls to look out on landscaped gardens and court-yards. Now the hospital, like a body, pulled in to the center, keeping alive the parts that best survived the firestorm and amputating the parts that didn't.

Turning right would take Rachel to the cafeteria where patients with tickets could get one meal a day during a specified time period. Adam would need food as soon as he woke up. Glancing down, Rachel saw that she was an hour too early to redeem her tickets.

To pass the time, Rachel walked left toward the hospital's doors. Security guards were spread out to protect the entrance. This part of the hospital gave her a different view than from her room. She could see up the street where the grocery store was still in use. The building was more than half intact. Rectangular with a blue roof and an unlit sign that read Shop'n'Save and a tarp thrown over the side with a hole. Chain-link fence yanked from someone's yard was spread across the tarp. More worry about looters than the weather. It hadn't rained since the firestorm.

There'd been a gunfight for control over the store a week ago.

Soldiers, the National Guard back then, enforced the waiting line. Only a few people were allowed into the store at one time. Another line, much shorter, entered through a side entrance reserved for those who had something to sell.

While Rachel watched a red-haired man come out of that side door. He looked to be in his early twenties, freckled, and relaxed. He wore khaki shorts, hiking boots, and a flannel shirt over a white T-shirt. A duffel bag was strapped onto his back. Rachel stepped closer to the wall and peered through to watch him as long as she could. There was something familiar about the man. Instead of walking toward the hospital, and toward the stadium, he was walking away. Toward the boundary. His step was light. Rachel imagined him whistling as he meandered along. And with a snap of the fingers she recognized him. He was a park ranger up near Cacapon where she and Craig had bought a log cabin. She'd taken Adam to an outdoor lecture about owls last summer and he'd been the ranger giving the talk. They'd seen him around afterwards because their property was adjacent to the park.

Suddenly a face jumped into her vision and an impact against the glass wall made a loud thump. A white man with a hat and weeping sores on his face—a symptom of firestorm burns—banged his hands on the glass again to either side of Rachel's head. She leaped back and the man screamed "Hospital bitch!" Outside, the clouds were dark, the wind blowing trash along the street below.

The security guards inside snickered. "That wall looks like glass, but it's stronger than anything they can throw." She wondered if they were laughing at her or the people outside.

"Better stand back, Miss. They're hot tonight." The nearest guard was thin, tall, with a beard. He lowered his eyes and kept a respectful space back.

A crowd gathered, banging on the Plexiglas, demanding to be let into the hospital. In the mob, Rachel recognized Jackers from the bomb shelter. And there was the teenage girl, Brie. They chanted with the crowd.

Rifle shots split the air. Rachel ducked down, but it wasn't the crowd shooting. Instead, a group of soldiers approached from the outside. They'd shot to break up the crowd. A guard from the inside moved forward to unlock the Plexiglas and allow them inside. The group looked tired. Their leader, Major Griffin, took off her helmet. "Grab food and we'll meet in twenty minutes for debriefing." She stalked toward the stairs.

This was one of the exploratory parties that had gone out. Rachel grabbed the sleeve of the nearest guard. "Please, can you tell me what you saw out there?"

The soldier—hollowed cheeks and ashen skin testifying to hunger and fatigue—jerked his arm away. "Let go, Ma'am. I have to eat."

The other soldiers were already gone. Fear gripped Rachel. "They're making me leave the hospital tomorrow. Can you tell me what direction you went? We have no news here. No way to make a decision."

The guard looked toward the cafeteria.

Rachel's hand clenched on the extra meal ticket she'd earned with her blood. "Here," she said. "I'll pay you."

He reached out, but Rachel jerked her hand away. "Tell me first."

"We marched up to Pennsylvania. Found individual survivors, but no government control." He shook his head. "Nothing much to the east. A lot of death. Didn't see plants or animals. The ground looks like black sand. Using binoculars, we could see the Atlantic Ocean a hell of a lot closer that it should have been. Survivors moving inland, abandoning homes and villages. Making their own cities."

Rachel nodded. "Sounds reasonable."

Odd noises came out of his throat. "Naw, it's all messed up."

"What do you mean 'messed up'?"

He swallowed, searched for the right words. "One night this giant golden bull came thundering across the sky. Flames at its heels. Solid and real as could be. The next night it came again. One of our guys shot at it. The bull, it just turned around and looked at us. Then it galloped down onto the ground and gored Ryan. We all shot, of course, but nothin' touched it. Not one bullet. Ryan fell down, dead, bloody hole in the middle of him. This smoke rose outta him. The bull opened its mouth." The guard trembled and shook his head. "The goddamn thing inhaled Ryan, then galloped off into the sky. Disappeared into the clouds."

Golden bull galloping across the sky? Rachel shook her head. "I don't understand." But goosepimples spread down her arms. This was not so different from a winged dragon sending her and Adam tumbling head over heels. She'd avoided thinking about the encounter during their stay within the false security of the hospital, but now she was going out into a different world.

The soldier wiped a hand over his face. "We're not supposed to talk about it till we've met with Dr. Abramson."

Rachel's mind churned. "So, minus this golden bull, what do I do?"

"Major Griffin said no one's to leave city boundaries. You'd be crazy to anyway, the things I saw. Just follow the group to the stadium like you're supposed to." He snatched the meal ticket from her hand.

Rachel looked out into the twilight at the people shuffling outside and then turned toward the cafeteria, two tickets left. Her mind crowded, sounds muffled; she couldn't think. Too much input without time to process. This was how her depression started, the feelings that paralyzed her, kept her from being able to move. *One thing at a time. Get food.* She went to the cafeteria, gathered her allotted food into the tote bag, and moved forward into the hallway. *Go to recovery room. Use Purell on wall. Get Adam back upstairs. Help Adam climb into the bed of room 833.* She did it all, but couldn't stop her mind from looping.

Back in the room, Rachel crawled up into the window seat, and rocked back and forth. *Think. We're leaving the hospital tomorrow. We'll be killed by the people outside or Adam will get sick from a random germ and die. If he dies, I don't want to live.* Adam curled up, tired from the aftereffects of the anesthesia. *What did the soldier's story about the golden bull mean?* Her fingers itched to draw the bull, the power in the shoulders, the bovine skull. If she could draw it, then maybe she could get the image out of her head.

"Mom. I don't feel good. My stomach hurts." His mouth twisted. "I need to eat."

There was something earlier, something that I need to remember, but I can't. What if Craig isn't dead? What if he comes here after we leave?

"Mom!" Adam was right in her face, still in the hospital gown from the OR, his expression angry. Rachel squinched her eyes closed. It was so hard to open them, to make her mouth move. Like she was the Tin Man from the *Wizard of Oz.*

"Leave me alone." She forced her eyes open and took a deep breath. She wanted to scream. *How am I supposed to figure this out if you keep bothering me?* Instead, she said through gritted teeth, "Sorry." *Congratulations, you're a real mother of the year.* She concentrated on breathing.

"I'm hungry." Adam said. "You were supposed to get food."

"The bag is over there." Rachel pointed toward the pullout couch. Her stomach growled. She replayed the memory of the redheaded park ranger in her mind. How he'd walked west toward the I-95 exits of Baltimore. She thought back to the first night, remembered the satellite picture showing the main force of the storm to the east and moving south. There was one place, if Craig was alive, that he would think to look besides the hospital. A place to go that wasn't living on the streets of Baltimore with gunfire every night.

The paralyzing force of despair was wearing off. Rachel became aware of her outside surroundings instead of only her interior landscape.

"Adam, slow down. You're eating everything."

He was sitting on the couch, already halfway through the second meal.

She moved to sit beside him. "I need to eat, too." Rachel snapped. "I gave blood today."

"Here." Adam picked up the last sandwich. "You can have the rest."

"That's alright, buddy. I'm sorry. You need to eat." Embarrassed about snapping, about the self-pity that caused it, Rachel leaned against his shoulder. "Besides, we have a big day tomorrow."

"We're in this together." He held the sandwich to her mouth until she took a bite. "A team."

Grateful for his kindness, Rachel whispered, "Thank you."

The dullness outside the window combined with the lack of electricity inside created a heavy, murky ambiance. She thought again of the park ranger. There had to be something better in that direction.

The parking garage looked intact. They'd just get in the NewWave and drive away. Except they'd be breaking quarantine.

Adam yawned. Set down the last bite on the sandwich wrapper. Closed his eyes.

She'd almost finished eating Adam's leftover crust when the gunshots started again.

EIGHT

Naomi came to walk them to the hospital's front doors. Rachel had her packed bag over her shoulder as she took one last look at the room.

"Adam, take this." Naomi held out a black bookbag. "It was my son's, but I convinced him that you need it more. You've got five minutes to grab whatever you want from the playroom while I talk to your mom."

Adam opened his mouth as if to argue, then shut it and grabbed the bag, racing for the door.

After the door clicked shut Naomi crossed her arms over her chest. "Alright Rachel, what's the plan?"

Rachel's head pounded and her stomach ached. Last night it had seemed such a brilliant idea to take off for their cabin in the mountains. This morning it seemed impossible. She wasn't adventurous or a fast-thinker. But, living in the stadium, exposed to germs, at the mercy of another freak storm wasn't an option. She pressed the palm of her hand to her forehead.

"Rachel," Naomi said. "We have to meet the rest of the discharges downstairs at the front door. Tell me you've thought of something."

"I'm going to throw up."

Naomi gave her a little shake. The movement was enough. Rachel sank to her knees and threw up her morning coffee into the wastebasket.

"Oh jeez," Naomi went to the bathroom and got paper towels. "Sorry, sweetie. I'm pushing you too hard."

"No," Rachel sat back. "At least my stomach isn't cramping anymore. I'd thought about driving away. Just getting in my car with Adam and driving to our house in West Virginia. But I don't know if the roads are passable, if the cabin is still there, if someone else has taken it over." She dug in her pack for toothbrush and paste.

Naomi followed her into the bathroom. "I know you're scared, but I've also seen your courage fighting for Adam. Being a cancer mom. That's not easy. Now there's another one of life's fires. You've got to be brave enough to walk through the fire, Rachel. There's no other way through."

"How do I go through this fire?" Rachel scrubbed to get the vomit taste out of her mouth.

"One step at a time." Naomi flashed a cheeky grin. "Go check out this cabin. If it isn't okay, you can always come back to the stadium. No harm done. If it is okay, then you have a place to stay. And if Craig shows up here I'll tell him to meet you."

"Do you think there's a chance of that?"

"No. But if, by some miracle he does, then I'll send him to you."

Rachel spit and rinsed. It didn't sound hard when Naomi said it that way—but that was one of Naomi's gifts. She was full of sass and practical energy. Last night's sense of possibility came trickling back to Rachel. She nodded. "Okay. Yes. Adam and I are doing it."

"Well, hurry up or we're going to get in trouble."

"Right." She threw the brush and paste into her bag and pulled out the car keys, sliding them into her front jeans pocket. The women grabbed Adam from the hallway and rushed down the stairs to join the group waiting by the front doors. Rachel didn't recognize the other patients who were being discharged today, but all were gathered by the giant Plexiglas doors of the front entrance. Dr. Abramson was taking back the hospital bracelets. Four armed guards stood waiting to escort the group across Baltimore to their new home at the stadium.

"Naomi," Rachel whispered as they stood at the periphery of the group, "those guards aren't going to let me leave."

"The parking garage is right around the corner. Walk there with purpose. Keep your eyes straight ahead."

Then Dr. Abramson was there and both Rachel and Adam had to surrender their bracelets. He checked the numbers against a list on a clipboard. Rachel wanted to grab hers back, a security blanket, and instead rubbed her wrist, feeling a loss that it was gone.

Dr. Abramson told the group that they were the fortunate ones, the survivors. He said they were being released into the community. It made Rachel think of unwanted pets being dumped outside. He finished by saying, "I counsel you to remember your goal as a citizen of Baltimore. Good day."

"Bet he was a real hit at commencement," Rachel muttered to Naomi.

"What's commencement?" Adam whispered.

The doors opened and two guards walked through. The discharged group began to file outside.

"One last thing." Naomi reached into her pocket and held out what looked like wadded up tissues. "I stole it from the OR for you."

Rachel shoved it—whatever it was—in her jacket pocket and leaned forward to embrace Naomi. "I don't know what to say."

Suddenly Rachel felt herself yanked away. It was a guard. A big man with a rifle in his hands. "Let's go."

Everyone was already outside. Rachel stepped through the door, Adam's hand in her own. The sun was hidden, as usual, behind thick gray clouds; the air smelled greasy and unclean. The group began walking, shepherded between two guards at the head and two towards the rear. Rachel and Adam fell in line, but each step was taking them farther from the parking garage. A tapping from inside the hospital drew Rachel's eye and she saw that Naomi was keeping pace with them inside the hallway. Naomi's face contorted as she gestured toward the parking garage.

Rachel slowed her steps. How was she supposed to know the right moment to turn around? In movies there was always a distraction and then the hero creeps away unseen. She grabbed Adam's hand and they stopped walking. The other patients and guards kept going. No one seemed to notice that they were falling behind, or maybe they did and just didn't care. Rachel and Adam stood at the edge of the block. The rest of the group and soldiers crossed the street.

This was it. They could either run forward and catch up with the others, or go their own way. With a swallow, Rachel pulled on Adam's hand, and placed a finger to her lips. They crossed to the opposite side of the street and stayed close to the building, looking for the opening to the parking garage. Each moment Rachel expected to hear a guard shout. *They can't shoot me because I'm leaving. But, maybe they can. Who knows.* A quick glance up showed Naomi across the street inside the hospital. She gave them a quick thumbs up and then disappeared into the building. Probably didn't want to draw any attention to them.

Up ahead, Rachel could see the parking garage entrance. There was a crater in the wall and the driveway was cracked, but the building looked solid compared to most.

"Come on, Adam. We're almost there." Rachel kept a hold of his hand with her left and dug the keys out with her right.

"Mom?"

"Shhh. I'll explain as soon as we get moving."

Rachel saw the SUV, parked like she'd left it the night of the firestorm, except for a new dent on the side. Like someone had kicked it. She clicked the remote button and the doors unlocked. Focused only on getting away from the guards, Rachel had already shoved Adam into the back seat when she became aware of the noises all around her, of the stench of unwashed bodies and rotting sores.

She hated haunted houses. The kind where things leap out of the dark. And here, in the semidarkness of the parking garage, she had that same feeling. Deliberately she pushed the button to lock the car and slowly pivoted, keeping her hand on the SUV as she walked toward the trunk to get around to the driver's side.

At the trunk she kept her back to the gray light of the entrance, and looked into the breathing darkness. This abandoned parking garage had become a squatter's camp for street people, the same ones who'd thrown bricks and debris at the hospital's glass walls. Their bodies were marked with hunger and with burns from the firestorm. Sheets were hung for privacy, barrels from somewhere had become firepits. That explained the spots of light in the cavernous space. Blankets were thrown on the floor for beds. Cars with broken windows turned into living quarters. Rachel touched the reinforced, tinted windows of the NewWave. They'd special ordered the windows to protect Adam's photosensitive skin. It had saved the SUV from becoming someone's starter house.

"Hospital bitch." The words passed through the street people, those who hadn't been let in, those in pain.

"Not anymore." Rachel said, turning her head to speak to the whole garage. "Now I'm like you . . . with no place to go."

There was the old man who'd called her a hospital bitch, and the youth with the rotten fruit and rotten teeth who sat on the empty street. They were all watching her, little camps of people interspersed throughout the space. Rachel had the feeling that one wrong movement would ignite a hate mob.

"What's in her bag? I bet she's got food." The voices seemed to be coming from all over and Rachel glanced up and around. When she looked back, the fringe group of street people nearest to her had crept closer. She tried to remember anything from her psychology classes in college. Maybe try to single out individuals? Break the mentality?

"Hey," Rachel called to the girl sitting cross-legged near elevators that had been turned off from inside the hospital. The doors down here were dented, as if someone had tried to force them open, like the dent on her SUV. "Brie, I remember you. I shared food with you. And the little girl. Daisy. While we were in the bomb shelter."

"You were in the hospital? You one of them?" The street people in the forming mob turned to the teenager, hostility against one of their own members.

Eyes wide, the girl shook her head, feeling the weight of the collective. "She a'right, but we're not friends. It was just the first night, the fire night, and then they kicked me out."

The SUV was between Rachel and the mob, but Adam was inside. And she was scared that more people were approaching from behind her. Through the window of the trunk, Rachel saw something white and yellow. She put the key into the trunk lock, not wanting to unlock the doors, and turned it.

"Hold on," Rachel said. "I have something." She kept one hand on the trunk hatch so it didn't completely raise. Her other hand swept the floor and pulled out two melted granola bars left from some other day. "Here." She pulled her arm back and threw the two as far into the garage as she could.

The people ducked down like she'd thrown a bomb. Rachel put her head down so she could see and grabbed the bottle of water and then a pack of Pop-Tarts. She lobbed these in another direction. Scrambling ensued. They'd figured out she was throwing food and not a weapon. The last thing was the white and yellow box of fish-shaped crackers, a big box from a discount store that she always carried around.

"Here, you guys can have this." Rachel tossed the box to Brie, hoping it would be payment enough that they could leave. She slammed the trunk and dashed to the driver's side.

The girl shrieked as the box landed in her lap. The mob jumped on her, trying to get at the food. Brie disappeared under the pile. Arms and legs flailed. Rachel imagined a multitude of desperate hands indiscriminately grabbing at anything that resembled food.

Rachel slid into the SUV and put the car in neutral. They rolled down the driveway. No one was paying any attention to them anymore, but Rachel and Adam could hear the girl screaming from underneath the pile of bodies.

Out in the gray sunlight, Rachel put the car in drive, but could hardly see. Sweat dripped off of her. *I didn't know they were going to swarm like that, but it's still my fault. I was just trying to break the mob mentality. They would have done that to me and Adam. No. I should have been smarter, figured out a way.*

"Mom."

"Yes, Adam."

"Why are they attacking Brie?"

"I don't know, sweetie. That's why we're getting out of here." *They are hurting her because I gave her food and they all want it and they'll be angry if they don't get it and blame her. I did that, son, so we could live. Difference is, next time I'll know what's going to happen. But I'll still have to choose what to do.*

"That's not fair," Adam said. "She probably would have shared. Now the package will break and the goldfish will be trampled and no one will get anything."

In the rearview mirror Rachel saw Adam frowning. He pushed the edge of his hand against his heart.

"What's wrong?"

"It wasn't right, what happened in there." Adam adjusted his hand. "My heart hurts. Like thumping hard." He rolled his shoulders and lifted his chest like he was trying to create space inside his rib cage.

"Adrenaline," Rachel said, but she remembered the moment in the hospital with the fake nurse. He'd had this feeling before. Could the chemo have compromised his heart?

There were no other cars on the road, but some pedestrian groups of two and three walked in the same direction that Rachel drove. Some pushed grocery carts packed high with their belongings and others had packs on their backs. A starving dog sniffed at the corner of a demolished building that had been a fast-food restaurant two weeks before. Rachel drove towards the I-95 exits.

PART II

INTO THE MOUNTAINS

She was petite, but her beautiful box braids were piled into a topknot and added to her height. Her skin was brown with a smattering of dark freckles. Her most startling feature, however, were eyes the green of an unfurled spring leaf.

NINE

A green sign marking Baltimore City's limits hung upside down. Wind swung it back and forth. Debris spread across the highway. Rachel swerved around a large pothole and pulled onto the interstate. Only twice did she see other cars and they didn't stay on the highway for long. She pulled off toward I-70.

"Mom, you're going the wrong way."

"I'm not." Driving west to the mountains should be a scenic tour during the summer, hardy maples and redbuds lining the road, but a flaming tornado had passed through. The remaining trees and brush stood like charred matchsticks. Scorched earth and melted pavement on one side. A pile of burned cars on the other. Their inhabitants had either been killed or run for cover. Rachel hoped they'd made it. "We're going to the cabin."

"What?" Adam pounced forward from his seat so that his face was right at her ear. "We have to go home. We have to get Dad."

Rachel struggled for calm. "We barely got out of Baltimore. I'm not wasting gas and putting us back in danger. I understand how you feel, Adam, but your father will know where to meet us."

"You don't even believe he's alive." The words were angry, a hurled accusation. Adam shook Rachel's seat and the car swerved. She slammed on the brakes in the middle of the road and swiveled to face him. Adam's nostrils flared. Tears stood in his eyes. Betrayal?

Rachel searched for something to say, thrown off by his perceptive comment. She'd thought she'd protected Adam from the truth and knew that any lie now would be immediately spotted. She couldn't keep underestimating him so she settled for stating the next step.

"Inland seems less affected by the firestorm. We've got to get to a safe place, Adam."

"You can't tell me what to do." He lunged for the doors. "I'll walk back to our house." Adam yanked at the handle, letting it smack back into position again and again. He punched the seat in front of him. "You're so stupid."

"You can hate me." Rachel said. "My job is to keep you safe and I will do that."

"He's waiting for us. He knew I wasn't feeling good and we'd have to go to the hospital. He's waiting at home." Adam threw himself against the back seat, pulled his knees up to his chest, and stared out the window.

"He's not." Rachel bit the tip of her tongue. Had Craig really dropped off Adam knowing he was sick without telling her? "Daddy left us before the firestorm."

Adam glared at her and shook his head. "He didn't leave us. He left you. Because you didn't love him enough."

She had to take a deep breath to control the immediate pain. *Was this something Craig had said to Adam or was Adam intuiting again?* "We aren't friends, Adam. I'm your mother. And you will not speak to me like that again."

She put the car into drive again and angled the rearview mirror to the back seat. Adam's forehead pressed against the window pane.

"I loved being pregnant with you. The total connection. Aware of the kicks and flutters that no one else could feel. This little person with me all day long. I was in love with you before I even saw you." He'd turned his head a bit. She hoped he was listening. "But I was so scared for you to actually be born. That I wouldn't know what to do." She swallowed. "I'm not perfect, Adam. Maybe I'm overprotective. Maybe I'm too cautious. I could list a thousand ways I've messed up, but I can promise you. I will protect you. Maybe not the way that you'd like, but the way that I, as your parent, believe is best."

Adam rolled his eyes.

About an hour into the drive Rachel passed a group of people walking toward Baltimore. They yelled and told her to stop, but Rachel kept driving.

"Should we give them a ride?" Adam asked. His tone was curious, the anger from earlier gone.

"No. I get that they need help, but I don't know who to trust." She glanced in the rearview mirror and then forced herself to look forward.

Soon after, I-70 began climbing and twisting around the summits and ridges of the Appalachians. The exposed sides of the mountains were shiny as if the rock had melted and then hardened.

"This looks like a nightmare," Adam whispered. "I wonder whose."

Rachel swallowed. The mid-Atlantic used to be featured in travel magazines for its colorful beauty, but color had all been drained away. The tree trunks were white, reaching up with limbs like bleached bones. Nature's graveyard. It was eerie.

"It's so empty. All burned up." He sighed. "I miss my friends and I want to see Dad. It's just lonely. No offense, Mom."

Rachel felt awareness stab through her. She'd been so focused on getting them to safety that she hadn't even considered Adam's point of view. During his illness, Rachel had tried to keep up communication with Adam's school class so he could still exchange emails with his friends. She'd posted medical updates on the CaringBridge site so neighbors and Craig's parents out in California would know what was happening. But, her parents had died in a car accident while she was in college. And she'd dropped all of her own friendships. There was no time to catch coffee together when Adam was constantly being treated or neutropenic, his numbers so low he couldn't be exposed to anyone new. Naomi was Rachel's only constant friend and that was because they saw each other at the hospital, not in spite of it. So, Rachel didn't feel any more lonely than usual, but Adam did.

He was offering a truce, she thought. Putting the argument behind them. "None taken."

"You just should have told me." His eyes met hers in the mirror. "About not going home."

Rachel nodded. "I'm sorry I didn't talk about it with you."

"I'm sorry, too." Adam sighed again and looked out the window.

Raindrops began to fall, slow at first, then harder. The water was gray as the sky, but turned clear the longer it fell. Adam stretched out across the seat. His right hand rested on his chest as if saying the Pledge of Allegiance. Rachel wondered if his incision from the port removal hurt or if his heart was beating irregularly again.

The road curved higher into the mountains, over the rain clouds, but tendrils of fog hung in the air only a few feet above the macadam. They hadn't seen any more people walking since they'd passed Frederick; pedestrians no doubt choosing the flatter path to the north rather than west. No other cars until a Volkswagen crammed full like a clown car careened around a switchback.

The driver—a black man with glasses—leaned out. "Can't go any farther. Fog's too thick. You could drive right over the edge. There's a runaway truck lane you can use to turn around about three hundred yards up."

Rachel nodded. "Thanks." She eased her SUV as close to the inside as possible so the car could squeeze past.

"Punch buggy," Adam said.

"Yeah. Maybe you could not hit me while I'm driving." The car disappeared in the rearview mirror. Rachel pulled to the center line and drove forward. The lack of visibility made her imagine they were all alone in the world.

"Are you going to turn around like the guy said?"

"Nope." Rachel leaned forward. The fog was much thicker up here. "I know the way. It'll clear after we summit and start going down the other side."

"Or over the edge."

TEN

"I've never seen fog like this." Rachel rolled down her window to see if it would help, but the air was so dense that when she extended her hand, it came back damp. She checked her watch. It would be dark soon and the fog wasn't going to burn off.

Rachel spotted the place the driver had mentioned. Last chance to change her mind. She shivered, but kept driving. The road ahead curved upward and Rachel knew that there was a nasty switchback, but they couldn't sleep on the side of the mountain. There could be wild animals or something worse. Rachel pulled at her necklace as her imagination conjured up the dragon in the firestorm and the golden bull described by the soldier.

"You know how I always tell you not to hang your arm out the window?"

Adam looked up from his book. "Yeah."

"I'm about to let you." Rachel pointed through the windshield. "Hang your body out the window and tell me if I get too far from the mountain. We should be right up close to it. I'll look out my side and make sure we don't go over the cliff."

Imaginary Craig smacked his head with his palm and mumbled, *What could possibly go wrong while driving blindly along the edge of a mountain?*

Rachel ignored him.

As if sentient, the fog surrounded her car and clung. Rachel kept her foot on the gas, going about 5 mph. As they drove around a curve, Rachel slammed the brakes. Gravel scattered. Ahead of them a chunk of road was missing, taking away both the guard rail and the outer lane. It looked like damage from a rockslide. She took a calming breath, unfastened her seatbelt, and opened the car door. The SUV driver's tire was on the edge of the hole. Everything below was lost in a thick white sheet of fog.

Don't panic. Her jaw ached from clenching. She wanted to quit, but she couldn't. Not like quitting art school and blaming her parents' death. No, if being a cancer mom had taught her anything it was to get to the next step. The doctors didn't tell her the *whole* three-year treatment plan on the first day. They explained the next step and then the next one.

She would get them to the next step: through the fog.

"Mom?"

She pulled her door shut. The passenger side door was impossible to open because of how close the SUV was to the mountain. Rachel popped the hatch.

"What are you going to do?"

"I'll climb over the NewWave and then see if the road ahead is passable."

"I'll come with you."

"Stay here." Rachel didn't want the distraction of wondering if Adam was going to fall over the edge of the cliff. She crawled out the back, shut the hatch, and then climbed on top of her car and slid down the windshield.

Blind, Rachel dropped to her hands and knees to follow the edge of the road, trying to judge if the width was enough for the SUV to pass. Blue light slashed through the fog, like miniature lightning. It smelled like after a storm. Ozone. She felt dizzy and couldn't think.

The voice spoke at such a low volume that Rachel didn't think it was real until it repeated: "What are you doing here? Who sent you?"

She stared into the fog bank as something—a vague shape in the whiteness—spread across the road. The shifting shape suggested the outline of several people bunched together.

"Was it Marduk?" The man's voice was querulous and scratchy like an old-fashioned record. "Ashur?"

Rachel pushed herself to her feet and thought through her options. It was too late to hide or get away. *They have me blocked from going forward and I can't reverse down the mountain.* Her only possible weapon was a screwdriver and that was back in the glove compartment.

"Nobody sent me." Using the opposite tactic, Rachel held up her hands to show she had no weapons. "I'm waiting for the fog to clear. Then I'll be on my way."

"You'd be waiting for a long time then. The fog isn't what you call 'natural.' Won't roll back unless I say, and I won't say." The tone made her think of an angry grandfather with hands on his hips.

"Why not?" Rachel peered into the fog at the shape. What did he mean "not natural?" Was this fog man-made?

"Because I don't believe you." The voice sounded angry. "What moron would try to come through my fog unless he or she is a spy? Turn around and go tell whoever sent you that I'm not playing. I'm neutral. Leave me out of it."

Rachel gave an ironic snort. "Me. I'm the stubborn moron who is trying to drive through an impossible fog. All my idea. I promise you, no one sent me." Rachel played along with his tirade. "I get that you want to be neutral. Like Switzerland."

"Yeah, I'm like Switzerland." He cleared his throat. "Who's Switzerland?"

Was he kidding? She just wanted to get to her log cabin. "I don't want any trouble."

The voice laughed and laughed, an ugly undercurrent to the sound. "Trouble's coming whether you want it or not."

"What kind of trouble?"

"You really want to pretend you don't know?" Blue lightning flickered to either side of where Rachel stood. The hair on her arms raised. "War. City-states are forming from the rubble. Everyone's going to have to pick a side. Humans aren't top dog anymore, y'know?"

"No, I don't." Her nose burned. She had to get back to Adam. "If you can really control this fog, just let us through."

"Us?"

Rachel frowned. She hadn't meant to reveal that Adam was with her. No use lying now. "My son. The two of us, that's all. We want to go home."

The voice sighed. "I always was a sucker for the little mice in the world."

Rachel bit her tongue to keep back an answering insult. It was hard to think with the smell of ozone all around. She swayed on her feet, head stuffy like she'd taken cold medicine. Uncomfortable, Rachel wanted to sit down. Even making conversation was difficult.

"Give me that gold around your neck and I'll give you a test. If you pass, I'll let you through." A hand beckoned from the fog.

Rachel's hand went to the charm around her neck. "It's special to me."

"It'll be special to me too. Only way to get through the fog. Hurry up before I change my mind."

It was their only chance. Feeling as if the flickering blue lightning was hypnotizing her, Rachel undid the clasp and held out her necklace toward the mysterious shape. An old man's hand darted through the fog to snatch it. Another hand fingered the charm and a third hand played with the clasp.

"Gold is so nice, so very, very nice." The voice sounded well pleased.

One of the hands grabbed her wrist. Rachel tried to jerk back, but found herself frozen. Images passed through her mind. Her first drawing class, her parents' death, her wedding to Craig, Adam's birth, the day that Adam was diagnosed. The night of the firestorm.

"Hmm. Guess you told the truth." He sounded surprised and then his voice softened, the anger gone. "Family. Home. Security. These are your primary concerns. You're scared of failing, would rather quit first. You have trouble letting go. Art is an escape for you, but you've ignored your own needs because of trouble in your family or home. Your heart leads the way, but you've lost belief in yourself."

The hand dropped her wrist and Rachel rubbed her chilled skin.

"So what do I do?" Rachel squinted into the fog, knowing she shouldn't trust a stranger, but with her head so foggy it was hard not to be seduced by his sympathetic manner. "I need help."

"Know yourself and then let go."

Rachel yawned. The air was so thin up here. "Of what?"

"Everything you clutch the tightest. That's freedom. A bird can't hold its perch and fly." He cleared his throat. "I mean, it could if it was strong enough to break the branch. Then it could fly and hold on, but that's a different metaphor."

Rachel shook her head. "I think . . . I think that's an analogy." Something in the air made her want to sleep. "I just want to be safe."

An old man's head swam into view. He wore sunglasses and a white beard so full that it looked like a cat glued to his chin. "Well, you won't be," he said in his distinctive voice. "No one—human or Misbegotten—will be. Have to change the world first. But, hey, find out for yourself."

The fog pulled away from Rachel and then rolled up from the ground like curtains rising over a stage. A perfect tunnel formed through the fog.

Like an automaton, Rachel walked back to the SUV, climbed through the hatch, and slid behind the wheel, her mind sharpening only when she stared at the tunnel. Everything that happened while she'd been outside was hazy, like she'd been hypnotized and the hypnotist just snapped his fingers.

"Where did you go?" Adam punched her on the shoulder. "What happened? You disappeared and I couldn't see you anymore."

"Enough." Rachel shook her head and steered through the tunnel. Her skin held the phantom touch of her missing necklace.

She turned off I-70. Night had fallen. Branches lay across the narrow lanes and twice she had to get out and drag them to the side so she could drive through. Finally she turned into her driveway, past where the No Outlet sign had blown over or been taken. It was difficult to assess the surrounding damage through the in the darkness of the gray rain. They parked in front of their log cabin.

"We made it," Rachel collapsed so that her forehead rested on the steering wheel and her fingers tightened around it with the strength of her relief.

Rachel ran through the rain to the front door and through to the garage, manually pulling the rope to open the door. Once the SUV was parked and the garage door closed again, Rachel helped Adam maneuver through the dark house to the bathroom. He was half-asleep and disoriented.

"Where are we?" he murmured.

"We're home, sweetie."

"What's going on?" His arms windmilled as she tried to move him toward his bedroom.

"Come on, hon." She pushed him through the doorway to the bed. "We can talk in the morning."

"I don't want any needles." He shoved at her as he fell onto the bed, pulling the covers over himself.

"No needles. We're not in the hospital."

In her bedroom, dusty after months of disuse, Rachel sank down into the thick rug in the middle of the room, adrenaline still pumping from the grueling drive. Her fingers combed the rug, she smelled the faint trace of a spilled perfume. They'd made it here, to the next step. Exhausted, she crawled into bed.

Twice that night Adam screamed out and Rachel went to his room, but his eyes were still closed and she smoothed back his hair and murmured that it was just a dream. She stumbled back to bed and hid in her pillows, listening to the storm pounding all around, branches scraping against the roof and other unidentifiable sounds, before returning to her own dreams of a beast with many arms caged by blue lightning and haunted houses with no escape.

ELEVEN

Raindrops freckled the skylight over the sleigh-style bed in the master bedroom. Rachel propped up the pillows behind her and stretched, enjoying the feel of satin sheets instead of the rough cotton of the hospital. She felt good. The relief was welcome after the danger of getting here. Rich green paint on the walls and thick rugs scattered across hardwood floors fed the feelings of warmth and comfort. At the base of the bed, a wooden chest held extra blankets and thick sweaters. A tapestry—*The Unicorn is Found*—hung on the wall. The medieval scene depicted hunters stalking a unicorn as it dipped its horn into a pond to purify the snake venom. According to one of her first college papers, the unicorn represented a sacrificial figure while the hunters embodied base motivations.

The bedside radio clicked on. Soft music played, "A Hard Day's Night." Rachel looked over at the nightstand, startled.

"Morning." Adam stood in the doorway. A patch of hair over his ear stood straight up while the other side was flat. Adam rubbed at his head and then held out a swath of hair. "It's coming out again."

"That's alright. It grows back." Rachel searched his expression, but he seemed matter-of-fact. "Besides. Last time. You're done with chemo now."

"How come we have electricity out here?" He dropped the hair in the wastebasket by her dresser. "And music?" He walked over to her nightstand and leaned over. Then he held up a cord that ended in a plug. "Electricity that doesn't need connections."

One more unexplainable thing to add to a growing list, but Rachel refused to think about it now. "Probably has a battery. That's why it's good in an emergency."

"Then why are you using it?" He climbed up and stretched out across the bed.

"It turned on by itself. Maybe a welcome home song." She hummed along, trying to remember the words.

Adam had lost interest. "What's for breakfast?"

"I'll make something, but how'd you sleep? Is your chest sore from yesterday?" Rachel brushed back his hair over the new bald spot, searched his eyes. He seemed so much older than eleven sometimes, as if his fight with leukemia had awakened him to the expectation of pain.

"Breakfast," Adam said, pulling away from her hand.

"Alrighty then." Rachel pushed back the covers. "Coffee for me and breakfast for you."

The music ended in hissing static. A voice boomed through the radio sounding like a sportscaster: "That's from a group called 'The Beatles.' I predict good things for them. Catchy. And that title. The night of a hard day. I think we can all relate.

"In weather news, we've got a storm system moving over the Appalachian Mountains. Two more systems gathering force. Today will be overcast with winds from the north. Gusts up to forty miles per hour. Not your typical July and not a good day for fireworks. Don't want to start a forest fire. Just a joke, folks. This is The Weatherman, returning you to your regularly scheduled silence."

The radio clicked off.

Adam and Rachel looked at each other. He said, "What the heck was that?"

"Who knows?" Rachel twirled her hands in the air. "Station could be broadcasting from anywhere." This was the radio personality from the night of the firestorm. Adam wouldn't remember because of his fever, and she wasn't going to remind him.

Adam cleared his throat. "He said Appalachian Mountains."

"The Appalachian Mountains go from Georgia to Maine," Rachel said. "Google it."

Adam rolled his eyes. "With what Internet? Sometimes," he said, "I don't know when you're trying to be funny and when you're serious."

Rachel shrugged one shoulder. "That's how I keep you on your toes."

They walked out of the master bedroom and past the wooden stairs that led to the upstairs bedrooms. A cozy reading nook with a shelf full of books had been built at the stairway's landing. Floor-to-ceiling windows in the great room looked out on the front yard and one could see the gravel driveway before it snaked into the woods. A leather sectional couch wrapped the room and directed attention to the two-sided fireplace in the heart of the house. Rachel and Craig had worked with an architect to design the cabin years ago, when Adam was still young, wanting a place to get away and enjoy nature. They'd named it Hiraeth. Then, with Adam's diagnosis, they'd all but forgotten it until fall of last year. They'd come up here to reconnect. Echoes of the full house remained and teased at Rachel's senses, reminding her that her family was incomplete.

A picture on the shelf caught her eye. She wiped the dust away with the edge of her shirt. In the picture Craig and Adam had returned from a boys' fishing trip. They were both grinning in matching fishing hats. Craig angled the container so that the fish could be seen and Adam stood behind him giving bunny ears. Rachel held the frame with one hand and covered her mouth with the other. A lump formed in her throat. *I'm sorry, Craig. Maybe I should have tried harder. You could have tried harder, too. We were supposed to be partners.*

She looked to Adam to gauge his reaction, but he was already in the kitchen.

Breakfast was easy: open the stocked pantry and make a trail mix of BBQ sunflower seeds, dried cranberries, and granola. Bowls—pretty things with a flower pattern along the rim—in the cabinet exactly where they should be. It was disconcerting. Over the past eleven days her mind had accepted that Craig was dead, that Baltimore was in ruins, that the world had ended. But there were still flowery bowls and granite countertops. There was a big-screen television in the great room. It only took a little imagination to think that Craig was on a business trip, that he'd be home later and they'd put on a movie and relax in front of the fireplace.

"I'm glad to be out of the hospital." Adam grinned at her.

Rachel smiled, trying to quiet the ghostly whispers. "Finish your breakfast. We have a lot of work to do today."

In winterizing the house they'd unplugged appliances, gotten rid of all food in the fridge, and stocked the pantry with cans and sealed containers. Twelve gallons of water that, at the time, had seemed overkill.

"Hey Mom, look! Lemonade mix. Can I make it right now?"

"You know a vital ingredient?" Rachel raised an eyebrow. "Water. We need to find another source to supplement what we have stocked. Grab this," she handed him an empty pitcher, "and I'll take this cleaning bucket. Follow me."

They exited through the garage. Rachel's hand went to the light switch and toggled it. Grimacing, she walked forward to grab the rope that manually opened the garage door so they could have light. A few years ago they'd felt the push, as many people did, to become more self-reliant as climate change and natural disasters headlined every news source. Two rain barrels were on either side of the house, but Rachel didn't want to drink from them. They'd been sitting there for months and, even boiled, the water could be too contaminated for Adam's weakened immune system.

Outside, the air felt damp and heavy. No sun. Their cabin was on an acre of land inside forest on three sides, and a meadow to the north-east leading to the forested state park. The garage opened to the west where the private driveway curved away to a one-lane road. Between the house and the stream that ran perpendicular to the driveway, Craig had labored over cutting out a garden with a fence intended to keep out deer and rabbits.

The wind blew, shaking the trees in what used to be the state park. The boundary line between forest and house was about a half mile, but that edge of forest looked sinister, different than the woods closer to the front yard. Like the trees they'd seen on the drive, these had no leaves and no bark. Skeletons scraped together with ominous moans.

Together Rachel and Adam walked to the creek that ran along the west side of the property. Rachel dipped her hands into the clear water and felt a tingle. Startled, she removed them and dried her hands on her jeans, wiping the sensation away. Peering at the water, there appeared to be an opaque ribbon running through the middle. Adam was already following the creek around a bend, so Rachel wiped her hands one more time and then followed him into the trees.

After about ten minutes of walking they came to the junction where their creek doglegged off from the larger river. The river was maybe thirty or forty feet across, the water carving a path down from the top of the mountain. A few feet upstream, a short drop caused background splashing to fill the silence in the absence of birds or squirrels. A large tree, blackened by fire, had exploded through its top—the sap boiling inside and then erupting like a volcano—but its limbs still hung over the water. Hairs raised on Rachel's arms. Beyond looking different, the river—this whole place—felt different than the last time she was here. It felt sacred, somehow. Looking closer, Rachel examined the round stones lining the riverbed, the way the air above the water shimmered. If she squinted a certain way, shadows appeared in the clear water; an opaque current, larger than the one in her little creek, as if certain parts of the water were out-of-focus.

Motion caught her eye across the river. Dead birds had fallen from the sky. Ravens, maybe? Twenty or more, their bodies were scattered on the brown grass, black feathers still shiny and beaks open as if to call out a warning. An unkindness; that's what you called a flock of ravens. Rachel shivered. Last time they'd been up here, they'd gone to a ranger talk on the birds, one of the most intelligent creatures on the planet. In art they represented memory and thought.

It was Adam's sharp eye that saw one black bird still alive, hopping among the rest as if searching. "One survived, Mom."

The bird went to the river and then back to a body, dropping something. It repeated the action several times, hopping from bird to bird, until Adam gasped.

"It's feeding them water."

Rachel shook her head. "That's not possible." But, that's what she was seeing. The raven was bringing water to each of its brethren. A wing seemed to flutter.

"It's windy," Rachel said. She wrapped her arms around herself. "We should get back to the house."

More feathers ruffled. Maybe the birds weren't dead. They were just dehydrated. This clever bird knew to be a field nurse, bringing river water in its beak. Rachel hadn't known ravens would go to this extent to save their friends.

"Yeah," Adam took a step back. "We should leave."

"I think," Rachel licked her lips, "we should collect water from the creek outside our house." She didn't have a rational explanation, but she didn't want to drink this river water.

"Yeah," Adam said again.

The bird paid no attention as the humans headed home, but Rachel heard cawing behind her as she walked. It sounded like it came from more than one bird.

Later that evening they threw themselves into chairs on the deck, exhausted. It was darker, harder to see. No sunset pinks and golds.

"I'll bring out some cans of food and we can eat with a fork. It'll be like we're camping." Rachel said. "Just give me a minute to sit."

"Don't get up. I'll do it."

"Really, bud?" Rachel gave him a hopeful look. "There has to be a vegetable involved."

"Black olives count, right?"

"Um," Rachel said. "Sure." She searched the sky for ravens, but didn't see anything. She remembered sitting out here at sunset and watching the deer come onto the lawn. Maybe a rabbit and her little babies peeking above the blades of grass.

Adam came back out carrying a can opener, a can of olives, a plastic container of pineapple bits, two cans of tuna, and a package of M&Ms from the candy box. He set the items down on the picnic table.

"Ewww," Rachel said, poking at the candy wrapper. "Those things are so old."

"Really? Are they older than the fish we're going to eat?"

"You have a point."

Adam set down one last thing. It was hard to see in the semidarkness, but Rachel had seen the picture only hours before. She began turning the can opener.

"Is it my fault," Adam asked. "That you and Daddy fought so much? Because I have cancer?"

Rachel left a bit of lid connected and drained the olive liquid over the side of the deck. She opened the tuna cans and then arranged a fork on top of each napkin, sliding Adam's across to him. It was easier to talk when Adam was only a shadow, when she couldn't see the yearning or confusion on his face. Or worse, blame.

"You had cancer," she corrected. "And no, it wasn't your fault at all. Relationships are hard. Daddy and I met in college. He took a renaissance art history class for his liberal arts credit. I was in the class. There was a group project and your dad joined me."

She made a point of eating a bite of pineapple so that Adam would too. It had no taste to her, but he seemed to enjoy it.

"My parents had died the year before so I was lost and feeling lonely. Your dad was outgoing and had all his friends at the fraternity. It was easy for me to join his group."

"So why'd you fight?" He leaned forward as if he didn't want to miss whatever she was going to say.

"We didn't have much in common. He liked current events, I liked researching symbolism in historic paintings. He wanted to go to a baseball or football game, I wanted to go to a museum." Rachel swallowed. "I guess what I'm saying is, you should marry your best friend. Doesn't matter what a person looks like or where they're from. When you find someone that you can talk to for hours and makes you want to be a better person." Rachel nodded. "That's the one you go with."

"Daddy didn't?"

Rachel licked her lips. Like with the story she was creating in Adam's scrapbook, she wanted to present a balanced version of the truth. "He let me replace my dreams with supporting his. He wanted a nice house, dinner on the table when he got home, a companion on the weekends. Normal, healthy, perfectly fine things to want. But, I didn't go to any more art classes because it was too far to drive, because exhibit openings were on the weekend, because I didn't make friends among our neighbors."

"But Daddy didn't tell you to stop drawing."

"No," Rachel said quickly. "And I wanted to build a strong family, to build something lasting since my parents were gone. And then all my time was taken up with a baby named Adam Michael." She cleared her throat.

"And then I got cancer."

Knife in the gut. *That's how he interpreted what she was saying?* "I didn't say that and I don't think that, Adam." She tried to breathe through his accusation. "I'm not blaming you and I'm not blaming your father. You can't make someone else responsible for your own happiness. I'm just trying to explain to you how your dad and I grew apart. He was a good guy and he loved you very much."

"He loves me very much," Adam corrected.

Rachel tapped the photo. "Why don't you take this into your room for a while?"

TWELVE

By the end of the week Adam's incision had healed; the skin a healthy pink. In a perfect world, he'd have had labs drawn each month to check if the leukemia cells were multiplying in the absence of chemo, but there wasn't time now to worry about the cancer coming back. The priorities for survival had to be water, food, and fuel.

They tramped past the Paulownia tree down the path through the southern woods to gather firewood. Rachel kept a careful eye on Adam as he pushed the wheelbarrow around. Sweat lingered on his neck. Despite the lack of sun, his skin was less pale than before; the glowing white of an invalid wearing away. The outside temperature remained a steady, sticky hot. It was mid-July now, but if they stayed until September, they'd need firewood for light and warmth, not just cooking. Adam pushed the wheelbarrow up to the deck and dumped it.

"Can I get the next load by myself?" Adam said.

Rachel looked at the woods. *I can't follow him everywhere.* She nodded. "I'll be right here if you need me."

A half hour later Rachel took a break to stretch. Her back and neck muscles were sore, but she'd almost finished stacking the firewood under a blue tarp. A sudden crashing sound came from the woods and Adam emerged, running. "There's a man! He's hurt."

Rachel followed Adam through the woods to where a man lay on the forest floor, unconscious, a fallen tree pinning him across the chest. His arms wrapped around the trunk as if he'd fallen asleep hugging it. Divots by his feet showed where he'd tried to brace himself and slide out.

Adam said, "I tried to lift the tree off, but it wouldn't move at all."

Rachel stared down at the redheaded man she'd seen in Baltimore. He was younger than she'd thought, mid-twenties at most, wearing khaki shorts and a T-shirt with an embroidered patch of a sequoia tree, mountains, and a white buffalo. A backpack sat a few feet away.

"No," Rachel said, "We aren't strong enough to lift. We'll have to use a lever. Quick, find me a long thick piece of wood."

Adam dove forward. "Here's one."

"Perfect." Rachel positioned the lever and shoved a log under to be the fulcrum. "When I count to three, you'll grab under the man's armpits and pull him toward us."

It took several tries, but Rachel stood on her end of the lever and Adam pulled and together they freed the man. When he was clear, Rachel jumped off and the tree crashed down.

"That was really smart, Mom."

"Thanks."

The man's chest rose and fell with breath. Adam reached down and shook his shoulder. "Mister? We got the tree off of you."

The man's blue eyes fluttered open and he groaned, looking around. "Scott, not mister," he said, hand wrapping around his chest. "I was trying to clear out underbrush when this *Acer rubrum* fell on me."

"Racer-what?" Adam asked, brow furrowed.

"Red maple," Scott said. He tried to sit up, but fell back.

"Rachel Deneuve. This is my son, Adam. Her hand reached for a necklace that wasn't there anymore as she calculated whether he could be a threat to her or Adam. "Is anything broken?"

Scott shook his head. "Bruised, I think, but not broken." He lifted his shirt to reveal a nasty bruise. "Thought I'd be trapped there until I was a skeleton. Thank you for rescuing me."

"You're welcome," Rachel said. "Well, we've got things to do so we'll see you around." She turned back to the house.

"Wait!" He dropped his shirt. "You saved my life. I'll help you with whatever you're doing today. It's the least I can do."

Rachel licked her lips. If he'd wanted to hurt her, he already would have, bruised ribs notwithstanding. And, they could use the help. And, she did kind of know him. "Fine. You guys are on firewood duty. And Scott?" She waited for him to look at her. "Be careful with my son. I don't want to pry up any more *Acer rubrums* today."

Scott and Adam made several trips and then began chopping. It was the first time since arriving that Rachel had a moment to herself. She went inside and watched through the kitchen window. Adam laughed at something Scott said as they came up to the door.

Rachel heard whispering. Then Adam said, "Knock, knock."

"Who's there?" Rachel said.

"Mikey."

She closed her eyes for patience. "Mikey who?"

"Mikey doesn't fit in the lock." Adam opened the door and looked over his shoulder at Scott. "Funny and relevant."

Scott shrugged. "Shut it and let's see what I got." Adam swung the door closed. "Knock, knock."

Rachel said. "We should just leave him out there. How long do you think he'd wait?"

"Not nice, Rachel," Scott said through the door. "Knock, knock."

"Who's there?" Adam said.

"Ice cream."

"Ice cream who?"

"Ice cream if you don't let me in."

"I don't know." Adam made a face. "Middling."

Rachel opened the door.

"No way." Scott stepped through. "It was classic, also relevant because I would scream, and I got a bonus point because your mom was mean to me." He made a face like 'what can you do?'

"Hey Rachel," Scott said. "Can we get something to drink?"

"There's some watered-down grape juice." Plastic containers of grape juice with forty-five grams of sugar each for when Adam woke up after fasting before a lumbar puncture and his blood sugar dropped. Now they're diffused into a gallon of water to tickle memory of taste.

Adam pulled two glasses from the cabinet and they gulped the pale liquid. After refilling their glasses, they wolfed down granola bars and a can of cold soup each.

"Hey," Scott said to Adam, "can you stack those last logs we cut? Then I can help you guys with one more thing before I leave."

"Sure." Adam set his glass in the sink and trotted out back.

"Thank you for letting him help you." Rachel leaned against the counter. "It makes him feel useful."

"It's not an act. You've got to give him more responsibility if you guys are going to make it out here." Scott leaned forward to put his glass in the sink, too. "Are you serious about staying?"

Rachel tilted her head. "Did you think I was joking?"

She glared at him until he held up his hands in surrender. "Okay, okay. But, unless I'm wrong you don't know how to hunt and even if you did, there aren't a lot of animals out there. You need to go shopping."

"No way." Rachel's eyes widened. "I was in Baltimore. I saw the grocery store with armed guards."

Scott laughed. "This is different. We need the wheelbarrow, thick gloves, and a hammer."

After grabbing the supplies, the three of them hiked up the long gravel drive.

"Where are we going?" Adam asked, eager and jumpy.

Scott wouldn't answer. Rachel had a suspicion, and when they rolled the wheelbarrow up to her nearest neighbor's house she balked. "No way. Scott. No. Unacceptable. This is someone's house. They could be coming back here."

"Honestly, what'd you think we were doing with those?" Scott gestured to the hammer and gloves.

"What's going on? What are we doing?" Adam insinuated himself between them.

"Rachel, you're the only nut who is coming out here to live. Everyone else is gathering together to share supplies. How do you think those guys in Baltimore had stuff to sell to the grocery store? They were breaking into houses where people were turned to ash and grabbing out cans of food. This is better. You don't have to worry about accidentally stepping on someone."

Rachel walked a few feet away, arms around herself, stopping by a pine tree to breathe in and out.

"What's my mom doing?"

"She's realizing I'm right."

"Oh. How long is it going to take?"

"Not sure," Scott said. "How often does she have moral dilemmas?"

"I can hear you!" Rachel shouted over her shoulder.

"Sorry," Scott shouted. He didn't sound sorry. "Hey, Adam wants to know how much longer you're going to be."

Rachel rolled her eyes and walked back. "Okay. Here's the deal. We will take what we need, but I'm going to write everything down and leave a note. That way, if the owners come back, I can return what is theirs or give them something in exchange, at least apologize."

"No, you're not." Scott's voice was flat. "No owner is coming back and you're not leaving an invitation to looters to come to your house. Do you need me to explain why?"

Rachel's face went pale. She shook her head 'no,' tried to recover. "I'll keep the list at my house then."

"Waste of time, but your call. Personally, I think you'd be safer burning these houses down so they aren't attractive to anyone looking."

"But then Hiraeth—"

"Here-ith-what?" Scott asked, wrinkling his brow.

"Our house's name."

"You named your cabin?"

Rachel brought the conversation back on track. "If we burned the other houses then wouldn't ours stand out as the only one around?"

Scott opened his mouth and then shut it. "I don't know. Honestly, it wasn't in the manual. Park rangers are supposed to tell you civilians not to burn things down."

She put her hands on her hips. "Okay. Well. I'm not really qualified to burn houses down."

He shrugged. "Alright guys, get your gloves on. Let's see what's in the store for us today. Bonus points to anyone who can find flour, salt, honey or sugar, and powdered milk." He picked up the hammer. "Oh, and also beer."

The window broke with a bright crash.

A raven cried out from the top of a nearby tree and spread out its black wings before settling and tilting its head. Beady eyes studied the humans.

Scott looked up and he nodded his head in greeting. Rachel was close enough to hear his muttered, "Hey, Jude."

Rachel followed the two through the window, wondering what Scott knew about the ravens.

THIRTEEN

It was late when they got back to the house, the wheelbarrow overflowing, Scott's backpack filled, Rachel carrying bags full of anything they'd thought might be useful. They stowed it all in the garage.

Scott whistled to get Rachel's attention as she followed Adam to the door, and then held out the rifle. She'd refused to carry the rifle and two boxes of ammo that Scott had found so he'd carried it himself.

"Oh no, I have no idea how to use a gun. I'd probably kill myself. Or the bad guy would take it from me and kill me." She made a gun with her thumb and index finger and shot herself in the temple. "Bang."

"Learned helplessness is not cute," Scott said. "Hold it."

Stubborn redhead.

"Fine." The rifle was lighter than she'd expected. Rachel could feel scratches on the composite stock, squinted through the scope, smelled an acrid, metallic odor, and ran her hand down the thin metal barrel.

"Up here, the hunter was probably after deer. Rifle cartridges like these 30-06 come in boxes of twenty, but one of them has been opened." He pronounced it "thirty-oh-six."

"So there's less than forty bullets? That's not very many. Why wouldn't the hunter have more?"

"Big game hunters would fire maybe two to six bullets to check their sights." Scott raised an eyebrow. "It only takes one to kill a deer. This is enough for a standard hunting trip."

She handed the rifle back to him.

"I'm serious. You don't wait for the emergency to debate if you're going to use a gun. Decision has to already be made."

She shrugged, an angry gesture to show that she didn't like being forced into action, and then changed the subject. "Hang out for a minute and we'll have a beer. I think today's capture counts as something to celebrate. Let me make sure Adam brushes his teeth: he skimps when he's tired if I don't check." She walked into the house and heard his footsteps behind her.

Scott had the curtains closed and candles lit on the bookshelf and on the fireplace hearth when Rachel came back out to the family room. Adam was asleep already, exhausted from the day. Rachel grabbed two green bottles from the unplugged fridge—an attempt to keep them out of the warm air—and brought them to the coffee table. It was a long time since she'd entertained a male guest and she didn't quite know what to do. Scott stood in the corner of the room looking at the copy of Raphael's *The Madonna of the Meadow*. The Virgin Mary sat in a bucolic landscape with two toddlers: Jesus and St. John the Baptist.

Turning at her approach, Scott said, "Are you religious or an art collector? Maybe got this at a yard sale?"

"Keep your voice down, please, or you'll wake up Adam." It was something that Craig would have known. "I'm familiar with Bible stories because I had to be; I studied medieval art." Rachel moved around the table to stand next to Scott. He was taller than her and gave off a not unpleasant aroma of sweat and pine trees.

"I bought this while I was in Rome during sophomore year. I loved the details. See how the mother takes up most of the picture? But look at how the children interact. St. John is kneeling before Jesus. And the top of the reed St. John is holding?" Rachel pointed. "It's a cross. Jesus is grabbing it, embracing his destiny even as a child."

"I see that now," Scott said. "I guess you'll be our museum curator." He grinned at her as he reached for the beer and flopped on the couch. "In our post-firestorm society."

"That was a lifetime ago. Now I'm worried about whether Adam and I will even survive this nightmare. I keep waiting for it to end."

"Rachel," Scott took a swig of the beer. "What if this is the world? Can you live with that?"

She walked to the other side of the couch and sat down, making sure to keep distance between them. "I guess I have to. But I don't understand why the firestorm happened, what it was."

Scott cleared his throat and sat up straighter. The green bottle rolled back and forth in his hands. "I have a theory. I spend a lot of time outside, you know. Looking up at the stars. A lot of crazy things happened in 2012."

"No," Rachel said. "Please tell me you aren't one of those end of the Mayan calendar doomsday people."

"Listen. The Mayan long count and prophecies got a lot of press because their astronomers were amazing scientists. Our solar system did pass through the galactic equator, just as the Mayans predicted. They saw it as the crossing of the Sacred Tree. 2012. The same year of a conjunction between Venus and the Pleiades. That year was also the environmental tipping point. The black rhino had just gone extinct from poachers, fracking was connected to earthquakes, and the coral died in Australia because the oceans became too hot. I think it's all connected to the firestorm."

"Like divine retribution?" She shrugged. "Seems like it should have been more immediate." Rachel tucked one leg underneath her and leaned against the couch cushions. "2012 came and went a dozen years ago."

Scott set the bottle on the coffee table. He'd seemed like a voice of sanity in the wilderness, someone who could be trusted. She felt a surge of disappointment that he was espousing pseudoscience the way people used to claim the earth was flat.

"When did the firestorm fall?"

"June 21, 2024." The date had seared into her mind.

"Summer solstice. There's astronomical relevance."

Scott held up his hand and ticked off the list on each finger. "Climate change, droughts, the increasing power of hurricanes as the oceans warmed. These issues were ignored, but the firestorm was so big that everyone noticed. It didn't just change the earth; it was the catalyst for a worldwide energy transformation."

Rachel shook her head and rubbed at her neck. "I have no idea what you're talking about, Scott. One beer and you're buzzed?"

"Come with me," he said, pushing against his lanky knees to stand. "I want to show you something."

"Adam's sleeping." Rachel glanced at the stairs as if to confirm the boy hadn't appeared.

"I know. It won't take long." He held out his hand to help her up off the couch. "You have to see it for yourself." He gave her a teasing grin. "What are you, scared?"

Rachel looked down at her hands. She knew Scott in general as a park ranger, but he was asking for her trust. On one hand he'd helped them so many ways, but he'd also just claimed that there'd been a worldwide energy transformation. Honestly, she didn't even know what that meant. Still, if this was something that would help her and Adam to survive, then she needed to learn about it. Whatever "it" was.

"What are you, five?" Rachel accepted his hand.

FOURTEEN

She hadn't been outside at night since the firestorm, choosing to close the blinds and lock the doors. The night air was warm and dark, muffling sounds like a cocoon. Constant cloud cover diffused the moonlight creating swirls in the sky. Rachel felt as if she'd stepped into Van Gogh's *The Starry Night* where the black mountain was represented by the sinister forest in the former park and the gentle village was their homestead.

They tiptoed out the front door. Scott didn't let go of her hand.

"This way," he said, guiding her across the driveway and into the woods. They followed the creek that went past Rachel's house, the creek they used for washing clothes and watering the plants. Of course they were going to the river. She'd known, somehow, that they would.

"You scoffed when I said worldwide transformation because you thought there was no way I'd be able to tell without radios and telephones." He ducked around a tree and Rachel mimicked, still joined by hands. "But water. That goes everywhere, right? Into the atmosphere, into the ground, out to the oceans," Scott said. "Have you ever heard of ley lines?"

"No."

"It's the idea the earth has certain pathways of energy, natural walkways connecting special landmarks or energy nodes. We humans used to be tuned into these spiritual energy lines, but we lost the ability when we became modern and chose to live in cities apart from the natural world. But, historically, in every culture there are sacred spaces, or otherworld entrances, or special guardians of those holy sites, gods with a little 'g.' "

"Scott, this sounds very mystical." She tripped over a root and caught her balance. "And, I don't see the relevance."

"Why is this part of the Appalachian Mountains doing alright compared to the surrounding areas? Why is the creek right there comparatively clean when Baltimore's harbor is filled with ash? Your house is near a ley line intersection."

They came to the dogleg where the creek veered off from the river. A thin jet of light flowed from the river into the creek and diffused. It would be too faint to see clearly during the day. Scott led her farther upstream, to the same place where she and Adam had stood and watched the ravens. The whole river glowed like a million white candles.

Insects, more specks of light in the forested darkness, flew in the air. Lightning bugs, but no, these were shaped like lady bugs and were bigger. To Rachel's right trees were growing. Maybe three feet high with gray trunks and evergreen needles. They seemed healthy.

"The forest is coming back?" She pulled her hand from Scott's. "Is that what you wanted me to see? New trees?"

"Not new," he said. He was distracted, looking for something on the forest floor. "Unless I'm wrong, those are *Cedrus libani*. Cedars of Lebanon. The species grows in the Mediterranean dating back to the earliest human civilizations, if not even earlier. The question is why are they growing in Appalachia?" Scott bent down and picked up a twig about eight inches long "Ah-ha! Here we go." He presented the stick to Rachel with a flourish, turning it like a magician to show there was no trick. "Watch this." He threw the stick in the glowing creek. It floated on the surface and sank.

"Hold on. It doesn't always work perfectly." Scott grabbed two more twigs. The second did the same thing. The third, however, sank and then floated back to the surface, the twig emerging as a thick, three foot long branch. It swirled to the edge and Scott picked it up with the tips of his index finger and thumb. He squatted and dug a hole, planting the branch and then wiping his hands on his shorts. "Tingles," he said with a grimace, shaking out the hand that had touched the stick.

Rachel's stomach contracted with recognition. She'd felt that tingle in the creek. "What the hell just happened?"

He said, "I don't know if it'll grow. But, it definitely changed. You saw that."

It had changed. There was no denying it. Was it magic? Did turgor pressure fill up the twig's veins with water? Too many questions to ask. She settled for, "How did you do that? I don't understand."

"I don't understand either, exactly, but it's no trick." Scott held up one finger. "I think the firestorm was deliberate." He held up a second finger. "I think the earth, and the energy on earth, changed the night of the firestorm." He held up a third. "Plants and animals are changing in unpredictable ways." He flicked out his pinky. "Fourth, I think there are people or maybe creatures who know how to use this new, or maybe old, kind of energy."

"Right." Rachel shifted position so that she was facing toward her house, wanting to make sure that Adam hadn't awakened and come outside to look for her. She rubbed her arms. "Those are some wild claims."

But her thoughts went back to a raven dipping its beak into the river and feeding the rest of its tribe. Fluttering wings. A nurse who wasn't a nurse from the "land between two rivers" who said "they" would come after Adam because of something the boy had. A voice in a fog, the smell of ozone, the warning that war was coming. Rachel shook her head. Too many unexplainable things, but the big picture still wasn't clear.

Scott came around to face her. "Listen, don't freak out, but I knew you guys were here before today. Lucky for me that you were willing to move the tree."

Rachel nodded, kept her face blank to mask her fear, her burgeoning awareness of their vulnerability. Scott had known they were here, and she hadn't even thought about who might be planning to take their house, steal their food.

"What's the story with Adam's dad? Does he actually exist?"

Rachel reached up to touch the necklace around her throat, but the chain wasn't there. After clearing her throat, Rachel said, "Craig. My husband. We were married ten years. Adam and I were in the hospital, safe, because Adam had a fever. Craig wasn't with us."

"Why not?"

"What do you mean?"

"If my kid had cancer and got a fever, I'd be at the hospital with him."

"No, it's not like that." Rachel said. "It's an emergency, but it's not an emergency. Blood cancers suck." She shrugged. "You can't be on the highest of high alerts for over two years without a break. I wasn't mad that he didn't come. If the doctors said it was a virus or Adam didn't respond to broad spectrum antibiotics, then Craig would have come.

"We'd separated." She made a face. "It was nasty." Then she corrected. "We were nasty. Trying to hurt each other. I don't know if we could have gotten back together. I'd like to think we could have been amicable, put Adam first, all that."

"If he was alive then he would be looking for you." Scott sounded confident. "Maybe he's in Baltimore now."

"We can't go back to Baltimore. Adam can't take it." Rachel looked down at her hands and then met Scott's blue eyes, visible in the ambient glow of the creek. "What do you think our chances of making it out here for another three months?"

"You're stubborn. And strong. Otherwise you wouldn't be out here trying to set up a homestead." Scott nodded. "But, you've got to let Adam be strong, too. You saw how he stepped up packing supplies in that house, but only after you stopped trying to do everything yourself."

Rachel's jaw clenched and she folded her arms across her chest. "I need to take care of him. Adam doesn't even have the most basic vaccinations because he's had over twenty blood transfusions. He could die from germs if he falls down and gets a cut; common germs that you and I wouldn't even know that our bodies were fighting."

Scott was quiet. Rachel wondered if she'd come down too hard on him, but all he said was, "So he's a fighter. Bet he gets it from you." He shifted his feet. "Thanks for sharing the beer with me. Think about what I've said about ley lines. It's not magic; this is a science with rules. We just don't understand them, yet. I've got to get going, but I'll try to check back on you guys."

"Where will you go?"

He pushed his chest forward. "I'm the last ranger. Everyone I worked with is gone. Our station was in the path of a fire tornado. I was out in the other part of the park. By the time I got there, the building was destroyed."

Scott picked at the edges of a scab on his hand. Rachel had to bite her tongue to keep from telling him to leave it alone or it wouldn't heal.

"I first became a ranger because I believe in conservation and love the outdoors. I'm outgoing and independent with a sparkling personality. . . ." He looked at Rachel for her reaction.

"Uh-huh."

"But now my job description's changed. I'm learning this new environment. I'm going to map out the area that I believe is protected between ley lines and try to guard this area of forest." He was so determined, so sure of himself. "Will you be okay getting back to your house?"

"Of course." Rachel looked at the creek and back at the ranger. "Be careful."

"Can't be. Park rangers always lead the resistance. Stephen T. Mather said, 'Though small in number, their influence is large.'"

Rachel frowned. "Who is that?"

Scott shook his head with a sad expression. "First director of the National Park Service. I will quote him often, so please remember the name." He faced her and walked backwards upstream. "Keep shopping, hide supplies away from the house so you have backup if your house is raided. I haven't seen any bears or coyotes around, but they'll be desperate for food too. Animals have a keen sense of smell so don't leave anything out. If you're still here in a couple of months I'll help you build a cool house over the stream. Practice with that rifle we got today. Sight through the scope without shooting so you don't waste shots. Just enough practice to get used to handling it and feeling comfortable. More survivors are going to be leaving the cities, possibly coming through here."

"I don't know if I can do this." She spoke without emotion. A kind of numbness had taken over until she could process the evening.

He misunderstood her, and kept talking about feeling confident with the rifle. Would Craig have hugged her? Ignored her? Kept talking like Scott was doing? "And, you can always use it as a club." He waved. "Alright. I'll be back when I can." He slipped on a rock and wobbled. "Try to stay alive."

"You too." Rachel said. "G'night."

Rachel watched him disappear into the forest and then walked home.

She'd joked that one beer had given Scott a buzz, but maybe it was affecting her too, because the sadness she hadn't felt since they'd arrived was coming back. This wasn't some fun homesteading experiment. If she messed up, she was the one responsible, and then she and Adam would die a stupid, horrible death. If Scott was right then it wasn't only a checklist of food, water, and fuel. It was knowing if strangers were watching you, planning to steal your food. It was some type of new energy and bizarre new insects and plants.

Humans aren't top dog anymore, a voice she almost remembered whispered.

Rachel went back into the house, locked the deadbolt, and grabbed another beer from the unplugged fridge. She was too wound up to sleep. The candles on the bookshelf were half burned. Still plenty of light. Rachel scrounged through the cupboards on the bottom of the bookshelves in the family room, pulling out a child's drawing kit she'd bought for Adam years ago. She'd hoped he would like art, but he'd preferred the new soccer ball and net Craig had picked out.

Rachel sank into the carpet in front of the coffee table and set her beer aside. She poured out the art materials and turned a fresh page in the sketch book. It was hard at first, clumsy, but then, in the comfort of the candlelight, she began to translate her tangled thoughts into images on the paper.

FIFTEEN

As days settled into routine, Rachel seized any free time to work on her charcoal drawing, trying to fit together the conspiracy of ravens, the ambient glow of the river, the twig becoming a branch. Would it grow into a tree like the cedar of Lebanon that had no business in the Appalachian Mountains? She should go back and check, just to know. But she put it off, just as she set aside thoughts of Scott and his stories of energy transformation and astronomical formations.

Capturing the images on paper was as much an exercise in her belief as in her artistic talent. This morning she rubbed the edge of her fist against the paper to wipe out the incorrect lines she'd drawn as she struggled to remember the way the bird had cocked its head in that knowing look. With a final sigh, Rachel rolled the paper up in frustration and took the picture and her art materials to her room, unsure why she needed to hide this from Adam. Actually, she knew why. Adam, typical eleven-year-old, would have no fear of a river with magical properties that acted like magic.

As she tucked the materials into her bedside table, the radio clicked on by itself. The Weatherman was already speaking, in his own sportscaster way.

". . . Detroit is still burning. Where's Nero and his fiddle now? Replaced by Ashur. His followers call themselves Hotheads, and that should tell you something. Stupid Babylonian. They continue to move south, recognizable by the red paint they wear on their faces and their enjoyment of setting anything and everything on fire. Meanwhile, winds sweeping across the mountain tonight. Make sure your windows are shut tight. This is The Weatherman signing off."

Great. Even a post–firestorm news program was sensationalist. "Would it kill you to run a human interest story?" Rachel asked the radio. She picked it up and shook it. No loose wires. Nothing to indicate when or why this radio kept turning itself on and off. Or why the information was always accurate to this specific region. Rachel stalked around the bedroom, still frustrated by the drawing, by what she'd seen at the river, by the radio.

Rachel went out to the porch. "Hey, Adam?" He came around the corner of the house. *He's grown*, she acknowledged. In the two weeks that they'd been at Hiraeth, she'd been watching for unexplained bruising or lack of appetite; instead, his body had responded to the lack of chemo by shooting up a good two inches. His hair had grown longer and she'd had to trim it a few days ago to keep it out of his eyes. She didn't remember any of the other moms talking about growth spurts so soon after treatment ended.

"I'm almost done with the wood pile," Adam said.

Rachel looked at the sky. Overcast. Like every day. The wind blew, but it didn't help. There was no warm, clean summer smell; just the faint, rotting scent that came from the dark forest northeast of the house.

"Let's go shopping. You can work on the wood pile later." Rachel pointed to his shorts. "We should look for longer winter clothing. There's no way you'll fit into your jeans."

"Cool." He took off the gardening gloves. "Can we take the car?"

Rachel shook her head. "We need to save gas in case there's an emergency."

"Come on, Mom, we haven't used it since we got here. It's always walking here and walking there. The wheelbarrow doesn't even hold that much. If we just took the car we could fill it all the way up."

It was tempting. And he had a good point.

Feeling her weakening, Adam walked up to her and gave her puppy eyes. "I'm a growing boy and I'm hungry. You don't give me enough to eat even though it's summer because 'it has to last us.'" He mimicked her tone.

"Alright!" She grinned at him. "Let me find the keys."

The engine started, but an error message popped up on the screen: 'Warning: hybrid battery fail imminent. Seek technical assistance.'

"What's that mean?" asked Adam.

Rachel touched the screen box closed. "Nothing good." She drove down their long driveway. The track was even more pitted after the heavy rains. The steering wheel almost jerked out of her hand.

"If we gather enough supplies, we might stay here for winter. What do you think about that?"

"Cool. I can grab some books from this house since we brought the car, right? I got the second in a series from the hospital, but I need to read the third. It's a cliffhanger."

"Of course," Rachel said with a frown. First cancer and now the firestorm meant Adam was isolated from playmates, from the library, from sports teams. He was losing his childhood. She sighed. Something else to feel guilty about.

"I mean, it's a community service. You said we should preserve culture for when the electricity returns."

Rachel took a right onto a gravel road, drove a mile, and pulled over. "Let's park here. There's a huge pothole up ahead and I don't want to get a flat tire or break something I don't know the name of."

They stopped about twenty-five feet before the driveway. The house was straight ahead; the chimney rising into the sky was visible through bare trees and piles of brittle leaves that made it look like late autumn rather than midsummer.

As soon as they opened the car doors Rachel smelled smoke. She took in the surroundings, but didn't see anything.

"My heart." Adam had a pained look on his face. "I feel like I sprinted up a hill."

Rachel frowned. "Are you able to walk?"

Adam nodded and dropped his hand from his chest. "We're already here. Let's get the supplies."

"Okay." Rachel shook off the feeling that made her want to turn around. Instead, she led the way from the road straight through the forest toward the house, crunching through leaves. First came the sound of breaking glass, and then thick black smoke rose into the sky. Rachel fell into a crouch behind a log, pulling Adam down with her, and then peeked over. The smoke smell. *Careless,* she thought.

They stared at flames licking along the window frames of the lower level. A man, chest bare with his face painted red, ran out the front door, baseball bat in hand, smashing at windows, and using his hand over his mouth to whoop like he was a cowboy. More people with red-painted faces wrenched open the garage door. Five of them were pulling items off the wall, stomping, breaking, hitting, screaming incessantly. This wasn't looting, this was destruction. One, possibly a woman, leaped outside the garage and ran around the house in laps, panting. She looked like a cartoon character with her tongue hanging out, eyes wild, arms pumping, knees in the air. *Some kind of drug,* thought Rachel. She shoved a fist against her mouth to keep from making a sound as she made the connection between the painted faces and the radio announcement: these were Hotheads.

A man, larger than the rest, wearing a spiked collar around his neck came outside followed by five more wearing loose clothing with sashes. They looked like demons with their white eyes standing out from the thick paint; race, gender, and age obfuscated. These six were different than the first group. Serious. The man with the collar watched the running woman. *Spike*, Rachel named him. He grabbed a metal trash can lid and held it up at shoulder height. As the woman came flying around the corner of the house, her face hit the lid and she fell flat on her back.

Spike looked at his crew and they all laughed. He nudged her with the toe of his boot. "You want to run?"

The woman stared up, blood flowing from her nose. Flames from the house now reached toward the sky from the second level.

"Light her up," Spike said. One of the Hotheads leaped forward and pulled out what looked like a large cigarette lighter. The woman's hair hissed into fiery life.

Rachel gasped and shoved Adam's head down behind the log.

With a screech, the woman leaped to her feet. Around the house she went again, her burning hair streaming behind her. The woman kept running and screaming, pausing only to suck in breath, cough, keep moving. After another lap, she doubled over, patting at her head, falling to the driveway, and scraping her face and head along the concrete until she was a bloody mess.

Spike stepped forward. He must have taken the baseball bat from the cowboy Hothead smashing windows earlier, or found another one. "Praise Ashur. Accept our offering. Let the energy vultures eat her soul."

He used the bat like a club and the demon-people behind him chanted praises. Rachel wanted to back away, but knew that they would attract attention if they moved. She pressed her body farther into the space under the log. A puff of smoke floated out of the woman's body. The Hotheads cheered.

"What was that?" Adam whispered. He'd resumed peeking over the log.

Rachel shook her head, put her finger over her lips.

Hands on hips, Spike said, "Where's the real sacrifice?" One of his crew moved out of the shadows of the garage, pushing something in front. A young Asian woman—Rachel guessed around twenty years old—with an athletic frame. Blue streaks colored chunks of her short black hair, cut in a downward angle from the back. Her arms and legs were muscular; almond-shaped eyes set in; skin the light brown of a cherry tree. The Hothead removed the young woman's backpack and the black pouch she wore like a purse and set them aside.

Spike caressed her cheek, but she kept her eyes on the ground.

"A more pleasing sacrifice to our god." He forced her to her knees and Rachel saw that her hands were tied together. "But, let us make this interesting." To his crew of five he said, "Gather the initiates."

Soon all the red-faced people were gathered in the driveway. The difference between Spike and his crew and the four others with painted faces was clear. The first Hotheads stood ready, serious, their faces completely red. The four initiates, including the cowboy, looked haphazard and stoned, their faces only streaked with red.

Spike pointed at each in turn. "You are An, Nammu, Enki, Aia." He looked at the Asian girl. "You'll be Utu. You don't mind being male in our little play, do you?"

She didn't look up.

"Mom, we've got to help her," Adam whispered.

Rachel's insides were frozen, immovable. She knew Adam was right; she remembered the bitter guilt back in Baltimore when they'd left the Brie to the mob in the parking garage. But she didn't have a plan.

The initiates shuffled their feet, couldn't seem to concentrate.

"We," Spike said gesturing to his crew, "are Marduk, Enlil, Geshtinanna, Ashur, Ninhursag-Ki, Ninlil. Understand?"

The initiates looked at each other. "Yeah man, we're in," said the cowboy. He sniffed and wiped his hand under his nose. "Can I get some more of that stuff from you first though, cuz?" He rubbed his hand on his chest.

"I don't think you understand," Spike said with feigned sadness. "I'll explain to you. We've been trapped away from this world and Utu, god of justice, thought he'd be heroic and block the gate with his body. So, we're going to tear Utu apart," he kicked the Asian girl to get her attention, "and then we're going to kill all of Utu's friends." He looked at the Hothead initiates. "You," he said, "are Utu's friends."

It took a moment for the message to process, but when it did the initiates scattered.

Spike shrugged. "Off-script, but we can kill Utu's friends first." He and his crew loped after them as if they'd done this before.

Rachel's eyes closed, the images too ugly.

A sudden cawing made Rachel's eyes snap open. From a nearby tree a raven launched itself through the bare forest.

Beside her, Adam groaned, his hand on his heart. "This isn't right."

The Asian girl had realized she'd been left alone and had made it to her feet. She tried to get the ropes off her hands.

"No, it isn't." Rachel leaned forward, staring in the direction the painted people had gone. *Courage,* she told herself. "Scoot all the way under the log and I'll cover you with leaves. Don't move." Rachel took a deep breath and then she ran from tree to tree getting closer to the driveway.

The house whistled, pressure building and releasing in gasps, flames licking at the sky.

Movement from the right—the direction the Hotheads had run— caught Rachel's attention. She ducked down at the base of the tree and peeked around. The four initiates had been gathered like cattle, herded back to the driveway. Smoke poured from the house, making Rachel's nostrils and throat burn with the need to cough. The Asian girl was gone.

Spike noticed a moment after Rachel did. He cursed.

"Shall I hunt her?" one of his crew asked.

A crack of lightning split the air above.

Spike looked all around and bowed with a mocking expression before addressing the sky. "Is this the great An? Ashur sends his greetings to the former pantheon leader."

Rachel used the distraction to crawl away from the inferno, covering her mouth to cough as she slid into position beside Adam. She touched his arm through the leaves and felt a surge of reassurance.

"Who's he talking to?" Adam whispered, brushing leaves away from his face.

Before Rachel could answer, a bolt of lightning struck the trees nearest the driveway. Another hit the other side in rapid succession. The smell of ozone filled the air. Spike ducked and covered his head. So did his crew.

"Come on, guys." Spike and the Hotheads ran for the side of the house Rachel couldn't see. Engines roared to life and she saw them drive off down an access road on motorcycles.

Big wet flakes fell from the sky interspersed with balls of hail. Astonished, Rachel caught a flake on her hand and watched it melt into a dot of water. She and Adam looked at each other. It was snowing in the middle of July. Not the beautiful white of postcards, but a gray heavy sludge. Scott had said the earth was changing. To Rachel, the important part was that the flakes were wet, blanketing the flaming house, and would keep the fire from spreading.

"Cold." One initiate wandered in a tight circle.

The cowboy answered him, "Cold." It seemed all they could say, the group of four painted people left behind in the driveway. A dark cloud of smoke rose into the air.

Waste, Rachel thought, angry. *We should have come yesterday or the day before. Everything is gone. Batteries, flashlights, more water, rice, books, art. All burned to ash.*

Too little snow, too late to save the house. It swayed back and forth, about to fall.

"Cold. Cold." Their eyes were cloudy, the manic energy gone. They stretched out on the concrete, painted bodies still, arms crossed their chest. The painted people stayed on the concrete, spread out in what in yoga is called corpse pose.

Rachel and Adam sprinted to the SUV. Back at the car they heard a giant whoosh as the house collapsed. Rachel struggled to see as she drove, wipers swishing on the fastest setting, SUV jouncing and sliding over the icy road and swerving around potholes.

She shot a glance at Adam. "Those people were scary. Are you okay?

"Yeah. My heart hurt, but it's okay now."

When they pulled up to their house Adam jumped out to manually open the garage.

"Um. . . . Is it okay if I come inside too?"

Rachel whipped around. The Asian girl was in the back of the SUV.

SIXTEEN

Dark brown eyes pleaded with Rachel. "Please let me stay here." The girl placed her palms together in a prayer pose. "I swear I won't be any trouble."

Outside, the July snowstorm swirled. What if she was a trick by the red-painted people to find other occupied houses? But, the young woman didn't even have a coat. Sending her away into the snowstorm would be a death sentence.

"You can come inside," Rachel said. "For now."

Rachel popped the trunk and stood aside so the girl could climb out. Snowflakes fell across Rachel's bare neck like needle pricks. She shivered. With a groan of metal tracks, the garage door opened from inside and Adam stood there. His mouth fell open. "That's the girl—"

"Yeah," Rachel said. After the adrenaline rush at the house, she was exhausted. "Let's get inside and out of this wet mess."

Inside, the girl sat on the stone hearth while Adam built up the fire. From the kitchen, Rachel heard them talking in low voices. She heated water for instant soup and tea and lit candles. Outside was a white blur, impossible to see even to the forest line, but still Rachel kept listening for something that would tell her they were about to be attacked, that they'd been found by Spike or the painted people left behind.

Coming into the family room, Rachel noted that the girl had left her red-marbled combat boots in the doorway. She wore a black jean skirt with biker shorts underneath and a tank top overlaid by a ripped concert T-shirt for a band Rachel had never heard of. A black pouch strapped across her front and a backpack sat at her feet. She'd grabbed her things when running away. *Must be something important in there.* Ink, something written in Asian characters, crawled down the left side of her neck and a tiny jeweled stud nestled in the side of her nose. Rachel noticed a slight limp when she walked and attributed it to the shiny pink scar on her left leg—it looked like a chunk of flesh had been bitten—or hacked—out.

Rachel cleared her throat. "Did you come with the Hotheads—"

"They kidnapped me."

"I see." Looking at the scar on the young woman's leg, Rachel was struck by all the things that she might have gone through, the things the Hotheads might have done to her. "What's your name?"

"Tamaki."

"Where's your family?"

Tamaki twitched and looked down. "I don't . . . I'm all alone."

Rachel's heart melted. *How can she survive without anyone to look out for her? What if Adam didn't have anyone?* "I need to understand the Hotheads. They were praising someone named 'Ashur.' Is that their leader?"

Tamaki shook her head. "That's the god they serve."

"Huh," Rachel shook her head. "I'm familiar with most Roman and Greek mythology—"

"He's the god of war in Mesopotamia."

Rachel swallowed. "The land between two rivers."

"Hey." Adam tilted his head. "That's where the fake nurse said she was from."

"I remember," Rachel said. She also remembered the threat the woman had made: *the others will come for you . . . be drawn like wasps to honey.* "The land between the Tigris and Euphrates. The cradle of civilization. What's the connection for the Hotheads?"

"I guess they believe Ashur is willing to listen to them. That's religion, right?" The girl bit her lip and glanced around the family room. "This is a nice place."

"Thanks," Rachel said. She understood the nudge, the question underlying the comment. "Adam, may I speak to you for a moment?"

He followed her down the hall to the master bedroom. Rachel shut the door most of the way, leaving only a crack. Tamaki sat on the hearth, elbows balanced on bony knees, her chin resting in her hands, the longer strands of dyed blue in her hair falling forward to frame her face like birds' wings.

Facing Adam, Rachel whispered, "She wants to stay here."

"Of course, Mom. Why not?"

Rachel exhaled, made her shoulders relax from where they'd bunched around her ears. "It's probably okay. But, maybe she works with the Hotheads and is going to let them know where we are."

Adam shook his head. "You're paranoid. They were going to kill her!"

Rachel walked over to the window and lifted the curtain. The snow had stopped. Enough had fallen that their SUV tracks were filled in. The sky looked like a gray winter's day instead of the middle of July, like maybe it wasn't finished snowing.

"Alright," she said. "Let's go invite Tamaki to stay."

Adam walked out ahead of her. "This is going to be cool."

"Come on, you can sleep in the spare bedroom." Rachel grabbed a candle and led the way upstairs, going into the room across from Adam's. The flame revealed a round bedroom painted dusky rose. A decorative net nailed to the wall held stuffed animals, gifts Adam had received after diagnosis, and a bookshelf overflowing with paperbacks.

A wooden giraffe stood tall in one corner, a gift from Naomi that Adam had appreciated, but had not wanted in his own room. "Sorry it's dusty in here."

"Thank you. For not kicking me out, and for treating me like a guest." Tamaki set her backpack on the bed. "Everything from my old life fits in this bag."

"I can lend you clothes and you're welcome to anything in the bathroom closet. We survivors have to look out for each other." Rachel waved away her thanks. "You said you were kidnapped. Isn't someone looking for you?"

"No." Tamaki shook her head. "Gran and I left Ohio after the soldiers came through; wanted to find a city or someplace safe to live. Then the Hotheads captured us." Tamaki met Rachel's eyes, but her fingers snuck down to her scar. "They murdered Gran right in front of me when we tried to get away."

"I'm so sorry." Rachel reached out to touch Tamaki in sympathy, but then stopped, afraid of being too familiar. "There's juice and boiled water in the fridge if you get thirsty." Rachel's hand hesitated on the doorknob. She needed to know more about the Hotheads, their strange ritual, and what Tamaki had seen in her travels. But the girl had been through enough for one day; they all had. And Rachel's bones ached with complete exhaustion.

That night Rachel dreamed of red-faced people and burning houses. She dreamed of her husband and neighbors from the community pool. She dreamed of Adam and Naomi back at the hospital. She dreamed of bad, faceless things coming from the forest.

In the morning Rachel didn't want to get out of bed. She didn't feel any less tired, didn't want to see whatever a new day would bring. Rolling over toward the center, Rachel realized that she still slept on "her" side of the marriage bed. Craig's pillow was smooth, unmarred by a human head. She reached out and punched it, just to make wrinkles. The diamond on her engagement band winked on her left hand.

She'd told Scott that the ring represented a trick—a nonexistent husband to scare strangers away. She'd told Adam that his father was dead. The reality was that dead or not, Craig wasn't coming and she was on her own in a dangerous world.

Rachel took off the two bands of gold. She expected some sort of punch to the gut, a physical reaction to her decision to let go. She flexed her fingers to see if her hands looked different. They did, but not because of the missing rings. The knob of her wrist poked out because she'd lost weight. Her hands had calluses from dragging wood and working in the garden. *Not all change is bad.*

Moving like an old woman she placed the rings in her jewelry box and crossed the room to open a curtain. Snow everywhere. She went back to the bed and curled up amongst the tangled blankets. Adam and Tamaki's voices drifted from the front of the house. Rachel knew she should get up, make sure Tamaki wasn't crazy or going to hurt Adam, make sure they didn't eat too much of the food, but she couldn't seem to move.

Yesterday the Hotheads would have killed them. Would have burned this house down without a thought in their drugged-out minds. Hiraeth wasn't safe. They couldn't make it here. She was kidding herself. Rachel felt her eyes close as she got closer and closer to the black hole of depression.

"Hey Mom, can we eat the raisins and oatmeal?" Adam yelled from the kitchen.

She had to swallow several times, make her voice sound cheery. "That's fine."

With a groan she rolled back over to hide her face in the blankets. *Enough. Get out of bed.* Raising her voice she called out, "Could you heat some water for my coffee, Adam? I need something to get me going this morning."

"I'm doing something, Mom."

"Right," she said, feeling a surge of resentment. "Not like I deserve help or anything."

The radio clicked on to the chorus of The Beatles' "Help." Rachel pulled her face from the blankets and stared in disbelief.

The Weatherman's familiar voice interrupted, "Can you believe those four guys? Even their names are cheerful: John, George, Paul, and Ringo. Ringo, maybe I should take that as a name." He deepened his voice, "In breaking news, a militant group calling itself New Babylon has moved into the vacuum of power left by the United States government. New Babylon has issued an invitation of citizenship to anyone seeking to rebuild civilization. That's the carrot. Here's the stick. Once people are inside the city, they are at the mercy of its dictator. New Babylon has sent search parties to the surrounding areas to find mutations in the plant and animal life that survived the firestorm. It seems to this newsman, however, that mutations aren't the only thing these search parties want. And what's with the name? New Babylon. What's next, the hanging gardens? This is The Weatherman, signing off."

A fist pounded on the front door. Rachel jumped in surprise. Red painted faces jumped to her mind, followed quickly by the new threat of a New Babylon search party. She yelled, "Don't answer it! Don't open the door! I'm coming."

She grabbed the rifle from where she'd stashed it in her closet and ran toward the door. More pounding. Adam and Tamaki stood back, away from the window.

Rachel called, "Who is it?"

"It's Scott. Open the freaking door; it's freezing out here."

Rachel unlocked the dead bolt and threw the door open, still holding the rifle, breathing heavily from her sprint.

Scott bounded in like a puppy, shaking snow everywhere. "Wowza, Rachel. Could you have kept me waiting any longer?" He noticed the rifle in Rachel's hand and froze. "Hey, what happened here?"

Rachel slowed her breath, but couldn't control the snarkiness in her voice. "Oh, I don't know. Hotheads. Looting and burning down one of the houses while we were there." She hefted the rifle. "I wanted to make sure that wasn't them at the door."

"Because they would have stood out in the cold knocking? That makes sense."

The effort of trying to be tough while she was terrified, of trying to hold it together in front of everyone, made Rachel's throat close up and her eyes tear.

Scott searched her face. His voice softened. "Oh, I'm sorry. Don't cry. Please don't cry."

"I'm not. I wouldn't. That's dumb." Rachel scrubbed at her face with a hand, trying to wipe away her weakness. "But, we need to make this house secure. I don't want anyone to get in. And I need you to show me how to use the scope on here. Like, right now. I'm ready to learn."

"I guess I don't have to worry about whether you're willing to shoot." Scott puffed out his cheeks while he thought. "I'm a park ranger, not a soldier. But, if you'll tell me which house, I can go check it out, see if they left the area."

"Actually, I think they might have frozen to death." The image of their painted bodies, flat on the driveway, while the snow fell on top, made her hurt. She covered her face with her left hand, bit her knuckle to make it stop.

Scott took the rifle from her. "I'm going to put this . . . somewhere else."

Emotions stifled, Rachel dropped her hands. "Sorry, Scott. I got really scared." She gave him a little smile. "Just need a strong cup of coffee and I'll be fine."

"Now I know what makes you happy. Bet they knew your order at the local coffee shop, right?" He grinned back at her. "Where's the little man?"

"I'm over here," Adam called from the couch. "Mom told us to stay away from the door."

"Oh yeah?" Scott glanced across the room looking for Adam and his eyes locked on Tamaki. Rachel started to ask him what was in the sack over his shoulder, but stopped when she saw the expression on his face.

"Scott, this is Tamaki. She got caught in the snowstorm. Tamaki, this is Scott. He's a park ranger who keeps an eye on us."

Scott, flushing, wiped his hands on his pants, and then stepped across the room, his hand extended. The sack slipped off his shoulder, pulling him off balance.

"Flowers for you," he said.

"Flowers?" Tamaki leaned away.

"Err, flour rather. For everybody here." He swept his arm around, finished the sentence like he was a game show host giving away prizes.

Rachel hugged her arms across her chest, still feeling breakable, like she was made of glass.

"I'll take that," she said stepping forward for the gift. "Adam, can you please get a towel for Scott so he can dry off?"

"Oh, I can't stay long. Just wanted to make sure you guys were okay with all this snow." Scott couldn't stop staring at Tamaki. The girl had slipped her hands in her front pockets and settled back against the fireplace, letting her blue hair fall forward to obscure her features. *Hiding*, Rachel thought. *And who wouldn't after being held by those drugged Hotheads?*

Adam said, "Hey Scott, wanna have a snowball fight?"

Scott scoffed, "Yeah, if you want me to kick your butt." He walked away from Tamaki, but said over his shoulder, "'Cause I'm strong. And fast. And a great conversationalist."

"Scott, Scott," Adam was hanging off of the ranger's arm. "What does a penguin have that nothing else has?"

"Adam!" Tamaki frowned at the boy. "You promised you wouldn't say anything."

He waved her away. "Baby penguins. Get it?"

Rachel felt like she'd missed part of a conversation, but she retreated to the kitchen to fill a teakettle and set it on the stove. It worked as long as she used a match to light the gas, but she should get in the habit of hanging the kettle on the hook over the fire, save the gas for emergencies like lack of wood. She looked inside the sack while the water heated.

"This is great, Scott! Where'd you get it?"

"I procure things," he called. "Because I'm a good provider. That's the kind of man I am."

Rachel rolled her eyes at the ceiling. "And a good performer for attractive young ladies." She tried to squash a twinge of jealousy. "Here," Rachel pushed through the swinging door. She flapped the bag at him, "you can reuse this sack. I poured the flour into one of my plastic containers. That must have been almost ten pounds."

"Yeah, that should hold you for a bit. I'm gonna pelt your son with snowballs and then check out the burned house. Let you know if I see any people with painted faces."

"Any excuse to come back here soon, no doubt," Rachel muttered to herself, standing in the kitchen doorway, watching Tamaki stand at the window and watch Scott and Adam play in the snow.

SEVENTEEN

Rachel knocked on Tamaki's bedroom door.

"Hey," she said. "Do you have a minute?"

Tamaki unlocked the bedroom door and stood there, her body blocking entry.

So this is what it's going to be like to have a teenager. "Did you want to grab a beer? We could sit outside on the porch swing. I don't even know if you're old enough . . ."

"I'm nineteen. Not that there are rules anymore."

"No," Rachel agreed. "No rules."

"But I don't drink alcohol."

"Okay, well, that was really my way of saying that I want to talk to you." Rachel headed for the stairs, trusting that Tamaki would follow her out. She grabbed a blanket off the couch for each of them. Rachel wanted to have a conversation with the young woman without either Adam or Scott around as a distraction. Everything with the Hotheads had happened so quickly that Rachel didn't really know anything about their guest.

Outside, in mid-July, Rachel exhaled, watching her breath turn to vapor in the cold air. Almost a month had passed since the firestorm, but it felt like so much longer.

Tamaki shut the door and accepted a blanket. She wrapped it around her shoulders and took a seat on the swing.

The silence turned awkward.

Rachel rubbed her hands against her jeans. "I thought we could get to know each other a little more."

"I'm biracial, Japanese mother and all-American dad. My grand-mother was very traditional. We lived apart, spoke Japanese in the house. She thought my mom was betraying her culture, her values, her way of life. They argued a lot. One night my mom dropped me off with Gran and didn't come back." Tamaki recited the information as if it were boring.

She acts tough because she's been hurt in the past.

"Adam and I are going to try to live here through the fall and then I'm not sure what we'll do. This cold weather is running through our resources." Rachel cleared her throat. "But what's your plan? Do you want to get back to Ohio?"

"Are you tired of having me? Are you saying I'm the reason we're running through resources?" She sounded hurt.

"No," Rachel said. "I'm trying to figure out what everyone wants."

"My grandmother taught me a lot about plants. I can help you." Tamaki played with the black pouch strapped across her chest. "One of my earliest memories is following her around her house, listening to her talk to her orchids like they were her pets. She grew her own herbs and sent me outside to pick mint for the tea. She tried to teach me to speak Japanese too, but that didn't go so well." She gave a little laugh.

"It sounds like you miss her very much."

"I do." Tamaki took a deep breath.

"I know that the Hotheads," Rachel picked through her words, "hurt you. Do you want to talk about it?"

"I wasn't prepared." Tamaki tilted her head. "I may not look like much, but when I'm ready, I will hunt them down and I will kill them." Her black eyes glittered in the darkness. "But, the Hotheads aren't the only danger out there." She gestured toward the woods.

"Is there something you aren't telling me?" Rachel said. A memory of the hospital flashed in her mind. The soldier she'd bribed with her meal ticket claiming that the land to the east had been devoured by the ocean. That a golden bull had eaten a human. "Did you see any-thing . . . fantastic?" The question made Rachel wince, but she had to ask. "Any giant creatures or mutations?"

Tamaki swallowed and hung her head.

"You can trust me," Rachel urged. "We're not going to hurt you. And . . . I'll believe you."

"The things I saw on the way here . . . rocks that moved by them-selves, a bridge with destroyed supports just hanging in the air, a place where it was a desert with sand and nothing else and two steps later you stood in a forest with trees reaching to the sky. . . ." Tamaki pushed her blue streak back behind her ear and met Rachel's eyes. "I don't want to be scared anymore, wondering if I'll find food and shelter or be attacked. And, I don't have another home. This is where I want to be. Part of your family."

Tamaki is about the same age I was when I lost my parents. She needs a safe harbor. Rachel nodded. "We call this cabin Hiraeth. Do you know what that means?"

Tamaki shook her head.

"Homesick for the home you never had." Rachel took a deep breath. "It's for all of us. You can stay as long as you want."

"Thank you," Tamaki whispered. Her shoulders dropped as she relaxed.

※

She'd asked him one hundred times, and it was about to be one hundred and one. "But have you made your bed and brushed your teeth?"

"Why should I? Who cares about making a bed? You just get in and mess it up again every night." Adam scowled.

"I care, that's who." Rachel stood in the doorway to Adam's room. Dresser drawers open, a pile of clothes in the corner too small for him, his bedspread—for some reason—actually under the bed.

"Leave me alone!" Adam shoved past her to go downstairs.

"Don't yell at me," she called after him. With a sigh she went into his room and pulled his bedspread out. She should discipline him, call him back and make him straighten his room, but Rachel was also sympathetic to Adam's feeling stir-crazy. Five days since Scott stopped by with the flour and it had snowed again. Outside was freezing; ice covered the porch and the water in the rain barrels had frozen solid. The three of them—Adam, Rachel, and Tamaki—had taken turns bringing in wood from the stack, which no longer seemed so plentiful.

A knock at the kitchen door and then voices. Rachel hurried down the stairs to see Adam chattering to Scott, who was holding ski poles and wearing long pants, a puffy jacket, a face mask, gloves, and his bag over his shoulder like Santa Claus.

Rachel felt tension melt, the fight with Adam fall away. Scott made her feel lighter, more buoyant.

"Ahh, hold on, Adam. I've got to get these snowshoes off. I'll meet you at the fireplace." Adam pushed past Rachel. Scott maneuvered the snowshoes off and set them outside. Whispering so that only she could hear, "I found the house, but there was nothing alive there."

Rachel nodded. "Thanks." *Great. Frozen to death. Doesn't make me feel better.*

Scott sat on the hearth and opened his bag. "On my last trip, I went west beyond these mountains and found a functioning Amish survivor community. They are on another ley line, so beyond our jurisdiction, but I marked it on my map. I think I'm starting to get it, how finding the ley lines means I can predict where the next cities or settlements will be. No more state lines, of course, but the United States are essentially over anyway."

They stared at him.

"Right. Sorry." Scott grimaced. "I'm on my own a lot so sometimes I forget how to have a normal conversation."

"Whose jurisdiction?" Rachel asked.

"You know," he turned a full 360 degrees. "Ours."

"And what do you mean," Tamaki said, "that the United States are over?"

"I mean," he faltered. "From what I've seen, which is only around here, that ley lines are the new way to determine where survivor settlements are." He looked at their attentive faces. "I'm not an expert or anything."

"You're talking like an expert," Adam said.

"I'm not. I'm a park ranger and that is all. Look, you guys are missing the big point."

Rachel took a deep breath. "Right. So, the United States being over isn't big, but something else is. I'm almost scared to ask."

Scott beamed, "The point is . . . I have a gift. The cold helped. I don't know whether it would have lasted otherwise." He reached into his backpack and pulled out a glass bottle.

"Is that—" Rachel leaned forward.

"Oooh," said Adam.

Scott watched Tamaki. She perched on the stone hearth like a contortionist, knee pulled into chest, the other leg wrapped around. "I'm lactose intolerant."

"What? No!" He looked at the milk bottle in horror and then back to her. "I carried this all the way here. I had to trade a whole bag of flour for cocoa powder mixed with brown sugar."

Tamaki laughed. "I'm joking. That looks amazing. I love hot chocolate."

"Okay." Scott needed to recalibrate. "Because you're not intolerant. You're tolerant."

"Yes." She blushed. "I'm quite tolerant."

Rachel cleared her throat, feeling a flicker of irritation. "Hand me the milk and cocoa powder, Scott. You guys can keep discussing your tolerances."

Adam followed her into the kitchen. He said, "I can't wait to have a bowl of cereal. I haven't had any with milk in so long. And I'm a growing boy."

"Yes, you are a growing boy." She kissed the top of his head, surprised that he already reached her chin.

Scott pushed open the swinging door and stuck his head into the kitchen. "Come on, guys. Let's all walk to the creek first. Fresh air will do wonders."

As they walked, Rachel noted cracks in the ice. She took off her glove and held her hand in the air. Warming up.

Tamaki and Scott walked a little ahead. Rachel gritted her teeth. She was a third wheel in her own household.

"We have to enjoy it while it lasts. Soon we'll be back to warmer weather," Scott said.

"How do you know that?" Rachel heard Tamaki ask.

"I have it on good authority," he said.

Adam nudged Rachel. "Watch this." He sprinted forward, pushed Tamaki aside, and pulled down a branch. Scott was left behind as the branch rebounded and raindrops pattered down all over him. Scott shook his fist in mock rage and took off after Adam. Adam's giggles echoed until an answering smiled tugged at Rachel's mouth.

After the four of them were back in the house, Scott insisted on making the hot chocolate. Tamaki disappeared upstairs.

"Adam, go get your pj's on." Rachel said.

"But Scott's making hot chocolate."

"You can take it with you. I need to talk to him alone."

Adam's head cocked to the side.

Scott came through the swinging door balancing a tray with the mugs. He set the tray on the coffee table and Adam opened his arms for a hug. Scott picked Adam up under the armpits and swung him around before kissing the top of his head. "Goodnight, sport."

Adam stared at Scott with hero-worship. "Goodnight." He took a mug of hot chocolate. "Too bad we don't have marshmallows."

"I'll work on it." Scott exhaled noisily as he plopped on the couch.

"This hot chocolate looks great." Rachel scooted closer. "You know, you should spend the night. It's too cold to travel. Leave in the morning." The invitation was rushed, but it came out casual.

"You don't mind?"

"Not at all. There's a built-in loft bed halfway up the stairs or you can sleep on the couch, whichever you want." Rachel touched his shoulder with hers. "You really saved us. We were irritated and claustrophobic. You turned it into the most fun day of all summer with hot cocoa and a hike."

"I'm glad. I'll leave early in the morning, though. There's someone I have to see."

Surprised, Rachel looked at him. "There's someone around here? Where?"

Scott looked flustered. "Well, not exactly. I'm . . . it's hard to explain."

"Try." It wasn't a suggestion.

"I kind of work for someone. I mean, I bring information to someone in exchange for other information."

An idea niggled at Rachel. Information. Around here in the Appalachian Mountains. Scott making a map. The only one who had updates. "You work for The Weatherman, don't you?"

She could see by his face that she was right.

"How do you know about—"

"I hear his reports on my radio. Unlike regular forecasters, he's always right. Like the morning we ran into the Hotheads, it was on the radio. Later I thought how lucky that had been. Wasn't luck at all." Rachel squinted at him. "Are you his spy?"

"Spy? No." His eyes looked to the right. He was a terrible liar. "Yes. Kind of."

"And what is happening that you have to go see him first thing in the morning?" She folded her arms across her chest. The last time she'd challenged Scott he'd shown her a river that performed magic.

Now, Scott looked past her shoulder and Rachel tracked his gaze to see that Tamaki stood at the bottom of the stairs. She'd brushed out her hair and put on green pajama pants with a frog face sewn near her feet, one of the few pieces of clothing she'd brought from her home and kept in her backpack. The seriousness of her expression didn't match the frog's cartoon grin.

"The snow is over for now." Scott said. He swallowed. "That means they'll be on the move again, coming in to our territory."

"They who?" Her heart hammered in her chest.

Scott looked at her, scratched his hand through red hair. "New Babylon."

Tamaki hissed and fled back up the stairs.

Rachel watched Scott. *This was not how I intended the evening to go.* "Okay. I'm exhausted and I'm confused. What do you know about New Babylon?"

Scott stood up, walked around the coffee table away from Rachel. Toward the stairs. "It's the name of a city near what used to be Pittsburgh. The group is the most organized of any survivors. They're trying to expand and The Weatherman wants to make sure they don't cross into our territory."

Rachel nodded. "I heard The Weatherman say something about military regime on the radio. So what's the problem?"

"Nothing definite. But, they're gathering up weapons and materials. We'd like to know their plans. That's all."

Rachel's eyelids felt so heavy. "It doesn't sound like there's any immediate danger. The Hotheads aren't coming back, right?"

"No." He took another step away, toward Tamaki.

"Okay. Then I'm going to bed." She hadn't even made it all the way to her bedroom when she heard the creak of the stairs.

Rachel wanted to slam the bedroom door, again and again, but she didn't want them to hear. Any of them. Not Adam. Certainly not Scott and Tamaki. This was her house. Did they even realize that? She could throw them out.

"Yeah, for what, Rachel," she muttered. "Because Scott prefers Tamaki?"

Yes, that's exactly why. Because I'm not good enough. They are young; she's nineteen and he's in his twenties and I'm too old at thirty-four or too maternal or I worry too much or too . . . something.

The feeling—that terrible sensation—of being made of glass returned. Breakable. See-through. Jagged. Shattered. Rachel paced the bedroom. Why couldn't Craig have been an alcoholic and stashed a bottle of wine in here? Or vodka. Or anything. She ran to his bedside table and pulled out the drawers. Nothing.

She knew there was nothing in hers, but pulled out the drawers to check, looking through the clothes she knew by heart. She pulled out the dark blue hoodie she'd worn when she left the hospital. Her right hand felt a wad of tissues and when she pulled it out she remembered Naomi handing her something. Rachel unwrapped the tissues and there, nestled, was a tube of lip balm.

"Ha!" Rachel smiled through a huge lump in her throat. "Oh, Naomi. I wish you were here, my friend."

She searched the medicine cabinet next. Adam's medicines winked at her. Methotrexate. 6-MP. Prednisolone. Zofran for nausea. Senna to counteract Vincristine's side effects. They'd forgotten them the last time they'd come up and Rachel had to drive down to Hopkins and get new scripts from the oncologist because he needed them that day. Included was a headache-inducing call to the insurance company who almost accused her of lying.

She groaned and shoved the meds aside. All that was left was a green bottle of aloe, Neosporin cream, and Benadryl.

How pathetic. If I can't get drunk, at least I can sleep. Rachel poured out four pink tabs and tossed them back. No more feeling. No more pain. She grabbed a pillow off her bed and slid down until she reached the floor. Hot tears of self-pity and hiccups were muffled as Rachel buried her face in the blue hoodie, fingers clutched around the lip balm, eager for drowsiness to overwhelm her.

EIGHTEEN

As Scott, via The Weatherman, had predicted, the outside temperature had risen something like thirty degrees in one day. The air was thick and damp, settling deep into the lungs. Adam, Tamaki, and Rachel cleared branches, stacked firewood, and drained the garden by digging a shallow trench toward the creek.

Rachel said Scott's name to herself, probing for reaction the way a tongue might feel the space of a missing tooth. That was the worst part of her anxiety. Panic attacks made her feel ridiculous the next day. Like she should be able to control her emotions and act like a normal human being. *What if Adam had seen you feeling sorry for yourself, crying on your bedroom floor?* she chided herself. Another internal voice answered, *Then he'd know you were a real person and not a paragon of martyrdom.*

"Rachel?" Tamaki sat on a branch of the Empress Paulownia, strong legs dangling from either side as if she were on a jungle gym. "Are you and Scott. . . ."

Rachel's stomach flipped. "Are Scott and I what?"

"You know . . . together?" Tamaki stared down at her.

"Not at all. I saved his life so he feels indebted. Nothing romantic." Rachel gave a laugh. "I mean," she wrinkled her nose, "he's a bit of a goof, isn't he?"

Tamaki's cheeks flamed with either anger or hurt and Rachel felt like a jerk. She was so focused on no one knowing she'd felt humiliated that she'd just hurt the girl. Scott liked Tamaki, not Rachel. That wasn't anyone's fault. Rachel let go of her crush, her hopes that Scott was falling in love with her, that she was special, romantically, to someone else.

"But, a good guy." Rachel looked around, trying to find something to smooth over the awkwardness, to prevent her snarky comment from breaking up the delicate strands of their relationship. "Thanks for your help today. If the sun shines tomorrow, maybe we'll make some more progress with the garden."

"Whatever." Tamaki leaned against the trunk. The rapid change in temperature seemed to have convinced the tree that—instead of the end of July—it was time for spring. Buds popped all along the branches of the giant tree.

Looking away from Rachel, Tamaki twirled a strand of blue hair around her finger.

Trying to keep the conversation going to smooth out rough feelings, Rachel's eyes fixed on the color. "Tamaki?"

The girl tilted her head.

"How is your hair still blue? I've been wondering, but I can't imagine you've been coloring it and I haven't seen any black roots."

"It was this way during the firestorm and it stayed like this." Her tone of voice suggested that Rachel was boring her.

"Okay," Rachel said. She scuffed her boot in the dirt. "Come in for dinner when you're ready."

Adam followed Rachel into the house from where he'd been stacking the wood. "What's the matter? You don't seem very happy today."

I'm trying not to mentally replay all the conversations where I mess up or sound stupid. It takes a lot of energy. "Just tired." Rachel walked back to her bedroom and shut the door.

She went to her bed and lay there, face down in the pillow. Tamaki and Adam could make themselves dinner.

Rachel opened the door to Scott a few days later.

"I need everyone outside," he said, bouncing on the balls of his feet. "And, are you wearing lipstick? It looks pretty."

"ChapStick," Rachel said. "We'll be out in a sec."

When they'd gathered, Scott clapped his hands. "Alright guys, our project today is to keep the roots of the trees and shrubs safe. For today that means getting rid of this." With his boot Scott nudged a fungus growing up through the wet leaves on the forest floor. The mushroom was brown and slimy with a bright orange tip. "It spreads underground and then pops up." He took a stick and dug down to the egg-like bulb and showed the white threads spreading out.

"What's so bad about it?" Tamaki asked.

"Good question." Scott said. He was using his park ranger voice. *Showing off for the tough punk-haired girl with the almond skin.* Rachel reminded herself to be nice, to keep the family together.

"Between the forest fires, the strong winds, and the torrential rain, this ecosystem has been pummeled. While its immune system is down, the balance is off, and these seeds and spores from other ecosystems move in. They grow fast and strong and there's no natural checks and balances. So, we become the guardians. Now, if I wanted to be mean, Rachel, I'd point out that you really shouldn't have the Empress Paulownia tree in the Appalachian Mountains."

"Ahh," Rachel protested. "We wanted a tree that would grow fast so we could hang up a tire swing for Adam, maybe even a tree fort, but close enough we could keep an eye on him. It's been here for years and hasn't done any harm. And," she finished in a rush of words, "there's a legend that a phoenix will only land in that type of a tree."

Scott closed one eye and stared at her. "That's the best you can do?"

"You can't cut it down. It's my house," Tamaki said, matter-of-factly. "As soon as the weather cooperates."

"Something wrong with the guest room?" Rachel asked.

"No, but it'd be nice to have a place of my own. A treehouse."

Adam clapped his hands. "Will it have a rope ladder and a zip line?"

Scott raised his voice. "I'll let it go for now, ladies, but only because we have more troublesome vegetation to collect. Don't touch the spores, use a long stick and dig the whole bulb up, put it in a pile right there, and then use your stick to disrupt the thin white shoots trying to spread out. We'll start in a circle around the house and move as far out as we can while we have light."

Adam interrupted. "It looks like a dog penis."

Rachel whipped her head around. "Adam! There's no need for that kind of language."

"He's right, it does," Scott said with delight, staring at the offensive spore. "We're officially naming it dog-penis-fungi. Get it? Fun guy?"

Tamaki shrugged, but her lips twitched.

"No. Nope. Not going to happen." Rachel shook her head.

"Mom. It's been named."

"Putting my foot down. We're not doing this. It may be the end of the world, but we'll maintain decorum." Rachel made a cutting-off motion with her hand. "That name is vulgar and gross."

Adam whispered, "Mom's cutting off the dog-penis-fun-guy."

Scott whooped. "Let's go dig up some DPF, folks."

Scott and Adam set off. Tamaki wouldn't meet her eyes. Rachel, outnumbered three-to-one, groaned then grabbed a stick and followed.

They worked until they'd de-mushroomed a circle around Hiraeth all the way to the clearing where the strawberry plants and blueberry bushes grew wild. Adam was the first to point out the white bells on the blueberry bushes.

"Not long now!"

Rachel walked closer to her son. "Remember when I took you to the farm to pick our own strawberries? You must have been about four years old, wearing overalls. Your face and front had so much juice, the farmer threatened to put *you* on the scale."

"That was when I was a baby. Come on, don't talk about that stuff. Are you going to bring up some diaper story now?"

She gave a surprised laugh. "Sor-ry, Mr. Big Shot!" Rachel made a production of walking over to Scott.

"Are we almost finished?"

He wiped the back of his hand across his brow. "Here's the thing, Rach. I don't really know the scientific reason, but this DPF sprang up both times we got one of those nasty storms. Maybe it's because the wind blows the spores in from somewhere else, but I wouldn't have thought they'd come with a snowstorm."

"Well, they're here because the ground was soaked. Right? Mushrooms like moisture."

He looked at her with a troubled expression. "You don't see any other kinds, though. Follow me farther away from your house and I'll show you why I dislike the DPF so much."

Tamaki and Adam fell in behind Scott and Rachel as they walked northeast beyond the clearing through the forest following the boundary between residential land and the national park.

"This is the worst area," Scott said. "You guys are taking care of yours and I'm in the park section, but this part is unclaimed."

Rachel could tell a difference. Without intervention from watering, trenching, staking, patting down the dirt, these trees and bushes were growing sideways, branches twisting over one another as if to get away from something. The foliage here was lighter because the leaves were curled up, but the impression amongst the trees was one of darkness and hiding. Rachel blinked, trying to clear away shadows that didn't make sense.

"That's what happens if you don't dig them up." Scott moved to the side and the other three stopped to stare. Thick white threads had grown up from the ground, surrounded what looked like a young maple tree, and had pulled the tree down so that it was strapped to the ground in a cocoon, white tendrils pulling off bits and pieces of the tree bark. The DPF grew all around. Rachel felt the urge to cut the tree loose, it looked so much like a tortured being. Other trees and shrubs were in earlier stages—the white strings still climbing up, making rope after rope before the victim would eventually be pulled down.

"Decomposition is a good thing, but this fungus isn't breaking down the vegetation so that nutrients can feed the soil to benefit the whole forest. Instead, it kills the plants and then uses the bodies to make more fungus."

Adam said, "That's spooky-looking."

Tamaki had wandered off, calling out from a few feet away. "Not just trees." They walked toward her voice and saw her squatting on the ground with a knife in her hand. She'd cut open one of the white cocoons. Bones, meat gone; a perfect skeleton lay inside.

"A fox?" Rachel asked. She looked to Adam to read his reaction. He seemed more fascinated than horrified.

Scott whistled. "A carnivorous fungi. Knew I hated those dog-penis-thingies."

"Should you really be making a joke?" Rachel snapped. "The fox went to sleep and this plant ate it. What's to stop the plant from eating people?"

"Nothing. Look, this area is terraforming. New plants and animals are appearing and we don't know their properties." Scott gestured around the dank forest. "We have to laugh sometimes. That's all we can do."

"I don't want to laugh." Rachel folded her arms across her chest, aware that she was being childish. "I want the world to go back to the way it was."

PART III

NEW BABYLON

Blue light slashed through the fog, like miniature lightning.
It smelled like after a storm. Ozone.

NINETEEN

By August 1, the pseudo-spring had caught up to summer. Rachel followed Adam down the path through the woods to the blueberry clearing. Despite the new leaves on some trees, the beans in the garden climbing up the wooden stakes, and the potatoes growing in the mounds, the view didn't lend itself to beauty. Overhead the sky was a dome of thick pus-colored clouds. Rachel brushed a pine tree. Needles fell at her touch. The fastest-growing, and healthiest-looking, were the post-firestorm plants that Rachel couldn't identify.

Adam disappeared around a curve. "Mom, come here!"

Rachel charged into the clearing, heart hammering. Adam crouched in front of the wild bushes, inspecting the berries. "The green blueberries we saw a couple days ago are almost ripe. There's a ton on here."

Rachel exhaled her anxiety. "That's great, buddy."

Wild strawberry plants were nearby, but they had succumbed to the DPF. Rachel pushed her auburn hair behind her ear and watched her son for a moment, proud of how strong he'd grown. Adam's T-shirt and jeans were shredding off his body from rough use, the knees frayed on both sides. His hair was less curly now, more of a wave, the chemo effect cut off with a pair of kitchen scissors.

A branch cracked somewhere across the oval-shaped clearing. Rachel froze, hand still on the bark. She looked to Adam and motioned him to be quiet, but the boy was singing to himself, head shoved into the bushes as he crawled forward to examine the berries.

"Scott?" Rachel's heart thumped. The park ranger was usually a shadow in the woods, knowing where and how to step.

A dark shape surged forward, the leaves moving, the creature lurching sideways. It stopped at the line of trees before the clearing.

Rachel moved closer to her son, crouching down to pick up a stick for inadequate protection. The rifle was back at the house. She used her right hand to reach out and grab the back of Adam's shirt, unsure whether to run, hide, or fight. The creature took a final sideways step into the clearing.

It was a bull moose, identifiable by its shaggy brown coat and its huge antlers. Rachel guessed he stood about seven feet tall. The bull shook his head, making a deep grunting sound. He rubbed against a birch tree and a big patch of fur fell off. He shook his head again, as if confused. His legs went to his left, knocking his face against a thin tree. The white tree tipped to the ground, its rotten roots exposed like a short petticoat.

Adam gasped.

Rachel looked down. Adam still squatted on the ground, his hand on the blueberry bucket, his mouth wide open.

Rachel tried to say that moose were vegetarians, joke that this was awkward for both parties. But then she followed Adam's gaze, tracked what he saw. Her own mouth dropped open.

A second head grew out of the moose's shoulder. It was covered in the same peeling fur as the rest of the body, but the unnatural angle gave the head limited mobility. A single asymmetrical devil's horn sprouted above thick-lidded eyes, creating a malevolent expression. The body lurched another step into the clearing and Rachel raised her hands to her mouth, understanding why the movements were so uncoordinated. It was this second, malformed head that was in control of the body. The head had turned the shoulder in her direction when she moved. Rachel froze. She had the feeling the second head was near-sighted, the way it hesitated, the nose going up in the air as if trying to smell, but the short neck preventing much movement.

"Adam," she whispered, her hand tugging on his shirt. "Adam. I'm going to count to three and then I want you to run for the house as fast as you can."

"No—" he whispered, shaking his head. "I don't want to leave you, but my stupid heart is burning. I don't want to be a coward."

She stared into his eyes. "You are not a coward. This isn't a choice. I need you to promise that you'll obey. Run to the house, lock the door behind you."

Eyes wide, the boy nodded.

"One."

The moose shuffled forward, each hoof as wide as Rachel's out-stretched hand.

"Two." She felt Adam tense, prepared to run.

"Three!"

Rachel waited the half-second for Adam to hit his stride, dodging trees, careening left onto the path back to the house. Then she leaped forward waving her arms and screaming: a clown at a rodeo.

The bull charged.

Fear flooded Rachel—her arms remained in the air, her eyes staring, her feet wide apart. Both heads faced her, white foam flecking their mouths, four legs scrabbling against the ground toward her. *Adam*. It was the one thought that could get her to move. Rachel turned around and ran in the opposite direction from her son, sure she'd be mowed down any moment, imagining hot, fetid breath on her neck.

There was a whistling sound, but Rachel didn't have time to wonder why the air whizzed by her face and past her ear, or why the moose was grunting and groaning behind her. Instead, she raced for a small dip in the hill where she could duck beneath an overhang and hope the moose ran over her and beyond. Not much of a plan, but it wasn't much farther. Suddenly two dogs ran at Rachel from either side. Rachel yelped, but kept running, falling off the overhang and crawling back underneath, pulling her knees to her chest.

She heard a grunt behind her, another whistling sound, dogs growling and then the moose was squealing. Rachel ducked her head down when she heard running footsteps, but they went right past her. More sounds of combat that she couldn't identify. Rachel poked her head up over the mud ridge and caught sight of two wolves.

TWENTY

One wolf was solid white and other solid black. Both had thick fur and sharp teeth exposed in snarls. They circled the moose, keeping it in position while a tall blond-haired man with a bow and arrow took aim. His face was stern, eyes clear, body humming with contained energy, all focus on the next shot. Two arrows protruded from the moose, one in the neck and the other in the withers. The deformed head kept gnawing at the shaft of one while the other head flipped back and forth making a distressed grunting noise.

The archer took a breath, set his feet shoulder-width apart and let the arrow loose on his exhale. It lodged right between the moose's eyes. The antlers slumped forward; the moose should have been dead. But the deformed head squealed again, the other head now bumping life-lessly against its own chest. The moose's body kicked out, hopping sideways, retreating from the clearing. The wolves nipped at his heels, keeping the creature in check, dancing out of his way when the ungainly hooves kicked out. The man nocked another arrow.

Cautious, Rachel got to her feet. Enough time had passed for Adam to get to the house and lock himself inside.

"Don't worry my dear, you are quite safe now. Captain Lewis is an excellent shot."

The rich voice came from behind her and Rachel whirled around. The man was slight, commanding more space than his build suggested. A patch covered his right eye, a faint scar leaked down the cheek like a rogue tear. Smooth, mahogany skin made it difficult to tell the man's age, but his voice was cultured, the pronunciation precise. He wore a long tailcoat with a double row of buttons down the front over black military pants and combat boots. An unfamiliar insignia of a seashell sat boldly to the left of his chest. A leather belt strap crossed his chest the opposite way and looped around his right arm. A gold chain, Rachel guessed that it attached to a pocketwatch, hung from his front pocket. Black hair was cut short on the sides and back, the top neat with comb marks.

Thunder rumbled, angry mumbling in the sky.

"I am," he said with a little bow, "Consularis Sharma."

Rachel wasn't sure if "Consularis" was his first name. The way he said it was like a title.

Sharma cleared his throat.

"Oh, Rachel Deneuve." Rachel held out her right hand.

"The other hand, my dear, if you don't mind. A bit of a war wound." He offered his left hand and Rachel suddenly understood the belt, that the right arm was a prosthetic.

"I'm so sorry." Rachel, flustered, shook the left. Reaction set in and she clasped her hands together to still their shaking "That moose. I've never seen anything like it. If you hadn't come—"

Two other men in similar uniform stood behind him—one Hispanic, one black, both serious. Foot soldiers, Rachel guessed. Consularis Sharma didn't introduce them.

Lightning flashed. The leaves in the top canopy made a rushing sound and the sky deepened from the earlier yellow to gray.

"The weather isn't welcoming." Consularis Sharma looked to the sky with a strange smile twisting his generous lips.

These soldiers had just saved Adam's life. Her life. Filled with relief, Rachel said, "You can stay at my house until the storm passes over."

"How very generous of you, my dear." Sharma smiled at Rachel, gesturing her toward the clearing with his stiff right arm.

In the clearing the archer knelt on one knee, pulling his arrows out of the dead moose. He wiped the tips on a cloth and then replaced the arrows in his quiver. The two wolves sat at attention, although Rachel could see red on the white one's coat as it breathed in and out.

"Captain Lewis? I would like to introduce you to Ms. Rachel Deneuve, our hostess."

The archer flicked a glance at Rachel as he got to his feet. Standing easily over six feet, the archer was blond, hair also cut short. He looked as if he'd stepped from artwork, a warrior from ancient Greece or Rome. Even features and intense blue eyes made his face classically handsome. Parentheses around his mouth made Rachel think they were about the same age, early thirties. His full lips could have been soft, but they were pressed together. *Cold,* thought Rachel. *And arrogant.* Unlike the Consularis, Captain Lewis did not wear a coat. Instead, he wore a tight black T-shirt over camouflage pants. The same shell insignia embroidered on Consularis Sharma's uniform hung from a silver necklace around his neck, the way some might wear the crucifix.

Rachel pulled her gaze from the archer to stare down at the dead creature in wonderment. *The energy mutations aren't just in plants. This is bad. Very bad.*

Captain Lewis slid his strung bow into the quiver with his arrows and settled it across his back, adjusting the leather strap so it didn't rest against his throat. His movements were efficient, a study in feline grace.

Drops began to fall as the wind picked up from the east. Leaves flipped back and forth on their stems. Rachel felt anxious to get to Adam. She turned toward the path that Adam had run up not so long ago. The Consularis stepped to her side as if he already knew how to get to her house. The other soldiers followed without a word.

Lightning flashed again across the darkening sky, bouncing across the atmospheric cloud cover like call and response. Raindrops fell, the rustling of the forest canopy masking any other sounds. Rachel hurried up the path to the door, then turned around to wait as the consularis sauntered. He touched the bark of an oak tree at the outer edge of her property. It hadn't sprouted any leaves yet. She needed to ask Scott if there was any way to take it down.

The consularis jutted his chin at the best specimen in the area, the only tree in the front yard. "Is that an Empress Paulownia tree?"

Rachel glanced at the tree. It had grown under Tamaki's care, the giant leaves spreading into a fort for the Asian girl. Pale pink, purple, and yellow flowers had bloomed and then remained on the branches. *Maybe a positive mutation*, Rachel mused.

To the consularis's question, Rachel nodded before twisting the doorknob. Locked. *Good boy, Adam.*

"It looks quite healthy, the topmost branches reaching your roofline. In fact, this section of forest is the most intact I've seen during our travels. And you have a garden. How very practical."

Adam opened the door. Threw himself into her arms. She hugged him back, inhaling his unique scent. When he stiffened and pulled back, surprised by the strangers, Rachel said, "These men are soldiers. They killed the moose and saved my life."

She read Adam's face and hoped his thought wasn't as obvious to the men. *Strangers aren't welcome.*

The consularis made it through the doorway just as hard rain rushed down against the house. Wind howled outside, shaking the structure of the log cabin.

"The animals need to stay outside." Rachel said. She was thinking of the blood and grit in their coats and in their teeth from the fight with the moose.

"They come with me," Captain Lewis said. "They are as much soldiers of New Babylon as the rest of us."

The wolves followed the archer, pressing past her legs. Rachel stood frozen, the term "New Babylon" resounding in her head. They were from the military regime that the radio had warned about. The two foot soldiers followed the wolves until Rachel stood alone in the doorway looking out at the storm. Her house, the place of safety, had become a trap. The worst part, Rachel realized, was that she'd invited the monsters in.

Suddenly a form scampered through the interior darkness, skittering into the kitchen, the swinging door moving back and forth. Rachel whipped around at the sound. Rain obscured the outside light, making it difficult to see.

The two foot soldiers fell forward into crouches, their hands ready to attack.

TWENTY-ONE

Rachel pushed through the soldiers, her own hands raised, wheeling about to face the men. "Stop! That's Tamaki! She lives here."

Consularis Sharma flicked his hand and the two soldiers stood upright.

Rachel walked backwards to the swinging door of the kitchen, nudging it open with her foot while she called in, "Tamaki? These soldiers killed a wild moose in the clearing. He had rabies . . . or something. Anyway, they need to stay here during the storm."

Adam followed her into the kitchen and went to stand beside Tamaki on the far wall against the kitchen counter. Behind the counter rainwater splashed like a fountain down the window making what light came in gray and flat. Underneath the window a row of plants lined the granite backsplash—vegetables grown from seeds planted in Tupperware, ravioli cans, anything that would hold dirt. The pumpkin vines curled out and up while the thin tomato stalk wobbled in unseen breezes, its sole leaf yellow.

"He didn't have rabies, Mom. He had an extra head."

"Right. We can discuss that later," Rachel said. *More pressing danger to worry about.*

"Let's pull the shutters on those windows—just in case this is the storm that's going to send flying shards of glass into our house."

Adam shook his head, an eleven-year-old's impatience with his mother. "They're open because I was watching for you."

Aware that the three of them could be seen through the dual-sided fireplace, Rachel stepped forward like she was going to hug her son.

"I'm just so glad you're alive," she said loudly with a sniffle. Adam gave her a horrified look and tried to duck her maternal embrace. Rachel grabbed him and shoved her head between Adam's and Tamaki's.

She hissed, "Listen! Do not give any information away about anything. We don't know what they want. There's a rifle in my room and knives here in the kitchen, but they have weapons too, and those wolves. So, we're going to go along with the charade that we are all friends."

Pulling back she spoke in a normal tone, "Adam, will you please light some candles and lanterns? Take them into the dining room and I'll make dinner." Rachel opened the swinging door and pointed, "Tamaki, this is Consularis Sharma and Captain Lewis and . . . I don't know their names," Rachel gestured to the still silent foot soldiers.

"Gentleman, you can take off your packs and leave them by the front door. Also, I'd appreciate if you'd take off your boots to keep germs out of the house. There's a shoe tray right there." She smiled at the recalcitrant looks. Again, the men looked toward the consularis. He met Rachel's gaze and gave her an inscrutable look before tipping his head. The men, archer included, bent down to remove their muddy boots.

"What the heck's a consularis?" Adam hadn't moved, except to cross his arms over his chest, playing man of the house.

Sharma ran his fingers along the chain of his watch. "A title is merely syllables strung together."

The archer spoke up, his tone warm, "He's too modest. Consularis Sharma is one of two elected officials from the patricians of New Babylon."

Rachel shook her head. "I don't understand." But she did. The terms hadn't meant anything at first because she'd never heard them, only read them. Roman titles she'd learned as background in her art history classes.

Captain Lewis narrowed his eyes, but Consularis Sharma spoke, "These men are part of my census team."

Rachel hesitated. "Would you excuse me? I need to secure the house." Out of the corner of her eye she saw Adam push off from the kitchen counter, hopefully to follow her earlier instructions. Tamaki eased away from the soldiers, following Adam.

Rachel used a crank to roll down an aluminum shutter curtain in front of the picture window in the family room. This shut out the weak outdoor light, but also dampened some of the storm's noise. Then Rachel moved to the fireplace and lit the fire, painfully aware of Captain Lewis approaching from behind her.

"I need a rag and some warm water to care for Dido's wound."

Rachel swallowed and nodded her head towards the swinging door.

The kitchen felt like it shrank when Captain Lewis and his two wolves entered. The man should have looked ridiculous walking around in socks, but he had such a commanding presence that he was still intimidating. That and he walked with two predators by his side who had big teeth and no visible restraints.

Rachel swallowed. "Are they going to attack me or my family?"

The archer looked down, laying his hand on the black one's head. "Only if I tell them to. Or if you make direct eye contact." The black wolf chose that moment to growl, a menacing sound vibrating in the throat.

"That's reassuring," Rachel said with a tight smile as she studied the animals. Both were slender, with powerful shoulders and heavily muscled necks, but the black one was larger overall. The white wolf pricked triangle ears forward as if listening to the conversation.

Rachel nodded, shut the pantry door and opened the drawer beside the sink. "I didn't see how it was hurt."

"She."

Rachel frowned, cracked her fingers. "I didn't see how 'she' was hurt."

"Caught a hoof in the side."

Captain Lewis knelt beside the black wolf and began unbuckling what looked like a backpack from off the animal. "This is Ceasar. He carries the med kit. Dido carries their food." He removed the dog backpack from Dido, making sure to avoid her injury.

Rachel compared the two wolves: Caesar's long, blunt muzzle and forehead were both thicker than Dido's. Despite a large head and strong jaws, though, Dido gave the impression of grace, her fur an impeccable white except for the bloodstain. She looked like a queen and probably had since she was a pup.

Rachel pulled out a dishrag. "I'll boil the water extra long to make sure to kill any bacteria so she won't get an infection."

"Is that your technique for the cooking water?" He looked at her with those knowing eyes. His lips pulled up slightly to the right.

"Yes." She drew out the word, feeling this was a test.

"That's very . . . interesting."

"Okay. I'll bite. Why is that interesting, Captain Lewis?"

"You insist on our taking off our shoes to control germs, but have no clue about actual survival basics. This area is high in nitrate. Heating water past boiling only causes liquid to evaporate thus making the nitrate concentration higher and more toxic for consumption." He snorted. "No thanks. Bring me water when it reaches a rolling boil."

"I don't think you really know what's in our water," Rachel said. Her cheeks burned with both anger and embarrassment. She fidgeted with filling the pot of water. So she, Adam, and Tamaki were all going to die of nitrate poisoning? Well, Captain Lewis hadn't seen dead branches grow into trees.

Walking back to hang the pot over the fireplace, Rachel tried to change the subject.

"Dido. That's surprisingly romantic. The queen in love with a warrior."

Lewis snorted. "I don't anthropomorphize my animals; they're soldiers like me. She's named after the 'Dido solution' to an isoperimetric problem. When Dido was founding Carthage, they say that she bargained for as much land as could be encircled by an oxhide. Then, she cut the hide into strips so fine that they cordoned off an entire hill. It's a practical, clever name."

"If you say so." Rachel shrugged, added a stick to the fire, making it pop. She leaned forward to look into the other room through the two-sided fireplace. Adam sat at the table with Consularis Sharma, but he didn't seem upset. An open math workbook, brought from the hospital, lay open between them. Adam was pointing at the shell on Sharma's shirt.

By leaning almost into the fire, Rachel could make out their conversation.

Adam said, "What's that shell mean?"

Consularis Sharma tapped the embroidered cross-section with two fingers of his left hand. Metallic threads of gold and bronze circled around and around, finally opening like the bell of a French horn. "Calculus, young man. The spiral of the nautilus shell is a classical image used to depict the growth and change related to calculus. Think of it this way. Did you know the ratio in a snail's shell is the same, mathematically, as the spiral in the Milky Way galaxy, and it's also the same as the spirals in human DNA?"

Adam's head tilted to the side. "That's cool."

"It is more than that, young man." The consularis stared into Adam's eyes. "You seem different than most children. Did anything . . . special happen to you the night of the firestorm?"

Rachel held her breath and glanced at the two silent soldiers still sitting at the end of the table. Everything seemed hinged on Adam's answer.

"Special?" Adam pursed his lips as if carefully considering. "Nope."

A boom of thunder shook the house. Rachel exhaled.

From the corner of the kitchen Captain Lewis cleared his throat. "Is the water boiling?"

Without acknowledging that she'd been caught eavesdropping, Rachel offered Lewis a rag and bowl of water. She poured more water for dinner and hung the pot back over the fire. Then, she crossed her arms over her chest and propped her hip against the cabinet. "I thought that wolves paired for life. So, it should be Dido and Aeneas."

"Stop re-naming my wolves." Lewis's tone was superior. "Aeneas abandoned Dido at the whim of the Greek gods and Dido killed herself on a burning pyre. I think I'll stick with my names."

Rachel shrugged. "Whatever."

His condescension was hard to take, but she had to get him talking, find out what the New Babylon census team wanted. "What brought you guys here?"

"We've been tracking the moose for the past several days."

"Is this the first time you've been in the area?" Consularis Sharma seemed familiar.

"Standard procedure is to scout an area."

That seemed like a non-answer. Rachel walked to the pantry, standing in front to block the archer from seeing how full or empty it was. "What do you guys like to eat?"

"We've been camping with field rations." He said it as if that were nothing.

"So I just have to compete with meal bars? I can do that." She grabbed the rice, a can of salmon, and canned mandarin oranges. There was still an unopened family-size box of rice and a package containing eight cans of oranges from one of their last raids. The salmon was a little harder to part with, but they needed protein, and the soldiers had saved her and Adam. It was the least she could do to say 'thank you.' And, maybe, good old hospitality would persuade them to leave this house in peace after the storm. Rachel poured more water into the kettle and adjusted it over the flames.

Captain Lewis asked, "You get your water from a rain barrel?"

Examining the question for a trap, Rachel nodded. She pulled a can opener from a drawer.

When there was no response she looked over her shoulder and found herself observing a private scene. Caesar, the black wolf, nosed Dido on one side while Lewis knelt on the other with the white wolf's head resting on his knee. The expression of concern on the archer's face as he washed her wound was so intimate that Rachel shifted her gaze to the shuttered window. Muted pelting came through the shutters. Hail. Rachel could picture the black hunks of ice and dirt. They wouldn't melt at first, but would stay on the ground, hard pellets of hate from the yellow sky.

While the rice cooked, Rachel walked past the archer and his wolves and opened the swinging door.

At the table Consularis Sharma was talking to Adam, their heads together over the workbook in front of them. Sharma looked up. "Your son is quite good at algebra. He caught on quickly."

That's what the tutors at the hospital had said as well; Adam was gifted. Was Sharma trying to show that she wasn't providing any education for her son or was he really nice enough to tutor a strange child while caught in a storm? Rachel caught Adam's eye and raised an eyebrow, asking if he wanted her to intervene. Adam shrugged one shoulder.

Rachel nodded, tried to smile, retreated into the kitchen.

Caesar raised his black head and fixed her with yellow eyes. He pulled up his lip to show teeth. Rachel backed away, saw a quick smirk cross Lewis's face. He was so self-assured it was annoying. He obviously thought of himself as the bold, handsome hero.

"I'd prefer for you to control your animals while you're in my house," she said sharply.

"I'm always in control," Captain Lewis said.

She struggled not to roll her eyes the way that Adam often did. A sudden spattering of rain came down the chimney and sparks scattered while the flames made angry sizzling sounds behind her. Rachel added another stick to the fire, worried that it might go out.

Captain Lewis squeezed the bloody rag into the bowl and gave Dido a final pat.

"Where's the other woman?"

"Tamaki? Oh," Rachel looked around as if expecting to see the blue-haired girl hiding in the corner, "she's like a skittish cat. Probably hiding under one of the beds or something." The water seemed to take forever to boil. Rachel leaned against the counter. "Listen, I really appreciate your saving my life out there." She gestured toward the window. "I had no idea what to do and if Adam had been hurt or killed . . . he's my everything."

Captain Lewis stood. "That's why you need to leave here. Go to New Babylon before winter. Not only is the city-state your only option for safety, it's your best option."

"Thanks, but Adam can't—" Rachel stopped herself from saying too much and finished lamely, "he gets sick really easily."

"That's irrational." His tone was dismissive. "If you're worried about his health, then you shouldn't be isolated in the mountains, you should be near technology and doctors."

Rachel's face flushed with anger. "How dare you make judgments when you don't know anything about me or my son?"

She walked over to the fire. After this storm they'd have to gather what the wind had blown down. Maybe store it in the garage to dry before the next storm.

Lewis was waiting for her across the kitchen. *Rehearsing*, Rachel thought.

"What did you do before the firestorm?"

"What do you mean 'what did I do'?" Rachel could hear the defensiveness in her tone.

"I already know. You're college-educated. Your vocabulary, familiarity with Greek mythology, they scream liberal arts to me. You look fit, your hair is brushed, all your teeth are there. Instead of doing manual labor you probably paid to go to a gym. You're too comfortable to be squatters in this house, so I'm guessing that this cabin with its picture windows and granite countertops belonged to you. Wealthy. Which means that you either had a white-collar job, or, more likely since you said Adam was everything, you stayed home to take care of your kid. How'd I do?"

It was like he'd ripped apart everything she'd been building at Hiraeth, including her independence. She wasn't qualified to survive post-firestorm with her art degree and her stay-at-home-mom experience. To hide her reaction, Rachel grabbed two large potatoes she'd picked from the front garden and began peeling them.

"I'll take your silence to mean I'm right."

Rachel added the canned salmon, potatoes, and mandarin oranges to the rice and put the stew back over the fire. *Take it however you want, you giant walking penis.* She took a deep breath and turned to face him.

"So, high school athlete. Lacrosse, maybe. Definitely a frat boy riding on daddy's money. Dated the cheerleader so you'd look cool. ROTC so you could wear the uniform but not worry about the pushups. A follower, always looking for a team to run with. No surprise you ran for the biggest gang on the block when the world ended. Bullies always run in packs."

Dido whined from her corner of the kitchen. Her head swung back and forth between the two humans.

"How'd I do?" Rachel put her hands on her hips and gave a savage smile. *You pushed me first.*

A thundercloud passed over his features. His fingers twitched as if he were imagining grabbing her by the throat.

Rachel felt a thrill of fear along with a sense of vindication. She'd pushed his buttons.

"You're not going to make it out here." He held up his hand and ticked off ways she could fail. "You'll run out of food, be killed by rogue humans, be caught in a mudslide, you'll get an infection from unclean water, or you'll die of hypothermia when winter comes."

Rachel faced Captain Lewis with her hands on her hips. "I'm not worried."

"Either you're lying or you're a fool." The archer leaned against the wall, striking a nonchalant pose. "In one year a person needs one hundred pounds of rice. Sixty pounds of honey or sugar. Fifty pounds each of beans, peas, lentils. Three hundred pounds of wheat. You got that —times three—tucked away in your pantry over there?"

The stew was finished cooking. Rachel carried the pot through to the dining room, bread made the day before balanced on top, and let the door swing back into Captain Lewis's face.

TWENTY-TWO

Rachel sat at the head of the oval table, the consularis sat on her right and the archer on her left. The other soldiers sat at the other end of the table. Rachel wondered if they'd left the two spots in the middle for Adam and Tamaki or if their lower rank meant they couldn't sit beside the officers. Adam brought in two more candles and set them on a mantel underneath a mirror before he sat down at the table.

"Mrs. Deneuve. While I don't wish to be indelicate, I must ask where Mr. Deneuve is."

Must you? Rachel wondered. She considered lying, but it didn't matter. If something bad was going to happen before the storm finished, she didn't think the threat of a husband on his way was going to stop it.

"He died."

Adam made a sound, but Rachel gave a subtle shake of her head. She was as outraged by the consularis's cavalier attitude as her son, but she was also afraid of him, and worse, what he purported to represent. Her gaze went to the insignia on his uniform.

Consularis Sharma picked up a fork in his left hand and served himself from the stewpot before passing it to Captain Lewis. "Ahh, salmon? Quite a fancy meal."

Rachel tried to smile. "Thank goodness for canned meat and rice."

Consularis Sharma tightened his mouth then deliberately set down his fork. He grabbed his right forearm with his left hand and began to twist. The forearm screwed off exposing a wooden stub with an attached serrated blade.

Rachel blinked.

"It is not goodness, my dear, but technology that needs to be thanked. For example, this fine German steel. And yet, I would have no hope of replacing this arm were the blade to break, the prosthesis to crack, were it not for New Babylon."

The consularis picked up his fork in his left hand and began eating the fish chunks, using his right knife-arm to cut. *Yeah,* Rachel thought, *that canned fish is really hard to cut.* Rachel glanced at Captain Lewis, but he was eating with quick, efficient movements. Feeling her gaze he looked up, raised his eyebrow, said, "Nice dinner."

She frowned, unsure whether he was serious.

A few seats away Adam's eyes bulged. He used his fork to point at the consularis in case Rachel had missed the unexpected form of prosthesis. She motioned with her hand for calm. Adam shook his head, but at least he didn't say anything.

They ate in silence until the consularis began his questions again. "I thank you for your hospitality, though I need to point out to you that living here is unsustainable. You have no access to clean drinking water, no way to stay warm when winter comes, and no ability to leave when you do realize that you and your son," he gestured with his knife-arm, "are going to starve."

"Thank you for your concern, Consularis, but we use the water from a stream not too far away, store it in a barrel with a mesh screen, and we have another rain barrel set up for the garden."

The archer snorted. "You're in West Virginia. There's coal contaminant in the groundwater. Drinking anything from your rain barrel means you're drinking the filth from the polluted cloud cover overhead."

Rachel crossed her legs. "We are managing just fine, Captain Lewis." Her foot tapped in time with her anger. "But why, exactly, is New Babylon concerned with us?"

Outside, the full force of the storm hit. The whole house shook and no one could speak for a moment. The candles flickered as wind came through tiny cracks and forced itself down the chimney.

"New Babylon has two goals: to bring citizens in to our city and to delete anything abnormal to civilization." Consularis Sharma settled back in his chair as if telling a story. "The firestorm caused crustal shifting. Most of Pennsylvania is under the ocean. In New Babylon we've built a desalination plant to provide the most essential element of survival: clean water. We have other teams right now gathering more resources."

He smiled. "My second task is equally clear. Fire has rained from the heavens, burning and scarring. The excess energy in our world is causing mutations in the plant and animal life. The moose was abnormal to civilization. We removed it." Consularis Sharma leaned forward across the dinner table. "That monstrosity began as an animal. Think about human mutations."

Rachel shook her head. "Everyone touched by the fire died. They burned up."

"Imagine a human with two heads, or devolving into something worse. Only the memory of reason twitting about in malformed brains. We've seen them."

He couldn't be right. Rachel shivered. She could tell Adam was uncomfortable by the way he fidgeted.

"Do you believe me, Mrs. Deneuve?"

The question hung in the air until Rachel pushed back her chair, letting it scrape against the floor the way she'd told Adam not to do a thousand times.

Consularis Sharma took his bread in his left hand and used it to wipe the stew off his plate. His lips glistened. Rachel looked away, but heard him chewing the bread.

"The roads are no longer safe. I do not wish to frighten either you or the boy, and yet I must."

Again with the 'must.' What is he trying to sell?

"We've just traveled through what remains of Baltimore. The city is filled with unrest, the few who remain sit on the filthy streets, covered with sores, trying to sell rotten food. Complete human misery."

Rachel looked at him, startled. "But the hospital . . . it's okay, right? The nurses and doctors? Do they still have oil for the generators? What about food? Naomi . . . my friend said they were starting a school in one of the buildings."

Captain Lewis said, "We've sent a census team into Baltimore. They'll meet me back in New Babylon to report and bring any citizens who wish to join our movement."

Rachel swallowed. Maybe these men were right. She could give up being in charge and join a community. Adam could play with other kids. No more worrying about food or the red-painted people coming back. No more two-headed moose. And what if, just by the craziest chance, what if Naomi and her children were in Baltimore right now listening to this other census team and they could all meet up?

Outside the storm continued. Rachel imagined the ground turning to mud, her plants battered. "New Babylon isn't a democracy, I'm guessing." Rachel chewed her lip. She'd almost told them about The Weatherman and the transistor radio.

Consularis Sharma leaned forward so that Rachel could smell his breath. His face filled her field of vision. The candle in the lantern flickered three times before going out, the wick surrounded by a puddle of white wax. In the resulting shadow, Consularis Sharma's face seemed to spread outwards, deepening in color to an eggplant hue.

"I think, Mrs. Deneuve, that you have some expectation that if you gather a few sticks of firewood for the evening meal and plant your little garden, that everything will be okay. But, you are delusional."

He whispered so that only she could hear. To Rachel, his voice sounded like a record player set too slow. "You are an attractive woman. The candles catch the red hidden in your dark hair, the shape of your breasts, the irises of your eyes as they struggle to see out of your beautiful face. If I were you, I would be very afraid." He held her gaze, his expression carnal.

Rachel fought the urge to leap up and away.

Consularis Sharma straightened and spoke in a normal voice. "But, strength may be wielded for the greater good, as well. New Babylon is the cavalry, the help for which you have been subconsciously waiting. Yearning, even. Our job is to protect you from the mutations caused by the firestorm. New Babylon will rise to become even better than we were," he clenched his fist on the last word and Rachel flinched from the spittle on her cheek with a small sound of distress, "before."

Before what? She didn't raise her hand to wipe away the flecks, more frightened than when the moose had charged. What the consularis said was logical, she was a mom who'd spent the last years learning medical jargon and the side effects of various chemotherapies. If there was ever someone unqualified to survive winter, or beyond, in an isolated cabin with dependents, it was her. These men invading her home were scary because they were strong and unknown. But, Rachel forced herself to examine the possibility. She and Adam could pack up what they needed. Tamaki could come too. A new, safe beginning. Rachel found her head nodding in agreement to her thoughts.

The swinging door to the kitchen moved an inch and Rachel knew Tamaki was listening.

Sharma said, "When we leave tomorrow, I hope you and your family will allow us to escort you to New Babylon."

"Thank you for the invitation. It's a lot for me to think about tonight."

Suddenly a loud crack sounded from above, perhaps a tree falling, perhaps lightning directly overhead. All eyes looked up, but the roof held. Tamaki pushed through the door carrying another lantern. Rachel looked at Consularis Sharma in the extra light and saw his face had returned to a neutral expression, hiding what he'd whispered to her a moment before. *Too late,* she thought at him. *I've seen your true self and you are a monster.*

Consularis Sharma turned to her as if he could hear her.

"Tamaki, please clear the plates." Rachel stood. "Adam will sleep with me, so there is a bedroom and the couch for you and your men to use tonight."

Consularis Sharma also stood, began screwing his arm back on.

Across from Rachel, the archer—still seated—tilted his head. "Where will the other woman be?"

"There's a guest bedroom." Rachel pushed her chair back under the table.

Even by candlelight Rachel could see his blue eyes assessing, calculating. There was more here than Captain Lewis and Consularis Sharma were telling.

TWENTY-THREE

Rachel pulled her bedroom doorknob taut and turned the lock, not caring whether the soldiers heard it or not. She looked around and saw the heavy wooden chest at the foot of her bed. With a grunt of effort Rachel dragged it over in front of the double bedroom doors, and then leaned her forehead against the door, exhausted. It wasn't enough that they had no electricity, clean water, or transportation. Now two-headed animals were roaming the woods and the human beings left on the planet either worshipped an obscure Middle Eastern war god or were a military cult determining what was allowed and what was a mutation.

"Mom?"

Rachel lifted her head. "Yeah, sweetie?"

"I wish the soldiers had killed the moose and then kept walking." Adam sat on the floor with the lantern in front of him, his hand crossing back and forth through the orange flame. The storm still raged, but the hail had stopped.

Rachel sat down next to her son, her legs stretching out next to his. He'd gotten tall, his ankles exposed by his pj pants.

"I know. I shouldn't have invited them." She didn't say the second part of that statement: *My invitation may not have mattered.*

"Why did he say he wanted us to go to New Babylon?"

Rachel looked down at her hands, used her index nail to clean the dirt from underneath her other nails. "They are trying to get the largest group possible so they can run their city. You know, like our neighborhood back home. We all got together and chipped in for the pool and worked together to make our lives better. Don't you miss that at all? School and hospitals and other people."

"Yeah, I guess."

"Living here is hard, Adam. Winter is coming and I don't think we have enough food."

"You worry too much." He was dismissive. "Hey, can I check the weather? Make sure the storm will be gone by morning? Please?" Adam turned his face up to her, expectant.

That's what you get for trying to get advice from a child, Rachel thought. *He doesn't realize that I don't know how to fix the house if we get a leak, don't know how to fight off two-headed moose and Hotheads.*

"Yes," she said as Adam started to scramble up, "but keep it at a whisper, okay?"

He was already at her bedside table fiddling with the transistor radio. "I know. Those guys out there won't think this is 'normal,' right?"

Rachel nodded, getting up and going over to listen with him.

Adam flipped the switch on and static answered. He turned the volume down. They both glanced at the bedroom door but nothing happened. He turned the dial, surfing stations up and down the graph until, through the static, a man's distinctive sportscaster voice emerged.

"The Weatherman," Adam grinned, triumphant.

". . . unexpected pressure system brought nasty hail and winds gusting at 30 mph. If the system leaves on its own, we'll have rising temperatures. If it doesn't clear out on its own, we'll see what kind of pressure this mountain range can bring. No music until then." The speech was followed by a fumbling sound like someone hanging up an old-fashioned telephone.

Adam replaced the radio on the nightstand.

"Come on." Rachel walked back over to the lantern and picked up the Star Wars quilt he'd brought from his room. She snapped it open and spread it out, then grabbed a pillow from her own bed. "Here you go."

Adam yawned as he lay down. "Those guys didn't know what they were talking about. Scott brings us all the stuff we need so we don't even have to go into Baltimore."

"I know, sweetie, but let's keep that to ourselves. They don't need to know anything more about us."

"Okay. I love you."

Rachel leaned down and kissed his forehead. "I love you, too."

For a moment she allowed herself the luxury of just watching Adam. He lay on his side, cheek resting on his folded hands, eyelashes sweeping as he blinked. Rachel felt like she could see Adam's mind swirling with thoughts, going through everything he'd seen today from the moose to the soldiers.

"I didn't like when that consularis guy was talking about dad." Adam licked his lip as he stared straight ahead. "It's none of his business." A tear slid over his nose and dropped on the pillow.

Rachel settled onto the floor next to her son. She rubbed his back until Adam's eyes closed and his breathing settled into a regular rhythm.

Rachel blew out the lantern. The house was silent, but Rachel couldn't sleep, listening for any sounds from either outside the house, or from inside. She didn't know what time it was when she heard the sound she'd been dreading since the episode at dinner. A scratching at the door. Rachel's heart thumped so hard it hurt. The scratching turned into a quiet knock. The consularis's face filled her mind as if the zoom feature on a camera wouldn't turn off.

Someone whispered her name.

Rachel leaped up. She shoved the chest out of the way and unlocked the door. Cracked it open a few inches. A little light from the fireplace helped Rachel see Tamaki's outline. Rachel stepped back and the young woman slipped in. Rachel let out her breath as she relocked the door and shoved the chest back in position.

"I was wondering where you were," she told the young woman. "I thought maybe you'd gone outside into the storm."

Tamaki climbed up on the bed wearing her button-down pj top and matching cropped pj bottoms with the frog faces. She had the black pouch she always wore still on, the strap over her right shoulder and around her left hip. She tucked her hair behind one ear and peeked over the side of the bed to see Adam asleep on the floor.

Rachel propped up her pillows, and settled next to Tamaki. Outside the wind keened again, last efforts of the dying storm. Rachel struck a match and re-lit the lantern. Sitting on her bed with another girl, by candlelight, felt like the weirdest sleepover she'd ever had.

Tamaki whispered, "Rachel, you were really brave at dinner."

"Thanks. I didn't discuss it with you first. . . . Do you want to go to New Babylon in the morning?"

Tamaki shook her head. "No way."

"I didn't think so either, but I've been thinking. We're all alone out here and mutations are real. We've seen it in the fungi, and today I saw it in an animal. Once cold weather comes, we can't change our mind, even with the SUV. A blizzard could trap us here with no food and no heat. And, even if we do survive, what's the point? Adam doesn't have even the most basic immunizations. This city might have doctors and access to medicine that Baltimore didn't have." Rachel sat up in the bed, a feeling of excitement catching hold of her imagination.

"You don't understand," Tamaki said.

"What don't I understand? This could be our chance to join a community. Instead of day-to-day survival, we can look to the future. Adam could have a real life. Grow up, get married. I could become a grandmother one day. When you arrived, I was so excited to see another person who hadn't gone crazy like the Hotheads or the mob in the car-garage when I left Baltimore."

"I've met New Babylon soldiers before." Tamaki closed her eyes and gave a great sigh as if she had to gather her strength. "I lived with my gran outside of Dublin, Ohio, just like I told you. After the firestorm, all the survivors gathered at the high school. There were about a hundred or so after we all trickled in." Tamaki pushed hair behind one ear. "New Babylon soldiers came through, just like here. They said the Hotheads were a threat and they'd help us. So, we were happy."

"The Hotheads are a threat." Rachel folded her arms across her chest.

"They rounded up all the Hotheads." Tamaki gulped. "They killed them. Right there in the school courtyard. This black smoke came out and the soldiers said it was the energy of evil. They said we all needed to go to New Babylon. But, some of us didn't want to. My gran had lived in her house her whole life. She knew how to live simply. Another woman had just had a baby. She didn't want to travel and her husband said they wouldn't go. The soldiers said—" Tamaki closed her eyes. "They said, 'Fine, you will be food for the bull.'"

Rachel stared at the girl. "What bull?"

"The next day the soldiers and most of our community left. And then these horrid little imps came, like people who had turned into monkeys, somehow. I know how that sounds, but I don't know any other way to describe these creatures. They had humped backs and jumped around. They attacked everyone who'd stayed. Suddenly, there was a great sound and everyone looked outside. My grandmother grabbed me and we hid in the janitor's closet of the school hallway, but we could hear. Those things took the baby from the woman. She screamed and screamed."

Goosebumps broke out all over Rachel's body. "Then what?"

Tamaki looked at Rachel. "I swear I don't know. We stayed in the closet as long as we could and when we came out there was nobody there. Nothing.

"My gran and I left. We started south and stayed off any roads, but she got sick. We had to eat plants we didn't recognize, new plants. We were captured by Hotheads. The ones you saw me with." Tamaki rubbed her leg with the scar. "You know the rest."

Rachel stared at the Asian girl with anger in her eyes. "You kept that information from me? After I gave you a place to stay? And you couldn't bother to tell me something that might hurt my son or me?"

"I wasn't being malicious. I wanted to tell you that day when we were talking on your porch, but I knew you'd never believe me." Tears glistened in Tamaki's black eyes.

Rachel rubbed her face. "That . . . is . . . something." She wanted to discount all of it, but it was too much of a coincidence to hear of a bull from the soldier in Baltimore and then from Tamaki. The question wasn't whether there was a bull, but how was it connected to New Babylon? And, if they didn't go with the soldiers, would the bull mutation come here?

"Please, Rachel," Tamaki said. "We can make this homestead work. You said we're a family. We can do this."

All Rachel could do was nod her head in acknowledgment at what Tamaki said. "It's late," she said. "Get some rest." What she meant was, *I don't want to think anymore.* Babies and bulls and Tamaki's grandmother murdered in front of her and God knows what else they did to her before she escaped. Enough to make her imagine things? *And yet, I didn't imagine a two-headed moose.*

Rachel leaned over to blow out the lantern, but changed her mind. Instead, she lay back against the pillows with the lights on and listened to Adam and Tamaki breathe, both asleep. Worry sat on Rachel's chest, collapsing her ribs and squeezing her heart. Like the first night at college after her parents' death. Before: the dreams of being an artist, of maybe opening a gallery in New York and hosting galas. After: no family, no support, no mentors. Panic and fear. The need to make the pain stop, even if it meant forgetting about drawing and becoming a suburban wife. A wife who didn't fit in with the neighbors even before Adam's diagnosis, who felt like she was acting a part in exchange for not being alone. This choice—move to New Babylon or stay at Hiraeth—was so much harder. Because she was afraid of both options.

TWENTY-FOUR

The next morning Rachel put an "X" through the date on the calendar hanging on the kitchen wall. Forty-seven days post-firestorm, but that didn't account for her queasy feeling. Today was the anniversary of Adam's diagnosis. She reached for her necklace, but it wasn't there. Some families celebrated the diagnosis date, but they'd chosen to look ahead, look toward the five-year anniversary of chemo completion instead, towards Adam being pronounced cured. "The date," she told herself, "has no power. It's a normal day."

She adjusted the teakettle hanging over the fire. The soldiers were staying for breakfast, but she'd had to offer. After she said it was too soon for her to leave the homestead, the men, minus Consularis Sharma, had climbed up on her roof and rigged a pulley system to bring down the tree that had fallen across the roof during the storm. The offer of help was unexpected and she'd agreed. The least she could do was cook them something to eat before they left. So, there she was in the kitchen using up precious resources to make bannock bread for seven people. Flour, only one more bag in the pantry, baking powder, getting low, mix together and make a hole for the water, powdered eggs, and then add in the raisins and coconut. The bag of shredded coconut had been a bonus find in the McHenry's abandoned house a week ago. Rachel poured the batter into the cooking pan and then put it over the coals of the fireplace.

Sharma's face popped into view as he leaned into the fireplace from the other side. "I wish you would reconsider, Mrs. Deneuve. I feel like I'm abandoning your family."

Rachel nodded. "Thank you for your concern, Consularis Sharma. You've given me a lot to think about, but I'd want to pack up before we left."

She pulled off the kitchen mitts, self-conscious about being studied from the other room.

"There will be another storm with a larger tree falling on your house. Or perhaps the bull moose's mate will come looking for him while you are deciding."

Rachel shuddered at the thought of another mutant moose. To cover her reaction she turned away and reached for the French press and the bag sitting on the counter. She smelled the coffee grounds, rich and pungent. A treat. Rachel filled a teakettle and hung it over the fire before pushing through the swinging door into the dining room.

The soldiers had already finished the can of peaches and the small fried potatoes from the garden that she'd set out before starting the bread. Tamaki was nowhere to be seen and Adam was outside bringing in water from the creek.

"Thank you for helping us with the moose and with the tree, but we don't need to rush into a decision. I have a . . ." she stopped herself from saying "an SUV." *Would they steal it if they knew?* ". . . legs and can go north to New Babylon before the weather turns." Rachel went back into the kitchen and returned with the French press and five matching mugs. "We're managing without electricity. I even have coffee to offer before you leave."

Rachel set the tray on the table and was straightening when she felt the room change. Something was wrong. Sweat broke out under her armpits. She swallowed and tried to think of something to say, some-thing to chatter about, to restore the idea that she was just a hostess and everything was fine. All four soldiers stared at the coffee. Rachel looked at it too, regular brown grounds inside a glass container, the plunger at the top, until the teakettle's whistle broke the silence.

"Coffee?" the archer asked her, too softly. "Don't tell me you grow that in your garden as well? You must have quite a supply up here."

Rachel nodded, forcing herself to move to the fireplace, prepare the coffee. Why had she tried to show off?

"Yup. Got to have coffee. Save it for special occasions. Like this one." She tried to laugh, but her mouth wouldn't work.

"Rachel," said Captain Lewis.

Startled by the use of her first name, she looked into his blue eyes.

"Someone stole our rations on the way here. That's punishable by death."

"I don't—" Her hands shook as she poured. Water swirled. "I hav-en't left this homestead since we came out here."

She cleared the table and in the privacy of her kitchen leaned against the cabinet. Adam walked in from the other side carrying the water.

"What's the matter, Mom?"

Rachel covered her mouth with her hand. "Nothing." She didn't want to worry him. "I just want them out of here."

"Why don't you tell them to go?"

Rachel nodded. Took a deep breath and pushed away from the counter, the same motion her son had used last evening. In the dining room she pushed the plunger on the press and poured coffee into the cups. "I guess you'll be anxious to go while the weather holds." Gripping her own mug, Rachel walked around the men and opened the front door.

"One last thing, Ma'am." The black foot soldier, who hadn't said one word to her during the past twelve hours, spoke up. "We gotta take care of that moose."

"Oh. Well, let's go." Rachel used her arm to usher them forward, out of her house.

Storm damage was everywhere. Leaves had been whipped off the Empress Paulownia tree, branches were down, and the garden to the right of the porch looked like a giant had stepped in it. Puddles were everywhere in the overly saturated woods. Worse, in the short hours since yesterday, DPF had popped up from the ground. Each stem was about six inches, the head a slimy brown, the body bright orange. They thrived in this new climate of heavy storms and no clean sunlight. Tilting her head, Rachel thought she saw Tamaki in the trees and gave a wave. Probably already using her stick to dig up the fungi and expose the white bulbs that webbed unseen below the dirt.

The soldiers were halfway down the path to the clearing when Rachel turned back around. Adam came out of the house behind her and Tamaki emerged from the forest line, leaned her stick against the fence.

"Is it bad this morning?" Rachel asked.

Tamaki nodded. "Dog-penis, poison ivy, and those new vines that strangle other plants are thriving. The storms make them stronger."

"I guess because of all the moisture."

Tamaki gave a noncommittal shrug. "Maybe because the water falls from ley lines."

Scott must have told Tamaki about his theory. Rachel looked up. "There are ley lines in the sky too?"

"No, I mean, I don't know. Guess there could be. I meant it's like the water cycle." Tamaki rotated her finger. "The energy is inside the water droplets that evaporate into the clouds and then the storm spreads it around. A higher concentration of energy creates mutations."

"Right." Uninterested in speculating about the theory of supernatural energy, Rachel gestured toward the ruined garden. "More practical question, can we salvage anything from there?"

Squinting at the sky, Tamaki nodded. "If we could get a break from the storms."

"Mom," Adam interrupted. "What are those guys doing?"

"Let's go see."

The three walked down the pathway, splashing through the mud, smelling smoke just before they reached the clearing. A soldier held a branch with a struggling flame, the damp wood refusing to cooperate.

Space had been cleared around the carcass. Captain Lewis stood to the side, Consularis Sharma near the forest as though ready to go.

Rachel glanced at Tamaki to see her reaction to the mutant moose. The woman's eyes searched the two heads, the one crooked horn, and the shaggy coat peeling away from the skin. "It's not dead."

As if in answer, the front leg twitched. A wave of horror swept through Rachel. The moose was terrifying, but no animal should suffer.

"It will be." Consularis Sharma raised his hand and then dropped it as a signal. The soldier with the lit branch leaned forward; the moose burst into flame. Thick, greasy smoke rose from the carcass, hanging above it. The overwhelming smell made Rachel's eyes water—like hydrogen sulfide gas from the paper mills where she'd grown up in Pennsylvania—not a byproduct from a living thing.

"My blueberry bucket." Adam darted forward toward the bush where he'd been yesterday.

"Adam, no!" Rachel turned around a second too late.

Captain Lewis lunged toward the boy, grabbing his arm, and pulling him back toward the others, but as he did the cloud of smoke rose into the air. Adam pulled forward, only his arm trailing behind so that it passed through the noxious smoke. Captain Lewis took the brunt of the smoke across his face. Seconds later the two joined the others on the perimeter. The captain grimaced and exhaled. He rubbed his hand across his face the way one does when they've walked through a spider web.

Rachel grabbed Adam, "Are you okay? Why did you do that?!"

Adam jerked away and ran up the path toward home.

Rachel groaned and pulled her hand through her hair.

Consularis Sharma said, "Last chance to protect your family, Mrs. Denueve."

"We're fine. I—"

A familiar voice called out from the east, "Ladies. What the hell smells so bad? Must have been Adam's turn to cook."

Rachel froze. Scott. Beside her Tamaki made a moue of distress, her dark eyes flicking from the men to the forest.

Consularis Sharma looked to the women and used his prosthetic arm to place a manufactured finger over his mouth in a signal to silence. The soldiers stood at attention, waiting, all listening to Scott's monologue.

"Your grocery man has arrived and I think you'll be pretty happy, although the road has gotten even worse and this storm made some nasty mudslides. I brought you some more coffee and I even—" Scott stopped short when he entered the clearing. He wore his typical uniform of shirt and long shorts, black lace-up boots. Over his shoulder was a bag. On his face was realization.

Immediately Scott turned to run, but the two foot soldiers lunged toward the smaller man and tackled him only a few steps outside the circle of the clearing. A rough wrestling match ensued with Scott scrambling to escape. The black man, the one who'd called Rachel "Ma'am," punched Scott in the face, again and again until the ranger stopped struggling. The New Babylon soldier pulled Scott up by his wrists, nose broken, blood streaming down, the position making him a human punching bag. The other soldier hit Scott in the kidneys with a right and then a left before straightening his own uniform.

Rachel cried out, in shock. The attack had happened so fast. "What are you doing? Let go of him!" She ran forward and shoved the soldier holding Scott. He staggered a bit, but didn't let go. A fist slammed into her solar plexus. She doubled over, and couldn't breathe. Her ribs wouldn't expand and her mouth gaped. Breath rushed in with a wave of pain and nausea. Never in her life had she been punched by someone who meant it. She straightened up, both hands clutching her middle just as the same soldier punched her again in the back.

Rachel cried out as she fell to the ground. Stars filled her tear-filled vision.

"That's enough. I think Mrs. Deneuve has learned her place." Consularis Sharma stepped closer. "Open the bag, please."

"Captain Lewis?" Rachel pleaded with the archer, looking up at him from the ground, but his blue eyes were only on his consularis.

Tamaki rushed Consularis Sharma, her head down, arms wrapping around his waist.

He pulled her arms apart and knocked her to the ground. He put his boot on her back and pressed down, digging the heel into the small of Tamaki's back. When he removed his boot, a mudprint remained as if he'd marked her as property.

The Hispanic foot soldier upended Scott's knapsack. Small plums rolled out, a brown banana, a bag of squished bread, and, last, falling in slow-motion, a bag of coffee grounds. The golden logo of a nautilus shell on the dark blue bag was unmistakable.

"Execute the thief."

"Stop it," Rachel moaned, unable to stand up, the pain making her dry heave. "Leave him alone. He's a park ranger."

The consularis ignored her, stepping forward to confront his prisoner. "You've been found guilty of theft by officers of New Babylon."

Scott struggled, trying to use his body to twist out of the soldier's grip.

Tamaki crawled across the clearing to cling to Scott, insinuating her body as a shield.

Rachel got one knee up and used it to push herself to a standing position in front of Captain Lewis, grabbed onto his arm. "Take the food back, we don't want it. Just take it back."

Captain Lewis looked down at her, his jaw clenched. He shook his arm away from her grasp.

"Come now, pull the girl away and let's be done with it." Sharma sounded impatient, as if Scott's death would be inconsequential to his day. This was the true Sharma, a monster, not the honorable soldier he'd portrayed.

"She won't let go, sir." The first soldier had his hands full with Tamaki clawing at his face. At that moment Scott ripped free from the distracted man. A shout of encouragement rose in Rachel's throat, but Captain Lewis had his bow up.

The arrow flew. Hit its mark.

Scott fell, his body smashing into the muddy ground.

"He was a thief, my dear hysterical ladies," the consularis finally looked at Rachel as the first soldier, embarrassed, shoved Tamaki against a tree. "Hang the body."

Rachel couldn't do anything as Scott, bleeding, was forced into a noose. The rope, same one used to pull the tree from her roof, stretched over the broad limb of an oak tree, one foot soldier holding the rope taut and the other rolling a log into the clearing, shoving Scott onto the makeshift stool and holding him in place. Scott wouldn't, or couldn't, stand on his own.

"Stand up, criminal, or we'll beat you until you do." The soldiers grinned at each other.

Beat you until you can stand? That's the circular logic of the Salem witch trials. Rachel jumped to her feet, frantic plans swirling through her mind. *I'll leap on Sharma, and give Scott time to get away. I'll shove the men together and Tamaki will free Scott. I'll start screaming and distract everyone.* Reaching for a miracle, she even wished the stupid moose would come back to life.

Captain Lewis's hands seized on her upper arms, holding her.

The consularis turned calm eyes on Rachel as if he could hear her thoughts.

Then, Scott was on the log, noose around his neck, rope tight. He looked to Tamaki. She reached out a hand as if she could touch him from across the clearing. The soldier kicked the log away. Into the silence Scott fell, a crack like a breaking branch, but it wasn't the branch. Scott's body swayed back and forth.

Captain Lewis's hand fell away and Rachel sank to the ground.

Tamaki crawled forward and grabbed onto Scott's leg, the white flesh over his ankle socks. "You're a murderer," she cried at Consularis Sharma. "I hope you rot in hell."

"Leave his body there," said the consularis. "A warning."

Rachel felt cold, and the edges of her vision became foggy.

"I hope this was not a friend of yours, Mrs. Deneuve? That would certainly change things. Right now you are making a poor decision to stay in wild lands, but should I believe that you were accepting stolen goods. . . ."

Numbly Rachel stared at the ground. She couldn't make her teeth stop chattering. Consularis Sharma bent forward, his face filling her vision, the scent of incense emanating from the man.

"Say that he was not a friend."

They were only words. Scott was already dead. Hate flashed inside of Rachel. Scott was dead over coffee beans that he'd been bringing to her and this man, this monster, wanted her to betray that? *Never. I will never betray my family.*

Rachel lifted her gaze to Sharma's. An exultant smile spread across his face. His eyes glowed with ferocious madness. *He's enjoying this.* She knew this in her innermost being to be a true fact. And though it meant death, being strung up beside Scott, she would not betray him.

She snarled, "I won't." The words were no louder than a whisper, but the silence of the clearing was complete. Her statement dropped like rocks into a well. "Are you going to hit me again?"

The archer cleared his throat. "Consularis? The time?"

She didn't know if he interrupted at that moment to save her life. She didn't care. She didn't owe anything to Scott's murderer.

Thunder boomed from the sky. A sudden wind moved the clouds in a strange swirling pattern.

"Of course, Captain Lewis." The consularis pulled a pocketwatch from inside his tailcoat. The watch was golden, the size of his hand, with elaborate gears that matched his prosthetic arm. "Time to go, gentlemen. We don't want to be late for pick-up."

The thunder rumbled again, as if in answer to his statement.

Sharma snapped the cover closed. "Mrs. Denueve, I'm sure we will meet again. If you live that long." He looked up at the sky with that same mysterious half-smile he'd made when first arriving behind the two-headed moose. They left the clearing, the wolves trotting beside the archer.

The shaking wouldn't stop, her whole body vibrating, teeth chattering. Scott, their friend, had been killed right outside their house, their safe place. Adam. At least he hadn't seen.

"We have to cut him down, Tamaki." Rachel shook the heartbroken girl. "Adam can't see this. At least we can bury . . . it." She couldn't call that thing Scott. She wouldn't. "Come on, I need help getting the ladder."

Tamaki unfurled. Tears marked her face, her chin quivered, but underneath was determination as she faced the body hanging from the tree. Approaching with solemn grace, Tamaki touched Scott's leg and then ran her delicate fingers down his heavy boots, untying the black laces and pulling off the boots and socks. Then she placed her hands together, spoke another language, and bowed to Scott's body as she walked around it in a circle. She chanted words full of vowels, lilting, almost singsongy. After three completions, Tamaki stopped and closed her eyes. One more inhale–exhale cycle and then Tamaki bowed again.

Tingles ran up and down Rachel's arms and legs. Sadness nestled deep in her heart. She stepped forward and touched Scott's leg. "I'm so sorry, Scott. I'm sorry that I couldn't protect you. I'm sorry that you were bringing supplies for us. You were my inspiration. You will be missed, my friend. And I wish I could say it better, but I am so grateful to you and this was so wrong. So unfair."

When Tamaki laid her head on Rachel's shoulder, Rachel could feel her shaking and worried that the young woman was going into shock. She rubbed Tamaki's arms to create warmth, tried to keep her talking. "What was that thing you were saying earlier?"

Tamaki gave a great shudder and stepped back from Rachel. She took deep breaths before she was able to talk. "My gran's people believe that the soul and the animating spirit are two different things. Scott wasn't ready to die so I said a prayer, told his soul I wanted it to stay. I took off his shoes so that his energy might be free. I didn't see any smoke when he died. I think his spirit is still here."

Rachel nodded her head. "It was beautiful. He would have . . . he would have liked it."

Tamaki pressed her lips together and nodded. "I never told him. . . ."

"He knew," Rachel said, leading Tamaki to the path. "Come on, let's go back to the house. We need to find Adam."

TWENTY-FIIVE

Inside the house Rachel went to the kitchen making a mental list, trying to prepare instead of think about what she'd just seen: ladder, garden shears to cut rope, and shovel to dig the grave. First, though, she needed to find Adam, make sure he didn't see what they were about to do.

"Adam?" Rachel walked through the kitchen, and looked in his bedroom. He wasn't there.

She went into the dining room. "Adam?" The house felt empty. Her voice louder, she shoved aside the chairs to look underneath the table, running into the family room and climbing over the sectional to look behind. *Kidnapped. They'd stolen her son.*

Last place to look was her bedroom. She ran in, hand still reaching for the light switch even after all a full month of no electricity. Glanced at the empty bed, shoved aside the clothes in the closet. No other place to look. And then, through the pounding in her head, she heard a moan. Rachel threw herself to the floor to look under the bed. Adam was curled up, wrapped in his blanket from the evening before.

"What did they do to you? Come out!"

Her son kept rocking in fetal position.

"Adam." Rachel tried to keep her voice calm. "I need you to come out now. If you can't, then I will pull you out. But, I need to know what happened so I can fix it."

He moaned again.

Rachel shoved her hair behind her ear. "Okay, baby, here we go." Rachel took a hold of his ankle and eased him toward her. Feet first, then stiff, curled body, and finally head came out.

"What hurts, sweetie?"

"My arm." Adam choked out the words.

She unwrapped his body from around his left arm and then had to hold back a gasp. His skin, from above the elbow to an inch below was bruised, blue blood pooling under the skin. A black blob about the size of a pencil eraser had formed in the middle. Red pinpricks scattered all around the bruise's circumference. Someone else might think it was a rash, but Rachel knew. Petechiae. Tiny broken capillaries. Not enough platelets to seal off the broken blood vessels.

"The smoke." Adam's eyes shimmered with tears. "It burned me. I could feel it and I ran inside to put water on it, but the burning doesn't stop."

Rachel hugged her son. This was no burn, but it had to be because the alternative was unthinkable. "Come on, buddy. We're going to get you fixed up." She heaved her son to his feet, wrapped the blanket around him, and supported his weight across her bedroom to the bathroom.

Adam, calming down in response to her tone, sat on the toilet and held out his left arm. From the closet Rachel grabbed the first aid kit and smoothed on green aloe vera gel, even as she knew that it wouldn't help. "I don't see any blistering, so I think you'll be okay. I want to check this black spot, make sure it isn't ash stuck to you or charred skin. . . ."

"Ow! Stop!" Adam leaped up so hard that his right shoulder hit the opposite wall. "What did you do, Mom?"

Rachel, still kneeling, shook her head. He'd been so healthy. "Adam, I barely even touched it." The brief thought of cutting the blackness off, like she'd done in the hospital after the firestorm, disappeared. This was larger and the blood vessels were already compromised.

"It hurts!" Her son's face contorted with anger and pain.

"Okay, no problem," Rachel said, getting to her feet, trying to project calmness although her heart raced and she wanted to punch the wall and scream. Adam was a stoic kid, used to needles from the oncology ward, used to surgery and routine lumbar punctures, used to headaches from the anesthesia. He never complained like this. "Let's let the aloe work and in the meantime I'll give you something for the pain, alright?"

Rachel faced away from Adam, her hand sweeping through the medicine cabinet, her vision blurred by tears. She didn't know what had happened; Adam's arm had been fine this morning. Now a huge, painful bruise was spreading around the mysterious mark. That meant his blood vessels were too weak. That meant abnormal white blood cells were crowding out the good cells. That meant Adam's blood marrow was cranking out abnormal cells.

It was August 7. Three years to the day since Adam was diagnosed. The leukemia was back.

TWENTY-SIX

After a dose of oxycontin, Adam fell asleep on the couch. The prescription was for pain related to cancer—no good giving regular Tylenol or Motrin because they could mask a fever and a fever meant dropping everything and getting to the emergency room. Rachel had never intended to fill the prescription, telling her husband the drug was too strong, only to be used for an emergency. She'd never forget the haunted look in Craig's eye when he said, "This *is* the emergency."

Rachel walked outside to the porch. Tamaki sat on the swing, using her foot to push off and then coming to a complete stop before starting all over again. Dark eyes, wide and staring, suggested Tamaki was lost, floating in her thoughts. The afternoon sky was light yellow, and one had only faith that there was a sun behind the clouds, struggling to get through.

"Tamaki," Rachel shook her head, leaned her forearms on the railing as she looked out toward the blueberry clearing where Scott's body waited. The couple had had such a brief time together. It was hard to know what to say. "I'm so sorry for your pain."

The girl kept moving through her ritualized motions on the swing. "I was mad at Craig when . . . when the firestorm came. I wish—"

"Shut up, Rachel." The words burst from Tamaki. "Don't you dare talk as if you know." She shoved a finger into her mouth and bit down as if it would bring distraction from the pain. "I swore I would never stand by and watch someone I loved die. But, I couldn't stop it. Again."

Rachel held up her hands to signal surrender. "We won't talk about Scott. But we have a problem." Rachel looked back through the open front door to see Adam's outline on the couch. "Adam's sick. He needs to go to the hospital. That means either Baltimore or New Babylon."

"How could you even think about going to New Babylon after what's happened?" Tamaki glared at Rachel.

"Tamaki," Rachel clenched her fists and then spread out her fingers. "I have to do what's best for Adam. I need medicine for him. I need to know we'll have enough food for winter."

"I'll manage the garden. We'll be fine if we have good weather."

The numbers from Captain Lewis rolled through her mind. A single person needed one hundred pounds of rice. Their family had two adults and a growing boy. Why hadn't she kept better track of how much they'd used?

"You think the city dwellers will be better than the soldiers you met? They won't. They're liars. They make people scared so that we'll do what they want."

"What are they lying about? The condition of the roads? That Baltimore is full of riots?" Rachel remembered the lines outside the marketplace, the gunshots, the garage full of angry homeless people. She had no problem believing that murder was a serious threat for those who'd stayed behind.

"They're lying about mutations." Tamaki spoke in a flat tone.

Rachel shook her head. "I would be dead if Captain Lewis and his wolves didn't kill the two-headed moose."

"Yes, and the carnivorous fungi are dangerous too. But—"

"But what?" Rachel glanced inside again, but Adam hadn't moved.

"Not all mutations are bad. Like my Empress tree. Have you noticed how fast it's grown?"

Rachel scoffed. "It's one of the fastest growing trees on earth. That's why I planted it there, for shade."

"Okay." Tamaki leaned forward on the swing, her eyes narrowed. "You're not going to like this."

"Like what?" Rachel said. "Can I decide for myself please?"

Tamaki stopped the swing with her foot and unzipped the black pouch she always wore, reached in, and brought out her cupped hand. In her palm she held a small turtle shell, maybe five inches across.

"That's your big secret?" Rachel rolled her eyes. This argument was a waste of time.

"This is Saki," Tamaki crooned, holding the shell up to her face. "Come on out, baby."

Slowly a webbed foot extended, black nails first. Then Rachel saw the gray fur at the top of the leg. Out came another leg, then two furry flipper arms, and finally a soft-looking head, black and white coloring around two black eyes and a black bill.

Rachel blinked. "That . . . looks like a baby penguin."

Tamaki used one finger to stroke the creature's head. Saki rubbed the side of her head against the finger. "She is. I think she'll get feathers, but I don't know. I followed the Hotheads, hiding in their shadow so that they would encounter any danger first, keeping a slightly different trail. I found her by a stream."

A strange comment suddenly made sense. A joke that Adam made about penguins and Tamaki's angry reaction. "You showed this thing to Adam." It was an accusation.

"I showed Adam and Scott, but I didn't show you because I didn't want you to freak out."

"I am freaking out. That thing could spit fire or . . ." Rachel waved her hand in the air. "Who knows what it could do? You had no right to go behind my back and show it to Adam without my permission."

Tamaki glared at her. "I knew it! You aren't any better than the soldiers. Anything different must be killed. Destroy and then dissect."

"Cancer is a mutation," Rachel hissed. "Abnormal cells crowding out—"

"Open your mind, Rachel. You might be surprised." Graceful as a cat, Tamaki stalked past Rachel, down the porch steps, and out to the forest, still cradling Saki.

A rumbling started, pulsing vibrations. Disoriented, Rachel thought something was coming from the forest, set off by Tamaki's entrance, or it was another earthquake. But the sound came from above. A helicopter emerged over the forest line, propellers rotating. A nautilus shell gleamed on the side.

Rachel backed into the house, closing the door. In her bedroom, she turned on the radio, but nothing came through even after the sound of the helicopter was gone. Rachel wanted a moment, a time out to process New Babylon, Scott, the penguin-turtle, but, most of all, Adam's arm. She needed to know if the weather was going to cooperate for the plants, long-term worry, and whether it would hold for travel in case Adam's arm didn't get better, short-term worry.

Frustrated, Rachel slammed her hand against the radio. "Is it safe or not? Red-painted people? Freak snowstorm? What!"

Static.

"You're The Weatherman! You're supposed to tell me when the next storm is coming and when it's safe to travel. You're supposed to tell me what roads are gone and which I can use so that I don't take a dead end and lose time and my son gets worse."

She picked up the radio and shook it until her arms grew too tired to hold her anger any longer.

Tamaki was in the clearing when Rachel found her an hour later. Scott's body lay on the ground, the ladder from the garage still set up. His backpack lay where it had fallen, the stolen fruit and coffee beans still there. Anger burned through Rachel. They'd killed Scott for stealing, but hadn't even bothered to recover the food. It made the whole, awful ordeal feel like a show designed to intimidate.

Rachel set the bag upright and heard a rustling sound. She reached in and pulled out a thick piece of paper with seemingly random lines drawn on it. *Must be the map of ley lines that Scott was talking about,* she thought, shoving it back in the bag.

"I would have helped you get his body down."

Tamaki knelt on the ground. The blue streak of hair slipped forward to hide her face.

Rachel walked over to Scott's body and dropped to her knees. Tamaki had closed his eyes and removed the rope from his neck. His face did not look peaceful—the emotions from the vicious encounter hadn't receded.

Seeing his body was so final. There was no hope that he'd saunter up to the house again with his cheery, light-hearted boasts.

"Burning is cleaner than burying." Tamaki's voice held no expression.

Rachel got to her feet. She felt old. "I don't like the way the moose burned. It wasn't right."

"This won't be the same."

"How do you know?"

Tamaki pulled up her lip in a snarl. "I asked his spirit to stay."

Unnerved by Tamaki's vehemence, Rachel cleared her throat. Together the women pulled the body to the middle of the clearing, away from any brush, and crossed his hands over his chest. Rachel looked away as Tamaki said her goodbye. They gathered large, dry tree limbs blown down during the storm into a funeral pyre and lit it. The orange flames reached toward heaven, licking at sticks, consuming everything.

Tamaki was right. No greasy smoke hung in the air, no smell of paper mills. Just the smell of burning meat.

"If we're going to stay here, I need a weather report," Rachel said as she watched the flames. "And if I have to take Adam to the hospital, I need a weather report. But, I couldn't get anything on the radio." Rachel fidgeted. "I wish I knew how to find The Weatherman instead of waiting."

Tamaki kept her gaze on the ground.

"How long are you going to ignore me?"

"Saki's my pet." Tamaki stroked the black pouch. "She doesn't breathe fire."

Rachel clenched her jaw. The optimism of youth was frustrating. "She might breathe fire. She might fly. We don't know, Tamaki. That's all I'm saying."

"Okay." Tamaki crossed her arms over her chest. "Do you agree that she might also be something new and wonderful?"

"Is it necessary for our friendship that I agree?"

"Yes."

"Okay." Rachel nodded her head. "I concede that I do not understand the mutations that are happening, but Saki might be something new and wonderful. Now are we good?"

Tamaki wiped her hands on her thighs. "As long as you hate New Babylon." She moved away to drag another tree limb to Scott's funeral pyre.

"Should I get some water to put out the fire?"

"No. I'll stay here until it goes out." Tamaki sank down in front of the fire and crossed her legs.

"Okay." Rachel hesitated, but Scott was dead and Adam was alive. She had to focus. First, she launched the stolen fruit and bread into the forest. They were still edible, but there was no way she would be able to choke down Scott's gifts. Unsure what to do with the bag of coffee—she'd never drink or serve it, but it had New Babylon's logo on it—she finally shoved it back into the bag. She left the bag in the clearing in case Tamaki wanted to look through it later for personal notes or pictures. All Rachel needed was the map.

She pulled out the heavy paper and took it back to Hiraeth. There was no legend, no reference for a reader because it wasn't intended to be read by anyone else. No state boundaries for Rachel to use. Instead, two sets of branching lines, one in black and one in yellow. Once Rachel figured out that black was water, then the yellow had to be Scott's mysterious ley lines. She found the circle by the black that should be Hiraeth and the creek. The mountains, little triangles to the west with a circle past them could be Scott's Amish settlement where he traded for supplies. A huge circle with a star around it near what used to be Pittsburgh that she guessed was New Babylon. But, it was the circle—decorated with four ovals—to the north of Hiraeth that interested Rachel. What were the little ovals supposed to be? Flower petals, a settlement with four occupied houses? Could it be The Weatherman and a little settlement?

Afternoon turned to evening with no report from The Weatherman, but Rachel, restless, carried the radio throughout the house. Finally, Rachel felt Adam's forehead once again, checked his bruised arm, and went out to Tamaki's tree. "I'm going to look for The Weatherman first thing in the morning if we haven't gotten a report. Can you watch Adam and listen to the radio?"

Tamaki leaned down. "How do you know where to go?"

Rachel shrugged. "I don't really, but I have Scott's map. It looks like there is something to the north of us. His black and yellow lines run right past a decorated circle."

"That sounds random."

"I've got to do something. Besides, even if I don't find The Weatherman, I'd like to know what's walking distance of us that Scott found important enough to mark. I'll stick to the river so I won't get lost and I'll be back by nightfall."

TWENTY-SEVEN

The radio was stubbornly quiet all night. Rachel left at daybreak. It wasn't long before she was farther into the forest than she'd ever been before. Going north meant following the river, leaving private property and entering the state park, now overgrown and wild. Rachel took a deep breath, fear tugging at her heart. New Babylon soldiers had flown away in the helicopter, but that meant no help if another mutant moose attacked. Saki may be a pet, but what if other animals hit a ley line and combined? Her knees went weak. "You have to keep going," she said aloud. Rachel put one foot in front of the other. She had to find The Weatherman; they were running out of time. At least due north wasn't like the forest to the northwest; the dark forest where Scott had shown them the skeletons.

The strange choking vines and the ugly orange DPF grew in spots, but there were also large trees that had kept their green leaves, still fighting for summer, for life. No time to dig the fungi up, but Rachel kicked the orange and brown heads off of any that were close, making a face at the resulting muck covering her boots.

After close to two hours of hiking, Rachel heard a new sound: water splashing. She didn't know of any waterfall in the state park.

Curious, she followed the sound around a bend in the river and saw a gristmill. The building was three stories high: the first floor was made of stacked river rock, the other two of faded wooden planks. A red roof matched the color of the huge overshot wheel attached to the right of the building. The wheel was two stories high, water from the top sluicing down a chute over the paddles making them dip into the water below and keep turning. Rachel stared at the process, marveling. It still worked.

There could be flour inside, or even bags of grain stored from before the firestorm. Maybe this wasn't The Weatherman, but it had to be where Scott got the flour he brought them. Could the four ovals on his map be a flower for flour?

She inched forward and stared through the dusty pane of glass in one of the bottom windows. Inside she saw a long wooden shaft reaching from the floor up through a hole in the ceiling, a large wooden gearwheel, apparently attached to the overshot wheel through the wall of river rock, and a smaller gearwheel near the ceiling. No evidence of anyone inside. Rachel imagined how happy Adam and Tamaki would be if she brought back food. This could mean surviving the winter, at least from hunger.

Cawing from a nearby tree made Rachel look up. An unkindness of ravens perched in the branches of a nearby evergreen, watching her. Rachel pushed down on the metal handle. One raven hopped forward on its branch and made a loud caw sound three times. Was it warning her about something? Maybe to stay away from its food source. She wrestled the heavy wooden door open. It was dark inside, although light filtered through the dirty windows. Cobwebs clustered in the corner and the boards creaked under her feet. It smelled musty and unused.

"Hello?" she called, not expecting an answer.

To the right a set of narrow wooden stairs led up to a trapdoor. She crawled through the trapdoor onto the next floor. On the near wall a large window looked out on the chute while the overshot wheel turned below. In the middle of the room, a circular contraption sat by itself. Creeping closer, Rachel saw two huge flat stones. On top sat a hopper, a square funnel underneath a chute in the ceiling. Grain had fallen from the chute, down the hopper, into the middle of the millstones. What looked like cornmeal seeped out underneath the bottom millstone into a rectangular collection box on the floor. *This place must have been working until the firestorm came. Maybe the rangers used it to teach park visitors?* Rachel fell to her knees and dipped her hand into the powder, bringing the yellow grit to her mouth and tasting it, rolling the rough texture on her tongue. She laughed out loud with joy. Cornmeal for cornbread. Corn muffins. Cornmeal-battered everything.

Her imagination went wild. Maybe Tamaki and she could get this mill running again. After all, the waterwheel still worked. She looked around for a bag to carry the cornmeal, but didn't see anything except the last set of stairs. There could be bags of corn stored above, or at least empty bags to carry cornmeal back to Hiraeth.

This staircase, like the first, was narrow. Emerging into the third story, Rachel blinked, taking a second while her eyes adjusted to the dimness. Unlike the other floors, the window to the outside was small and seemed even dirtier.

This floor was filled with equipment unrelated to millwork. In the farthest part of the room, wires hung from the ceiling. Hoses and gears dominated the middle space. Close to the stairs sat a large wooden box, uncovered and filled to the top with corn kernels. A few steps toward the back wall of the gristmill Rachel saw what she'd been looking for: bags of grain piled on top of each other. Rachel pulled on one of the sacks, trying to get a feel for how heavy it was, concentrating so hard that it was a moment before she noticed a new sound, a whisper of movement. She jumped back from the pile, heart thumping. Of course there would be rats. *I hate rats.* They could have gnawed their way into the bags; there could be a nest of them underneath. She hadn't seen any droppings, but she also hadn't been looking, so excited to have found food.

"Rats? No. I do not have rats." The voice was masculine, older, heavy with breath.

Ice ran through Rachel. *I didn't say anything out loud.*

"But I do, apparently, have a thief." The voice was louder, approaching from the darkness.

"I'm sorry." Rachel swallowed, unsure of what else she could say. "I saw this mill and I was curious."

"You came in to steal my food, you mean." The voice was testy. Querulous and scratchy as an old-fashioned record, it sounded familiar. "Not a very well-prepared thief, though." An arm came out of the darkness into the dim light, its fingers pointing at her.

"I didn't know I was stealing. I thought the mill was abandoned." She remembered New Babylon's form of justice. Was this an outpost of some type? Rachel's heart beat so hard she thought she was going to throw up.

The scratch of a match. The man in the shadows held up a small lantern. A thick white beard and black sunglasses couldn't fully conceal the baggy skin of an old man. He leaned forward as if hunchbacked, bald head shiny in the reflected lantern light. The white dress shirt and old-fashioned vest with thick lapels and a bolo necktie made Rachel think of a storekeeper in a spaghetti Western. The man set down the lantern to cough into the crook of his elbow. The smell of ozone wafted toward Rachel. Abruptly her head ached and she had to press her palms to her forehead. The smell triggered submerged memories, images flashing too quickly to be examined.

"You," said Rachel, dropping her palms as the images ceased. "I know you. You were the one who stopped me in the fog. Where are the others?"

A loud jangling came from one of the instruments and the man turned to the side, pulling down from the ceiling what looked like a submarine's periscope, a hand on each side as he turned the lens from direction to direction, muttering to himself about the wind sweeping down from the other side of the mountains.

"There's no one else here. Just me. That's enough."

"You're The Weatherman."

He pushed the periscope away and glared at her through the sunglasses. "Whatever gave me away?" His arms gestured into the darkness. "I'm surrounded by a lab of meteorology equipment and the girl thinks she's a detective."

"I don't think that. Normally Scott comes here, but he was killed and now I need to talk to you, to find out if it's safe—" Rachel's chest heaved with emotion from talking about Scott.

"Course the boy's dead. Told him not to mess with those fools from New Babylon, but wouldn't listen to me. Oh no, thought he was tough shit."

Guilt that she couldn't save Scott, that she hadn't shouted a warning before he came into the clearing, converged on Rachel. Her vision blackened as if she was going to faint. She fought the panic by biting the inside of her cheek, using the pain as distraction, counting, picturing a line of numbers. A trick she'd learned at the hospital, listening to the doctors state what Adam would have to go through. Rachel had learned how to wrestle down panic and stay in the moment.

"Stop that now; I don't like it. You're sorry you tried to steal from me. Okay. You're a dummy who doesn't know how to barter. I'll let you off, but you owe me."

Sudden clacking sounds filled the room. The Weatherman scooted past Rachel and began twisting knobs and pulling levers until it was quiet again.

"Hate noise." The Weatherman grabbed a pencil, licked the tip, and began to scribble in a notebook. "What! Why are you still here? You want to thank me for being merciful?" His back was elongated, disproportionate to his two legs, so that he scuttled rather than walked.

"I want to know if a hailstorm like the one from the other day is approaching. That storm brought down a tree on my roof."

"That was my storm. Speaking of which, would you like to explain why you let the New Babylon people into your house? I made a storm so they'd leave, and you gave them shelter!" The sunglasses couldn't hide his look of derision.

"I didn't know." The blame felt like a punch in the gut. Rachel's mind churned through what-ifs. What if she hadn't given them shelter? What if she hadn't offered to make breakfast? "There was a moose and then they helped me—"

"They shouldn't have been here when Scott returned!" The Weatherman yelled. He pulled at his beard until it poofed out. In a quieter voice, "It shouldn't have happened."

Rachel wrapped her arms around herself, miserable with guilt.

"I didn't know you would invite them inside. You didn't know Scott would steal their supplies. Scott didn't know New Babylon soldiers were at your house. It's not your fault the ranger is dead. That's the problem with free will." The Weatherman's voice was gruff, but Rachel heard emotion. He'd cared about Scott, but hid it behind crankiness. "You humans are a bunch of buzzing bees swirling about in clouds of your own chaos."

Anger sparked into a tiny flame. It felt better than self-blame. "Could you stop calling me names?"

"I'll call you whatever I want. I'm your elder. By thousands of years. Humans," he chided, "you think you're so special. It's all happened before, but this time, this time it won't happen again." He began cackling, slapping his legs as if he'd told the funniest joke.

Uncertain, Rachel shuffled her feet. "The firestorm happened before? Like an asteroid?"

"An asteroid?" He grimaced at her, baring stained teeth. "You moron. The Misbegotten have returned."

"Who," Rachel had to clear her throat, "are The Misbegotten?"

"How?" he moaned. "How have humans managed not to die off like lemmings?" He rubbed a hand over his bald head. "All hell has, literally, broken loose from its chains and you want to hear a story. The Nephilim are at war again, Anunnaki versus Igigi, and humans are once more jumping in and making it all worse."

"No." Rachel shook her head, but her resistance was crumbling, too many clues gathering together and leading to this moment. She knew the word "Nephilim" from her art history classes. According to ancient texts, Nephilim were a mythic breed created by the coupling of the "sons of God" and the "daughters of Adam" that resulted in heroes, monsters, and gods and goddesses bearing supernatural powers yoked with human emotion and pettiness.

"Yes," said The Weatherman, answering her unspoken thought. "That's a pretty good description."

Rachel's mind continued to spin. The creatures in the firestorm falling to earth, the mysterious summer snowstorm when the painted people were here, trees and plants from a different ecosystem thriving here in the mountains. Even the ravens outside weren't ordinary birds. Rachel understood that they hadn't been warning her, they'd been warning The Weatherman about her. The smoke from the two-headed moose somehow awakening the cancer cells within Adam. This was the moment when she was asked to accept that the world would never go back.

"Energy patterns are occupied elsewhere for the moment so I don't have to defend my territory. Forecast is clear for the next three days. Garden or take your son wherever you want. Now go away, I'm busy."

Rachel held up her hand. "Wait! Are the roads clear to the hospital?"

"Why?"

"My son's arm is burned, but—"

"What kind of careless mother burns her son?" He snorted.

"Not me, the moose."

"The two-headed moose burned your son?"

"No. Yes." Rachel tried to explain. "Adam's arm went through the moose's smoke and now there's a painful burn, a black mark in the middle of a bruise."

His chin tilted down to his chest. "Black like car oil?"

"Yes, how did you know?" Rachel stepped forward. "It's cancer, isn't it?"

"No hospital can help you. You've got to go to the Bathhouse. Ask The Lady of the Bath for help. She's the only one who might be able to heal him."

"What bathhouse? Why?"

"I told you, it's all energy now. This isn't Newton's world, girl. That little construction's been swept away. We're back to raw materials, the stuff of original creation activated by the firestorm. Earth is ripe for all kinds of alchemy." The Weatherman dropped his snarkiness. "That moose was bad energy, unbalanced *etemmu*. It activated the poison dormant in your son. He's dying."

Rachel felt time stop as her greatest fear was said out loud.

The Weatherman coughed. "Anything else you want to know? Not like I'm getting any work done with you bothering me."

"Well," she said, "how do you know all this?"

"You know why you're stupid? You don't ask the right questions." He stared her down.

"I'm one of the original and most powerful Misbegotten." He put a hand on his hip and smoothed out his white beard. Preening. Then, he jerked his hands into the air. From out the window a crack of lightning split the clear sky followed by a roll of thunder.

Rachel jumped in surprise. No sign of a storm.

The old man stuck out his chest and grinned like a naughty child. Behind him, the roof of the mill that had surely been made of wooden planks was now a dome of blue-black night sky. White lights blinked in constellations that Rachel felt she almost knew.

He doesn't forecast, he's actually controlling the weather. "I believe you," Rachel said, feeling a swell of hope. "You can heal Adam."

"Oh no, I don't do that. You want him healed, you'll have to cross territory lines to get to someone who cares."

"I don't care about territory lines. I only care about my son."

He threw his hands into the air. "You better care. We're fallible, selfish creatures. Our last war created the schism between Anunnaki and Igigi."

He'd said those words before, but they still made no sense to Rachel. She guessed, "Those are the teams of Misbegotten?"

"Teams?" He frowned. "That's . . . not quite it. In Babylonian, Anunnaki means "gods of earth" and Igigi means "gods of heaven," but it's more philosophical differences than domain rights."

"So, you're Babylonian?"

"I am not." His bushy browns moved up and down in obvious agitation. "I'm Sumerian. Many cultures rose and fell in Mesopotamia."

"Fine." She tried again. "Which side is the good side?"

"Just like any other war." He snorted. "Each side thinks it is."

Rachel nodded. That, she understood.

The Weatherman jutted his neck forward and shook a finger at her. "Right now each of The Misbegotten is scrambling to set up a city-state, raise followers, shore up alliances, and create a square on a chessboard. And then they'll battle like it's a game, using humans for their armies."

"They'll battle? You're not involved?"

"Nope, no how."

Another memory fragment swirled up. "You're Switzerland."

"That's right. Minding my own business. The others should too, but they won't."

The others. "I think I met one of you before. In the hospital. She told us we could come to her territory because I offered a drink of water."

The Weatherman raised his puffy eyebrows until they almost reached above his bald head. "Rookie move. Who did that?"

"I don't know. She had these green eyes and reminded me of a deer, but a human deer, if that makes sense."

"Pfffft. Aia. Shamash's widow. Most of us feel bad that Shamash was killed, he tried to be fair and impartial, but no one will feel bad enough to let her control a territory. She's weak and inexperienced. I give her three months before New Babylon takes over her territory." He shrugged, "Here's a freebie to get you out of my house. The answer to the question you should have asked: LaPorte. That's where you'll find The Bathhouse."

LaPorte. The door. A little town north of the Susquehanna River. She and her husband had taken a dinner cruise starting from a neighboring town, Havre de Grace, a lifetime ago.

The Weatherman was still talking, "Fill up a sack of cornmeal on your way out. You already owe me for trying to steal it, so might as well take it with you."

Rachel grabbed a sack and began filling it before he changed his mind.

Cawing came from a tall tree outside the window and then another raven cawed from its perch on a rafter over the bags of grain.

"Which one is Jude?" she asked, remembering how Scott had spoken to one. That bird must be The Weatherman's spy.

"They're all named Jude." The Weatherman waved his arms in the air. "Now, go!"

Outside the gristmill Rachel adjusted the sack and checked Scott's map. She didn't need directions—she only had to follow the river back to Hiraeth, but she felt lost after the conversation with The Weatherman. Ancient gods and goddesses who could wield energy like magicians walked the earth again. These Misbegotten were going to war with each other and humans would be nothing more than fodder.

"If The Weatherman is so powerful," she said to the map, to Scott, "then why didn't he attack the New Babylon soldiers with lightning and save your life?" A wave of sadness for her friend rushed through her bones.

The Weatherman had created that catastrophic storm while the New Babylon soldiers were in his territory, but he hadn't been able to save Scott. He knew that they were here, but he couldn't get them out. The old man was feisty, but he couldn't take on Consularis Sharma or Captain Lewis. They, or the Misbegotten they worked for, must be stronger than The Weatherman.

Shoving the map into her pack, Rachel followed the river, her mind a riot. Most importantly: if The Weatherman spoke true, she and Adam would have to cross a supernatural chessboard for a chance to save her son's life.

TWENTY-EIGHT

Exhausted from hiking, Rachel ate dinner, checked that Adam was still sleeping, and fell into bed. She didn't know what time the screaming started, the sound reverberating in her head. A mother's call to duty: illness in the night. She tripped in the darkness, made it out of the bedroom to the couch. Adam's forehead seared her hand.

"Oh, hold on, honey. Let me light a candle."

"Mooom," he moaned, writhing on the couch. "Don't leave me."

"Alright, baby, alright." Panic beat in her chest, but Rachel kept a low, soothing voice. She stretched out beside him on the couch, balanced on the edge, listening to Adam whimper, watching him move, unable to get comfortable. It took almost a minute for the wave of pain to ebb.

"I'm going to get the oxycontin, okay? Give me a second."

Rachel eased off the couch, not wanting to shake it, and felt her way to the lantern on the mantel of the fireplace, lit it, and brought the orange plastic bottle and a cup of water to the couch.

He swallowed the pill—years of training.

"Give it a couple minutes to work. I need to look when it doesn't hurt so much."

Adam held out his arm. The affected area had expanded—almost up to the shoulder and down to an inch below his elbow—but now it was swollen as well as red, and the black blob had grown from the size of a pencil eraser to a penny, puffy with irregularly shaped edges. Rachel used the tip of her finger to probe. Adam's arm felt dense. The black blob seemed to pulse. She imagined the black breaking off, replicating cells, killing her son.

His eyelids drooped, but his cheeks were red, his breathing labored. He looked so young as he cradled his hurt arm. Rachel wanted to smooth away the parentheses of pain that shouldn't be around an eleven-year-old's mouth. Instead, she kissed his forehead then set the lantern on the coffee table and walked to the window. Pulling back the curtain, Rachel wondered if Tamaki was asleep in the Empress Paulownia. Outside there was an eerie high-pitched screech. Rachel felt more than saw a black shape wheel across the navy sky with no stars. Too large to be a bat.

"Hey, Jude," she whispered.

The next morning Adam said he felt better. ChapStick on his chapped lips, the morning dose of narcotic administered, sweat-hardened hair pushed back, Adam was unable to recall the nighttime wake-up. Rachel gnawed her lip. The wound wasn't getting better. And it wouldn't without medical intervention. It would grow and grow, taking over his body until it reached his heart or his brain.

Seven days of thinking it would get better, would go away on its own, was how long it had taken before. They'd returned from a family trip to the beach. Adam had been tired, complained his ears hurt. Rachel took him to the pediatrician, picked up the antibiotic for an ear infection. Three days had passed, but Adam was still lethargic. Craig said to take him back to the doctor, but Rachel shrugged. "Let the medicine work, he's a growing boy and needs his sleep."

And then Saturday, the soccer game. Adam had been running, opponents chasing him as he went up the center toward the goal. As he gave the ball a final kick, a small guy in glasses, the last one you'd expect, had shoved Adam hard, knocking him over. It shouldn't have been a big deal. But Adam limped over to the coach and stayed out the last ten minutes. After the game, Adam pulled up his pants leg. His entire leg was one gigantic bruise.

Hours later, Adam had been admitted. Cancer, cancer, cancer. The oncologists had a one-inch book for her to read and a diagnosis: Pre-B Cell Acute Lymphoblastic Leukemia. The good kind. *There was a good kind?* she'd wondered. Craig asked questions, but the words blurred together for Rachel. Instead, she watched the body language of the attending and compared it to Naomi's. It was Naomi who had explained what the incomprehensible words would mean on a daily basis. About taking labs in the middle of the night so results would be back by morning. About the induction phase of treatment. Adam and Rachel didn't leave room 833 for thirty-one days, except to go to the OR to put in a port-a-catheter and lumbar punctures to inject chemo directly into his spinal fluid.

"You're not better," Rachel said. "Aloe vera didn't help, it's not a burn. We're going." The question was where: to the Bathhouse or Baltimore? No need to make a decision right this moment. The important thing was to get on the road. Moving from the bedroom to the kitchen with her backpack, throwing in food, trying to make a plan, Rachel couldn't stop thinking: *His cancer has mutated. Like the plants and animals, his disease has changed into something else.* She packed a bag for Adam too.

Outside, Tamaki had Tupperware containers of sprouting pumpkins, squash, and carrots sitting by the garden fence while she used a garden hoe on the soil. Adam walked out the door and Rachel jiggled the car keys in her hand, nervous about leaving, about going into the unknown.

She waited for her son to enter the garage before telling Tamaki, "It'll take about two and a half hours of driving to get to Hopkins and I don't know how long we'll have to stay. It's naïve to imagine that the city healed itself in the months we've been up here, but maybe the hospital has been able to hang on."

"Be careful." Tamaki picked up the first container, tipped it up and gave it a shake until the whole plant fell into her waiting palm. "Don't trust anybody. Get to the hospital and get back out."

Rachel nodded. "I'm scared."

"You've got to go." Tamaki shook her head. "I heard him screaming last night."

Rachel swallowed. "I put a bag of cornmeal in the pantry yesterday. Help yourself to whatever's there. And listen to the radio."

"Don't worry about me. I can take care of myself." The young woman picked up the next container, her brown hands confident in their work, hair shining in the muted sunlight. "Hey, Rachel?"

Tamaki looked over her shoulder to make sure Adam was still in the garage.

"While you were gone yesterday, that guy came back here." Her lips curled into a sneer, "The one with the wolves from New Babble? He wanted to know where you and Adam were."

The one with the wolves and blue eyes. The one who'd shot the arrow that pierced Scott's chest. Coldness threatened to swallow her whole.

"What did he," she wouldn't give him the respect of calling him by name, "want?"

"Didn't say." Tamaki shifted her feet, dirt falling from around the plant in her hand. "Couldn't be anything good."

"Right." *Consularis Sharma sent him to kill me. Because I wouldn't deny Scott.* Rachel shook her head. Couldn't worry about that now. "If he comes back—"

"He won't find me." Tamaki was matter-of-fact. Rachel nodded. Tamaki could melt into the forest like no one she'd ever seen, but then Rachel wondered if the comment meant more than that. With Scott dead, was Tamaki going to leave too?

"I won't say goodbye. We'll see each other again." Rachel opened her arms inviting Tamaki in for a hug. "If not here, then somewhere else. We're survivors."

"Yeah," Tamaki's dark eyes made no promises to Rachel as she stepped forward. "You remember that too. If anything happens to Adam." Her arms clasped Rachel like a butterfly's caress and then dropped away.

Sadness settled on Rachel as she walked away, a feeling that with Scott's death their little family had died too.

In the garage, Rachel remembered that the last time they'd driven was the night of the Hotheads in the surprise snowstorm. So, as she and Adam stood in the dark garage looking at the SUV, she cleared her throat.

"Get in. Nothing to do but try it."

Adam slid into the passenger seat, careful of his arm in the sling. The interior smelled moldy, and nothing happened the first time she said, "On."

Rachel inserted the key, attempting the manual method to start the engine. She pumped the gas.

"Mom, you're going to flood it."

"Flood what? The carburetor? The engine? You don't know. I don't know. Just give me a second." Rachel tried to calm down. She didn't want to tell Adam about Scott or her premonition that it would be a long time before they saw Tamaki again, but the secrets were a heavy weight inside her chest and the emotion was spilling out.

Adam threw himself back against his seat with a huff and Rachel turned the key again. Bright yellow flared across the screen. Black letters spelled out: 'Hybrid engine failure.'

Rachel looked out the window, shaking her head. *Of course. This has been a problem since before the firestorm and I didn't take it in to be fixed and now, at the most important moment, it failed.*

She jabbed her finger at the screen over and over but the message didn't disappear.

"Mom, we've gotta be a team. That's what you always say. I don't know why you're mad at me, because I didn't want you to flood the engine."

Exhale. Control anxiety.

Rachel turned to her son. "You're right." She managed a smile around the brittle feeling threatening at the edges of her mind. "I'm not mad at you, I'm mad at myself." She made a fist and punched the dash.

The screen went black. She shook out her wrist and rubbed her knuckles.

A whirring sound came from the engine. The screen flashed a message: 'Partial engine failure. Battery not charging.'

She and Adam exchanged a look. Partial was better than complete, right? "Let's get out of here before this thing breaks. We're not stopping till we hit Baltimore."

Rachel checked the mirrors, backed out of the garage and drove down the bumpy driveway toward what used to be US-522 North. The path to the blueberry clearing, to Scott's grave, grew smaller in her rearview mirror.

PART IV

THE ROAD

The whisper came: Do you believe?
The ground rumbled. The largest boulder of the collection
cracked open so that tiny pebbles fell away. Water gurgled
out—the pace of an elementary water fountain—tracing a
path through the dust down the boulder.

TWENTY-NINE

They entered Maryland state limits and kept right at the fork, merging east. There was no one else on the road. At one point several ravens flew overhead. Rachel slowed down to watch.

"Hey, Jude," Adam called from the back seat. At her look, he said, "What? Scott told me to say that whenever I saw a raven."

Abruptly the birds all switched direction, winging off to their right. A sudden tingling swept through Rachel's body and disappeared.

"Did you feel that?"

"Yeah, like we went through an electric fence."

Rachel jerked her attention back to the road. Navigating the compromised route was tricky but possible without The Weatherman's blinding fog. A familiar runaway truck lane popped up in the rearview mirror. The spot with the wall of fog that had marked The Weatherman's territory.

Driving through the mountains was complicated by rockslides that had covered the interstate, but it looked like other travelers had gouged out passes. Abandoned vehicles collected around each rockslide, gutted and ripped apart, the doors torn off. Some of the vehicles had been set on fire, their frames blackened and sparse. Rachel shivered. Hotheads must have come through.

To distract Adam from the pain of his arm, Rachel chattered. "It'll be good to see Naomi and her kids. She's not going to believe how tall you've gotten in just a month."

She glanced at Adam in the rearview mirror. "It feels like we've been in a cocoon. Do you think I've gotten weird from being isolated? Don't answer that." She slowed down as they approached the debris of another rockslide. Metal scraped against the side of the mountain and then the SUV jounced over larger fallen pieces on the road. "We're making slow-going, but still progress. Nothing we can't get through."

And then they came to a rockslide that hadn't been cleared.

"Mom," Adam sounded exasperated. "Why did you jinx it?"

"It won't take long. We only have to move enough rocks to drive over."

"What?" Adam scrunched up his face. "This isn't a tank. You can't just drive over a pile of boulders."

"It'll be fine. I'll leave the car running since the battery isn't charging. Grab your pack and we'll have a picnic after." She didn't want to eat in front of anyone in Baltimore who didn't have food.

Adam put on his backpack and went over to inspect the pile. Rachel grabbed her backpack and searched the trunk for anything to use as a lever.

A sudden stillness sent goosebumps up her arms.

"Adam?" Rachel leaned out from behind the trunk. She held the tire iron, an unwieldy four-pronged metal thing. All she could see was the rock wall. The wall that, from this perspective, looked constructed rather than random.

Scuffling sounds came from the other side.

She scrambled over the wall to see Adam lying face down on the road, crimson matting his brown hair, making it dark and slick. An old white man wearing a grimy undershirt knelt on Adam's back and yanked at the backpack straps.

All rational thought left Rachel's conscious mind. Maternal instinct kicked in.

"Hey!" Rachel screamed. "Get off him!"

She charged forward, skittering on pebbles, her arms pumping, the tire iron weightless in her hands.

The old man looked up and gaped at her, no teeth except filed incisors on the top and bottom. Like a monkey, he screamed and bounced off Adam's back onto his bowed legs. Wispy hair covered his head, his face, and emerged from the sides and bottom of his undershirt where a loincloth tied around narrow hips.

Rachel lifted the tire iron in her right hand, took the final step, and slammed the iron into the monkeyman. There was a thudding sound as the momentum pushed him to the side.

The monkeyman wheezed and grabbed his shoulder. She'd opened a gash on his arm. She hoped the arm was broken. He scampered toward the rock wall, agile in a way that defied his age, and perched on top.

Rachel stood over Adam's body and looked at the blood on the metal weapon in her hand. She would have hit the monkeyman again if he hadn't run away. As many times as it took to get him off of Adam.

Two more monkey-people emerged from the scrub brush near the mountain. These had to be the imps that Tamaki had described. They kept setting the same trap for drivers. Create a rock wall, hide, and then attack the people when they stopped to move the rocks.

Rachel fell to her knees beside Adam, touching his shoulder. He was unconscious. She found the lump on his head, but the bleeding had stopped. His jeans were ripped, revealing a bloody gash through a jagged hole at the hamstring.

She called his name until Adam blinked his eyes and looked around. She said, "Are you dizzy? Can you sit up?"

"My head hurts." Adam rolled to his side. "But, I'm okay."

Relief and then rage filled Rachel. The rush was so powerful, she shook. She stood up, tire iron in her hand.

Rachel ran at the white-haired creature. He chomped his jaws, pulling back his lips to show the four remaining teeth. When Rachel was a few feet away, he dropped down the other side of the rock wall. Rachel chased him and yelled, "Get out of here."

Then Rachel saw the other two had climbed inside the SUV. One looked like an old woman, hairy, torn blue dress, red lipstick smeared as if a child had done it. The other was another loin-clothed male. The female crouched in the driver's seat while the male hung out the window, hitting the side like a jockey whipping a horse.

"That's my car." Rachel spoke slowly, like she would to a toddler. "Get out of it. Now."

The first old man, the one who'd attacked Adam, lifted his loin cloth and squatted. He stared at her while showing his teeth. A foul smell wafted. He was pooping, just like a monkey at a zoo.

Suddenly the SUV surged forward, hitting the rock wall. The impact caused Rachel to stumble backwards. It almost knocked the monkeyman out the window and he screeched at the female.

The older monkeyman grabbed his feces and threw it at Rachel with a high-pitched squeal. It hit the wall.

Rachel ignored him, watching as the SUV reversed, hitting the side of the mountain with a metallic shriek and then veering back across the road.

"No, no, no," she muttered.

The male grabbed the wheel and the SUV hit the mountain hard, crumpling the front of the frame. The front tires grabbed against the rock, finding purchase so that the SUV climbed vertical. The monkeys jumped out the windows. The SUV tottered. It fell, in slow motion, onto its back, the tires still spinning.

The old monkeyman raced toward the others on his knuckles. He screamed back at her, "Food for the bull! You're food for the bull," in a thin, nonsensical voice.

Rachel dropped to the ground and pounded her fists. "Dammit." She retrieved the tire iron before walking back to Adam. *Don't let him know how bad this is; how very, very bad. Just like when the doctors said his port was infected for a second time. Focus on action.*

"Hey buddy, you're still bleeding." Rachel examined the gash on his leg. *Germs, infection, good thing the monkeyman threw his poop at me and not on Adam.* She used the edge of her shirt to apply pressure. "Hold still. I have bandages in my backpack. Always prepared, right?"

Adam's eyes were huge, disbelieving. "I was just standing here when that old guy popped out. He walked up and started kicking me. He even tried to bite me."

Rachel finished with the bandage and gave him a hug. She could feel his whole body shaking. "I'm so, so, so sorry. You didn't do anything wrong." Part of her was desperate to start walking so they could find shelter before night fell, but Adam had never been attacked before. He'd suffered pain from his cancer treatment, but he'd always known that it was part of a healing process. Today's attack had been premeditated evil.

Rachel looked at her son with his arm in a sling and a bandage on his leg, his hair still sticky with blood. "I'm proud of you."

"For what?"

"For putting one foot in front of the other." She swallowed. "Let's keep going."

THIRTY

Walking. Monotony broken only by panting and sweating as the road climbed. The packs grew heavier with every step; the gravel underfoot slippery. The road had buckled during the firestorm, great chunks of asphalt heaved up like mini tectonic plates. Heat pressed down, burning the thin line of scalp where her hair was parted. Rachel inventoried the packs in her mind, trying to figure out if there was anything they could leave behind.

A rumbling sound shook the air. Rachel looked over her shoulder, her first thought that The Weatherman had been wrong and the weather was about to turn. An immense brown cloud of dust swirled around a center of blinding light. Rachel coughed and squinted. The noise deafened. Rachel grabbed Adam's hand, pulling him to the side, but there was nowhere to hide. They stood and watched. Rachel's other hand tightened on the tire iron.

As the cloud came closer the vision clarified into three creatures of wheels and tangram shapes—riders on motorcycles. The riders came straight at them, at the last minute driving in a single-file circle around and around Rachel and Adam.

Adam gasped. "What the heck?" He squeezed her hand, and she felt the sweat slide between their skins.

"Stay back, I'm warning you." Rachel shook the tire iron in the air. She tried to shield Adam with her body, but couldn't be all places in the circle.

The lead rider pulled to a stop, the other two fanning out behind as the dust cloud dissipated. He tugged off his helmet, dark green with a three-pronged red flame, and shook out a mass of shoulder-length braids. He had dark skin and a heavy, muscled body like a professional football player.

"What are you going to do, tighten my tires?" His laugh boomed out, filling the air, deep and full.

"I'm not afraid to use this." Rachel shook it again.

The other two riders took off their helmets. Both had an olive complexion, dark hair, and yarmulkes under their motorcycle helmets. The closer rider was about Rachel's age, attractive with a head of perfect springy ringlets, a shy smile, and wire-rimmed glasses. He wore a white shirt and a black vest. A sheathed knife hung around his waist.

The farther rider was older with a full beard streaked with gray and *peyos* hanging in front of his ears. He wore a black shirt and long pants. Sliding his leg over the bike, the rider stared at Rachel from dark eyes. He pressed his outstretched hands against the air between them and called out in what Rachel assumed was Hebrew. After a moment he nodded, dropped his hands, and said something to the leader.

Rachel turned her attention back to the black man still straddling his bike.

He flashed white teeth, "I'm Jeremiad. And, yes, I am very afraid . . . for you to scratch my bike. It's a Harley-Davidson Ultra Classic Electric Glide. Only about fifteen hundred made, and I'm not sure how many survived the firestorm." He hooked a thumb over his shoulder. "These men are my gang. Go ahead and put that thing away; no one's trying to hurt anyone. Elijah says you're alright." Jeremiad's voice was molasses; Rachel could almost feel the words hang in the air.

Rachel let her weapon slide to the ground. "What do you mean we're 'alright'?"

"He tested you. You're not a follower of Ba'al, the Golden Bull." Jeremiad rubbed his palm across his thigh and waited, as if what he'd said made sense. Her gaze followed the movement. His torso ended where the motorcycle began. She hadn't noticed because he was black, his clothes were black, and the bike seat was black; they all matched seamlessly. The man was attached to his motorcycle. A modern-day centaur.

Rachel's mind tried to form connections. They'd left The Weather-man's territory. Was it possible? "Are you a Misbegotten?"

"Ha ha, I'd like to think so, but no. The three of us are bikers, cow-boys, nomads of the road. The only ones who need to be scared of us are the ones doing something wrong." His tone was wry. "Didn't think we'd find ourselves being attacked by a lady with a tire iron."

She felt red creep into her cheeks. "Our car was stolen a few miles back." She held out her hand. "I'm Rachel. This is my son, Adam."

Jeremiad's hand engulfed hers. "You guys hungry? Why don't you help Levi with the fire and we'll break bread together."

"Adam and I need to get to the hospital in Baltimore."

"Have some food first. It'll give you strength. Adam can help me," Jeremiad said.

Rachel looked to Adam, who shrugged and followed Jeremiad to the side. Rachel joined Levi at the side of the road where he'd pulled sticks from his motorcycle's pouch and was arranging them on the ground.

He gave her a friendly grin. "A-frame or teepee?" He had a slight accent. Israeli?

"What?"

"Uh-oh. Not a Girl Scout." Levi leaned the sticks together and applied a lighter to the bottom.

"Actually, I was. Only for a year though. I was more interested in the cookies. Love those peanut butter ones covered by chocolate. I used to put them in the freezer and eat them frozen."

"No, the best were definitely the ones covered with coconut."

"The purple box?"

They looked at each other and smiled.

"What's that look?"

She shook her head. "I feel like I'm in an M. C. Escher drawing. I'm putting one foot ahead of the other, but it's all gone topsy-turvy."

"He the one with the upside down stairways?"

"Yup." Rachel pulled out the blanket she'd shoved in her pack for the picnic with Adam and they settled in front of the fire. These flames emanated cold, little bits of frost floating up like white sparks.

"Never had a fire like this before," she said.

"Wait till you see what Elijah can do." Levi motioned toward the other rider. "There's a reason we call him a miracle worker."

"Elijah? Not the Elijah from Sunday school lessons, right?" Rachel teased, but she could hear the uncertainty in her voice.

"Why don't you tell me about these upside down stairs you're climbing?"

Rachel cleared her throat, looked around for Adam. He was still with Jeremiad. Watching Jeremiad, Rachel wondered how the man slept since he was attached to the motorcycle, if he was comfortable. She brought her attention back to Levi's question.

"Two days ago my son and I went to pick blueberries to put into breakfast pancakes. Antioxidants, you know." Rachel met Levi's gaze for a moment and then looked back at the ice fire. She'd adopted a light tone, but felt her throat swell with emotion. "We were attacked by a two-headed moose, an archer rescued us and then, the next morning, the same archer murdered one of my best friends while I stood there, helpless. Then, just a few hours ago, we were attacked by these horrible monkey-people who crashed our SUV."

"That's a lot to happen." Levi shook curls back from his face, poked at the fire with a stick.

She nodded, her mind returning to the most painful experience. "Scott was a really good guy. A park ranger. Showed us some tricks to living up there, brought us supplies."

"Helped out a mother and her son in their time of need." Levi gave her a sympathetic look, his brown eyes warm. "Definitely one of the good guys. Losing a friend is sad; murder is even worse."

Rachel tried to lighten the conversation, "What does your gang do? Meet with random people on the road and have lunch?"

"That seems to be today's agenda, but no, our purpose is a little bigger." He studied her. "I'm from Israel, but a week before the firestorm I arrived in New York to meet with a group of rabbis. It was a meeting arranged a year in advance. Yet, I believe that is where I was meant to be. Through prayer I heard the call to go west. I met with Jeremiad and Elijah. They'd also been given the meeting place."

"You're all so different from each other," Rachel said. "I don't have a lot of experience with gangs, but aren't you supposed to have something in common?"

"The three of us have all been called by El-Elyon." Levi waited for her to nod before he continued. "Our gang is looking for the Golden Bull."

Tension pounded in her head. The guard in the hospital. The monkeymen. Was this Golden Bull a Misbegotten? Rachel shrugged one shoulder, tried to make a joke. "Why? So you can go bull-riding?"

"No. So we can defeat it. The bull is named Ba'al. He's ancient and he's evil. He corrupts everything he touches."

Levi seemed straightforward. His gaze was intent, focused. Waiting for her to trust him.

"What does he look like?"

"We hear that he's large, and glows like burnished gold. His horns are filed to points and his eyes gleam with insatiable greed. We haven't seen him, but we've gotten close enough to hear his hooves and see what he leaves in his wake. It's not pretty."

"It's all hard to believe. There are supernatural beings and territories and—" she gestured toward Levi, "groups who don't belong to any territory but follow a divine plan."

"Difficult to see a plan in the middle of chaos."

"Here's the thing." She leaned forward. "I don't think my son and I are part of any plan." She shook her head. "I mean, I'm a failed artist turned stay-at-home mom with a son who has no immune system." She held up her hands like she making an announcement. "Voted 'least likely to survive the end of the world.'"

Levi shrugged. "In my culture we tell the story of a woman who thought very much like you. She later believed that she became queen for 'just such a time as this.' Esther is her Babylonian name. She took it from the goddess Ishtar to hide her Jewish identity until the right moment." Levi met Rachel's eyes. "And then she saved the Persian Jews from genocide."

Rachel did a quick mom check: Adam was still talking to Jeremiad, looking at the man's motorcycle.

Just then the ground in front of Elijah rumbled. The earth cracked open and a small stream of water glugged out, like the water fountain in an elementary school. Elijah turned around and gave two thumbs up to the group.

Levi called out something in Hebrew and the men laughed.

"What did you say?"

He looked at her. "I said that trick never gets old."

"Right," she said, allowing a sardonic tone.

"It's not really a trick, though. Anyone can pray to El-Elyon. Call out and He will answer you."

Adam walked over to the blanket carrying a messenger bag that strapped behind a motorcycle's seat. Contained in one side were chunks of thick bread and in the other was a porcelain dish filled with silver fish sitting in yellow sauce.

"Sardines? With mustard?" Rachel said. "I would not have guessed."

"Mom, you've got to try this, it's so good." Adam stuffed a piece of bread in his mouth.

A surge of relief made Rachel exhale. *Thank God*. He was eating, even with his wound. Appetite was one of the first things to go, suppressed by either narcotics or by pain.

She used her finger to put a sardine on top of the bread chunk and took a bite. Adam was right, it was spicy and flavorful, the bread chewy.

Jeremiad had driven his bike to the very edge of the blanket in time to hear her comment. Once again his laughter boomed out, making the flames waver. Meanwhile, Elijah had brought a dented tin mug over, filled with the water from the ground. The bag and the water passed around the group. The water was cold, crisp, and Rachel savored it. They ate in silence, everyone hungry, reaching again and again into the messenger bag.

Stomach full, Rachel leaned back on her elbows. Her gaze moved to Jeremiad.

"Well?" he said.

"You guys are great hosts. The best-tasting water I've ever had, fish and bread which are," she tilted the bag up, "yup, still full, a fire that burns cold, and a man who really loves his machine."

The big man grinned, friendly. "Seems like you're taking that right in stride."

Rachel shrugged. "In the past forty-eight hours I've seen a two-headed moose and a man who unscrews his arm to cut his meat at dinner. And Elijah over there who can find water in the middle of the dry, dusty road. I'm starting to think that I'm the weird one."

"Some of us changed on the outside, but maybe there are changes that are less obvious."

Rachel gave a little laugh. "Well, I've always been a late bloomer. Maybe flowers will start springing up from my footprints in a couple of days. Or I'll be able to fly. That would be a very cool mutation."

"These changes aren't random. They are an outward sign of the unique 'you.' That monkeyman I heard you telling Levi about? To me, that sounds like a human being who made a bad bargain with Ba'al. Someone who likes power from hurting other people. His body changed to reflect his insides."

Jeremiad raised his eyebrow and then seemed to lean back. "I was riding away from Chicago when the firestorm fell. Looked like a meteor shower from hell. A voice—later I realized it was El-Elyon—told me where to go, and I went.

"I'll never forget that night of fire, riding through it, the energy running over my body and as I rode it was like never before, the motorcycle responding to each thought, mind and machine perfectly in sync until there was this warmth in my legs and BAM, this is how I roll."

Adam snickered. "That's funny."

Rachel turned to look at her son. His eyes were clear, but he cradled his arm.

"So, what's your story, Adam?" Levi said.

Rachel started to answer, but Levi flashed a smile. "I asked him."

Heat stained her cheeks. "Sorry."

Adam cleared his throat. "Yeah. So we were at the hospital during the firestorm, but then they said we had to leave. I wanted to go home so we could get my dad, but Mom said if he was alive he would find us. He never came. I really miss him."

"That's hard, son." Jeremiad held out a fist and Adam tapped it with his own.

In the distance a wolf howled. A moment later the howl was echoed in a higher register.

Rachel scrambled up. "We'd better get moving. Thank you so much for sharing your lunch with us, but we're in a hurry."

"Why don't you ride with us for a while?" asked Jeremiad. "We're heading east."

She hesitated. "It might not be safe for you. I think we're being followed."

Levi seemed amused, Elijah whistled as he smoothed the fountain back into the earth.

Rachel looked at Levi. "Remember that archer I told you about?"

"The one that—"

"Yes," Rachel interrupted. She glanced at Adam, but he hadn't noticed. She needed the right time to explain what had happened. But learning about Scott now, in the middle of strangers, was not that time. "That's him."

"We're a motorcycle gang. Who's going to mess with you?" Jeremiad waited for Rachel's nod, her acceptance of help, before he gestured, "Move out, people."

THIRTY-ONE

They'd been riding for about two hours, Adam behind Jeremiad and Rachel behind Levi, before the smell, a combination of rotting trash and unwashed bodies, struck them in the face. They could see the camp a few miles before the 695 and 95 junction. A wooden sign read DROSSVILLE. Rachel ducked her head against Levi's back. Elijah pulled up alongside Levi and pointed. Rachel hoped he didn't mean that they should stop. The older man's *peyos* flapped in the wind and he gave Rachel a thumbs-up before pointing again at Drossville.

"We're not going there, are we?" Rachel shouted, but the wind whipped her words away. It didn't matter anyway, the motorcycles were already pulling off and heading toward the neglected town.

It looked like homeless people had moved away from the boarded-up townhouses, the burned roads, and rotting bodies in Baltimore. Perhaps it was an outgrowth or relocation of the squatter's camp in the hospital parking garage. This wasn't the type of town to have a town hall; instead, the center was the saloon. Four outhouses stood alongside the bar. One-room shanties made of cardboard and scrap metal alternated with tents, sloppily erected, created a wagonwheel of uneven pathways to the center. Filth lay wherever it was thrown.

Graffiti covered available spaces, bubble letters reading BULLSHIT with screaming heads for decoration and HELL AIN'T FOR THE FAINT-HEARTED. A primitive pictograph of a bull's triangular face with horns dominated, drawn over and over. The style reminded Rachel of something she'd studied in art history class. Lascaux, France. 17,300-year-old European cave drawings showing up outside post-firestorm Baltimore. More evidence that these Misbegotten, these gods, really had been here before.

Jeremiad rode the uneven paths through the camp. From behind Levi, Rachel saw faces popping out of tents, peeking out of shacks; an unwelcoming audience. All different nationalities here, but something about the faces seemed uniform, disaffected. The riders pulled right up to the saloon, the only building with actual construction. TENEMENT HOUSE BAR was written in red spray paint.

Rachel climbed off and went straight to Jeremiad. "What's going on? Why are we stopping?"

"Seems like an okay place to get a drink."

Rachel looked at the saloon dubiously. "Adam and I will wait for you out here."

Jeremiad shrugged. "Suit yourself."

Levi and Elijah walked up the three wide steps and through the swinging doors. Jeremiad revved his engine and drove up through the splintering wood into the bar. A shrill voice from inside shouted, "Hey, you can't ride a motorcycle in here."

Jeremiad called back, "Well, I can't leave it outside."

A youngish blond woman with greasy hair and the same blank eyes as the rest of the town poked her head out the doorway, "And you busted up the steps. You'll have to pay for those." She went back inside.

Jeremiad answered, but he must have moved away from the door because Rachel couldn't make out the words.

Alone with Adam, Rachel said, "We're almost to the hospital. How's your arm feel?"

He pulled off the protective sling and showed her. The redness around the wound hadn't calmed, his whole arm remained tender to the touch, the bruise still purple as blood leaked from vessels. The black mole in the center pulsed, its edges covered the bend in his elbow.

"I need more pain medication."

Rachel nodded. She looked over her shoulder as she shrugged off the backpack and became aware of people emerging from the shacks. Not so much a mob scene as individuals, men and women, wandering toward to the center of the wheel, shuffling forward to see if anything interesting was going to happen.

"You know what, Adam? Maybe we should join Jeremiad and the guys." She touched his unhurt arm to lead him up the steps.

"Hey!" The voice came from one of the men with greasy hair and rough stubble on his face. "You don't have to hurry off, pretty girl. Maybe we'll put your picture up on the wall."

"Put that boy up there, too!"

The crowd laughed, mean, but somehow tired. As if cruelty was to be expected, just another task on a to-do list. Cut off puppy dog tails. Hurt a mentally ill young man. Intimidate a single mother and her kid. Check.

Rachel hurried Adam up the stairs and through the swinging doors.

It took a moment for her eyes to adjust from the outside, but she could smell an overworked generator and hear the clacking sound of balls on a pool table. Straight ahead was a bar with a back mirror surrounded by ghastly green light bulbs and holiday tinsel hanging down the sides. To the left four men, locals, stood around the pool table while a man and woman slouched in the corner by a pinball machine. Stairs in the far corner led up. Rachel looked to the right and saw the gang sitting at a table made of stacked tires with a piece of plywood for a top. Rachel grabbed an extra chair for Adam and sat.

"Change your mind?" Levi grinned at her.

"I think we should go. These people don't seem to like strangers."

Levi nodded. "It's going to be alright. We're supposed to be here now."

The woman who'd yelled about the steps came over to the table. "I'm Tiffany." Two words to express complete disdain. "Are y'all here to go upstairs?" Her right hand plucked at the knot holding the two sides of her shirt together.

"No." Jeremiad's tone was firm.

"Then you'll have to buy a drink or leave." She glanced toward the seat closest to the bar. A man wearing a suit with black hair, black eyes, and thin lips sat half in the green light playing cards by himself. He checked the mirror periodically before going back to his game. "Mr. Lee don't let anyone just sit around here. This is a fine establishment."

"Alright," Jeremiad said. "What do you have?"

"We got little bits of this and that from Baltimore and also we got a still set up in our courtyard. Fresh moonshine."

"We'll take three of whatever is easiest."

"And you?" Tiffany's eyes went over Rachel's head.

Rachel swallowed. "Do you have anything um . . . non-alcoholic?"

Tiffany finally met Rachel's eyes. She even smiled as she crooned, "Oh, yes, we have some milk for you and the boy. It's what I give all the children."

"Milk?" Adam said. "I've only had it once in the past month. How did you get it?"

The last time had been with Scott during the freak snowstorm. The unexpected memory was a jab of pain to Rachel. She really missed him.

"We have a cow, a present to Mr. Lee 'cause this is all his. Gotta stay on his good side." She giggled. "We keep that old cow in the fence so no one steals it."

"That'd be great, thank you." Rachel smiled and then let it drop when the blonde walked away. Tiffany's exuberance was as creepy as her earlier reticence.

Elijah got up from the table and walked out the front door.

"Where's he going?" Rachel asked.

Jeremiad said, "He's just going to look around, see what he can see."

"Okay."

Adam grew quiet, pressed his hand against his heart in what was becoming a familiar signal of distress. His eyelids fluttered so it looked like he was falling asleep propped up against Jeremiad's muscular arm. She sighed and looked around the saloon. Four photo frames on the wall, hung where TV sets might have gone pre-firestorm. A cold pit formed in her stomach. The photos showed women in various states of undress and at the end of each cycle of pictures a screen came up reading RATE YOUR WHORE! This time when the pictures cycled through Rachel understood the various stars at the bottom. Her horrified glance went to the wooden stairs at the far end of the room. This was what that terrible man had meant about putting her picture up. And Adam's.

Rachel felt sick. "Levi, I do not want to be here. Can we please go?"

Levi gave her hand a sympathetic squeeze. "Not much longer, Rachel, we're just waiting for Elijah to come back."

Tiffany set down three mason jars with murky brown liquid on the table and a fourth with a white liquid.

"Go ahead, drink up." She waited as if she intended to watch them. Then she saw Levi. Tiffany practically purred. "Oh, how did you sneak in here without me seeing you?" She put her arm around his neck and tried to sit on his lap. Levi smiled, but removed her arm and half-stood so that she couldn't complete her move.

"I don't think Mr. Lee would like that," Levi said with a knowing tone.

"Yeah. I'm his girl, but he won't mind as long as you pay."

"Psst."

Rachel looked over. Sitting by himself was a black teenager wearing a sleeveless white basketball shirt, a diamond earring, ripped jeans, and what looked like new sneakers. He'd been so quiet that Rachel hadn't even noticed him. Rachel narrowed her eyes at his busted lip. The young man pointed to the milk and then shook his head.

She touched the mason jar and tilted her head. "What?"

Again he pointed to the liquid and shook his hand horizontally. Rachel still didn't understand.

"Don't drink that," he hissed.

"Why not?"

And then the man who must have been Mr. Lee was there, pulling the boy out of his seat. The Asian man gave off a sense of collected energy, of a person used to being in charge. Not afraid to use his fists.

"You have something to say, Tyrez?" He had a slight accent.

"Naw, Mr. Lee, I didn't say nuthin'." Mr. Lee was a great deal shorter than the boy, but Tyrez cowered.

"And you," Mr. Lee looked at Rachel. "Do you have any trouble?"

A chill passed through Rachel and she couldn't even swallow. The man was terrifying.

Mr. Lee put a hand on Tyrez's arm and whisked the teenager away.

Rachel turned back to the table to see if anyone else had seen. Jeremiad was watching the other side of the room where the locals glared at their table. Levi was busy disengaging himself from Tiffany, who kept suggesting that he come upstairs with her. Adam was rubbing his arm.

"I'll be right back," she said to the table and then followed the path Mr. Lee and Tyrez had taken.

Behind the bar was a small kitchen area. Rachel went through and out the back door of the saloon to a small courtyard, maybe twelve feet by ten feet, fenced in with wooden boards and barbed wire. Corncobs sat in a stack by a wooden still. On the opposite side stood the most pitiful cow she'd ever seen tied to one of the fence boards. The beast's flanks protruded, a walking skeleton, eyes rolling around in its head. Rachel stepped closer and the cow tried to step away, tottered off-balance, and almost fell, toothless jaws opening and closing.

"It's drunk!"

The smell was unquestionable. No corn or grain in the feeding trough; instead, the mash remains from the moonshine still. A milking pail sat on a wooden picnic bench. Inside was a chunky green soup that smelled like soured milk. Rachel's gaze flicked to the stirring spoon beside the milk pail, the chalk powder, the dirty water, the bleach. Chalk to turn the swilled milk white, water to dilute the chunks, and a touch of bleach to mask the smell.

Disbelieving, Rachel whirled around, arms out in front of her to feel her way back to the door. Her eyes felt as if they were hot, burning. The mason jar sat in front of Adam, untouched, he was still re-wrapping his wounded arm. Rachel pushed her way to the table, smacked the mason jar off the table so that white liquid spattered through the air, and grabbed the arm of Tiffany, who was still trying to writhe around on Levi.

Only a few minutes had passed, but Rachel felt as if she were going to explode. Her body shook with indignation and her vision wavered as if her very eyes were on fire.

"This is what you feed all your children?" Rachel waved her arms to gesture outside the saloon before grabbing Tiffany by the shoulders and shaking her. "This is how you protect and nurture little ones? What is the matter with you!?"

Tiffany yanked free and screeched in a voice to break glass, "There are no more. They're all dead, all dead, all dead. No more babies for the bull to eat." She ran behind the bar and flipped her middle finger at their table.

As if that was a signal the locals on the other side of the bar stood up, arranged themselves in front of the pool table, all eyes on Rachel's side of the room. The saloon doors crashed open and Elijah came through, yarmulke askew. The older Jewish man waited until he had Jeremiad's attention, then shook his head, lips pressed together, eyes expressing sadness. Jeremiad gave a tiny nod.

"Rachel," Jeremiad said, "You and Adam should wait outside."

Unsure what was happening, Rachel felt Levi's arm at her elbow, nudging her from the chair. Adam, also physically prompted by Levi, stood up.

The motorcycle man drove forward until he was in the middle of the room. He and his reflection spoke together. He announced, "This is a den of robbers. Not one person here has been found full of justice. You have sold your souls to the Golden Bull. In the name of El-Elyon, this town is condemned."

Jeremiad revved his engines until the sound reverberated through the whole wooden saloon. The locals surged forward with pool sticks. Jeremiad unfolded sunglasses and then reached behind his seat to pull out what looked like a long, thick rifle with metal tubing. He drove across the bar to meet the charging locals: a modern joust with motorcycle and pool sticks.

Dazed, Rachel's mind tried to make sense of what she was seeing. The bullets of a gun that size would have to be six inches across. But Jeremiad had the strap across his chest and stabilized the butt against his own leg. By now the locals had surrounded the motorcycle man, were beating him with sticks and fists. Jeremiad pulled the trigger and a spray of flames burst from the muzzle of his weapon. He swung the flames in an arc. Screaming and the smell of burning clothes filled the saloon.

Rachel allowed Levi to push her through the doors onto the porch. Adam came out right behind her and she wrapped her arm around his waist, bringing him close to her. She could still see into the saloon.

One burning man staggered into the wall. The dry wood caught fire. Footsteps came from upstairs and girls in ripped negligees, cheap material catching on fire, ran down the steps and through Jeremiad's flames.

From behind the bar Tiffany pulled out a baseball bat.

"Hold still, you idiot!" she screamed at one of the burning men rolling on the ground in agony. "You're going to light my bar on fire." Tiffany hit the man square in the head and Rachel closed her eyes, the screams echoing in her head. She gave no resistance to Levi as he pushed her further from the doors.

The situation on the porch was no better. The town's occupants had gathered from the tents and lean-tos, standing in a wary semicircle while Elijah used his own flamethrower.

"They're not human anymore. You have to understand that." Levi's voice was in her ear. "Elijah already checked. The bull has been here."

Rachel's eyes met Levi's before he left her to retrieve his own weapon from the back of his bike. Where she'd been sitting. Hysteria bubbled up. But there was something bothering her, trying to be remembered.

Looking at the crowd of blank eyes and slack jaws practically standing in line to be burned alive by two Jewish men in sunglasses with flamethrowers, it was easy to believe they were no longer human. But there had been one, that boy who warned her about the swilled milk. The boy that Mr. Lee had dragged away. Rachel had followed them to a dead end in the courtyard with the drunk cow. The only other place they could have gone was upstairs.

The gang's mass slaughter wasn't her fault, she'd had no idea that would happen, but that boy, Tyrez, that was her fault. He'd told about the milk and been dragged upstairs for speaking out. If not, maybe Elijah would have seen one good person here. At least Tyrez would have been downstairs near the swinging doors and could have saved himself. She had to do something.

"Adam. Stay right there, behind Levi and Elijah." Rachel pointed to a spot away from both the fighting and, hopefully, fallout from this saloon's collapse. "I'll be right back."

Adam nodded, his face looking as shell-shocked as hers probably did. For crying out loud, she'd monitored Adam's vids for violence and language and now he was experiencing what she hadn't let him play.

The structure creaked, but Rachel pushed through the doors, knowing there wasn't any more time to think. The screams had mercifully stopped, but vague imprints of bodies on the floor remained. People had burned so hot there was nothing left but ashes.

Jeremiad was parked in the middle of the floor with the flame-thrower strapped across his chest. Blood trickled from a cut on his stomach. Tiffany stood behind the bar, her eyes wild. She'd figured out that Jeremiad, strange centaur, couldn't easily get to her. The mirror behind her was partially melted which created a funhouse reflection of damage to the saloon. Glasses from the shelves had been hurled at Jeremiad; pieces littered the floor and then pooled together at hot spots.

"You got nothing left to throw, girl," Jeremiad called to Tiffany.

They both looked at Rachel when she came in. "Get out of here, Rachel," Jeremiad said. "The whole thing is gonna fall."

"There's a boy, Tyrez, I think he's upstairs."

"Better take your own advice," Tiffany shouted.

Jeremiad snorted, "Why don't you take a wash before you start giving advice?"

Tiffany let loose an outraged scream and tore off what remained of her shirt. The triangular head of a bull with horns that was graffitied around town was stamped across her chest in scar tissue like she'd been branded. "How dare you! I'm gonna be handmaiden to the Queen of Heaven." Tiffany reached down and then held up a corkscrew, metal part between her first two fingers, before standing up on the bar.

Jeremiad pushed forward, arms shoving tables out of his way, engine straining to get him closer. As he pulled up his flamethrower,

Rachel heard the snarling whoosh. Tiffany burst into flames. Rachel forced herself away from the door and toward the staircase. The smoke burned her lungs, it was so hot. She crouched down and tried to get closer, but she couldn't breathe. Her eyes stung and she felt like she was going to burst into flames. Her foot was on the first step, and then she was abruptly shoved backwards into the pinball machine. The metal burned through her shirt and she jerked upright.

Mr. Lee stood on the steps blocking her way. Like Tiffany his shirt was off, exposing the bull scar across his hairless chest. He didn't look scared, though, as Tiffany had before being incinerated. In his hands, Mr. Lee had a coiled bullwhip. Even through the smoke Rachel could see red. Didn't take much to guess it was Tyrez's blood. He could be dead. Rachel's lungs felt like they were going to explode. She had to give up.

Rachel dropped to all fours, pulled her shirt up to cover her mouth and nose, tried to get underneath the worst of the smoke. The burn across her back felt like it was continuing to sear the layers of her skin. Only a few more feet and then she was in front of the saloon doors. Here the outside air diluted the heat and Rachel sucked in a deep breath. Behind her the whip whistled, an ugly noise. The resulting wet sound was worse, the whip pulling out of flesh. Against her will Rachel looked over her shoulder to see three red stripes against Jeremiad's chest. Mr. Lee grinned with triumph as he came down the stairs, fire crackling overhead. Another groan from the building as the walls shook. Jeremiad roared forward into tables, grabbed the whip and pulled Mr. Lee into tug-of-war, trying to get the Asian man off the stairs and into flamethrower range.

The men were too intent on their fight to notice, but Rachel finished crawling out of the saloon. Fire out here, fire everywhere, but no longer the smoke that burned when she breathed. Instead, the smoke rose into the air as tents and lean-tos burned, Elijah and Levi systematically moving throughout the spokes of the wheel that made up

Drossville. Piles of ash scattered on the ground, no way to tell what they'd once been.

Behind her the saloon groaned as if alive. She pulled herself off the deck and felt Adam's hands helping her. They watched the saloon collapse, flames shooting out the top.

"Mom, Jeremiad didn't come out. I was watching the door the whole time."

Rachel tried to speak, but no sound came out of her burned throat. Instead she just nodded. A wind picked up, helping to spread the fire. Adam stepped close, let her lean against his right shoulder as they stared at the remains of Drossville.

"Rachel," Levi came toward her, exhaustion written on his face. "We'll stay here to clean up. I'm sorry we can't get you to Baltimore. Remember that you can call out to El-Elyon. He answers anyone with a sincere heart."

Rachel nodded. She touched her throat to show she couldn't talk and held out her hand. Levi covered it with both his hands and gave it a squeeze.

"Wait!" Adam cried. "What about Jeremiad?"

"We follow El-Elyon's orders, no matter what it means for us as individuals." Levi frowned, put his hand on Adam's shoulder, and looked at Rachel. "I fear the Bull's influence is spreading in this area. It will make the next part of your journey dangerous. Be safe."

THIRTY-TWO

It was strange turning off 695 onto Edmondson Avenue, having never before walked off a highway and up to a non-functioning traffic light. Probably a better way to get there, but Rachel had a driver's map in her head, not a pedestrian's. This area used to be known for drug corners, shootings, and abandoned houses.

"Pretty crazy back there." Her voice sounded hoarse and her throat and lips ached.

Adam's shoulders slumped. "I'm getting tired."

Rachel nodded, unsure if he meant tired of fires or tired of walking. Probably both. "Only about sixteen more miles. Then we'll be at the hospital."

"Sixteen!"

"Lot easier in a car, right?"

"Yeah, or the gang could have taken us the whole way. They're so cool with their flamethrowers. They were like—" Adam planted his feet and held both hands like he had a gun.

"Adam," Rachel stopped and put her hands on his shoulders. "Those men believed they were doing the right thing, but killing in the name of religion is a slippery slope. Now Jeremiad is dead. And so is a young man named Tyrez. And, they could've gotten us killed. We were lucky to get away."

"They had to burn it down." Adam's eyes were impassioned. He was still young enough to be an idealist. "It's justice. Jeremiad told me about the bull. Elijah's job is to see if a camp can be saved. If it can't, they have to burn it before it spreads."

"Adam, they're vigilantes, people operating outside of the law."

"Mom! Look around. There isn't any law anymore. Jeremiad said—"

"Don't care. This discussion is over."

He was disappointed, his facial expressions honest to his emotions. They'd had a long day and they'd both been pushed hard.

She tried to sound positive. "Let's keep an eye out for a place to crash tonight. We'll have a dinner from the backpack and we'll wake up early and get to the hospital. We can pretend that there will be taxis running and we'll catch one. Okay?"

Adam nodded, but he wouldn't meet her eyes.

Vacant lots stood gaping, homes blasted away to nothing but a black crater of scorched earth. No one sat on the steps, no cars drove down the street. Some of the nearby bungalows seemed intact, their low-pitched roofs overhanging porches. A few of the drapes seemed to twitch over front windows when they walked past, but that could have been Rachel's wishful thinking that there were more survivors in the city than she was seeing. Baltimore looked so broken and empty.

A lupine howling echoed. Rachel's spine straightened, causing the burn to shoot pain through her back, remind her where it was. Another howl joined the first. A random pack of wolves or the archer? She'd forgotten all about Captain Lewis when Drossville went up in flames. He was a professional soldier, they were a single mom and her eleven-year-old hurt son. No contest who could travel faster.

Adam seemed to catch her fear and they shifted into a running jog for a block, walking for two, until that turned into a few running steps and then back to a walk, heavy breathing and shoulders protesting. It wasn't long before she had a stitch in her side, her throat so dry all she could think about was cold water. So dehydrated. Each step became harder.

"Mom, I can't keep going."

"Me neither."

This time the wolves' howling didn't faze them. Adam and Rachel pulled off their packs and slid down against a set of broken stairs leading up to an abandoned house. The howls might have sounded closer, but if there was a trick to triangulating the sound, Rachel didn't know it. She opened her backpack and pulled out a thermos of water she'd packed at Hiraeth that morning. It seemed so long ago.

"Let me see your arm." Angry red streaked from the black spot through the bruises down to his wrist. The black mole had tripled in size, a tarnished half-dollar. She held Adam's hand while he gulped and tilted out the painkiller into his palm. Not much left, but they should make it to the hospital the next day.

"Slow down. If you drink too fast you'll vomit. And then I'll be mad that you wasted the water." Rachel tried to grin, but her lips were too cracked. And if they hadn't been, it was too much effort. She took the thermos, closing her eyes to drink.

"Anything to eat?"

"Yup, hold on." Rachel closed the lid of the thermos, though she really wanted to drink the whole thing. She distributed their food, knowing she should hold more back, but rationalizing that it would make their packs lighter. "Would you put some of this aloe on my back? I got burned in that saloon."

"Why'd you bring aloe?"

"It was in the first aid kit. You know me, I always overpack."

Adam took the small packet and spread it on her burn. He tried to be gentle, so Rachel gritted her teeth instead of screaming like she wanted to. "Thanks, buddy." She reached out to touch his cheek.

"I'm sorry you're hurt," he said.

"I'm sorry you're hurt, too. Let's find a place to crash."

"Hey, Mom?"

Rachel raised her eyebrows.

"What's something only penguins can have?"

She shrugged, not wanting to talk anymore because of her burned throat.

"Baby penguins."

She gave him a double thumb's up and nodded, an image of Tamaki's pet penguin-turtle popping into her head. She didn't mention that he'd told this joke before, understanding it was a sign of his mental exhaustion.

They trudged forward, hunger sated, eyelids heavy, when they heard someone call out. A priest stood in the doorway of a brave little church with stained glass windows and a tiny steeple that barely reached the top of the rowhouse next to it, a graveyard on its other side.

He said, "*¡Vamonos! ¡Vamonos! El Diablo esta llegando.*"

"Ow," Adam cried. He clutched his hurt arm. "Something's happening."

Exhaustion forgotten, Rachel and Adam ran, backpacks bumping against scrapes and burns.

Rachel heard running footsteps behind them and looked over her shoulder. As the figure got closer, Rachel could make out a man. His eyes were huge, his arms pumping as he ran. Rachel moved to the side, but he wasn't running toward them, he was running away from something behind him.

"*¡Prisa!*" shouted the priest. It was obvious he was urging all of them to hurry.

Rachel grabbed Adam's arm and they cut across the graveyard. Behind her the man screamed and she looked back.

The man fell to his knees, clutching the crucifix around his neck with one hand, holding it up toward the darkening sky. He screamed, "The soul-eater is coming!" while his other hand clutched at his heart.

Rachel felt her hair rise away from her face as it became difficult to move. The closest thing she'd ever experienced was the Gravitron ride at the amusement park. The force pressed her and Adam to their knees and then to their stomachs.

Blue light split the sky and thunder rumbled like hooves. A figure, outlined by the supernatural light, walked toward the man on the ground. Rachel didn't want to watch, but she couldn't look away. Another bolt of the blue lightning and this time Rachel recognized the figure. Her eyes widened. It made no sense, but there stood Mr. Lee from Drossville. He wore a long black duster and his chest was bare.

The lightning zigzag disappeared but the eerie blue glow remained over the scene.

The priest came down the church stairs and faced Mr. Lee. "*Vete, diablo.*"

Mr. Lee laughed. His chest began to glow as the lines formed the familiar outline of the bull's head. "You dare challenge a prophet of Ba'al?" He extended his hands and then shoved through the air. The priest flew backwards down the street and landed in a heap.

The man kneeling on the road screamed.

Mr. Lee pulled out a bullwhip and held it up, seeming to relish the man's fear. Mr. Lee shook the coiled whip, then rubbed it across the man's upturned face like a caress. The man panted, head shaking, fingers scrabbling at the ground in front of him. He screamed out "*¡El diablo!*"

The church. Rachel grabbed on to that idea. It was safety. It took an enormous effort to pull herself to all fours. Sweat broke out on her forehead.

Another crack of lightning. Mr. Lee stared at her from where he stood over the man. He tilted his head. She saw recognition spark.

He lifted the handle of the whip and pointed it at her. "You were in my bar. With the men who burned down my saloon and killed my bartender. How very fortunate that we should meet here when I'm already on an errand." Terrified, Rachel sank back down on top of Adam.

Mr. Lee whirled around, duster flaring, and kicked the man in the head. Blood poured from the man's nose. From above, two black vulture-like creatures swooped down. More absence than structure, their forms were outlined by the strange blue light.

The creatures swooped above the man as if hungry. He looked up and once again screamed out, "*¡Diablo!*"

Mr. Lee met Rachel's gaze as he, with an almost lazy movement, circled his wrist until the whip coiled around the man's neck. He pulled tight. The man grabbed at the whip, kicking out his legs, eyes bulging. His head hung. Gray smoke oozed out of the body and floated into the sky. Mr. Lee let the body fall forward to the ground and coiled his whip with efficient movements.

With reptilian screeches, the vultures dived toward the gray smoke, snatching at wisps, consuming whatever had come out of the man. Mr. Lee watched them, a small smile playing around his thin lips. He reached inside his duster and brought out a large glass jar. Then his whip snapped at the first flying creature, wrapping around it. Mr. Lee reeled it in as if he were fishing.

As the creature struggled in the air, unable to free itself from the whip around its body, Mr. Lee pulled the ends of the whip so tight, the creature melted into shadow. All that remained was a glowing cloud. Within the cloud, Rachel saw gray smoke.

Holding out the glass jar, Mr. Lee's hand lit with blue light. The glowing cloud drifted into the jar. Mr. Lee twisted the lid. The other creature shrieked as it flew away into night. Mr. Lee tucked the glass jar of glowing light into an inside pocket of his duster.

That poor man had been bait for Mr. Lee to capture one of those creatures. He'd use her and Adam to bait another trap. The creature would come and eat their psychic remains and then get stuffed into another glass jar. Chills ran up and down her spine. That black smoke caused the cancer to grow in Adam again.

Mr. Lee snapped his whip, holding the end in his right hand. He held the other hand outstretched. Blue fire, the same as the lightning, sparked in his palm, growing larger until an arc snaked from his hand to the corpse. The dead man's body jerked upright, a puppet with Mr. Lee controlling the movements by twitching the handle of his whip. The corpse did an awkward jig, limp body jouncing about.

"Scared yet?" Mr. Lee let the body drop into the dust and the blue dissipated. "Maybe you would like to dance like that?" He grinned, but his steps weren't hurried as he walked toward them. Rachel's body quaked from adrenaline, but she couldn't seem to move, couldn't even look away from Mr. Lee's eyes. There was nothing she could do against this man. He was too strong, too powerful.

The howling caught up to them.

"Stop!" The order rang out. "I command you to halt in the name of New Babylon."

The archer strode out of the darkness of Edmondson Avenue and into the blue light, flanked by his two wolves. Captain Lewis looked the same as she remembered. Tall with wide shoulders, narrow waist, tight black shirt, bow already in hand.

Mr. Lee stopped, but didn't turn his head to look at the newcomer. Instead, he maintained eye contact with Rachel before deciding that she wasn't moving, and then pivoted to face the captain. Neither man said a word as each sized up his opponent.

Finally, Mr. Lee said, "New Babylon? How interesting. You should go back there."

Captain Lewis tucked his chin and spoke with space between each word. "Put down your weapon or you will be considered an imminent threat. This woman and child are under New Babylon's protection."

Now Mr. Lee laughed. "By all means, consider me an imminent threat." His whip snaked through the air just as the wolves lunged forward.

Lewis dived to the ground and rolled away. Up on his feet, he pulled an arrow from the quiver and waited for Dido to move so he could get a shot. The white wolf snapped at Mr. Lee from the right side while Caesar circled to the left, lips pulled back to expose long canines, hackles raised.

Rachel gathered her resolve. This was their miracle. No wasting it. With Mr. Lee distracted, it seemed that the invisible force pushing down on Rachel and Adam had eased. She pulled herself into a crouching position and helped Adam to his knees.

"Let's go."

They crawled through the graveyard, the stench of charred grass hovering over the dirt. She heard an arrow thrum through the air behind her. Ahead, the stone steps climbed up to the wooden door of the church. Her hand reached for the door, but the knob wouldn't turn. An angry yelp sounded from one of the wolves and then the thrum of another arrow. The vultures screeched. Maybe telling Mr. Lee that she and Adam were getting away? Panic seized her. They could be hit by an arrow or blue light at any second.

Try again. The voice was a whisper inside her mind.

Rachel reached out a second time, grasped the knob, and it turned. She and Adam fell into the church, shutting the door behind them.

Rachel sucked in several shallow breaths as she bolted the lock and slid to the ground. From somewhere in the darkness of the church, a scratching reached her ears.

THIRTY-THREE

Rachel scanned the vestibule for the sound. It was hard to see in the blue light streaming in through the stained glass windows. Long pews with old velvet seat cushions lined the wall with doors to the sanctuary. A wooden table stood in the middle with stacked offering plates while signs to the left and right pointed out restrooms. A small shadow ran across the cloth on the table, its tiny nails scratching, and then shimmied down the side of the cloth, disappearing through a crack in the corner where the walls met.

"A mouse," Rachel muttered. "At least it didn't have two heads." She pushed on one side of the pew. It was heavy, but she could move the whole thing by shuffling forward a few feet and then running around to the other side and scooting that side forward until the pew barricaded the door. She wiped her hand across her forehead.

"Mom, we need to tell Captain Lewis what that guy did! How he collected that—"

"Shh. Let me think for a moment." Rachel put her aching head in her hands. Both of the men out there were her enemies, but Mr. Lee was evil. Should she have shouted a warning? Watch out, this man somehow survived a burning building and doesn't seem any worse off?

Oh, and he just executed someone right in front of us without flinching and then shot lightning out of his hand. But, Captain Lewis had shot Scott. Captain Lewis's job was to eliminate anything strange that didn't work for New Babylon's vision of the world. Third option: they could kill each other.

"Did you see how brave he was?" Adam adopted a heroic pose. "'Stop in the name of New Babylon.' That was cool, wasn't it?"

Rachel nodded. "Captain Lewis is certainly bold." *Ugh, my head hurts.* "All I could think about was getting away before we got killed."

Adam plucked at his jeans. "But, why was Mr. Lee going to kill us?"

"Just because we were there, Adam."

She read the confusion in her son's eyes and it broke her heart. He would be a teenager soon. These too-simple explanations wouldn't work much longer.

Crouching down next to the pew blocking the door, Rachel peeked out. The view was distorted because of the red stained glass window. Mr. Lee had gotten away from the wolves. He wrapped his duster around himself and disappeared in a glow of blue light. Captain Lewis stood there, his wolves pacing circles and whining. He glanced around and then walked towards the church.

Rachel ducked down, her eyes glued to the handle.

It jiggled, but the lock held.

She saw a shadow press against the stained glass window. Captain Lewis peering in. If he looked down he would see the top of her head.

The shadow disappeared. Footsteps rang against the stone steps. A whistle summoned the wolves. There was one last scratch against the door.

Rachel exhaled. Adam crawled from underneath the pew still against the vestibule wall and stretched out, using his backpack as a pillow. He yawned. "Why didn't you tell Captain Lewis that we're here?"

"Because," Rachel said, thinking fast. "We're going to the hospital. He's busy with New Babylon."

"Oh." Adam closed his eyes. Within minutes he was asleep, but Rachel wondered what Captain Lewis was planning. She pushed through the doors into a one-room sanctuary lined with stained glass windows. Communion table up front, piano to the left, organ to the right. A plain door tucked in the far left corner. Rachel checked that it was locked—it was—and then pulled the piano bench across it. They'd hear, at least, if someone tried to come in and they could go out the opposite way.

Rachel returned to the vestibule and leaned her back against the post of the pew so she was physically close to Adam. She wanted to be able to hear him breathing, just like when he was an infant. Her exhausted mind wouldn't stop spinning. Overstimulated. *That's what parents say when their children get this way.*

She kept staring at the door, worrying about it, imagining she heard sounds from outside. It was like the monster under the bed. She'd have to check again. No sign of any person or wolf outside. From far away she heard the screech of one of the energy vultures.

Finally, she stretched out parallel to Adam and fell asleep.

Rachel couldn't move when she woke up. Not like the night before— the Gravitron effect—but a rebellion of all her muscles. She groaned as she sat up, hamstrings, biceps, all the words from art anatomy careened through her mind as their actual parts screamed in agony.

"Hey, Adam?" She looked to the pew, but he wasn't there. "Adam!"

"Right here." He bounced through the sanctuary doors.

"Ugg," she wiped her face, "aren't you sore at all? That's so unfair."

"Check out the bathroom. There's running water and everything."

"Really?" Hope was enough to get her on her feet. The bathroom was like the rest of the church, serviceable and cozy. Adam had been right; the toilets and sink still somehow worked. There were paper towels in the dispenser, flower-scented hand soap, and little paper cups in a neat stack. Even a mirror. Rachel washed her face then stripped down to take a sink bath, running water through her auburn hair. She used a paper cup to drink the icy water over and over. It felt so good pouring down her burned throat.

The sanctuary smelled clean, like the lemon scent in furniture polish. Outside light filtered through the colorful stained glass windows—various scenes of Jesus's birth, death, and resurrection. Worn red carpet covered the floors. Two rows of pews and an aisle up the center that led to the raised altar. Behind that the standard choir area, podium, tables with golden communion dishes. Adam was over at the table.

"Look what I found. Bread!"

"That's for communion. I'm not sure you should be eating it."

"There's no one here, Mom. Stop being such a scaredy-cat."

Rachel walked toward the altar, letting her hand drift over the pews as she walked. A plain wooden cross stood in a circle of thorns. *Crown of thorns*, she corrected herself. Little white votive candles were set out in neat rows. A book of matches sat nearby.

"Hey, look what's under here. Coloring pages and crayons. Why would they have crayons in a church?"

"Some churches have children sit with their parents during the sermon. These activity sheets would keep the children occupied."

"Oh." Adam continued to dig through the cabinets of the communion table. "Did we ever go to church? I think I remember."

"We used to. But we quit going after you were diagnosed. We spent so much time at the hospital. You were considered high-risk because of your initial white blood cell count. And then you got a fever. So, we pretty much moved in to the children's hospital." Her foot moved against the carpet, making the sound of corduroy pants swishing.

"There was a little desk in all the rooms, remember? I set up my laptop, plugged in my cell phone. There was even a post office off the lobby of the main hospital."

He made a noncommittal sound.

She kept staring at the votive candles. "There was a chapel at the hospital too. I guess we could have gone. But, I really didn't have anything to say to a God who allows children to get cancer. You were young, but . . . some of the children there were so little, running around in teddy bear hospital gowns pulling their IV poles behind them. I couldn't stand it."

Adam came to stand beside Rachel and slipped his hot hand into hers. They stood together staring at the candles.

Then Adam broke the moment by dashing forward. "Look at this!" Adam waved one of the coloring pages he'd spilled earlier.

The paper showed a cartoon drawing of a man in an Old Testament robe holding two stone tablets while standing on a mountain. Below him a group of people were kneeling to an idol in the shape of a bull.

She shrugged, "The Ten Commandments. It's a story to explain how humans are supposed to get along. Don't murder, don't steal, that type of thing. The point is that while Moses was getting the holy rules, the people were already making Ba'al." The name came to her easily, after hearing Levi and Mr. Lee both use it the day before.

Adam studied the picture. "What's a Ba'al?"

"One of the gods people in the Middle East used to believe in." Even as she spoke, Rachel wondered: the creature from the Old Testament was back in the world.

Adam wasn't listening. He'd set down the coloring page and was leafing through the others. "This stuff is cool."

"I know, but we've got to go."

"Eat." Adam held out the basket of bread pieces. She ate two pieces, then her stomach rumbled and she took a third piece. They weren't that big. Feeling guilty she held it up in the air toward the altar and said, "Erm, thank you. And, also, please bless our journey." She raised the bread from forehead to chest, right shoulder to left in the sign of the cross. "Sincerely, amen."

Adam jumped down the stairs and ran down the aisle to the lobby of the church.

"Go to the bathroom and then fill up our thermoses with water, okay?" Rachel started to follow Adam and then did an abrupt about-face. Almost against her will she approached the candles again, her hand hesitating over the matchbox. She lit a match, closed her eyes, and whispered a prayer before lighting candles. For both her parents. For little Daisy. For Craig. For Scott. For the priest who told them to run to the church. The lit candles flickered and then remained steady as Rachel walked away from the sanctuary.

Outside, scorch marks on the street were a sign of the previous night's fierce battle. Suddenly a door from a house down the street opened. A middle-aged Hispanic woman supported the priest from the night before. He stumbled and favored his left side.

"We saw you walking yesterday," the woman said. "But, we didn't know whether you were with that devil. Then we saw him attack you."

"Right." Rachel was too tired to even argue about how unfair that was. "We know him as 'Mr. Lee.' Does he come and do that thing with the lightning and jars often?"

The priest said something in Spanish and the woman translated. "The devil has come three times. He tells us to leave out a tribute or he will pick whom to sacrifice to his god. We know that he is coming when we hear the thundering hooves. Last night John should have been hiding. He shouldn't have been out." The priest covered his face with his hand.

Rachel nodded. "I'm sorry. For John."

Rachel nudged Adam and they walked down the road, leaving the neighborhood behind. It wasn't long before they came to the I-95 junction. Adam started to go south, following the sign to the hospital.

"Hold on, Adam."

"Why?"

Rachel swallowed. The road looked the same in both directions, north and south. Nothing to differentiate the choices, except, if she squinted, black somethings. Energy vultures, or soul-eaters, or whatever they were, swooping against the yellow cloud cover over Baltimore's center. The hospital was familiar; that's where you went for medicine and healing, pre-firestorm. But, post-firestorm—this was a world where ancient gods walked and magic worked. Without a vehicle there wasn't time to try both.

"Come on. We're going north." *And may God have mercy on us if I'm wrong.*

THIRTY-FOUR

They'd only been walking for half an hour when Adam suddenly dropped to the ground, groaning. "My arm."

Rachel kneeled down and, with Adam's help, unwrapped the bandage. She couldn't hold in a gasp. During the night the black blob had grown from the size of a half-dollar to a solid black ring around his arm, the tar-like substance sitting two centimeters off of Adam's skin. The area of the arm below the ring was pale, the blood supply cut off.

Rachel's stomach clenched. "Can you wriggle your fingers for me? Do they feel numb at all?"

"No, they hurt. The whole arm hurts. All the way to my shoulder." He shook, his legs jittered, his face contorted. "Mom! Make it stop."

"Can you wait an hour? Try to get to the next green sign?"

He ignored her, banging his right fist on the ground.

"Okay, alright, hold on." Four capsules left. She could give him a double dose—all four at once—or try to make it last. The pain wasn't going to stop—the argument for pacing it out—but they needed to move fast, before he was too incapacitated.

These were the moments when she hated being a single mom. She was tired of being in charge, trying to guess what to do.

"There are four pills left. Two is a normal dose." Rachel touched his shoulder. "How many do you want?"

He looked at her, his mouth hanging open, panting.

"You know your body." It was hard to let him make the decision, but she had to trust him. "We have to keep walking."

"Two of them. I need two." His hazel eyes pleaded with her. "I'm sorry. After that, I'll walk."

Choked up at his determination, Rachel shook her head, "You don't need to be sorry." She handed him the water.

He popped the pills.

They walked again.

Mile after mile, the landscape didn't change as they headed northeast up the I-95 corridor. No people, no animals, no cars, just the road and the burned out vegetation that used to be trees on either side of the highway. The sun hung in the sky, a dim lightbulb behind yellow clouds. Anxiety clawed at Rachel, soured her stomach. When she saw beads of sweat on Adam's forehead, she kept walking, one foot in front of other. Just like him. There was nothing else to do.

Daydreams came easily with walking. She remembered how happy they'd been when Adam was released from the hospital. How she'd arrived with one bag of pajamas and socks and come home with stuffed animals, toys, gifts, and a seven-inch binder of instructions from the hospital. Dividers in the binder with headings like: General Information, Diagnosis, Treatment Plan, Drug Information, Blood Counts, Family Needs, Nutrition, Glossary. That first night home, Adam had walked ahead of her into the house and then run into his father's open arms. Pure joy. She wasn't sure which of them had teared up first, but soon Craig, Rachel, and Adam were in a tight hug, reaffirming, reminding each other through touch that, for the moment, all was well.

"This is our exit." It was hard to speak, the air hot and dusty. She passed Adam the thermos, before taking a drink herself, and put it away.

By midafternoon they were away from city streets and into a flattened suburbia that would soon be rural. They followed a main road with abandoned neighborhoods by the side. Where had all the residents gone? Pre-firestorm they would have seen tractors in the green corn fields, cars zooming to the big box department stores, parents buying school supplies or planning one last trip to Ocean City. Now trees that survived grew and twisted into improbable shapes or were half shorn off, as though cut by a giant razor.

Finally, the road sloped down. Wild grasses grew along the sides of the road here, an indication they were getting close to water. They followed the road as it curved under a metal bridge and they reached the banks of the Susquehanna River. Rachel wrinkled her nose at an unpleasant odor of rotting vegetation. Across the river, a speck in the distance, Rachel could see a town. It had to be LaPorte.

"Do we have to go across?" Adam asked. "It's creepy."

She heard his fear. "This is one of the tributaries of the Chesapeake Bay. Even if we try to walk south, we'll eventually have to cross. This may be our best chance. So," Rachel exhaled, "yes, we need to cross here."

"There's something in the water," the eleven-year-old said. "I saw it over there." He pointed to an area about the size of a swimming pool covered by bluish-green scum. "It smells gross." Adam frowned.

Rachel looked but there was no ripple or movement. "That's an algae bloom. It stinks because it's decomposing. Give me your pack." She adjusted the straps and put his bag on top of hers. Her shoulders protested and she rolled them forward to stretch.

"This bay used to be beautiful, scenic, the largest estuary in the United States." Couldn't blame the Mesopotamian gods, though. It turned rancid long before the firestorm. "The oysters couldn't filter all the crap people put in the water. Crabs died, fish developed lesions and then died, the dead zones spread until there was nothing." Rachel put her hand under Adam's chin until he looked at her. "The good news for us is that it's safe to cross. It is not, however, safe to stand here." She gave him a confident smile and took a step into the water. "We can do this."

Silt swirled up into water already lacking clarity. Warmth surrounded her boots as she moved forward, the sucking sounds making her cringe.

She reached her arm back, and pulled him forward into the water.

A few feet from the shore the silt gave way to stones. Rachel slipped to one side, the weight on her back unbalancing her. "Be careful, the rocks are covered in algae. You can't see where to put your feet through the dirty water."

Adam said, "I can't think right because of the pills. My head's fuzzy."

Rachel had to concentrate on not slipping. When she looked back at Adam, his face was white with fear, his arms out for balance as he slid one foot at a time across the rocks. His bangs were wet with sweat. Rachel's heart squeezed. She looked across to the other side. It shouldn't be taking this long, but their pace was tortuous. They were only halfway there. The river was shallow, maybe four feet in the center, but that came up to Adam's chest. The smell from the bloom was becoming more intense. *This is the worst part,* she thought. *If there is something, it will come now, when we are farthest from both sides.*

"Mom, I can't do it."

Guilt about putting her son through this, anger that she had to, made Rachel sound harsher than she meant to. "You have to! This isn't a ride where you can get off in the middle."

With a whimper, Adam closed his eyes.

"We have to keep moving," she said. "This is the hard part where we can't give up, even though we're tired and thirsty and we can't see the end. I can't walk across for you, I wish I could." She took a deep breath and struggled to soften her tone, "But, I can walk with you."

Rachel waited for him to pass her so she could help steady him from behind, but she wasn't fast enough when Adam slipped. His eyes and mouth flew open as he tilted forward, his wounded arm going into the brackish water. Her outstretched hand clutched at his shoulder.

A zing pulsed around them. Like touching an electric fence, the vibration ran from her toes up her spine to her clenched teeth, leaving a metallic taste in her mouth.

"Go." Rachel whispered from a throat too dry. "Be brave and go as fast as you can."

"Stop it!" Adam screamed at her. His face contorted with emotion too strong for words. "You're the one who is scaring me."

"I'm not scaring you!" Rachel felt something happening in the water, energy running over her body. "I'm the one who is saving you!"

She couldn't breathe; the packs were too heavy, but she didn't want to let them go. They wouldn't survive without their packs. She pushed Adam forward, using her own body to force him into his fear.

The blue-green scum of the algae bloom undulated, the smell nauseating, the motion its own rhythm in water that was still. Brownish shells bobbed to the surface, each one about two feet long, a spike-like tail behind, widely spaced eyes that looked like bumps. Five pairs of jointed legs. Except that some of the legs were missing, the shells had holes, the gills didn't bother to move. Rachel urged Adam, tried to shield him from looking at what was swimming toward them.

Zombie horseshoe crabs.

THIRTY-FIVE

Rachel scanned the other side of the river. A combination of dead and living trees started a few feet from shore and climbed up the sides of a steep hill topped by boulders. Near the top she could see the entrance to a cave. They could take refuge amongst the boulders or start a fire with dead wood and go on the offensive. Why hadn't she grabbed the matches from the church? Rachel looked to her left. The crabs were closer. Three in the front, a few behind them, more erupting from the blue-green scum downstream.

Adam was retching from the stink engulfing the bay, but still flailing toward land. It was shallower now, and the water only reached his knees. Rachel stopped moving, stayed in the water to give him time. She pulled off one of the packs so she could move, dropped it down onto the rocks below. It was pulled away in the current, dragging against the rocks. The rocks. Rachel reached down and grabbed a slimy rock. She wound up and threw it at the lead crab like an opening pitch.

The rock hit the shell and bounced off. It turned to her. Horseshoe crabs weren't supposed to be violent, but Rachel had no doubt of their intent to pull her apart. The energy from the crabs pushed against her, as if already pulling her under. Rachel threw another rock, but it splashed harmlessly between two. Glancing at Adam to see he'd made it to shore, Rachel snapped her attention back too late. The first crab was upon her. The hard shell bumped her a moment before the creature's legs hooked her clothing, climbing her body. The topmost leg sliced open a gash in the skin of her abdomen. Rachel shrieked in surprised pain. Numbness radiated through her body in concentric circles.

Rachel backed away, swinging the pack off her back and knocking it into the creature. It fell with a splash. Two others closed in. She stood in the water up to her thighs and swung her pack again and again in a circle. The ice in her abdomen began to thaw, burning as sensation reluctantly returned.

"Mom!"

Rachel looked over in time to catch the branch that Adam threw to her. It was the size of a staff and Rachel used it to push the closest zombie away. It swam towards her again.

"Stab it," Adam yelled. "Right through the shell."

Rachel sent the butt straight down. It cracked the shell. The body broke into pieces and floated downstream. Wisps of black smoke rose into the air. Remembering the two-headed moose, Rachel ducked away. Another horseshoe crab was nearby. She speared it with the staff. Again and again she repeated the attack, working her way through the swarm. Finally, all the broken pieces of the zombie horseshoe crabs had floated downstream.

Rachel struggled toward shore. She dropped her pack on the ground and threw her arms around her son, burying her head on his bony shoulder.

She looked out over the water and saw black wisps continuing to rise.

"Are they on fire under the water?" Adam asked her in a whisper.

Rachel shook her head. "I don't know, but we should climb up to that cave and take cover. I'm guessing those vulture things will come soon."

Rachel and Adam were almost to the cave when the shrieks began. Uncanny voices raised goosebumps on Rachel's arms. She watched through the bare trees as black creatures with diaphanous wings swooped through the air, opened their beaks, and sucked in the black smoke. They were oddly graceful in flight.

She followed Adam into the cave. Slanting light revealed bright green moss growing along one wall where water trickled down through the rock. The air inside smelled cool and fresh.

His cheeks flushed with excitement, Adam said, "Are those crabs gone now or do you think they'll attack the next people who cross?"

"I think they're all gone now, but I don't know what that black smoke is. It's not a soul, like I thought when Mr. Lee murdered that poor man. These crabs were moving, but not alive—like robots that got turned on by something."

"My arm," Adam interrupted. "Remember? After my arm went into the water, the algae bloom began to move. It's like energy."

Rachel nodded. *What had The Weatherman said about this not being Newton's world anymore, something about being back to the raw stuff of creation?* "Sounds right to me. Energy vultures. They suck up the animating energy from animals or plants or . . . zombies."

Adam shivered. "I'll make a fire so we can dry off. I saw some sticks outside. Do you have the lighter?"

"I do," she said, holding it up like a trophy. "I'll put together dinner." She went to the wet backpack and unloaded the contents, spreading them out to dry. "We lost a pack, but I have some zucchini in olive oil and half a loaf of bread inside a plastic bag."

Rachel set the food down and crossed to her son, kissing him on his forehead. "I know that was really hard, crossing the water. And really scary. I'm proud of you."

"Yeah." Adam lay on his side, quiet and still in front of the fire. He had one arm tucked under his head, but his gaze jumped around the cave, taking it all in as if he expected the shadows to come alive and attack him. Rachel sat down and stroked his back.

"Am I going to die?"

One of the logs in the fire popped and sparks leapt. "No."

He searched her face. "Are you lying?"

"Go to sleep. You need your rest." She straightened his shirt and kissed his forehead again. "We've been in tight spots before. This," she gestured at the strangeness of the cave, "looks new, but it isn't. By the time your birthday comes, this'll just be a memory."

"My birthday?" He was getting sleepy. His mouth fell open, his brows furrowed together. A feeling of tenderness swept over Rachel at his vulnerability.

"Yup. Three more months and you'll be twelve. We should have a party or something. Cake and balloons. What do you want for presents?"

"I don't need anything."

Rachel tilted her head. He lay there sick, with only the clothes on his back, no books, no iPad for games and music, yet he didn't have a list of things he wanted. *You're such a good kid. I don't deserve you.*

"You can't think of anything?" she asked.

"I've got you and Scott. Tamaki." He blinked and lifted his head. "You're getting me a cake, right? That sounds good." His head went back down.

"Yup." She swallowed past the lump in her throat.

"And candles," he whispered. His eyes closed. "Don't forget to invite everybody."

"Sure. I'll mail out invitations when we get back. Should we have a theme or will you be too old for that?"

His breathing—not quite a snore—was the only answer.

Rachel retreated to the mouth of the cave, rolled up her outer shirt to use as a pillow and stretched across the opening, knowing it was merely a show, as if she could keep anyone safe.

Standing at the entrance, Rachel stretched her shoulders and neck, muscles tight from carrying the pack. It should be sunrise, but was difficult to see with the cloud cover. Deeper in the cave, Adam snored. In sleep he sprawled, arms flung out, claiming space.

Rachel hated to wake him, but they needed to move. She tapped his calves and then his lower back, finishing by shaking his shoulder. The same ritual she'd used countless time before school.

"Go away," he groaned, rolling over.

Rachel tried food. "Ready for breakfast? You must be starving after all that walking yesterday."

Adam opened his eyes. "I don't want zucchini."

"You can have the bread. And I made you some tea."

Adam pushed himself to a seated position. "My arm hurts."

"Let me see." She took Adam's arm by the wrist and elbow, unwrapping the gauze to study the black patch. Rachel's heart beat faster. The area still looked like burning tar had been thrown on the arm, but it had expanded up past his elbow. Black lines, like magic marker, streaked down toward his hand. Adam hissed in pain although Rachel was using the barest touch.

Her son had been examined this way countless times in the pediatric oncology ward, sitting on tables decorated with decals of soccer balls and fire engines. The sterile white paper was always the same, crinkling with every movement. Before, the doctors checked outside the body to see what was going on inside. Now the wound on the outside ate its way in, inching closer to heart center. Her stomach turned. Desperation made her rub the skin over her eyebrow, the back and forth movement methodical.

Adam kept his gaze away from his arm, as if he disowned it.

Tears pricked, along with the old anger that she couldn't take this for him. She couldn't take the foul-tasting chemo, the poison that made his hair fall out in the bathtub and on his pillow, the endless needles, and the surgery to put the plastic port right up against his heart wall. It still hurt to see him in pain. Rachel pulled on her hair and shoved her feelings down deep.

"How is going to the bathroom like traveling the world?" she asked.

His open hand rubbed the wall, grating the palm as if causing pain in that hand could distract from the pain in his arm.

"First you're Russian, then European, and then Finnish." She chewed her bottom lip. "Get it? Rushing, you-are-a-peeing, and then you're finished?"

"Give me the pills," he said, his voice thick.

Rachel had to take a deep breath against his pain. "They're the last we have."

"I know."

Sending out a quick 'thank you' prayer to the universe that the pills hadn't been in the pack that swept downstream, Rachel brought them over. Adam swallowed them without acknowledging her, keeping his face to the wall. She shifted her weight from one foot to the other, desperate to do something, anything. "I'll be right outside. We'll leave as soon as you're ready."

Rachel climbed on top of a boulder and watched the water. She heard Adam rustling in their backpack. Her feelings bubbled up and Rachel felt like a failure. She imagined herself sitting on this rock and freezing into an ice sculpture. Then a giant hammer swinging down and smashing through her so that pieces flew everywhere, melting and disappearing. *That's my depression talking,* Rachel acknowledged. *I've got to keep going.*

Rachel sighed as she returned to the cave, filled the thermos with the rest of the boiled water, and zipped the pack. "Were you looking for more food earlier? Nothing is missing."

"I was looking for more pills. Like maybe one fell in the pack or something."

"Oh." Rachel felt Adam's forehead. It was warm, the fever return-ing. Glassy eyes and a lethargic, pale face; the same way he'd get when he needed a blood transfusion. Or platelets. He'd had plenty of both types of transfusions, typical when dealing with a blood cancer. The chemotherapy kills off all the cells. How had that doctor explained it? There were weeds in the flower garden. The combination of chemo tilled the whole effing thing under. And then Adam would need blood.

Plastic bags, each the size of Rachel's palm, were hung from Adam's IV pole. Crimson dripped down the tubing and into his chest. Some kids needed anti-allergy medicine before a transfusion. Not Adam. His body was starving for it, welcoming the thick liquid. They'd joked that on college applications he could put 'mixed-race' and get some type of scholarship. He had blood flowing through his veins from men, women, white, black, brown, and every other characteristic of a good-hearted volunteer. She and Craig had become regular donors after Adam's diagnosis. It seemed only fair given how much Adam had needed.

"Come on, buddy. We're almost there." *Except they weren't.*

Adam was malleable, letting her pull him to a standing position. They set off from the cave, Adam leaning on Rachel. When they got to LaPorte she'd find out whether this gamble was the correct choice. If it wasn't, Adam wasn't going to make it back down to Baltimore. She knew this. She suspected he did too.

THIRTY-SIX

Rachel found their location on Scott's map. What she guessed was LaPorte sat right where the Susquehanna River fed into the Chesapeake Bay, the furthest navigable point upstream for ships. Rachel and Adam were now skirting the county where their house used to be. This area had belonged to the Nanticoke Nation, the 'tidewater people.' Then the French colonials had set up a trading post, but the British took it over. The Americans took over from them and the town traded lumber, grain, coal, whiskey, and tobacco. Finally, LaPorte became a day trip destination of historic lighthouses, charter boats, and charming sidewalk cafés.

Scott's map suggested another reason for the town's rich history. He'd drawn one ley line underneath the King and Queen's seat in Rocks state park and another extended underneath the Susquehanna River. The lines intersected right through the middle of town. If Scott was right that energy paths ran across the lithosphere of the earth connecting land forms and significant natural monuments, and The Weatherman was right that energy was the key to understanding the post-firestorm changes, then . . . Rachel's mind stopped there. She didn't know exactly what it meant, except that this LaPorte place was something special.

A small blue sign reading WELCOME TO HISTORIC LAPORTE leaned on a metal post at a forty-five degree angle. Giant boulders dug out of the granite quarry surrounded the base and formed a rock garden. Rachel and Adam passed through an uncomfortable tingle that Rachel now recognized as the boundary between territories.

They stopped walking. Adam was unable to go any farther. Rachel shrugged off the backpack and stretched her shoulders. She'd been carrying it and letting Adam lean on her since they'd left that morning. Her lower back ached, her toes rubbed raw inside her shoes, the burn from Drossville throbbed and the scabbed over gash on her abdomen from the horseshoe crab was tender, but all Rachel could think about was Adam. She watched him and rubbed at the forehead over her eye, not stopping until she felt the skin start to peel off.

Adam slumped over on the ground, holding onto the pack like it was a body pillow. His face so pale that she could see through his skin to the sporadic beat in his exposed throat. Eleven years old. Cancer warrior. Son. She knelt down and felt his cheek. His skin burned her hand. His entire left arm was swollen down to his fingertips and the black blob had oozed even more, groping its way toward his wrist and up to the shoulder, seeking his heart.

"I'm cold. Can I have a blanket, please?"

The sun burned down. It was dry and dusty. Rachel didn't argue. She unzipped the pack and spread the blanket over his body.

Adam rolled his head away from her, mumbling.

"Adam! Look at me," she cupped his chin, tried to make him meet her eyes. "I solemnly swear that I will fight for you. But, you've got to fight too. This is not how the story ends."

What she didn't say was that she wouldn't know what to do if she wasn't taking care of him. Yes, she realized it was unhealthy. But, that's what she'd needed to do to survive the cancer crisis. Make her life about Adam. Now, in this post-firestorm world of mutations and Misbegotten, she needed him more than ever. He was her history—no one else knew their story, their struggles and triumphs and losses. Craig was gone, Scott was dead. And Adam was her future—everything she'd invested in him, dreamed for him. For them.

Face to the cloud-layered sky, angry, Rachel shook her head. "We have come too far." Each word spaced apart, daring anyone to answer her challenge, wishing someone would, the same way she and Adam had visualized the fight with leukemia. *Mom, I just slurped up some Methotrexate smoothie. Cancer cells running in fear to the tips of my fingers and toes to get away and, uh-oh the Vincristine will be there waiting. Caught in a chemotherapy trap, you big dumbheads!*

"I will not lose you."

Rachel stood up, shoved the map into her pocket, and used the back of her hand to wipe her face. She couldn't seem to breathe. "I won't, Adam. I won't do it. Do you understand me?"

No answer.

She stared beyond the sign, down what should be Main Street, her vision tunneling, bringing the area into sharp focus. There was nothing there, only a gray mound. The town was gone. Historic houses, the marina, the public playground. Rachel rubbed her foot against the ground. Gray grit scratched underneath her boot. Could have been someone's soccer ball or doll. The smell of stale smoke lingered in the air. Rachel remembered the fiery tornado and dragon she'd seen in Baltimore. It had come in this direction. Ahead, on a black hill made of what looked like ripples of cooled lava, sat a three-story structure made of pale sandstone. An onion-shaped arch was carved from the middle, balconies crossing the open arch where the second and third floors would be. It sat above the gray desert like a palace from ancient Sumeria.

"That's it. That's the Bathhouse." The statement was true; she felt it resonate deep inside. "We're almost there."

"Mom," Adam said. His right hand pressed against his chest. "Something's happening. I don't feel right." His mouth dropped open as he panted for breath. Then his eyes rolled back in his head and his body jerked in convulsions.

Rachel threw herself forward, tried to use her body weight to hold him still so he wouldn't hurt himself.

Adam smacked her in the face with a flailing hand, his knee caught under her ribs and she inhaled with pain.

Then it was over.

Adam, limp, lay on his back and gasped for breath. He was close to tears, but held them back, his mouth twisting with some combination of pain, exhaustion, and fear.

Rachel scrambled to pull away the blanket and lift his T-shirt. Black streaks, thin like veins, snaked from Adam's shoulder to the middle of his chest, plugging into his heart.

Adam turned his head as if it weighed more than he could move. Bright red cheeks, but his eyes were clear for the first time in days.

"Honey?" Rachel pushed back his hair in an effort to feel his forehead.

He stared into her eyes as if he could see deep into her soul. A warm light glowed from the center of his chest as if his heart had lit up. "I caught a falling star." He spoke in gulps of air. "I made a wish . . . that you would be happy again."

Rachel looked down into a face lined with pain. "Shh. Don't talk."

And then Rachel heard a whisper so quiet it was impossible to hear: *Have faith.*

"I hope my wish comes true." The light dimmed in his chest.

Rachel wrapped her hand around his, squeezing his cold fingers.

Adam closed his eyes. "You're the coolest mom ever."

Rachel couldn't see through her tears. "Adam?" She used the bottom of her shirt to scrub her eyes. "Adam?"

His blanket didn't move; his chest didn't rise.

"No," she said. Felt for a beat. Grabbed his wrist for a pulse. Nothing.

"I . . . need . . . help!" Rachel's body shook. She screamed, "Please, someone, help me!" The words echoed in the empty landscape.

She placed hand on top of hand with palms over his chest. *Compressions. Breathe for him. Compressions.*

Sweat dripped from her forehead onto Adam's shirt.

Inhale, hold his nose, exhale into his mouth. Sour smell. Time passing. How much time? Her arms quivered. *Hand under nose. Just like with an infant. A sleeping infant who looks so angelic that you have to make sure they are still alive. But, no breath.*

No more compressions. No more.

Rachel collapsed in physical exhaustion.

Adam was dead.

PART V

REBIRTH

One night this giant golden bull came
thundering across the sky.
Flames at its heels. Solid and real as could be.

THIRTY-SEVEN

Every human is born dying, but Adam's life had been in imminent jeopardy for years. Rachel had feared, fought against, featured the possibility in her nightmares. It felt, as she melted down into the ground, as if this had always been coming. Cancer had caught up. *No parent should outlive her child.* Rachel's shoulders hunched over, her knees came in toward her chest. The shaking started. The coldness. Her body too heavy to move.

Time might have passed, seconds or hours, because the sky overhead changed, shadows from the boulders moving over Rachel's inert form. Her eyes open, unblinking. No thoughts. Just the shapes of light and shadow moving across the gray sand, moving across her as if she were in the way.

Sometimes she'd think about getting up, wonder why she was on the ground. Then her gaze would move to the blanket, to the body lying underneath, the arm exposed. And it would all start over, her mind skittering away from the sight, the reminder, the knowledge.

And then Rachel felt something in her mind. A tickle. A feather against her brain. Alien, not her own thought: *Do you believe?*

Like watching a movie, Rachel relived separate moments since leaving Hiraeth: a night of sanctuary in a church where she confessed to Adam she couldn't believe in a God who would let kids get sick, performing the sign of the cross and praying out of guilt, the motorcycle gang with their faith in El-Elyon, the lightning fight between the archer and Mr. Lee, energy vultures and zombie horseshoe crabs. Then the struggle of the last few steps to get here, so close she could see the Bathhouse. Adam dying.

The whisper came again: *Do you believe?*

"Yes," whispered Rachel.

Hope fluttered damaged wings.

Do you?

"Yes," screamed Rachel. She pushed herself to a seated position. Frantic, Rachel looked all around for the voice. "I believe." Kneeling, Rachel declared, "I believe it all."

Levi had said anyone could call out to El-Elyon.

"Please, El-Elyon. My name is Rachel. I need your help. Please help my son. Please."

If there were magic words to say, a bargain to be struck, an offering required, she didn't know.

The ground rumbled. The largest boulder of the collection cracked open so that tiny pebbles fell away. Water gurgled out—at the pace of an elementary school water fountain. Just like with Elijah. The liquid traced a path down the boulder through the dust.

Rachel felt a hysterical laugh bubble up. She'd prayed to Levi's god and it had worked. Water. Her son was dead and she got water. A gift that at any other time she would have been so grateful for, a gift that could have saved their lives if Adam *wasn't already dead*.

Inarticulate sounds poured from Rachel's mouth until she laughed. Laughed without humor. Oh, all the old stories were filled with the ironies of the gods and now she was experiencing it.

Rachel got to her feet, spinning in a circle with her arms outstretched. "Thank you." She screamed, "THANK YOU FOR THAT!"

She couldn't force anything from an invisible god, but maybe she could force The Lady if she were tangible. The thought gave her hope.

She scooped her son's body into her arms, cradling him to her chest. He felt lighter, a husk. She walked across the gray sand and up the sandstone steps that cut through the cooled lava. Her throat was sandpaper dry. Her arms ached and burned and her legs moved in slow motion but she urged herself faster. *Can't quit now. Got to keep going. Get Adam to the Bathhouse.*

The door was made of heavy wood. It stood open.

"Hello?" she called out into the darkness. "Is anyone in here? Answer me!"

One more step to cross the threshold, then Rachel lowered Adam to the floor so she could rest.

Beyond the entranceway was an open-roofed room with marble columns. Afternoon light fell on colorful tile mosaics decorating the walls. The huge palace seemed empty; the soft fall of her footsteps the only sound. Matching staircases climbed the sides of the room.

Not questioning how she knew, Rachel picked up Adam's body again and walked to the nearest stairs, going up and up as if she must climb to the sky itself. Her arms grew numb from her burden. Her mind ached with doubts.

Both sets of stairs opened onto a landing framing a human-sized door nestled inside a large green and gold arch.

Rachel walked through the door into an open room. White gauzy curtains covered the windows. Plush carpeting absorbed her footsteps. Low benches with cushions, throw pillows, and blankets hugged the walls. Like the ogee arches on the outside, Rachel recognized the style as Middle Eastern. Wall sconces provided soft lighting.

Rachel saw a set of closed double doors flanked by white columns. This was the inner sanctum.

Rachel held Adam's lifeless body close to her chest and kicked the double doors open.

THIRTY-EIGHT

Golden sconces, like in the outer room, provided light. Candles flickered with delicate scents, instrumental music played from a hidden source, and miniature alabaster statues decorated an alcove in one of the walls. A twelve-foot swimming pool took up most of the temple.

Rachel continued through the doorway and stepped down onto the tile floor. A colorful mosaic covered the center. Soft bubbling came from the black wall fountain on the side that fed the pool. Gauzy curtains covered the window view, same as in the outer room. A delicate plant rose from a vase on the window sill, stem arched to seek sunlight while vibrant ivy draped the entire frame. Rachel approached the water and looked down into a sunken pool filled with clear water and scented rose petals.

Darkness swirled up from the depths.

With a splash, The Lady of the Bath emerged from the water, rising up and up until she hovered over the pool, water falling in a rush from smooth, unblemished skin. The Lady's beauty was uncanny, built with ideal proportions no human had. Maybe six feet tall. Long, graceful arms and legs. Perfect sensuous mouth. Skin pale with the fragile whiteness found in creatures that live deep below the ocean's surface.

Black hair—the swirling darkness from the pool—fell in smooth ripples from her head down to her calves, a kind of moving clothing over The Lady's nudity held back from her face by a silver diadem with a giant green agate set in the middle. A silver arm band encircled her right wrist. Translucent fins fluttered at her calves and her triceps.

The Lady hovered in the air, her black eyes coming to rest on Rachel. "You dare disturb me, human?"

"My name is Rachel. This is my son, Adam." Fresh pain ripped through her gut as she arranged Adam's limbs on the lip of the pool. "We've come to you for help."

"Your child is gone. Even I cannot bring back the dead."

"You will look at him." Rachel was an empty tunnel and her voice a faraway echo, tinny and strange. "He is special."

"Everyone thinks their child's special." The Lady's feet touched the surface of the pool and she walked toward Adam's body. "I should have you removed at once, but I'm curious about you. The mother. What makes you cradle a lifeless body to you, what makes you dare to make demands of a goddess, what makes you think you have anything to offer that I would want? To satisfy those questions, I will look at your son."

Rachel crouched beside Adam and studied The Lady. She didn't miss the sympathy in The Lady's eyes or the whispered, "So much pain for one so young."

She looked to Rachel and sighed. "I'm afraid you will be disappointed, but I'll show you." She placed her hands over Adam's feet and slowly drew them up his legs. Nothing happened. "His *etemmu* is used up." Her hands moved past his hips to his abdomen and then to his chest.

A rhythmic vibration shook the chamber. The candle flames flickered with the heavy thumping that one hears from an ultrasound machine, one that Rachel was intimately familiar with from her pregnancy. "That's Adam's heartbeat!"

The Lady frowned. Her hands glowed as she spread her fingers above Adam's chest. A faint orange glow appeared in the shape of the sun, pulsating in time with the vibration. "That is not Adam's heart. That is the god Shamash's heart. Why didn't you tell me that?"

"I didn't know."

"What is it doing inside of your son?"

Rachel searched for an answer. "He caught a falling star during the firestorm."

"This changes everything." The Lady's fathomless eyes stared into Rachel's. "Does anyone else know?"

"The girl at the hospital. The Weatherman called her 'Aia.'"

The Lady's mouth twisted. "I'm not worried about her. But if Marduk is still looking for the heart then I'll be a move ahead."

Rachel cleared her throat. "You'll help my son?"

The Lady brought her attention back to Rachel and narrowed her eyes. "There is a price."

"I know."

She raised her eyebrows. "So quick to agree."

"It doesn't matter." Nothing would cost too much.

"I accept your word." The Lady's black eyes searched Rachel's. "With Shamash's heart still in his body, I can try to call Adam back, but he won't be the same."

Rachel shook her head. "I don't . . . what do you mean?"

"I am a creation goddess; I understand the human body at the cellular level. I can see your son's body, what happened to it. When Adam was ill, his bone marrow made poison. His blood was replaced over and over. We will do something similar. For his body to fight the effects of this toxic *etemmu*, I must transfuse some of my own energy to him. Then, hopefully, his body will be able to make its own again. He will be something new, and even I don't know exactly what will happen. There have been children born of Nephilim and mortals before, but not like this."

Rachel rubbed her hands over her face. If there was a chance to bring her son back to life, it had to be done. "Do it."

The Lady shrugged. "It's not your choice, Rachel. It's Adam's."

Rachel jerked her face up. "You said I was the one to pay."

"You must pay for the attempt. He will be given the choice of whether he—his soul—wants to return."

"He's too young to make a decision like that. He won't understand." She stuttered as she searched for words, but the only thing that came out was: "I'm his mother."

Have faith. The whisper was inside her mind again. Too wispy to catch at, something only heard when you turned away.

"Every moment you wait is one moment closer to not being able to bring him back."

Rachel nodded assent.

The Lady took Adam's hand in hers, closed her eyes, and then pulled him into the tub. The vibration of Shamash's heartbeat stopped.

Rachel gasped, surged forward, but the water in the pool glowed. Rachel could not see through it.

Minutes passed. Doubt crept into Rachel's mind.

Then green light shot up from the center of the pool and for a moment Adam and The Lady were outlined, shadows in the water, floating in suspended animation. Their hands were locked as though in a dance. The Lady's black hair spread out in ropy coils. Adam's body jerked. His chin lifted, exposing his throat. His mouth opened in a silent scream.

Rachel's eyes devoured the spectacle, trying to decipher what was happening. The blackness on Adam's arm was pulled into The Lady while green light lit up his arm from the inside.

The Lady broke the surface, pushing Adam to the edge.

"Take him." The Lady looked drained, her body streaked with bruises, head listing to one side.

Disbelieving, Rachel put her hands around his wet body and felt

Adam's heartbeat strong and sure. She grabbed at his left arm and turned it over. The black was gone, the revealed skin pink like when a scab falls off. The marking was still there, faint, but she could see it. Perhaps the discoloration would always be there, a scar to show what he'd fought. Rachel put her face against his wet clothing and sobbed.

"Mom?" His voice was weak, but he was speaking to her.

"Adam!" Rachel pulled her head back to examine her son. Relief and joy made her giddy, light-headed.

"Follow me, The Lady would like privacy now." A young woman had appeared. She led Rachel and Adam out of the temple.

THIRTY-NINE

They followed the young woman to the outer room, shutting the double doors to the temple behind them.

"Sit here," she said. "I'll bring you a meal." She wore a long white shift with one shoulder bare. Her dark brown hair was held back by a headband while a green jewel twinkled like a sequin on her right temple.

Rachel couldn't stop touching Adam, reassuring her senses that he was indeed alive. Soft instrumental music filled the room.

Sitting cross-legged on the floor, Rachel and Adam pulled a short table close. Their dinner consisted of a savory stew with meat and vegetables, grapes, soft cheese, flat bread, snap peas, hummus, and a bean-based paste that went on the flatbread. The young woman poured hot tea into round cups with no handles.

Rachel was so tired she felt like she might fall asleep sitting up. "Thank you for your hospitality. This cheese is delicious."

The young woman nodded, accepting the thanks. "You are guests of The Lady."

Rachel gestured with her spoon. "Adam, eat the stew, you need the protein."

Adam tried a bite. Then he finished the whole bowl and took a second helping. He reached for the grapes and then put a hunk of cheese on the flatbread and ate it together. Adam slurped down a cup of tea and then yawned. Rachel's eyes devoured every movement, measuring his actions against how she remembered Adam, looking for changes after his experience in the pool.

The instrumental music was getting on Rachel's nerves. She fidgeted.

"I'll take you both to your rooms now," the young woman said. "You must be exhausted."

Rachel started to ask about what The Lady's price would be, but chose to keep yet another secret from Adam. "We are, thank you."

Panic woke Rachel. She looked around the bedroom for Adam, swinging her feet from bed to floor and padding across to the door. A vague memory made her turn left and enter the next doorway. Her shoulders sagged with relief when she peeked through and saw Adam sprawled across white blankets.

She tiptoed in and sat on the edge of his bed. "Buddy? Are you asleep?"

Adam groaned. "No, I'm laying here with my eyes closed for fun."

"Right." Rachel nodded. "But yesterday you were dead, so I now reserve the right to check your status whenever I want."

He opened one eye to stare at her. "You're so weird."

"Again. You were dead."

"At least you aren't saying that I had rabies like you did with the two-headed moose."

She rubbed his back. "Do you remember anything? Did you see a light? Get yanked back?"

He yawned. "Something like that. Can I go back to sleep now?"

Rachel stood, but there was one more question that she had to ask. "The Lady said," she swallowed. "She said you could decide whether to come back or not. Did you hesitate? I mean, do you have any regrets about . . . coming back? Did I make you leave someplace beautiful and peaceful?"

"Mom?"

Rachel clasped her hands together, ready for judgment, to hear that her selfishness had robbed her son of Heaven.

"You've got to stop overthinking things." Adam pulled the blanket higher on his shoulder and rolled over.

Rachel blinked. "Okay, then. I'm in the next room over if you need me."

As she shut his bedroom door, Rachel turned to find the young woman from the day before outside her bedroom holding a stack of thick blue towels.

"Good morning," Rachel said.

"Good morning. I'll put these by your bath before I join the morning chorus. Do you need anything else?"

"I don't really know," Rachel said, unsure of how to answer. "Who are you?"

"Sarai. I'm here to help you."

"Sarai? That's an exotic name."

"It used to be Josie. I had to change it when I became a handmaiden." The young woman disappeared into the bedroom. Rachel followed. The walls were painted in a neutral tone, the bed was the main furniture in the room, with a wooden table and chair to one side. Colorful flowers emerged from a vase—either clay or limestone—with a swimming fish in relief.

Mesopotamian pottery. Thousands of years old, but I don't know enough to date it. She snorted. *Of course, it could be only two months old, post-firestorm.*

White curtains fluttered in a warm breeze. Rachel stepped through the curtains onto a balcony and realized she was on the opposite side of the palace from LaPorte's entrance. She stood in the middle of a matching ogee arch looking down a rocky cliff to what used to be the Chesapeake Bay, but now appeared to be an ocean. As if the entire eastern shore had been submerged. *Maybe it had.*

Then Rachel caught movement. She clutched the edge of the balcony and leaned forward. People. Lining up along the shoreline and facing the palace so the water lapped at their heels. A village of reed huts dotted the beach between the base of the cliff and the water. Emotion welled up at the sight: relief, surprise, joy. A dark-haired teenager a couple years older than Adam ran across the sand. A man pulled a flatbottomed boat onto shore and called out to him, but Rachel was too far away to hear the words.

The people began singing. To Rachel, standing in the balcony, it felt like being serenaded. A soprano voice came from behind as Sarai walked onto the balcony, her singing joining with the melody below. The song was lovely, the words unfamiliar. The last note held out into the stillness and then the line of people dispersed as they each went back to their previous task.

"That was beautiful," Rachel said. "Do you do it every morning?"

"Of course." Sarai seemed surprised. "We sing the morning chorus to recognize The Lady and thank her for the day." Sarai pressed her palms together at her heart. "Your bath is ready."

"Thank you, Sarai." Rachel gestured to the village. "Who . . . what is that?"

"Our families." The young woman touched the green jewel at her temple. "All the handmaidens are allowed to bring their families."

"Ah," Rachel said. "We passed so many empty houses on the way here. I thought everyone was dead."

"We came after the firestorm," Sarai said. She pointed to the doorway. "Please."

Rachel stepped inside a bathroom. A scaled-down replica of The Lady's room, the centerpiece was a tub of steaming, churning water carved from stone. Built-in shelves held towels, washcloths, scented soaps, and shampoos. A chest of drawers pressed against the wall. To one side was a toilet and sink with an ornate mirror.

"Please help yourself to anything. New clothes are available in the drawers." Sarai ducked her head and left.

Rachel tested the water temperature and sighed in pleasure. She dropped her clothes, grabbed an apricot scented soap, and stepped into the swirling water. Ledges were built along the sides of the tub. As she soaped in a circular motion, Rachel noted how the dirty water swirled down and fresh warm water streamed in from an opening in the wall. Jets of water pulsed against her skin.

After rinsing, Rachel settled against the side, letting her head loll back and her thoughts wander. Rachel adjusted against the jets so the pressure was just right against her sore muscles. A few minutes later Rachel, almost lulled into sleep, heard a sound behind her. Startling, Rachel gasped and ducked down so that the water covered up to her neck.

Sarai stood in the doorway. "Are you ready for me to help you wash your hair?"

"I can do it," Rachel said. "Seriously."

"It is my pleasure and duty. I used to work in a salon back—" Sarai swallowed her words. "Sorry, we're not allowed to talk about before. After I style your hair, I'll escort you to the dining room to break your fast."

It wasn't such a bad thing to have a personal stylist. Rachel's cheeks glowed with lotion, her auburn hair was clean and soft, held up with a gold pin. She'd chosen a cream shirt with crocheted lace at the bottom edge and sleeves, a thick belt, short fawn colored skirt and dark brown leggings from the drawer. New hiking boots completed the outfit. Sarai led the way to a long table on the bottom floor balcony overlooking the village and sea.

"Hey, you got a haircut," Rachel said.

Adam grinned and rubbed his head. "Sarai did it."

Rachel's knees buckled as a sudden memory invaded. Adam's hair coming out in clumps after chemo. She'd made them a hair appointment and gone first, sitting for the swirl of a black drape, the snip of her pony tail donation, the vibration of buzzers. A pixie cut, they called it. A smile to Adam. See? Just hair. Her hand rubbing her scalp while her son took his turn with the buzzers. How young he'd looked after. How naked and vulnerable.

This haircut was different. He looked older, his hazel eyes more pronounced now that there was less hair as a distraction.

"I like your outfit," she said. "Snazzy."

He wore a new pair of athletic shorts, a T-shirt for a hockey team that no longer existed, and black and red basketball shoes.

"Can you never say 'snazzy' again?"

"Why?" She sat down across from him. "It's fun to say. All the z's."

"Bow your head, please." Sarai folded her hands. "We give thanks to The Lady of the Bath, our protector and our patron." She handed a plate to Rachel. "Help yourself. The porridge is made from barley. It tastes like oatmeal."

Rachel scooped the porridge into her bowl and poured honey on top. She took a bite and rolled her eyes in pleasure. "This is delicious."

"Yeah," said Adam, his mouth full.

Sarai said, "The Lady will see you both this afternoon. In the meantime, you are free to explore."

Rachel looked around the palace. She needed information about these gods and their supernatural creatures. "Do you have a library here?"

"We do. The temple has everything we need."

"A library?" Adam's face lit up. "Do they have manga?"

Sarai frowned. "It's different for everybody. You are welcome to look."

"Cool," Adam said. He looked over the balcony. "Wait, Mom, can I go down into the village first?"

Rachel opened her mouth to say 'no.' Instead, her gaze dropped to the pink scar on his arm. She wanted to hold him tightly, wrap her arms around and never let go.

"Yes," she said, but then added, "Be careful."

"Really? I can go by myself?" Adam jumped up from the table as if afraid she'd change her mind. "See you later, alligators." He dashed down the hallway, his voice trailing after him. "Hey, how do I get out of this place?"

FORTY

"This architecture is amazing," Rachel said as they walked to the library across the atrium. The second and third floor rooms hugged the sides to create the octagonal open space. She could have spent weeks studying the tiles, the tapestries, the giant painting that covered the ceiling three stories above.

An attractive young woman walked by, wearing the same long dress as Sarai. The green jewel on her temple twinkled against dark skin.

Rachel sorted through all the questions she could ask, but failed to settle on one before they came to the library and Sarai excused herself. The room was beautiful, but there were no bookshelves lining the walls. It wasn't large, maybe the size of a personal study, but was two stories high. A Persian rug covered the floor, and an elaborate brazier hung from a chain. *Probably in case anyone wants to read at night.* Blue tile with a flower motif covered the upper portion of the room and surrounded elaborate stained glass windows.

The lower windows were open to the ocean view and the warm breeze. Rachel knelt on the cushioned bench in front of the window and leaned out. Soon she spotted Adam's light brown hair. He was running with the teenager she'd seen from her window this morning.

Rachel waved, but neither person looked up. A glance at the sky confirmed that even here, in the goddess's domain, the sun was missing.

Alright, Rachel. Let's get to work. Now that she'd made a promise to personally pay a price for Adam's life, now that her life had directly intersected with supernatural beings from an ancient mythology, Rachel wanted to learn everything she could. Rachel went to the cabinets built beneath the cushioned bench that ran along the sides of the room. In one cabinet she found clay cylinders that were stamped shut. *These must be either private letters or contracts. Stamps are used as a signature by kings, queens, and nobles.* She kept on looking, hoping she'd recognize if something was important.

She unrolled scrolls, admiring the cuneiform, but not understanding the symbols. Large books that told either stories or history, but Rachel couldn't read. *The pictures are nice.* She slammed the book shut and put it back in the cabinet. Wiping dusty hands on her new clothes, Rachel leaned against one of the benches. She had no idea how much time had passed, but she was frustrated. *I'm not a linguist, I study art.* Rachel gave a bark of triumphant laughter. *So that's what I should do.* After taking off her boots, Rachel climbed on top of the benches and studied the stained glass that she'd vaguely admired earlier. Seven windows. A plaque underneath read: THE COUNCIL OF SEVEN.

The first was easy. A figure stood in front a golden sun. His wife stood at his side. Rachel could read the script at the bottom. *Utu-Shamash and Aia.* Next a male figure stood on earth. His cheeks puffed out and a funnel of wind filled the edges of glass. *Enlil.* A woman in a gown sat under a tree while a man knelt before her, accepting a scepter. *Inanna-Ishtar and Dumuzi.* The next window used blue glass to show that the man was underwater. He sat on a throne and wore a horned headdress with a flowing stream of fish. *Enki-Ea.* An older female figure took up most of the next window. Baby faces fanned out behind her shoulders as if she carried a multitude of infants in a backpack. *Ninhursag-Ki.* Rachel nodded in recognition. This was a trope in most religions or myths. "Mother goddess," she said and moved down the bench to examine the last two. A male figure sat in a crescent moon, light pouring down to illuminate the world below. *Nanna-Sin.* Finally, a male figure stood on a mountain. He had a beard in typical Akkadian style and yellow lightning bolts zagged across the glass. *An.*

On the other wall was a separate scene. Blue glass symbolized water again. A woman and dragon stood in side profile staring into each other's eyes with their arms outstretched, hand to talon. Rachel expected to read two names, but only saw *Nammu-Tiamat.* She reached up to trace the glass. Was the woman married to the dragon? Why was the dragon underwater? Loch Ness monster?

Pounding footsteps echoed from the hallway. Adam came running up.

"Hey, Mom, the village is so cool." He tilted his head. "Why are you climbing on the furniture?"

Rachel jumped down and raised her finger to her lips. "Don't tell anyone."

While she tied her boots, Adam rushed into the library. "Wow. Look at all the books." He dropped to his knees to inspect the open cabinets. "Look at this." He waved a scroll in the air and it unrolled. Adam shook his head, a wide grin across his face. "Impossible."

"What'd you find?"

"It's the third book in the series. Remember, I started the series *Calamity: Next Generation* at the hospital? It's not even out yet!" Adam waved the scroll. "I thought I was never going to know the ending. Can I have it? Please? I'll read it tonight and give it back tomorrow."

Rachel looked at it upside down. Drawings suggested it was a manual for how to build a ziggurat. "What do you see?" she asked him.

Adam made a face at her. "It's a portal to an alternate dimension. See? He got turned into a falcon at the end of the last book. That's him, there."

"Am I crazy? Here, let me hold it right side up." She took the scroll and walked to the window to examine it in a better light. It still looked like an architect's plan. "I don't see any falcon."

Adam trailed behind her. "Can I have the scroll back now, please?"

"I'm glad you found what you're looking for," Rachel said, holding it out. "I've been through this whole library and learned more about the Mesopotamian gods and goddesses from the stained glass windows, but I still wish I knew what caused the firestorm." Tingles ran over her palms. The lines on the scroll began to move, rearranging themselves into pictures.

"Um, Adam. Do you see this?"

He peered over her shoulder. "See what?"

"It's rewriting itself." Rachel's head filled with the blazing sun of a desert sky. Screams and blood. A battle. Humans in ancient uniforms with spears and chariots. The Misbegotten were easy to spot. They were taller than humans with perfect bodies, some with animal parts, others made of metal or inhuman materials. One figure, high on a sandy hill, swept his hands through the air and the sand responded by covering the army below so that humans were buried waist-deep and others shouted as they clawed at their eyes.

Another army marched from a different direction. Blue lightning sizzled through the air. Horses, white-eyed with fear, bolted. An unkindness of ravens descended from above, talons extended. A Misbegotten figure—female—hovered in the air and changed form, her neck elongating, her body covering itself with scales to become an enormous dragon flying over the human armies to breathe fire on the figure standing on the hill. "Tiamat!" the figure on the hill yelled in anger. Beasts made of stone flew from the desert floor to smash themselves against the dragon.

One lone Misbegotten stood watching the chaos, sadness and despair etched on his face. Text appeared under the picture: "At this time he walked with two names. Born Utu to the Sumerians, he joined with the younger Babylonian gods and was renamed Shamash. A god of justice, he was the sun. It was Shamash who realized, under Marduk's leadership, the Igigi would kill all humans and rejoice in their death. When The Creator became enflamed against the Nephilim, it was Shamash who agreed to help, to betray his chosen pantheon."

The story filled Rachel's mind again. She saw a sudden monstrous sandstorm, passing over the humans in the middle of the battlefield to gathering up all the Misbegotten. Only Shamash was left behind.

The text appeared again: "And The Creator commanded: 'The Nephilim will remain locked away until the sacred tree aligns. As punishment for setting themselves as gods, they will be forgotten. As punishment for bowing to these false gods, humans will no longer have access to the prime source of energy. They will have to create their own through toil and invention.'"

Misbegotten swirled through the air, their faces peering out, arms reaching forth, desperate magic enacted within the sandstorm to break free. On the battlefield, chariots righted themselves, sand smoothed out, beasts of stone fell apart into inanimate rocks. Ravens departed and the human armies milled around without leaders.

The heavens split open so that blackness and stars appeared like a cut in the blue fabric of sky. The sandstorm spiraled through the split. Shamash rose in the air. His body unforming and reforming to become the thread that held the prison closed.

"What then?" Rachel whispered. She had the sensation of spinning in cold darkness, excitement building until the appointed time on the summer solstice when Marduk moved from his place of exile. He sliced open his former friend. Shamash's body ripped apart, *etemmu* flowing like blood. The Misbegotten were free. They fell to the earth as flaming meteors.

Rachel shoved the scroll at Adam. Her hands tingled with spider silk sparks of energy.

"Rachel?" Sarai stood in the doorway. "The Lady is ready to see you now."

FORTY-ONE

"Wait," Rachel said, taking one more deep breath. "This scroll changed while I was reading it."'

Adam looked at the scroll with renewed interest.

Sarai nodded. "This library is created by The Lady's *etemmu* and changes depending on who is looking for information."

"What's *etemmu*?" Adam asked.

"It's the animating energy of everything."

Rachel tried to say something that didn't make her look stupid, but gave up because there was too much to take in. "Right."

Adam laughed. "So cool." He tucked the scroll under his arm.

"Please follow me," Sarai said.

"I met this guy, Jesse, in the village," Adam said as the three of them climbed the stairs. "His dad set up a net for him on the cliff wall and we played basketball. He said his sister works here as a handmaiden and his dad has a boat and goes out and fishes, but he has to give some of what he catches to the temple. His dad doesn't mind, though, because he's so grateful to The Lady."

"Uh-huh." Rachel answered, not paying attention. Her thoughts were on the upcoming meeting with a goddess.

"We're all grateful to The Lady," Sarai said.

They passed the second floor landing and kept climbing.

"Why is The Lady up so high?" Adam asked.

Sarai said, "The sky is holy, so her quarters are closest to heaven."

"Has she thought about putting in an elevator?" Adam said. "Hey Mom, why do you think The Lady wants to see us?"

"I don't know, buddy."

That's what was bothering her. What was the price? Was she going to become a handmaiden? Carrying around towels to guests didn't seem that bad. She and Adam would be safe. He'd have a friend in the village. They'd get a message to Tamaki that they weren't coming back. Adam wouldn't have to find out that Scott was dead.

They reached the third floor. Walking into the room with the pool, Rachel had a chance to study the intricate mosaic on the floor. A green dragon with wings outspread and breathing fire fought a man in a multicolored robe standing beside a large beast with the body of a lion, an elongated neck, and a serpent's head. A forked tongue tested the air while the front foot, a predatory bird's claw, grabbed at the space in front of it. Flakes of gold in the dragon's wings caught the room's light.

Sarai knelt in front of the pool and motioned Rachel and Adam to do the same.

Water lapped against the sides. When Rachel looked up The Lady had emerged as before, hovering in the air while her black hair swirled.

"Welcome. You may stand," The Lady said. "How do you feel, Adam?"

He looked down, shy.

Rachel nudged him, embarrassed at his lack of manners.

"It's alright," The Lady said. "He probably doesn't remember me."

That, and you're a naked woman, even if you are covered by your hair. Maybe he doesn't know where to look.

"I'm good," Adam muttered.

"Excellent. We'll have a feast tonight in honor of you both. The impossible pair: the mother and the son. Sarai, will you make sure to inform the village and the other handmaidens?" The Lady waved her hand. "Take Adam with you."

Sarai bowed. "Of course, my Lady."

Rachel stared at the mosaic while they left, nervous to find out the price for Adam's life.

"I'm sure you have many questions."

"I do." Rachel looked up and pointed to the mosaic. "I've seen this before. The Misbegotten fighting. What was the fight about?"

"First," The Lady said in an icy tone. "You may call me Nephilim or goddess. I will not be insulted."

Rachel flushed. *Was "Misbegotten" like a racial slur? The Weatherman said it first.* "I'm so sorry, I didn't mean to offend. I'm still learning."

"I accept your apology," The Lady said. She floated down to perch on the edge of the pool. "The fight was about humans and their place in the world."

"I don't understand" Rachel said.

"The Divine Creator made humans and loves them. Some of us—the Anunnaki—accept this. Others—the Igigi—are jealous. They despise humans, finding them crass, base creatures. Mortals have *etemmu* like us, although their bodies are too small to contain as much, and souls, which we do not have.

"Marduk, the serpent-lion you pointed to in the mosaic, discovered that he could capture the energy of dying humans and use it to make himself stronger. He led the Igigi in a great battle and we were all punished by the Divine Creator. Locked away until now. But nothing has changed. If anything, Marduk wants revenge on all humans."

Think, Rachel. This is important. How did Ba'al relate to Marduk? "We went to this town, Drossville. They said a Golden Bull came through."

"Ba'al," she said with derision. "He's a minor deity, gathering *etemmu* for Marduk. Not particularly bright, despite the fact that he glows."

Rachel tapped her toe beside the mosaic while her mind spun. "If you hate Marduk, why do you have this mosaic in your throne room?" Rachel paced, trying to put pieces together, then stopped short as she made the connection. "This is you. You're the dragon. The one who fought Marduk before, right before the firestorm." Rachel took a step forward. "You are Nammu-Tiamat."

"Nammu is my Sumerian, preferred name. Tiamat is Babylonian."

Rachel nodded. "Like Roman and Greek. I got it."

Nammu gave a graceful shrug, her black hair settling like feathers down her back. "Others called me Lilith. Names are important." She shrugged. "And they are not."

Rachel exhaled, proud of herself. There was something else though.

"To fight Marduk, who learned how to steal human *etemmu*, how did you get your power?"

Nammu fingercombed her long hair.

She's not going to answer, but I think I know. "Gods and goddesses need to be worshipped. Prayed to. Sacrificed to. Loved or feared. It's all in the stories, I just never believed them." Rachel marveled. "But then you're dependent on humans. That's what you're doing here, with the palace. Setting up a village to worship you so you'll be strong."

"Aren't you clever."

The Lady's tone made Rachel snap her head up. The goddess was displeased. Rachel's heart thumped with dread. "You aren't going to make me a handmaiden, are you?"

"No," Nammu said, shaking back her hair with finality. "My girls are very sweet and love me without question. You don't really fit that, do you? Besides, you have a different talent; latent, but very strong. Come closer." The Lady beckoned Rachel toward the pool. "This isn't the first time I've saved Adam, you know. I was interested to see if he remembered, but neither of you did. Disappointing when one doesn't receive a 'thank you.'"

"The dragon at the hospital." Rachel fit together another piece of the firestorm puzzle. "Your wings pushed us inside. I didn't know if you were saving or killing us."

Nammu held out her hand. Rachel obeyed the unspoken command and placed hers inside Nammu's, closing her eyes in anticipation.

"You're trembling. Why?"

Rachel opened her eyes. Copying Adam's preteen cockiness, she said, "Well, one never knows the motivation of a deity, right?"

"I've fought to protect humans. I've met with you, personally, although I have a military campaign to plan. And, I've saved Adam's life twice. Why wouldn't you trust me?"

This is one of those moments where your life divides into before and after. Rachel nodded her acceptance. Warmth spread through her body and gathered in her chest as if she had heartburn while a buzzing filled her head until Rachel knew she was on the brink of a migraine. The buzzing stopped. A cold sensation swept across her head from the forehead inwards, accompanied by a crackling noise that caused Rachel to imagine her synapses popping and fizzling in a cellular fireworks show. When she couldn't bear it anymore, Rachel snapped her eyes open and pulled away from Nammu. She opened her mouth to ask what had happened, but became distracted by a subtle, luminous radiance that teased at the edges of wherever she looked. She blinked her eyes, but it didn't clear.

"I've awakened your ability to see energy, the aura around people and certain objects. It will make you better suited for our world."

"Can all humans do this?"

"Yes. It takes many years for a mortal to learn, but I gave you a shortcut."

Rachel turned to The Lady and was dazzled by the thick rainbow, a prism, surrounding the goddess. Protective tears sprang to her eyes and Rachel had to look away.

The Lady stood, the water from the pool forming a spout to support her. "And, I've awakened your spiritual gift."

Rachel blinked, "My what?"

"All humans are born with an innate ability to manipulate *etemmu* and a corresponding spiritual gift. Your instinct is to help other people. With instruction and practice, you can learn to heal. There are humans, descendants of our priests, tasked with guarding the ancient knowledge of *etemmu* and teaching psychic gifts." The Lady trailed her fingers across the surface of the water. "Now you're one of them. You're welcome."

"Thank you?" Rachel said, trying to make it sound convincing. Feeling like she'd been let off the hook, but still in shock, Rachel bowed and backed away from the pool.

The clarity and range of Rachel's sight had been doubled. Now color bounced everywhere, brighter than she'd ever seen, making every object worthy of study, a constant distraction. A repetitive sound intruded and she glanced at the waterfall across the room, her eyes focusing to watch a tiny drop fall from a collected puddle to the tile with an audible splash. Turning to go, her gaze was caught by a terracotta bowl with a broad body and two horizontal handles perched on a ledge near one of the sinks. Unable to stop herself, Rachel reached out her hand to touch it. A sizzle, similar to sticking a finger in an electrical socket, ran up her arm.

Immediately she knew it was called a *kylix*, Greek for 'cup,' and was a type of wine-drinking glass. The almost flat circle on the interior base of the cup was called the tondo. Scenes painted on the bottom would be revealed in stages as the wine was drained. An image of The Weatherman filled her mind, his white bushy beard and sunglasses, one pale finger swirling around in the wine.

"Rachel!"

Rachel blinked, aware that someone had been calling her name for quite a while. She dragged her gaze over to Nammu.

"I . . ." Rachel felt fuzzy. "I knew what that thing was called, but there was no way I could have known. And then I saw The Weatherman. He was stirring wine in that," she gestured over her shoulder, "kylix."

"After you leave my temple you won't be near such a strong source of *etemmu*, so it shouldn't be so distracting." The Lady gave a soft chuckle as she eased back into the water. "The Weatherman? Is that what he calls himself this time around? He gave me that kylix a very long time ago. Quite a character, isn't he?"

Rachel groped her way out of the room to the landing. She kept her hands pressed to her skirt as she walked down the stairs, concentrating on each step so she wouldn't become overwhelmed again.

Adam was on the first floor by the dining table overlooking the village. He waved at her.

"Mom." She couldn't understand his facial expression. He seemed to be trying to give her a message with that one word.

"Rachel!"

Her gaze moved to the figure standing beyond Adam. With a cry, Rachel ran down the stairs.

FORTY-TWO

Rachel threw herself at Naomi and they hugged, both trying to talk at once, the same questions overlapping. "What are you doing here? Are you okay? Where are your kids?"

Naomi held up her hand like a stop sign. "It's a long story, we're fine, we left the hospital about a week after you so we've been here almost a month, and my kids are in the village." Naomi stepped back, wiping tears from her eyes. "I couldn't believe it when I heard the story of the mom who kicked in the temple doors while cradling her dying son, but then I knew. It had to be you."

Rachel pulled back. "Wait, what? What are you talking about?"

"The handmaidens. That's how the village gets our news." Naomi grinned. Her face was thinner, but she had the same smile. "A surprise first, though. Follow me."

They walked to a nearby room where a few people had already gathered. Two large windows looked over the ocean.

"Our sunset yoga class. I remember how it de-stresses you." Naomi swept her arms in a broad gesture. "I'm kinda the village physician until we get someone better qualified. I found a former gym teacher and now we have a class every evening." She held up a finger. "One thing. The chant at the end is a little different, but it's not difficult to catch on. You'll see. Grab a mat from the pile."

Automatically, Rachel obeyed and then followed the teacher into mountain pose, rolling her shoulders back and inhaling the salty ocean air. Naomi set her mat to the right, Adam beside her. Moving through the yoga poses, Rachel's body popped and crackled until Naomi had to fight giggles.

"You're getting old." Adam grinned at her.

"Ugh. Been a while since I stretched. It feels good." Except for pigeon pose. That was torture on her hip flexors. Following the teacher's movements, Rachel brought her right leg forward and then grunted. Suddenly her hand slipped off the mat and touched the floor.

An image flooded through her mind of tea spilling. A handmaiden with dark hair on her knees wiping it up with a towel. Feelings of anxiety.

Someone shook her shoulder. "Rachel," Naomi said. "Are you okay? You spaced out."

Rachel looked around. Blinked. There was nothing on the floor.

"Here, I'll help you up." Naomi pulled on Rachel's right arm. "Are you okay?"

"I'll explain later."

Naomi held her gaze and then nodded.

They finished class and folded their hands in a prayer position. Rachel was used to the teacher saying "the light in me honors the light in you." Instead, the teacher said, "We praise The Lady of the Watery Deeps."

The class answered, "The Lady of the Bath."

The teacher said, "We praise the mother of the cosmos."

The class answered, "The Lady of the Bath."

The teacher said, "We praise the goddess who shows us favor."

The class answered, "The Lady of the Bath."

As the other people put away their mats, Naomi said, "I know your feast is tonight, but I'm starving. Let's grab a snack over at the table. You're a guest of the goddess, so you're entitled to the tithed food."

"What's tithed?" Adam asked.

"Everyone tithes to the goddess. If you want to live here, you join in the morning chorus and you give a percentage of what you make or bake or earn to the temple." Naomi folded her arms on the table. "Now, tell me the whole spiel."

With Adam's help, Rachel gave an outline of their time since leaving the hospital, leaving out Scott's death. When they were done, Naomi shook her head. "That's wild. We had a rough time, too. There was an uprising in Baltimore, the hospital was attacked. By that time we were almost out of supplies and fuel for the generator. The kids and I decided to leave with some others, safety in numbers and all that. After the first night, my daughter Lisa began having these dreams. She insisted we go in this direction. Our group came here, to the palace, and we were invited to stay. My daughter is a handmaiden and my sons are craft apprentices."

A smell wafted toward Rachel. Stew, thick and hearty. Fresh-baked bread. Even, yes, honey. Her mouth watered. "Can't you smell it?" she asked Adam.

"Smell what?"

A handmaiden appeared with a tray holding three steaming bowls.

"Coffee, water, or tea," the handmaiden asked.

Rachel shuddered. *Scott.* "I will never drink coffee again."

"Tea is better for you anyway," Naomi said. "Full of antioxidants. And makes people less excitable." She raised her eyebrows at Rachel, as if in accusation.

"Yeah, Mom. You are kind of excitable."

Rachel pursed her lips. "Whatever." She tried to change the subject, "So, do you like it here? I mean, compared to the hospital?"

"Honestly? Yes. It's slower paced. And working for a goddess is not that different from working for a hospital administration." Naomi gave a little laugh and turned to Adam. "And how do you feel? Back from the dead."

"I feel good." Adam shrugged. "Hey, can I go read my scroll?"

"Sure."

They watched him leave and then Naomi made grasping gestures with her hands. "Spill it, sister. What happened in class just now? You've done something stupid that I never would have approved of and now you need my help."

"I had to pay a price for Nammu, The Lady, to bring Adam back from the dead. Now I'm different. I can't see right. There are all these colors at the edge of my vision and if I touch something then I go into a trance and it's horrid." Rachel's breath sped up as her thoughts whirled.

Naomi looked out over the ocean. "Our goddess is older than humankind and incredibly powerful. She's also selfish and mercurial. Yes, she saved the people in the village. Now they think everything she does is for them. They won't hear a word against her. That kind of blind devotion is dangerous." Naomi looked at Rachel. "One of the things I love about you is how you always believe the best of everyone. Your dear Aunty Realism is asking you to do one thing. Look for motivation, look deep, for every move she makes."

Rachel folded her hands in her lap. "She said she was doing me a favor."

Naomi snorted. "Maybe she thinks she is, but a few minutes ago I picked you up off the floor because you were in a trance. By giving you powers that you can't control, she either made you more tantalizing to other gods or she, at the least, just complicated your life." Naomi shook her head. "I'm worried about you, Rachel. It's never good when the gods become personally involved in your fate."

A handmaiden walked to their table. Rachel knew without being told that they shouldn't talk in front of her. "The Lady of the Bathhouse wants to see you and your son in the morning for more training." She stacked their bowls.

Rachel felt nauseous. *I don't want to.*

Excited whispering, loud to Rachel's heightened senses, came from a group of handmaidens standing close to the window overlooking LaPorte. "What's happening?" she asked the handmaiden clearing the dishes.

"Oh," the girl's face lit up. "Dreamsinger must be coming." She hurried away.

Naomi snorted. "Probably wants a chance to check her hair before he arrives."

It was easy to understand the girls' reaction when Dreamsinger entered the palace. He wore an unearthly bucolic beauty that reminded Rachel of sculpted artwork from a pastoral scene, but with skin a warm Mediterranean gold instead of the cold white of a marble bust. Tousled black hair framed his face with a permanent five o'clock shadow, green eyes, and pouting lips. Trousers of soft brown leather hugged his legs and a white silk shirt opened at the neck, but his bare feet looked callused, as though he had not worn shoes for a long time. A shepherd from *The Arabian Nights*.

"Be careful," Naomi whispered. "Fertility god alert."

As if he'd heard, Dreamsinger glanced at their table. He flashed Rachel a wry smile before heading up the stairs, and Rachel found herself blushing.

FORTY-THREE

From Rachel's window in the Bathhouse, the beach looked like the sky. Hundreds of lanterns hung like twinkling stars, strung from one end of the cove to the other. Villagers scurried back and forth between tables in the deepening twilight, carrying baskets and platters as they prepared the feast. A bonfire glowed like a harvest moon in the center of the beach. A group of people with nets waded into the water up to their knees.

"I need you to finish getting ready." Sarai stood, arms crossed, at the archway to the bathroom.

Rachel touched her hair. The handmaiden had already swept it up to the side and fastened it with a silver clip. "What else do I have to do?"

"You're the guest of honor. I have a gown and your makeup. Everyone will want to see you."

Rachel looked back out the window.

Sarai stepped forward as if to physically herd Rachel into the bathroom and then looked out the window. "Oh. Well, I guess you can watch this part, but just for a minute."

A murmur rose from the crowd. Rachel leaned forward. The group in the ocean spread out, facing the tide, and then held up their arms. Rachel gripped the balcony tightly. She could see glowing swirls in the water that she recognized as *etemmu*. Incoming water surged and wriggling shapes emerged, leaping into the waiting nets. The crowd on the beach rushed forward to help pull the laden nets from the ocean.

"Dinner has arrived," Sarai said. "Hurry or you'll be late."

The gown was a forest-green sheath that clung to Rachel's curves. The front pretended to be modest, tracing her collarbone from one side to the other, but the whole back was open, revealing Rachel's spine. Delicate emerald pendant earrings hung straight and Sarai had stained her lips with a berry-scented balm.

"I feel undressed rather than dressed."

"You look stunning."

Another handmaiden stepped into the doorway, wearing the typical one-shoulder-bare white dress. She sneered, "I guess someone wants to catch the Dreamsinger's attention."

Surprised at the venom, Rachel stared. An aura around the young woman glowed dark green, blue, and purple, as if she were the center of an angry bruise. It took a moment for Rachel to see past the aura to notice the facial resemblance between the young woman and Naomi. "Lisa."

The young woman stiffened. "The Lady has renamed me Lyla and my life began three weeks ago."

"Oh," Rachel said, unsure how to respond. Luckily, Adam pushed into the room. "Can we go down now?" He stopped, his eyebrows going up. "Whoa. You look weird. I mean good weird. You know, not like yourself."

Sarai sighed, but Rachel laughed. "I still need shoes. If you don't want to wait, you can go down with Lyla to the party. Naomi said she'd meet us down there."

Lyla shook her head. "Sorry, I can't help. The Lady needs me." She flounced out of the room.

Rachel was secretly relieved. Even though Lisa/Lyla was Naomi's daughter and Rachel didn't know what aura colors meant, her maternal instinct told her that Adam was safer on his own.

"Newbies." Sarai rolled her eyes. "And, she's jealous. We all are after seeing the way Dreamsinger singled you out."

"Um." Adam seemed uncomfortable. "I'll head down now."

"Tell Naomi I'll be right there."

After he was gone, Sarai held up a pair of strappy, heeled sandals.

Rachel shook her head. "No way. How can I walk on the beach in those?"

"Trust me. They make the outfit."

Rachel held onto Sarai's shoulder for balance while she zipped up the back of the sandals. "Alright, I'm off. Thanks for your help."

Sarai said. "Promise me one thing. When Dreamsinger kisses you, stop everything you are doing and find me. Keep your lips in the exact pose and kiss me."

"No."

"It's the closest I'll ever come to kissing him. Don't deny me this." Sarai reached out. "One last touch. Literally." She tweaked Rachel's nipples so they stood out through the thin silk. "Perfect."

"Hey!" Rachel jerked back.

"What?" Sarai grinned. "You can take the girl out of New Jersey, but not New Jersey out of the girl. Bring me that kiss."

"I'm not doing that."

Naomi whistled as Rachel walked down melted lava steps to the beach, biting her lip in concentration.

"Don't distract me. These steps aren't the most even and the torches leave shadows."

Naomi held out an arm to steady her, but Adam knocked it away. "Let her fall. That would be funny."

"I see your impish sense of humor is intact," Naomi said tartly. "I don't miss this age. In my culture you only get another fourteen months before you're a man."

"What?" Adam made an indignant expression. "I get till I'm eighteen before I have to act mature."

Rachel made it to the base of the steps and looked around. Night had fallen, but the stringed lights, reflection of the moon on water, and the bonfire combined to cast a soft glow over the beach. The tantalizing smell of something like funnel cake drifted from one table, and spiced apples came from another. Sharp sticks had been loaded with fish and cooked in the bonfire, then the butts thrust into the sand so anyone could walk up and help themselves. All of the villagers were out, laughing and eating. Someone had brought a guitar and was singing a familiar song, the music emerging in the gaps of conversation. The perfect beach party, but to Rachel's heightened senses it felt overwhelming: everything a little too loud, a little too bright.

A sudden hush fell over the beach.

"Ah, here's my daughter." Naomi looked up the stairs with a face full of motherly love. Rachel turned to watch as the handmaidens glided down the stairs toward the beach, forming two straight lines, and then faced the atrium of the Bathhouse. Nammu appeared in a green maxi dress, hovering in the air as if were water, her translucent fins undulating in a current no one else could see. Dreamsinger stood a step behind and to the left.

"My children, chosen and special to me." Nammu spread out her hands in a benevolent gesture. "I give you this feast tonight so you might enjoy the hard work we've done in creating this Bathhouse and cove." She waited for the cheering to finish. "I introduce to you our guests of honor, Rachel and her son, Adam. Their heroic journey will begin a new set of stories for our world. A story in which humans and gods live in mutual harmony and cooperation." The Lady pointed and Rachel found herself the object of everyone's gaze. She gave a self-conscious wave.

"Enjoy the celebration!" The Lady smiled and withdrew into the Bathhouse. The handmaidens relaxed and melted into the crowd on the beach, laughing and greeting friends and family.

Naomi grabbed Lyla's arm as the young woman walked past. "Li—Lyla," Naomi stuttered. "Are you okay?"

Rachel noticed that the colorful aura surrounding Lyla a few moments before had dulled to a faint shadow.

Lyla's face was pale in the flickering light of the nearest torch and her shoulders hunched over. "I," the handmaiden put her hand to her forehead. "I think I need to eat." Her forearm was bandaged.

"What happened?" Naomi, ever the nurse, tried to look at her daughter's injury.

"Nothing, I hurt myself earlier. One of the girls helped me."

Rachel looked from mother to daughter. Lyla's arm hadn't been bandaged when she'd stopped by Rachel's bedroom.

"Well, let's get something to eat." Naomi gestured to Lyla to lead the way.

"Good evening," the voice was soft, but they all turned to look at Dreamsinger. Flickering firelight flashed on high cheek bones, caught the hue of his eyes. "I wanted to meet the guest of honor. I've heard so much about you." He spoke with a faint Middle Eastern accent.

Rachel swallowed, Sarai's stupid teasing playing in her head.

"I'm not hungry anymore," Lyla said. "I'm going back home." She stalked up the steps, cradling her arm.

Naomi frowned at her daughter's back. "I'm not sure what that's about."

"I'll check on her when I go up," Rachel offered.

Naomi looked at Dreamsinger and gave Rachel a significant look. "Later. No rush. Adam, do you want to hang out with my sons tonight? We'd love to hear about your adventures. News from the outside world is hard to come by here." She linked elbows with Adam and they headed to the nearest table.

Rachel turned back to Dreamsinger. "So, how'd you get your name?" *Brilliant, Rachel.*

"It's one that I use." He looked at her through thick black lashes. "But my given name is Emesh."

"Emesh," she said, so the "m" sound buzzed in her mouth. It suited him, made her think of beer hops and sex and summer.

Emesh raised an eyebrow. "Are you hungry?"

"Not really. We ate earlier." Rachel took a deep breath, afraid she was being boring. "And I don't really like crowds." *Tonight especially when I can hear several different conversations at once and don't know how to turn off that ability.*

"Then perhaps you would join me for a drink away from the crowd."

Unaccountably shy, perhaps with all the insinuation from Naomi that she needn't be a mother tonight and from Sarai that Emesh found her attractive, Rachel couldn't speak, only nod.

He took her elbow and turned her back to the stairs. She could feel his strength, noted that he stood only a few inches taller than her, perfect height for kissing. His skin glowed golden in the moonlight. His aura was a continuous glow around the edges of his body; a myriad of sparkles like liquid gold.

To make conversation, she said, "There's a moon at night, but no sun during the day."

Emesh turned his gaze away from her to the sky. "No," he agreed. "There's no sun."

"Because of the firestorm."

"Yes and no. Shamash the sun god is dead. The sun itself is still there." Halfway up the stairs, Emesh guided Rachel to the right. A path that she hadn't noticed before led into the dark, a garden walkway carved into the cliffside, parallel to the cove below. Excitement built inside her, knowing that they would be alone.

"The garden is my favorite place here," he said.

Rachel could understand that. As they'd left the beach, they'd left behind the overlapping conversations as well. Her shoulders relaxed from the unconscious, hunched way she'd been holding them.

A thigh-high hedge grew along the cliff, trimmed to resemble the motion of the waves, while a riot of tall wildflowers grew at the edge, mimicking a fence. Emesh led her along a walking path in between hedge and wildflowers until they reached a flat-topped boulder. Two small trees stood to the side. Moonlight shined down and the flowers gave off a faint floral scent. Heat from his fingers impressed on her skin.

"Sit." He reached behind his back and produced two glass goblets in one hand. A bottle of wine was in the other.

Rachel's breath caught in her throat. Yet, how was this stranger than Elijah creating a water fountain or a fire that burned cold?

He gave a self-deprecating smile and poured white wine in each glass.

"How decadent," Rachel said, trying to act calm, but her voice came out husky.

"Indeed." He raised his glass. "*Salamati!*"

She tapped her glass against his and brought it to her lips. She savored the tastes swirling in her mouth. Peaches and green apple. He refilled her glass, but Rachel set it down on the stone they used for a table. Her head spun and her skin felt flushed. "Who are you?" she said, emboldened by the wine.

"Just a farmer."

A peacock's raucous call broke the night from somewhere nearby. They both gave a surprised laugh.

"Gods and goddesses walk the earth again." Rachel leaned forward, until her hands splayed across Emesh's chest. "Are you a god?"

He gave an embarrassed half-smile. "I'm a patron of summer, of trees and growing crops. A minor deity, at best."

Summer. No wonder he smelled like hops and sex. No wonder his wine tastes of fruits and flowers.

"Drink," he urged, his mouth next to her neck. His breath caused goosebumps. He held out her glass. Again the tastes of the wine overwhelmed her senses and Rachel leaned into Emesh.

"You're very charming. Are you trying to seduce me?"

"Maybe." His thumb brushed against her mouth.

"Isn't that against the policy?" She swallowed. "In our myths, the gods are supposed to stay away from regular old humans. Bad things happen. Women get turned into swans and cows, men get eternal life without eternal youth."

"Technically yes, but you're not a 'regular old human,'" he said, his accent softening the words. "I have a feeling that you and Adam are going to be very important."

Rachel gave an unladylike snort and sat up straight to put a few inches of distance between their bodies. It was hard to think when Emesh was so close.

The peacock from earlier wandered out of the hedges and into the space where they sat.

"You asked who I was. Would you like to see?"

Rachel inhaled, scared of what she was agreeing to. "Yes."

He stared at the air above the stone table and hummed, his hands coming up and reaching forward. The air shimmered and then his hands tightened on a lyre. U-shaped, the silver instrument had ten silken strings and a carved dragon's head on each side. Emesh swung himself onto the stone and used both hands to pluck and play the strings.

Music flowed around them and with her new vision Rachel saw sparkles of *etemmu* in the air coalescing around the peacock. As she stared, the bird spread his tail, the feathers glowing as if neon pumped through the intricate patterns, swirling around into each eye at the top.

Rachel laughed in amazement. "How did you do that?"

The peacock, perhaps angry, threw back its head and pierced the night with its cry before wandering away, the tail showing its progress through the wildflowers.

Emesh struggled to explain. "Energy can be transformed, changed from one form to another, but can be neither created nor destroyed. I'm pulling *etemmu* from ley lines to call forth what could be, what could happen, but when I stop playing music the *etemmu* leaks back to the nearest ley lines."

"Why do you say 'ley lines'? I thought my friend made that up."

"The term, and idea, is quite old."

"I must have misunderstood," said Rachel. She put the pieces together. Scott had learned from The Weatherman, but wasn't supposed to tell about the old god, so had passed it off as his own idea. "Show me how you manipulated the *etemmu*."

"We're not supposed to."

"Oh," she felt disappointed, denied.

"But, I will for the lovely Rachel." Emesh began to hum while looking into her eyes. *It was the music that made his face light up*, she thought, staring back. His voice was beautiful and sad, a minor key. It created need inside of her, an urge to kiss and touch and talk about everything and nothing. When he took her hands in his own and pulled her up, she shivered. He placed their hands over the nearby hedge, stepping behind her so that she rested against his chest, and he sang to the plant. Rachel wasn't sure if she heard words. It seemed like she could almost make out lyrics, but then they slipped away. Underneath their interlaced hands, the hedge began to move. The wavelike motion parodied by trimming became real as the plants grew and retreated, all in semblance of the ocean below.

Rachel gasped. She felt herself slipping out of the song, but Emesh leaned in so she could feel the heat of his cheek against hers, his heartbeat intimate against her shoulder. The branches began to grow again, into the shape of a dragon's head, the green trembling with life as teeth and scales emerged. Rachel's hands were warm, as if energy poured out of her and Emesh shaped it.

Emesh stopped singing and Rachel slouched to the ground, leaning against the now still hedge. Emesh followed her, laying his head of dark hair in her lap. She was so tired; a little physically, but mostly drained in a different way. Like gestating, she thought. *I created that bit of beauty. Or, I helped to create it.*

They stayed like that, leaning against the hedge. He reached up his hand, caressing her cheek, his eyes watching for her reaction. Then he smiled and Rachel smiled back, heat rising in her face. She had to look away to breathe. *What a strange species we humans are to seek out a connection even after the world has ended.*

It felt good to have the weight of his head in her lap. She let her hand stroke his hair as the peacock, tail feathers fading, wandered in circles pecking at the ground. Emesh reached up and touched her auburn hair with one finger, twirling a strand round and round, then pulled her head down so close that their breaths mingled. "You are intoxicating, lovely Rachel Denueve."

"I think that's your wine," she dismissed with a smile. "You weren't here when I first arrived at the Bathhouse."

"No. I was looking for my brother."

"Your brother is lost?" Rachel frowned.

"He's the patron of winter."

"Of course he is," Rachel said, as if she heard such things every day. "But shouldn't there be four of you? One for each season?"

He smiled, showed white teeth. "Where I come from, there are only two seasons."

"Oh." Rachel nodded. "The nether world. Other world. Under world. What do you call it?"

"I believe you would call it Iraq." He laughed out loud.

"Right."

"Dance with me." He pulled her up, his hand going to the bare skin of her back. She breathed in his scent, and, again, it reminded her of summer. "Our meeting can be a secret from my mother, if you wish."

Rachel tilted her head while she tried to parse this strange remark. Why should she keep a secret? Who was his mother? And, just like that, any feeling of romance disappeared. Emesh didn't have any interest in plain old Rachel. He'd been sent as a spy for his mother, the goddess Nammu. How had she missed that connection? No doubt there were rules and consequences to any relationship between mortal and immortal and she'd almost been trapped again.

"I . . . can't." Rachel tried to give a polite smile as she shoved him away.

"I'd like to see you again." He pulled the silver lyre to his lap, strumming a new song. Walking was difficult. She knew the ground was in front of her, but images from the song filled her mind. Rachel leaned against a tree to unzip her sandals and leave them behind while Emesh sang of wandering in magic, creating dreams, and forbidden love. He wasn't using *etemmu* to make her stay, but he was making it difficult to leave all the same.

FORTY-FOUR

Inside the Bathhouse, Rachel remembered she was supposed to check on Lyla. Unsure what the woman would be doing in the empty palace since everyone else was at the beach party, Rachel searched from room to room. Finally, about to give up, Rachel peeked into one of the rooms where the handmaidens slept. Each bed was built into the wall of the circular room with a soft-looking pile of blankets on top and a nook to store personal items. Only one bed had a girl hunched over, face to the wall.

Recognizing the blond hair, Rachel crept inside. Lyla turned and looked up, her face white as her dress. Blood soaked through the bandage on her arm. No, it soaked through a different bandage on her opposite arm. Now each arm had a bandage. Rachel touched Lyla's shoulder. Immediately Rachel empathized with Lyla, felt her symptoms and pain, and recognized the reaction to losing blood.

"Don't let them find me," Lyla moaned. "Please."

Rachel removed her hand from Lyla so she could think without receiving supernatural stimuli and reached for her missing necklace. "Who did this to you? Who hurt you?"

"Hurry, help me out of this room before someone sees me."

"Okay," Rachel helped Lyla up, holding onto clothing rather than bare skin, and supporting her weight the way she'd helped Adam so many times. "Let's go to my room."

They didn't meet anyone on the way, and Rachel eased Lyla onto the bed, propping her up against the pillow. "Your color looks a little better. Do you want some fruit?" Rachel grabbed the basket and offered it. Lyla reached for an apple and took a bite. "I should get your mom."

"No, you can't tell anyone!"

The door opened.

"Where's my kiss? I want all the details." Sarai stuck her head in and took in Lyla on the bed. "Oh, hell." Sarai shut the door and pulled a chair in front of it to block anyone else. To Lyla she said, "You've really messed things up, haven't you?"

"Did you know about her being hurt?" Rachel demanded. Anger coursed through her. "Who is did this?"

"I did," Lyla said.

Rachel whipped around to stare at her.

Sarai walked closer and shook her head. Reached out to unroll the clumsy bandage on Lyla's arm and began again, pulling it tight. Rachel saw the thin line of blood from below the elbow almost to her wrist before it was covered. She demanded, "Tell me everything."

Lyla dropped her gaze, her mouth trembling like she was about to cry. It was Sarai who answered, "We give The Lady blood offerings." She glared at Lyla's bent head and held out a pricked index finger for Rachel to see. "Just a few drops into the pool, especially when The Lady is doing something difficult like the feast tonight."

"But the Anunnaki aren't supposed to hurt humans," Rachel objected.

"It's a gift," Lyla said. "The Lady would never hurt us. She loves us. We're allowed to give her however much blood we want." She'd finished the apple and looked calmer.

It wasn't the blood, thought Rachel. It's the *etemmu* that comes out with the blood. But, the handmaidens don't know that. She put a hand to her head. Emesh's wine wasn't giving her a headache, but all the secrets were.

"So what are you doing, slicing up your arm?" Sarai scolded.

Lyla's mouth trembled again. "I wanted her to know how much I love her. That I'm so thankful. And, the cutting feels good. Like, not the actual cut, but the release when I get upset. When I think about life before or when I feel lonely, I go up to give her blood so she won't forget me." Tears overflowed and Lyla grabbed the pillow to stifle her choking sob.

Rachel nodded as she replayed the evening. After Dreamsinger had come over to talk, Lyla must have been overcome by jealousy and run up to offer more blood even though she'd already given. It had been too much and, feeling faint, she'd gone to lie down on her bed, but was scared the other handmaidens would find out.

"Didn't The Lady tell you to stop?"

"She never says anything." Lyla's shoulders sagged. "If I could give more then maybe she'd notice me or say 'thank you.'"

"We have to tell your mom. This is serious."

"You can't," both handmaidens said together.

"Seriously." Sarai shook her head. "You can't tell anyone, Rachel. You could get us and our families all kicked out of here. Please, I'll watch over her."

"I'll be good," Lyla whimpered. "Please."

Rachel opened her mouth, but wasn't sure what to say. The Bathhouse had seemed like such a magical place with miracles and music, food and wine. Here was the darkness. Everyone trying to cope with the post-firestorm trauma. Defeated, she closed her mouth.

FORTY-FIVE

"Did you enjoy the feast last night?" The Lady leaned on the edge of the bathing pool, staring out the window framed with ivy.

"It was beautiful. I'm afraid I was too tired to enjoy all that was offered," Rachel said, after a hesitation to determine if The Lady was speaking to her or the plant.

"Hmm. Too bad." The Lady slipped into the water and swam over.

Rachel shifted her weight from foot to foot. *Is she making a reference to the time I spent with Emesh? Was he supposed to find something out from me or have I grown paranoid?*

"Adam, come here."

He approached the pool from where he'd been standing by the doorway.

"What are you scared of?"

He swallowed. "I'm scared of the monkeymen. That they'll come back and I won't be able to fight them."

The Lady nodded. "Courage is being scared and still being able to move. Heroes run toward the flames and endure the burn. That's how they become fireproof."

She pointed at Rachel. "What about you?"

"Ha, how much time do you have?" Rachel took a deep breath. "I'm scared about Adam. I'm scared that I'm not brave or smart or strong enough. I'm scared about Mr. Lee. He wanted to hurt us. I've never had someone want to kill me before."

"Humans who work for the Igigi will be just as evil as their masters."

Rachel's shoulders slumped. She was tired of worrying. At least they were safe in the Bathhouse now, under The Lady's protection.

"I will teach you to use your gift and that will make you more competent in this world. You can release your fear and enjoy what your life brings to you." The Lady raised an eyebrow. "Look at Adam. You'll see a psychic aura flow around him, almost out of the corner of your eye."

It was there, a halo of orangish-red streaked with violet.

The Lady nodded at Rachel's answer. "That shade is cinnabar or vermilion. It means happy. The violet indicates excitement. Once you are away from ley lines you will have to work harder both seeing auras and manipulating the healing power. Also, you can have a wrong impression of color—especially if you think you know what you will see—like a scientist manipulating data to get the outcome he or she wants. Ask questions and stay open."

The Lady patted her hand on the tile. "Sit here, Adam." Strand by strand she parted his hair to reveal the scalp wound from the day they'd left Hiraeth and been attacked by the monkeymen. It had already scabbed over, but was still swollen. The Lady took Rachel's hand and placed it on the wound, then placed her own hand on top.

"Close your eyes and feel what I'm doing."

Rachel obeyed and felt a knot of energy under the palm of her hand. Warmth, the same warmth as when The Lady had opened her eyes to auras, but moving over the wound, untying the knot, allowing the energy to run in smooth channels again. It was like when Emesh had grown the branches last night. She opened her eyes and saw that Adam's wound was no longer swollen.

"Does it hurt anymore?" asked Rachel.

He shook his head 'no.' "That's pretty cool."

"Yeah," Rachel tried to swallow. "Pretty cool." She heard Scott's voice in her head, *Where's your sense of adventure?*

"Please leave us, Adam. I need to speak to your mother." Rachel's imagination went into overdrive. *She IS mad about Emesh. Or, she overheard everything with Lyla last night and knows that I know about the blood sacrifice.* Rachel's heart leaped into her throat, tapping out an emergency message in Morse code.

Adam looked from The Lady to Rachel, a move that Rachel recognized as asking if she was okay. She nodded.

"'Kay. I'm going to get some lunch. I'll see you downstairs?"

"Yup."

The door shut behind Adam.

"It's time to pay the price." The Lady held out her hand.

"I didn't break any rules that I'm aware of." Rachel glanced to the doorway. *Could she escape?*

As if reading her mind, Nammu said with chilling nonchalance. "I can snap Adam's neck if you'd like to change the deal."

Horrified, Rachel came closer. "No. I'll do whatever. I thought you meant—" She swallowed as she tried to collect her thoughts. "The gifts yesterday and the healing."

"Correct. Those were gifts, given because I'm a generous goddess. Too generous, probably." Impatient, The Lady wiggled her fingers. "There is still the matter of payment."

Dread settled in Rachel's stomach, but she thrust her hand into the goddess's. Heat, painful, spread up to her arms and down to her fingers, gathering at the inside of her right wrist. Searing pain. Rachel cried out, arching her back and pulling away from Nammu. The pain receded to a throbbing drumbeat. Rachel opened her eyes to see a silver circle, the size of a quarter, embedded in the delicate skin of her wrist, her skin a thin red circle around it. Inside, a dragon with wings extended wore a diadem with a huge jewel. The same as the diadem that Nammu wore.

"You gave me a metal tattoo?" Rachel asked in disbelief. She touched the metal circle. It sent a shiver through her, like crossing a boundary line.

"This will be how we communicate when you leave."

"Leave?"

"You certainly don't have the gift of eloquence, do you?" The Lady sighed. "Your payment. I expect you to give yourself over to me like all who are under my protection. You will be my instrument beyond these walls, healing others for me and bringing them to my cause."

Rachel shook her head in denial. She didn't want to leave the comfort and security of the Bathhouse. Not when Naomi was here and Adam was making friends. "I don't want to leave."

"That's why it's a sacrifice. I believe you said you would do anything."

Rachel stood there, dumbstruck, the happiness she'd felt the night before ripped away.

"Sarai is waiting outside. She'll give you supplies to prepare for your journey back to The Weatherman's territory. There are still members of our Anunnaki alliance who are missing. Until alliances are confirmed, that must be my top priority." With that, Nammu slipped down into the pool, sinking and sinking until she disappeared.

Sarai gestured. "Take your pick."

Weapons hung on the wall. Not guns, but swords, European and Asian-style, crossbows, staffs, what looked like a Viking battle ax, and other things that Rachel had only seen on TV or in paintings. Rachel reached out a hand as she walked by and swept a wooden spear with a metal tip.

Immediately she was surrounded by the noise of battle, the clanking of armor, the stench of sweat. A horse whinnied and her hands wrapped around the spear. The tip plunged into something with a wet sound, the shaft trembled in her hand. With a grunt. . . .

Her hand separated from the weapon.

Sarai's brows pulled together. "Are you okay?"

"Fine." Rachel wiped her sweaty hands on her pants, trying to erase the sensations from the spear.

"This is a gift from The Lady. Every member of the village has a defensive weapon in case we are attacked." Sarai took a sheathed knife off the wall. "But you can choose something else, if you'd like."

The blade was six inches long with an elaborate curved hilt of antiqued bronze. Rachel wrapped her right hand around the hilt and her fingers slid into place around the whorls representing the ocean. A dragon rode the waves on either side, three claws balanced on the waves and one claw pointing towards the blade, and, Rachel assumed, toward the entry point of a victim. Darkness descended with the sense of wearing a cloak, of hiding. Maybe in an alley?

"I'll help," Sarai said. She untied the belt around Rachel's waist and threaded it through the loops on the sheath. The weight on the belt made Rachel self-conscious.

"Pull it out a couple times."

Rachel practiced until the movement felt more natural. Saria nodded and then opened the drawer of a short table and removed a red utility knife with several different blades. "For Adam."

Rachel nodded and put it in her pocket.

Sarai plucked a bow and quiver off the wall. "This is also for Adam. The Lady thought he'd like it." She held it out as if uncertain how Rachel would react.

Of course Adam needs a weapon, Rachel thought bitterly, *because we're not allowed to stay here. The payment for Adam's life is my happiness and my little boy's innocence.*

Gritting her teeth, Rachel said, "Just hold it out, please. I'll slide my arms through." No need to experience the last archer who used this set. As long as it didn't make contact with her skin, she'd be fine.

Naomi and Adam were waiting at the front entrance. Naomi said, "I'll take them down to the village."

Sarai straightened her shoulders. "They aren't going to the village."

"Says who?" Naomi said in her best bossy nurse tone.

"The Lady told me to personally escort them to the front gate." Sarai narrowed her eyes. "Do you want to argue with her?"

Adam gaped. "What is going on?"

"Why are you leaving?" Naomi grabbed Rachel's right wrist. "What happened?"

Rachel inhaled with pain.

Naomi yanked up Rachel's shirt sleeve and they both looked at the silver circle on the inside of her wrist. With a hiss, Naomi pulled the sleeve back down and pulled Rachel away from where Sarai and Adam were standing. Looking into Rachel's eyes, she asked "What is that?"

"It was the price," Rachel whispered, feeling a sense of shame at being exposed. But, it also felt good not to carry the secret alone and she wouldn't have to tell Adam. It might make him feel responsible. "I have to do what she says and she can communicate with me wherever I go. And, we aren't allowed to stay."

Naomi walked in a tight circle, cursing under her breath, before she stopped pacing and faced them. "So, you guys are going back to Hiraeth. Feels like we've done this before, huh?"

"I'm not leaving." Adam announced as he walked over. "This place is perfect. We have food, we have friends, and we can move into an empty house in the village."

Rachel looked up to the sky for patience. *Thanks, Lady, for putting me in this position.*

Naomi said, "When I found this village I wanted everything to be normal again. Even if that normal meant waking up and singing a song towards a temple." She sighed. "I wanted a house and food and not to have to worry."

"Not sure where you're going with this," Rachel said.

"Me neither," said Adam.

"That's not your path. You guys are the heroes, reluctant or not. The goddess chose you. I may be a secular Jew, but I know how the stories work. The heroes go to their adventures."

Naomi dropped her chin and stared at Adam until he gave a slight nod and dropped his arms. "Be careful out there," Naomi cautioned, giving Adam a hug.

Adam shrugged and wandered a few feet away, pulling at the front of his T-shirt. He looked at Rachel. "I just don't get why we have to leave. How are we heroes?"

Aware that The Lady might be listening, Rachel chose her words carefully. "There's a war coming. Soon. I have to be ready to help."

"What war? Why can't you help from here? They have supplies. Back at Hiraeth we're scrounging for everything."

"A war between gods and goddesses." She licked dry lips. "Yes, the village has supplies. That's why we have to go out to those who need my healing power. And we have to tell The Lady what is happening outside of her territory."

Adam cocked his head. "Wait a minute." He dropped his voice to a whisper. "Are you saying that we're going to be spies?" His eyes grew wide and he whisper-yelled. "That's awesome!"

"Umm, kind of." Rachel didn't like the "we" that Adam had used. She turned to Sarai. "We'll take those packs with food and supplies now."

"I guess I'll never find out how last night went," Naomi sighed.

"No kissing," Sarai called, obviously disappointed.

Naomi ignored her. "But, did you get a chance to talk to Lisa. Lyla. Is she okay?"

Feeling Sarai's gaze, Rachel struggled for a truthful answer. "She's lonely. And hurting, missing her pre-firestorm life, but I think the handmaidens are going to help her out."

"Thanks for talking to her." Naomi waited until Rachel had adjusted her new backpack and then pulled her in for a fierce hug. "I'm proud to be your friend. Take care. And Rachel?"

"Yeah?"

"Use the ChapStick."

Rachel looked back over her shoulder as she walked down the stairs leading away from the palace. Naomi was right. She usually was. As much as Rachel longed for a return to "normal," the choices made to save Adam's life meant that she'd given up that option permanently. Scary, but she'd make the same decision every time.

After they'd descended the stairs cut from the lava, Adam pulled something from underneath his T-shirt and held it up. The scroll. "Look like a labyrinth on the cover yet?"

"Did you steal that?"

He grinned. "I'll return it next time we're here. Seriously though, it's a book that changes. I'll never run out of things to read. Like a pre-historic Kindle."

"It's not prehistoric." She reconsidered. "Before history. Maybe it is."

There was no way they were going back. Surely Nammu knew he'd "borrowed" it.

Soon they felt the tingle that meant they'd passed out of Nammu's territory. Rachel saw their backpack, right by the blue historical marker that greeted travelers. Rachel marveled at how it leaned against the split boulder—no water coming out—as if at attention, that after

Adam's death she would have been so careful. But, of course, when her heightened senses heard the twang of a bow string she realized that she hadn't been so thoughtful. They'd walked into a trap.

"Sit down, Mrs. Denueve. Slowly." The archer's voice recognizable, although maybe a little deeper, a little more forced.

FORTY-SIX

Adam's breath quickened, but Rachel felt strangely relaxed, as if she'd known this was coming, this chance meeting not being chance at all. She smiled at Adam, trying to reassure him, noting the bright orange in his aura. Afraid.

"It's alright. He's not going to hurt us."

In direct contrast to her words, the archer stepped partially out from the shadows of a huge rock, nocked arrow first, string pulled back to his ear. The wolves were by his side, their ears pricked forward, ready to attack whomever their master commanded.

Rachel eased to the ground. She tried to sneak a peek at the man's aura, but it was hard to see because he hadn't fully emerged into the light.

"You've been following us a long way, Captain Lewis," Rachel said.

"Keep your eyes on the ground! You, boy, hold your arms out and turn around. No sudden movements."

Adam pivoted.

"On the ground. Do five push-ups."

Adam seemed confused, looking over his shoulder at Captain Lewis.

"Get on your hands and knees and do the push-ups!"

The archer took a step closer. Rachel saw swirling colors around the captain—red, brown, light green. She wasn't exactly sure what each color meant, but the speed of the colors was alarming. She guessed that red meant anger because it didn't take reading auras to see Captain Lewis was on the edge of losing control.

"You aren't hurt." It came out as an accusation toward Adam.

Adam shook his head 'no.'

Rachel's intuition kicked in. "But you are, Captain Lewis, aren't you?" She heard him turn toward her, felt his gaze, angry and bitter. "After you went through the smoke from the two-headed moose you felt a burning. Then you noticed a small black mole. It grew and burned and hurt as it spread."

She had his complete attention.

"Adam had the same thing. On his arm." She stopped, trying to remember back to the clearing when Adam had dashed for the blue-berries and Captain Lewis had pulled him back. How she'd wanted to thank him and then Scott had come to the clearing. And then Captain Lewis had shot Scott.

"Where's your wound, Captain Lewis?" she asked, but now she knew.

It was Adam who looked away when the archer stepped into the open, the black tar-like substance stretching up his neck, spreading like cancer around his throat, up to his jaw, creeping to his mouth, the top edge almost at the hairline, reaching across his eyes so that he looked as if he wore a black bandana. The bottom edge stretching, like on Adam, toward his heart.

He inched forward, the black wolf against his leg. A guide dog. But the bow was still up, the archer using their voice to point in the right direction.

That's why he'd stopped here and waited. Because Captain Lewis was blinded by the cancerous black energy.

"How did you get rid of it?" Desperation.

Adam spoke up. "We had to go to the Bathhouse. It's right up there." He pointed toward the sandstone palace, not yet aware that the archer's sight was limited. Rachel's head whipped around. But, of course, Adam was being helpful. He didn't know about Scott.

"Give me the medicine," Captain Lewis said. "Immediately."

The frantic speed of the colors in his aura had slowed.

"Point the bow down, Captain." Rachel watched him and then handed the food bag to Adam to carry, settling the backpack on her own shoulders. Her feelings were muddled. He was dangerous, but she didn't feel as afraid as she should. Captain Lewis wasn't evil like Mr. Lee. And Nammu could handle him. "You're almost there. Just a little farther to the Bathhouse."

"No." He dug his fingers into Caesar's thick fur. Dido pressed closer on the other side. "I'm not going anywhere. You'll give me whatever medicine you gave Adam or I'll kill you."

"There isn't a medicine." Rachel didn't know what else to say. She knew he wouldn't believe Adam had died and been brought back to life by a goddess. Or worse, he would believe and think that Adam was now a mutation to be murdered.

Adam stepped close to Rachel. "Hey Mom, I don't think he can see too good."

"I think you're right, buddy."

Rachel raised her eyes to look at the archer, watched him struggling to hide the pain. A curious calmness came over her. This meeting was meant to be. Which of the gods had orchestrated it, and to what purpose, she didn't know. Currents of energy were running, tingling, meeting underneath this place. All her senses were on overload, like drinking one hundred times too much caffeine.

"Hurry up," Captain Lewis growled. "Is this a trick?" His blond brows were drawn together over the blackness covering his eyes. He wobbled, struggled to stay on his feet. Rachel saw the sweat droplets running down his face, wetting his blond hair. As much as she disliked the man, she felt pity for his suffering. One foot stepped forward and, with a groan of pain, Captain Lewis lowered himself into a lunge, using the end of the bow against the ground to steady himself.

"No," Rachel said. She stepped next to him and wrapped his arm around her shoulders. Dido growled at her. "I'm helping your master, although I don't know why." Rachel did her best to lower him the rest of the way gently, but he was so tall and so solid that the end was more of a flop.

She spread him out on the gray sand under the one large tree that shaded the boulders. A shallow creek ran past the roots and then disappeared down the side of the lava hill. Captain Lewis's forehead was fire and his aura colors were weak, even though they should be clear to her here. *His life is in my hands in the same place that Adam died.*

He moaned in pain, shaking his head back and forth.

"Adam," she called. "Thoughts?"

Hands on his hips, Adam took in the scene. "You healed my head, but this looks really bad."

Rachel looked up at the palace again. Nammu wouldn't help. She'd kicked them out and Captain Lewis didn't have Shamash's heart as a bargaining chip.

"I'm going to heal him," she said. "All by myself."

Tentatively, so as not to hurt him, she let her hand hover over the blackness on his neck, sensing it without touching it. Sticky. What she imagined when seeing pictures of animals after oil spills. Rachel tried to take his black T-shirt off, but she couldn't get it over his head. Seeing a knife handle in his boot, she grabbed it, cut his shirt down the front, then pulled it off. She handed the rag to Adam.

"Go dip this in the stream and bring it back to me."

Rachel focused on her breathing, calming her racing heart. *You've got this, Rachel. Nammu taught you herself. Time to shine.* But inside her doubts shouted at her. She closed her eyes and practiced quieting the negative voices.

"Here," Adam said as he thrust the dripping cloth at her. "Can't wait to watch this." He laughed with excitement.

Irritated at his enthusiasm, Rachel took the cloth. Adam loved this new world. But this was serious. She didn't know if she could do it; nerves made her hands shake.

Rachel cleaned off Captain Lewis by starting at the farthest edge. She didn't know if it was working, but stayed with it, feeling her hands warming up as she smoothed the black energy away. White light surrounded her hands as she worked. The metal at her wrist bit and crackled in its flesh casing. She bathed the archer with the water, across the eyes and around the nose. She realized she was humming the lullaby that she used to sing to Adam first as a baby and later in the hospital, trying to soothe fears or pass the time when he couldn't eat before surgery.

It was working. The black was coming off his skin and onto the rag. It was harder on his neck; she had to scrub as if he were a dirty child on Saturday night. Still she kept going, scrubbing and cleaning. He moaned at times, as if what she was doing was painful. When his face was clear of the cancerous tar, he settled into a deeper sleep. Then she only had the last section at the bottom of his neck, reaching toward his heart. This was the hardest and by now she was exhausted, her arms and hands cramping from being conduits for the white energy. Physically and psychically drained, Rachel realized that the white light wasn't some mystical outside force. She was using her own *etemmu* to heal. It hadn't been so evident making branches with Emesh or healing Adam's small cut, but this was much more difficult.

She stood and stretched, her back cracking. Adam and Dido came in close, crowding the archer's unconscious body. "Looks good, Mom. Is it hard?"

"Move back." She pushed boy and wolf away. "It's like I have to picture it in my head at the same time I'm doing it. Like drawing. I don't know how else to describe it."

Caesar, the black wolf, whined at her.

"Don't worry, boy, I know there's more. I just needed a few minutes." She sank back to her knees and folded the T-shirt, looking for a spot that hadn't been used.

"This is taking forever." Adam threw an imaginary ball over the tree's lowest branches.

"Read the scroll. Take the dog for a walk."

"She's a wolf." He slapped his leg and Dido followed. "We're going to look around."

Yes, she was a wolf. Maybe that wasn't such a good idea, but the way she followed Adam around made her look tame. And Rachel needed time without distraction.

"Here we go," she said.

This tar seemed alive as it tried to move away, but Rachel gritted her teeth and wiped away the last bit. She sat back on her heels. His skin was clear. The patch where the wound had been on his face and neck was paler than the rest of his complexion, the same as when The Lady had healed Adam. Captain Lewis's fever had broken; his forehead and hair were soaked with sweat, but now a normal temperature. Caesar crept forward, nosed his master, and then settled in the sand beside his still form.

Rachel felt like there was something else she needed to do, but she didn't know what. So she offered up an uncomfortable prayer. On instinct she prayed to El-Elyon, the god who'd answered her with the gift of water instead of the goddess who'd answered her with a metal tattoo.

"Please don't let the black energy come back to Adam or to Captain Lewis. We're just trying to scrape by down here. Amen."

"You healed him!" Adam shouted an undeterminable time later.

"Shhh! Please don't yell. I have such a headache." Rachel settled her backpack under her head.

Adam's voice came from far away. "There's an apple tree. Can I climb it and get some?

"Yes, but be careful," she called to Adam as a cold nose breathed into her hand. "You're welcome, Dido."

FORTY-SEVEN

They stayed in the shade of the tree, enjoying the warm breeze coming off the sea. Together she and Adam had eaten about six of the apples he'd picked and then shoved more in their pack to take back to Hiraeth. After the first bite she hadn't been able to stop eating until her belly ached and her chin was sticky. Adam had planted the seeds by the creek, but Rachel didn't know if they'd grow in the gray sand. Would be nice to think a little orchard would spring up.

Rachel looked down at Captain Lewis, impatient, ready to get farther away from the Bathhouse. He was taking longer to recover than Adam, but she wasn't as good at healing as Nammu. She felt his forehead—normal—and checked his aura. Much stronger now and the swirling colors were green and light blue. She didn't know what that meant, but she sensed it was a good thing.

In sleep, Captain Lewis had flung out his arms, claiming space. His chest, exposed by lack of a shirt, was muscular with a flat belly. Fine blond hairs on his forearms. Too bad he didn't have a heart.

Watching him sleep, Rachel found herself comparing Captain Lewis to Scott. One was an athlete, arrogant and strong, thick shoulders, Roman nose, competitive with a desire for domination. The other had been a ranger, taller and lanky, red-haired and nurturing with a goofy sense of humor, playful and sensitive. One was dead and the other had killed him.

Rachel shook her head and looked for Adam, saw him sitting by the creek with the bow and arrows from the Bathhouse, admiring the weapons. He nocked an arrow and pulled it back, pretending to release. Looking away to say something to Dido, Adam accidentally let go of the arrow. It shot up into the tree. Dido stood panting at his side. They both stared up. Adam dropped the bow to the ground and scampered up the tree. Dido reared up so her front paws rested against the trunk. *A boy and his dog*, she thought. *He should offer her some water.*

Suddenly a hand grabbed her arm. She looked down in surprise to see that Captain Lewis was awake and staring at her.

"I can see."

Rachel nodded, his hand heavy, but she couldn't look away from his face. Where the archer's eyes had been a bright blue before, now they were almost colorless, like sea glass.

He blinked. His other hand came up, hesitated before cupping her face.

"The sky's so blue. The red in your hair. I can see everything."

His hand left her face to touch his own neck, search the skin.

"It's all gone." Her voice came out raspy. She cleared her throat, moved his hand off of her arm.

"Thank you. For saving my sight." His voice was full of raw honesty.

Rachel nodded, her feelings about the man confused. It was easy to hate an idea of a person; much harder when the person was right next to you, dependent and hurt.

"We'll be off now, Captain. No need to follow us anymore."

He whistled for the wolves. "The least I can do is escort you home."

"Again, no thank you." She raised her voice to carry, "Adam, time to go, sweetie."

The boy was back on the ground. He'd retrieved the arrow and was shoving it into the case. "Aw Mom, five more minutes, okay?"

"We need to go while we have daylight." *We can make it to the church and spend the night,* she decided.

Captain Lewis said, "I saved you from the whip-wielding crazy man. But you still don't like me."

If he'd smirked, she would have hit him. But, there was a question in his statement.

"No, I don't." Her eyebrows raised, inviting him to ask for clarification.

He got to his feet and held out his hand to help her up. "You helped me. Now I'll help you. We're not too far from New Babylon. I can take you there now."

She ignored his hand. Something strange about the way he said the last word. "What do you mean 'now'?"

He turned away, jerked a hand through short blond hair. "Just that. I've tracked you down. And now we can go."

"Nope," she said. "That's not all there is to it." Brown swirled through his aura. She watched, fascinated, as he struggled for calm and his colors changed in sympathy with his emotions. She heard his breath deepen at the same time light blue dominated.

"Come away from this," he urged, gesturing at the bleak gray sand. "Contemporary America has collapsed, but my city is amazing. We have leaders who are decisive and organized. Look, we can't use satellite technology to communicate anymore, right? But, did you know that engineers can daisy-chain microwaves to provide point-to-point communications? Did you know that car batteries can be linked together with a car's alternator to run generators? New Babylon is setting up outposts with those big drum-shaped antennas you see on radio towers. The High Frequency 3-30 MHz band is effective for long-range communications and can reach across the globe because the radio waves bounce between the ground and the atmosphere. They're unaffected by the cloud cover."

He waited for her reaction.

She shrugged.

"Don't you understand? We're going to have a one-world government. We'll finally, for the first time in human history, have true peace. If you live at your little homestead your entire existence is about day-to-day survival. New Babylon is about so much more."

She said, "I'm not an engineer and I don't know how to do any of the things you're talking about. But, it doesn't matter." Rachel rubbed the mark on her wrist through her sleeve. "I've seen how the world has changed and I don't need New Babylon. I also don't think all mutations are bad. There's a new—or old—source of energy and humans can learn to manipulate it."

"Manipulating energy with what? Your mind, like faith healers and psychics?" Captain Lewis snorted. "That's complete nonsense."

"Well, that nonsense is what healed you!"

"What are you talking about?"

"Do you see a hospital? Do you see a pharmacy?" Rachel's voice got louder as she gave in to frustration. "I healed you using my mind and my energy to remove the poisonous moose *etemmu* from your body."

He stared at her for a moment before throwing his head back and laughing. "Where's your magic wand? Do you have a special chant or will any rhyme do?"

"What do you think happened here, Captain Lewis?"

"Your son and I were obviously exposed to a type of virus. The virus could have been carried by the moose, maybe a flea that bit us, maybe the moose itself. After infection the virus spread through our bodies and distressed our skin and tissues creating abnormal cells that were extremely painful. The virus peaked with a fever and then our bodies were able to combat the virus and the effects."

"Interesting theory, but I think you know that you would have died if I hadn't healed you."

"When I had a fever you kept me cool. I assume that's why I'm shirtless?" He cocked his head at her and Rachel cursed herself as her fair skin showed a blush.

"Get a grip, Captain." She took a calming breath. "I used your shirt as a rag to wipe away the black stuff after I used my *etemmu* to separate it from you."

He laughed again. "Very professional description, 'black stuff.' After my fever, the cells were falling off because my body burned them off."

Adam walked over from his position by the tree. "You don't believe in mutations?"

"I believe in them," Captain Lewis said. "And I get rid of them."

"But," Adam shook his head, "my mom uses energy to heal, like the goddess in the Bathhouse taught her."

"Goddess?" Captain Lewis was on the verge of laughing again.

It sounded ridiculous. Rachel closed her eyes. At a loss, she said, "Fine, I'll show you. Does Dido still have the wound from the moose's antler?"

"Yes," he answered, drawing out the syllables. "But she didn't get 'black stuff.'"

"That's because it was a cut and not from the burning carcass. The moose had either too much *etemmu*, which is what happened to you and Adam, or someone deliberately made him that way. It does make sense, you just have to learn the rules. Call Dido over here and let me show you." The words were rash, and after they were spoken Rachel wondered whether her healing gift worked on animals or if she had enough *etemmu* left to spend after healing Captain Lewis.

He whistled for the white wolf but kept his new pale eyes on Rachel.

"Hold her head," said Rachel. "I don't want her to bite me."

After Rachel parted the wolf's fur, she could see the cut. It was about seven inches long and scabbed over, deeper on the end near her flank, more shallow at the top. The edges were puffy and pink, suggesting she was fighting an infection.

Rachel put her hand parallel to the cut. "It's about as long as my hand, agreed?"

"Do whatever you're going to do." He sounded brusque, but Rachel felt that he was becoming interested in spite of his tone.

Dido whined as Rachel spread her left hand over the cut, hovering about a half-inch off the skin. Nervous about being watched, Rachel closed her eyes, but she could still feel their eyes on her, waiting for her to perform a miracle. Warmth spread down her arm, the feeling of healing more familiar this time, but she couldn't psychically touch the wolf's wound. *I'm failing. This isn't working.* Her warmth fizzled out.

"Come on. Show him how cool you are," Adam said.

Without comment Rachel switched hands, but the same thing happened. The ability was there, the power was there, but she couldn't get anything to come out. Stomach cramping with anxiety, Rachel pressed her hand directly on the cut.

Dido leaped back, tossing her head, whining as she came out of her master's grasp, trotting over to where Caesar stared with yellow eyes. He nuzzled Dido, sending a reproachful look to the humans.

Captain Lewis rubbed his hands together, white hairs fluttering to the ground. "Is that how the healing ceremony works?"

Rachel stood there, humiliated. She'd given in to her nerves instead of staying calm and concentrating on the healing. She'd sabotaged herself. *I should have concentrated on helping Dido instead of how I appeared.*

Rachel glanced at Adam, but he was playing, keeping company with the wolves. She inhaled. "Captain, healing is a skill. It takes time and I'm just learning." Fatigue settled over her like a heavy blanket.

Done with Captain Lewis and his ungrateful attitude, Rachel motioned to Adam. He read her face, coming without an argument, walking away from LaPorte without a glance back. Behind her were the sounds of Captain Lewis strapping the packs onto his wolves.

"Don't follow us," Rachel said.

FORTY-EIGHT

Of course, he was following them. She released an annoyed huff of breath and kept walking down the hill of gray sand. Almost twilight—they'd wasted the whole day. New plan. They'd get to the cave and spend the night there. Not as secure as the church, but they'd be alright.

Captain Lewis called. "If you insist on going back to your house, I can take you there a better way."

She kept walking. "How about this? I don't want you anywhere near me and I don't want you anywhere near my son."

He caught up to her, grabbed her arm and spun her around. She realized how tall he was as he looked down at her and snarled, "What's your problem?"

Immediately Adam inserted himself between them, his hand on Captain Lewis's arm. "Let go of my mom."

Captain Lewis jerked his arm away, releasing Rachel.

Adam tilted his head and removed his hand. There was some type of silent communication. Rachel dropped her gaze to Captain Lewis's arm and saw a very clear red handprint. Adam had burned the man. Had he done it deliberately or an accident? Which would be better?

Shaken at her son's display, Rachel said to Adam, "Go ahead. I'll be right there." Adam gave her an unsure look, but she forced a smile and shooed him away. When he was out of earshot she said, "You killed Scott!"

He actually had to pause and try to remember who that was, which just made Rachel even more mad. Finally he said, "The thief with the coffee?"

She said, "He was part of my family. Gone with one thoughtless arrow."

"Not thoughtless. I'm a soldier and I obey a direct order. Your friend was a criminal, not Robin Hood. There's no time for a trial in the field. We knew our supplies had been breached and he walked up holding the evidence in his hand."

"No time?" Rachel said, her voice wavering. "You murdered Scott. I will never forgive you. And I don't . . . want . . . your . . . help."

"I'm going to see you both home safely," he said, his voice calm. "I gave my word. If you don't want me to walk with you then I'll follow behind."

"Whatever," Rachel's mouth twisted as if she tasted something bitter. "I won't stop you."

"You *can't* stop me."

"How's your arm?" she asked, hating herself for stooping to his childish level. "Need me to heal that too?"

"Do you have aloe in your bag or are you going to use your mind again? 'Cause that didn't work so well with the wolf."

She stared at him with what she assumed was the same disgusted expression Adam had given her in the hospital when she refused to acknowledge that she'd seen a dragon in the firestorm. What would it take to make him admit that a child had burned his arm with only skin to skin contact?

She and Adam followed the path to the cave.

The soldier and his two wolves followed them.

We're a miserable game of follow-the-leader. Rachel shook her head and kept walking. She and Adam got to the cave as night fell.

"I'll start the fire," Adam said.

Rachel felt a surge of pride. He was maturing, taking on responsibility. Scott would have been so proud that she was finally stepping back and letting Adam shine.

As if feeling her looking at him, Adam looked up. "It only took me one match to get the fire going!"

"Good job." *He still wants me to watch him.* "Wow. That's a big fire from one match."

"I'm talented like that." Adam sat down beside her, then laid his head in her lap so they could watch the flames together.

"About that," Rachel said slowly. "When did you develop an affinity for fire?"

"Affinity?" He wrinkled his nose like maybe he didn't know the word. "You mean when did I know that I could make things burn?"

"Yes." She swallowed. "It looked like you burned Captain Lewis's arm. Did you mean to do that?"

Adam bit his lip. "Kind of. Like, my heart did that beating thing. I used to think it was because I was scared, but now I think it's when I need to do something. Like, something's wrong and I need to act. I didn't plan to burn him. That happened by itself." Adam scuffed his heel in the dirt. "I'm not sorry. It was my turn to protect you."

"Hmm." Rachel wasn't sure how to feel about a rogue talent that manifested without Adam's direct control. Was some part of Shamash controlling her son?

She bent down to kiss his cheek, grateful once again that Adam was healed.

"Mom!" He rubbed the kiss away. "Why is Captain Lewis following us anyway?"

Rachel wasn't going to explain Scott's death now. But she'd have to soon. In a few days they would be home. So much had happened in one week. "He's going to escort us home as a thank you for returning his sight."

"He's sleeping outside."

"He's a soldier; he's used to it."

Adam yawned and curled up in a blanket off to the side. His breathing took on a rhythmic quality. Rachel pulled a blanket over herself and her sleeping son. Outside, a wolf howled and another joined the chorus.

She was dreaming, standing in the Bathhouse. The Lady leaned on her elbows at the edge of the pool. Angry, her eyebrows drew together, her eyes shot daggers. The temperature in the Bathhouse dropped several degrees. "You're already praying to other gods?"

A feeling of panic swept through Rachel. *I'm a grown-up*, Rachel reminded herself. *I don't have to stand here tongue-tied.*

"You sent me away." Rachel stepped forward. A deep anger surfaced. "And you're a hypocrite. You act like you're so kind and generous, but you don't care if the handmaidens kill themselves bleeding for you. Yes, I know your secret."

"I will not tolerate your disrespect."

"Really, because I've got another problem." Rachel stepped to the edge of the pool. "Even before the summer solstice my life has been about saving my son's life. The thing I wanted most in the world, but you let Adam die—right there outside your palace! Why didn't you step in sooner? Did you think it was funny? Oh, look how that little human cries." Rachel clenched her fists.

A massive ribbon of water gushed forth, surrounding Rachel, wrapping around her and lifting her off the floor, constricting her body. It was like being tossed under waves while still being upright, locked in an aquarium chamber. Terrified, Rachel kicked and fought, but there was nothing to hold onto. The water absorbed her blows, turned her screams into bubbles. Adrenaline spiked. She didn't know how she was breathing, but her nose burned and her eyes swelled. Her heartbeat drummed louder and louder.

Rachel's body gave out and she hung there, empty of fight.

The Lady rose up from the pool in a fountain of water. The rainbow aura pulsed and blazed until it hurt, the brightness piercing Rachel's closed eyelids.

"How dare you question me? I've been alive through countless generations of mortals." Through the water, Rachel heard the snapping of Nammu's black hair whipping back and forth. "Worshipped, adored, feared, until I was wrongfully imprisoned for protecting humans. For centuries I was locked away—by The Creator himself—with all the other Nephilim, not because I did anything wrong, but because of how I was born. The sin of my father and mother."

Rachel kept her eyes closed against the force of the rainbow aura, felt The Lady's mind pressing against hers like something physical. She distracted herself from the pain by holding onto Nammu's words. There was a Creator over the Nephilim who'd punished them all, not just the Igigi. Was there some design in place for the punishment's end or had the gods grown too strong to hold? Some reason that the sky opened above America instead of the fertile crescent or was this random violence?

The Lady said, "You've been given your task and you've pledged to obey. What is your task, Rachel?"

"To learn to manipulate *etemmu* to heal others. To tell you what happens beyond your palace walls. To stand against Marduk."

The water unwound and flowed back into the pool, dropping Rachel onto the floor. She pressed her forehead to the cool tile and coughed out water.

"One more task." Nammu smiled, cold and hard. "One that you are intimately familiar with. Guard Adam. Shamash must have had a reason to choose him. Marduk, and others, will be looking for the human that bears Shamash's heart. He'll look here first, but won't think The Weatherman would dare hide him, not right beside New Babylon." The Lady combed fingers through her hair. "Oh, And Rachel? To be clear, you are my property. I can find you wherever you go." She pointed to the metal circle on Rachel's wrist.

Rachel's eyes snapped open and she stifled a scream as she writhed on the cave's dirt floor, her wrist an agony of fire. She panted as the pain receded, but sleep was a long time coming.

"You're going the wrong way," Captain Lewis called from his place behind them. Rachel looked at the zombie horseshoe river straight ahead and reluctantly turned to listen.

"I know how to get home, thank you."

He took a step forward and used a hand to shield his eyes from the glare. "Yeah, but I moved faster, didn't I? Why cross the river and get everything wet when I know a bridge not too far from here?"

"A bridge," Adam said. "We are definitely crossing on a bridge." He stepped forward like he was going to talk to Captain Lewis.

Rachel threw up an arm across his chest, "I'll talk to him. You stay here."

"Why are you acting so weird?"

"Because that man did something that made me very angry. And, he's not even sorry."

Adam cocked his head. "If he isn't sorry, then why is he walking us home?"

A huge lump filled her throat. "Go practice with your bow and arrows. I'll map out our route with the captain."

With a grin Adam bounded away and picked out a tree for the target.

She watched, from her spot higher on the hill, as Captain Lewis rinsed the wolves' food dishes, efficient, leaving no mark of their camp. She noticed the way he put his hands on Caesar and Dido's heads. With her new vision she saw energy moving from the archer to the animals. He didn't even realize he was using *etemmu*, the innate ability Nammu had said humans were born with.

Forgiving him seemed disrespectful to Scott's memory. She remembered a night at Hiraeth when they'd all played board games. How they'd laughed and negotiated the rules when Adam insisted on doubling the money when landing on 'Go.' Tamaki and Scott cooking in the kitchen, wrapping chunks of canned tuna fish inside the grape leaves from the creek. Falling in love. Before New Babylon and the moose. Rachel had wanted the moment to last forever.

Captain Lewis noticed Adam practicing with his bow and called out, "That tree is tricky. Does it keep jumping?"

Adam ran to gather up the arrows. "The first one went wide, so I moved the bow and then it went the other way."

She didn't have to forgive Captain Lewis, but she did need to work with him to get home. Rachel walked up the slope, stopped a few feet away. "I've come to offer a truce."

Captain Lewis looked at her with an unreadable face. "Why is that?"

"Because this is ridiculous. I'm not going to ignore you or pretend you don't exist while you follow us around."

"You've been doing fine so far."

The only thing that gave him away was the mottled, shifting colors of his aura. Despite his poker face, he was feeling many emotions, probably because he was hurt. And she'd done that. "I'm not perfect. I'm just trying to figure this all out as I go along. Would you like to walk with us? I'd rather go over a bridge than through the river and it seems like you know a shorter way, anyway." She gritted her teeth. "I'd appreciate your help."

He got to his feet and they all set off again, Dido bounding like a puppy to walk beside Adam. Watching them, Rachel wanted to object. She saw the way he played with the wolf. It would only hurt when they had to separate, but she bit her tongue. She trusted Adam to know that this was all temporary.

By the time they stopped that evening only Captain Lewis knew where they were, setting up camp on the shoulder of a road halfway up a hill that he said meant they were moving into the Appalachians. They'd walked on the road for the last hour, but planned to veer west across the mountains in the morning. Baltimore wasn't too far away, they'd already skirted the southern boundary. No lights to show either the hospital or the stadium. More hours of walking tomorrow and then, if all went well, they'd be back at Hiraeth by nightfall.

After moving through camp routine, Adam found a spot away from camp to practice archery. Captain Lewis called out to Adam. "Bring your bow over here."

Rachel stopped gathering firewood and crossed her arms across her chest. Captain Lewis pulled on the string, made an adjustment and handed it back to Adam. Adam nodded his head as Captain Lewis said something. Adam nocked the arrow. It flew past the targeted tree to land on the hillside.

"Try again." Captain Lewis pointed to one farther away, stood behind Adam to make corrections.

Again the arrow missed the target. "I'm no good at this." Adam dropped the bow to the ground. "I want to play with Dido."

"Pick it up." Captain Lewis's voice was stern enough to make the wolves turn around and look at him. "That's not how a man treats his weapons."

Adam clenched his teeth, stared Captain Lewis up and down.

Rachel's face flushed with maternal protectiveness.

"You have enough light to hit the tree five times before it's too dark to see. Stand here until you do." Captain Lewis didn't raise his voice, his posture relaxed, but he expected Adam to obey.

Adam's hands plucked at the cloth of his athletic shorts.

And then he bent down and got the bow. Captain Lewis stood at his shoulder and corrected his stance.

Rachel shook with adrenaline. She'd stood by and watched while Scott was hanged. Hadn't believed they would really kill him. That man was beside her son now. If he did anything. . . .

"Mom!"

The shout had Rachel sprinting past the fire circle to where Adam and Captain Lewis stood.

"I did it," Adam said. He bounced on the balls of his feet. "Look at the tree!" Two arrows stuck out of the bark. He held up his hand for a high five, but moved it when she tried to hit it, using his hand to smooth back his hair. "Too slow."

Captain Lewis laughed and clapped Adam on the shoulder. "Three more to go."

Adam scrambled up the rocky hillside to retrieve the arrows he'd overshot. Bits of rock and debris showered down.

"He learned quickly, but he needs more discipline."

"Hmm," Rachel said. She walked back to the fire circle where she'd spread out her blanket between the fire and the hillside. The wolves still roamed in an almost perfect square pattern around the perimeter of the turnout. *Maybe Captain Lewis gave them instructions.*

"Adam," Captain Lewis called. "See that boulder on the hill? Looks like a natural ledge. Climb up there and tell me what you see."

Moving sideways, Adam picked his way across the steep hillside until he reached the ledge. "I don't see anything."

Captain Lewis nodded.

Rachel spread out Adam's blankets as she yawned. "Come on, Adam, we've got an early start."

"Aww, Mom! It's fun climbing around up here."

"Listen to your mother."

Both Adam and Rachel looked at Captain Lewis. *This is between my son and me. Who does he think has kept Adam alive since the firestorm?*

Adam crawled down the hill, slipping at the end and landing in a heap at the bottom. He rubbed a skinned elbow and gave her a grin. "I've got to finish the last three arrows."

She watched him struggle with the bow, the tip of his tongue clenched between his front teeth in concentration. *He's healed of cancer. I don't have to worry about infection. This is going to take some getting used to.*

When he was finished, he bounded over to her. "Did you see me?"

"Yup. Will you please go brush your teeth with canteen water?"

"Yup." He mimicked her tone.

"Good." She winked. "Cause there's no more dentists." In the semi-darkness he chuckled, baring his white teeth at her in a growl.

"Go to sleep. We have lots of walking tomorrow and then we'll finally be home." She waited while he adjusted the blankets. "I love you, Adam." His name came out garbled as she yawned.

"I love you, too. But I can't sleep." Adam poked her in the leg. "Tell me a story about King Arthur and Merlin and Mordred and Morgan the Fillet."

"Le Fay. She's not a steak." Rachel yawned again. "I'm so tired. I can't wait to sleep in my own bed. I'll tell you one when we get home. I'll go all the way from Uther Pendragon to Mordred's betrayal, okay?"

A shape moved through the darkness and Rachel sat up with a sharp inhale, but it was just Dido, the white wolf's yellow eyes glowing before she settled down with a whoosh of breath, leaning her back against Adam. Adam wrapped his arms around the wolf, burying his face in the thick fur.

Rachel looked over at Captain Lewis. He raised a blond eyebrow as if defying her to send the wolf away.

"Hey, Captain?" Adam said. "How come Dido and Caesar don't have any puppies?"

Captain Lewis's mouth dropped open. "Umm." He cleared his throat. "They didn't hit it off. Usually the alpha male and female of a pack mate for life and produce pups, but Dido keeps Caesar in the friend zone."

Rachel snorted. Adam adjusted his blanket so that his feet didn't stick out and closed his eyes.

"He's allergic to dogs," Rachel said. "I hope he's not going to be stuffy tomorrow."

Captain Lewis came over and sat beside her. Caesar pressed against his leg on the other side. "Being allergic to dogs doesn't necessarily make you allergic to wolves. It depends whether the allergy is to dust or fur or even the hair."

She rolled her eyes.

"I'm explaining something to you. Why are you always mad?"

"I'm not always mad." She used a branch to play with the fire. "But you are always explaining. Did you think that maybe I already understand how allergies work?"

He scoffed. "Are you serious? We're in the middle of an exposed camp, could be attacked tonight, and you're breaking up the team because I explained something to you?"

Rachel crossed her arms over her chest. "I'm not breaking up a team, I'm telling you not to explain to me how to parent my son. No, more than that. Don't parent my son. I've got that handled."

"Good for you, but I'm not going to talk every decision through. And I'm not going to apologize for telling your son to listen to you. I'm a soldier and I'm a man. I won't be nagged into tiptoeing around this camp. If you don't want me here, then say the word and I'll go back to following behind your group. I said I'd see you safely home. That's my assignment."

"And my assignment is my family, so butt out. Stop controlling everyone and respect my boundaries." Rachel felt like punching her blanket a gazillion times and pretending it was Captain Lewis's face.

"Fine." He got up, Caesar right with him, and climbed the hillside up to the ledge. Standing up, he held something toward the sky. A beam of light flashed in a series of long and short bursts.

"Is that your bat code?" Rachel called. "We're not in Gotham." She was trying to get them back on speaking terms. *We have to work together, just until Adam and I are home.*

He bounded down the hillside, keeping his balance on the slippery slope, and went to his own bedroll. She noticed he kept his back to her and his boots on.

She sighed, wishing Naomi was here so they could talk. After Adam's diagnosis, Rachel was on a different schedule, priority-wise and time-wise, than the other mothers in the neighborhood and didn't go to church or PTA meetings anymore. Her social group centered on the doctors and nurses at the hospital. Naomi became her best friend. Stealing a few quiet moments in the break room, they'd talked through Naomi's troubling divorce, through Adam's medical ups and downs, and Rachel's frustrations with her own marriage. *Lonely*, Rachel thought as she dozed off. *I've been so lonely, even before the firestorm. Since my parents died, maybe. Craig was right. I should have seen a therapist for my depression after Adam's diagnosis. It wasn't fair to him and it wasn't fair to myself.*

Sometime in the night Rachel woke to complete darkness. She reached her hand out, but couldn't feel Adam's blanket. She opened her mouth, but no sound came out. And then she heard thunder that grew louder and louder, building to a crescendo. A yellow glow illuminated the night sky. Rachel saw that she was hovering over the camp. Below she could see the sleeping figures, herself included. The glow expanded across her field of vision and she threw her arms up to cover her face and ears, but couldn't stop the wave of sound that sent vibrations through her body.

When the thunder decreased she cracked open her eyes, peeled away her hands, noticed the glow was in a different part of the sky. She saw what caused the glow: a giant golden bull. Almost as if it sensed her, the beast turned its head and she saw the ring through its nostrils, the pointed horns. The bull blew out through his nose, pawed the sky. Then it looked beyond her and began to run again, and when Rachel looked back she saw a metallic cyclone whirling through the sky. Wind swept around her and she tried to duck down, but couldn't move. Just when she thought she'd be pulled into the cyclone the noise disappeared.

Rachel opened her eyes to find Captain Lewis leaning over her, his expression worried. "You were thrashing around."

"There's a golden bull. Literally a giant bull that can run across the sky. I didn't know what Jeremiad was talking about, and a soldier back at Hopkins, but they were right." She choked on the words. "I saw him."

"It was a bad dream," said Captain Lewis.

Her eyes focused on the archer. "I'm fine now," she lied. She stared at the sky as lightning ripped overhead. *That's all it was. A dream caused by the weather.* But she couldn't forget the evil expression on the Golden Bull's face.

"It'll be dawn soon. Try to sleep for another hour." He rocked back to his heels and moved away, whistling for one the wolves.

Wind blew across the hill making dead leaves overhead brush against each other with a dry, chittering sound. Rachel shivered. Except the noise wasn't coming only from the trees on the hillside. There was another, more subtle sound and it was coming from ground level. Red eyes appeared out of the darkness at knee height, shapes backlit by the lightening horizon.

FORTY-NINE

Rats. Over a dozen of them. Each white with red eyes, bared fangs, and the size of a large dog. The group crept forward, spreading out. Snouts quivered while the sharp faces turned toward the biggest one as if waiting for a command. The largest rat made a hissing sound through its teeth.

Adrenaline rushed through Rachel. She grabbed a branch from the embers of their campfire even as Captain Lewis's whistle changed and Caesar, strong and sleek, arced across the campsite with his own teeth bared. Only seconds behind, Captain Lewis reached for his bow. Dido jumped to her feet, standing over Adam, hackles raised.

The foremost rat squealed as Caesar landed, the wolf grabbing its neck and shaking it from side to side. As if this was some signal, the albino rats converged on them. Captain Lewis shot off two arrows before dropping the bow and pulling out a professional-looking black knife, metal window-breaker flashing in the pommel.

Rachel looked over her shoulder. Adam was awake and huddled between her in the front and Dido on the side, his eyes wide.

Two rats climbed over Caesar as the wolf tossed his head and growled. Rachel rushed forward, using the barely lit branch in her hand to singe the fur of a rat. It slid off Caesar and slunk toward her, eyes crazed and teeth yellow. Rachel stepped back. The branch was no good. She threw it down and pulled the knife from her belt.

The rat crouched, its tail twitching. It leaped. Rachel screamed.

Dirty claws ripped at her clothing, the rat climbing her body. Pain flared in her thighs as nails dug in. Rachel could smell fetid breath as the sharp teeth snapped at her face. She held her face away and stabbed at the creature, felt the fur under her hands, but with it so close, she couldn't get enough movement. Using her elbow in a slashing motion, Rachel struck the rat's neck to the side and then used her knife hand to push the creature down. She felt its claws loosen and pushed harder until she could kneel on its ribs. She raised the knife over her head and plunged it into where the heart should be. The rat's face froze into a snarl as black smoke rose into the air. Rachel sat back and let out a shaky breath.

"Don't let the smoke touch you," she called to Captain Lewis.

He'd already stabbed one rat and grabbed another by the scruff of its neck before slicing it open with his other hand. "Get yourself and Adam up to the ledge," he called. The rock ledge that Adam had used to scout last night would get them to higher ground and keep them from the action. "Caesar and I will take care of the rest." He spun around to stab a rat who was biting Caesar's neck.

Rachel checked Adam. Only a few feet away, he stood by the fire circle holding a flaming branch for defense. Instead of scared, his expression was expectant. Ready. The fire on the branch flamed higher while Rachel watched.

"Adam," she called. "Take Dido and get up to that ledge." As long as Adam was safe, Rachel wasn't going to retreat.

He nodded.

Rat bodies lay in a heap across the clearing, but there were still too many of them left. Rachel looked for the largest one, the leader, but didn't see him.

A huge grinding sound came from the road.

"All clear over here," Captain Lewis shouted. His knife dripped dark. "I'll drive the rest toward the road." He whistled for the wolves. Dido loped from Adam's side to take the left side while Caesar took the right. Rachel tightened her grip on the knife and took a spot in between. The rats ran with a strange humping gait. Five of them. All running back down the road toward Baltimore.

"I hate rats," Rachel yelled as she chased them.

Dust built up into a cloud as the grinding sound grew louder.

An arrow whizzed by, hitting one of the retreating rats in the flank. Rachel jerked her head around to see Adam lowering his bow. The same grin as when he'd hit the tree target.

The rat stopped and squealed in pain while the rest of the group scattered before the wolves and humans. Reaching around with its snout, the rat bit the shaft of the arrow so that it broke off. It blinked red eyes.

Adam ran closer till he was near Rachel and raised his bow, but the arrow went wide. The creature lunged forward, its rodent feet scratching against the ground. Rachel held up her knife. She stepped into its path and sank into a crouch. At the last minute the rat changed course. It leaped toward Adam.

A blur of white. Dido had broken from her herding to protect Adam. Her teeth snapped together on the rat's injured haunches. The rat whipped its head around and scratched Dido's face with razor claws. Red gushed from her eye, from her face. She whined in pain, but kept hold of the rat with her teeth, pulling it away from Adam and Rachel.

The rat bit again, its nose burrowing through the wolf's thick fur to get at the neck. More red gushed. Rachel danced back and forth until she could get close to the frenzied animals. The rat's face was buried in Dido's white fur, but Rachel plunged her knife into its back, pressing forward until the entire hilt disappeared into flesh.

Both wolf and rat sank to the ground. Rachel kicked the rat's body away as black smoke rose. "Get me a blanket, quick."

Adam seemed unable to move as he stared down at the wolf. "Quick!"

Adam shook himself out of his stupor. He brought the nearest blanket. Rachel thrust it against Dido's neck. Her closed eyes lost in a mess of sticky redness. Peeling the blanket away, Rachel saw that the rat had bitten and then yanked the flesh—creating a gaping hole in Dido's neck.

"I'm sorry, Mom." Adam's voice trembled. "I should have gone up to the ledge. I should have listened. This is my fault. She's going to die and it's my fault."

Blood soaked through the blanket to Rachel's hands, coating them dark red. *I failed the last time I tried to heal this animal. I'm not close to any ley lines. I don't know what I'm doing.*

"Calm down, buddy." Rachel examined each fear and released it. "Come over and put her head in your lap."

Rachel moved the blanket. Thrusting her fingers down into the ragged hole, she looked up to heaven and said random words: "please," and "just this once," and "she's a good wolf," as they popped into her head. Tingling started in her hands. From warmth to a scorching heat. An amplified pounding kept her from hearing anything else but Dido's heartbeat. Plummeting into a trance, Rachel connected her *etemmu* with Dido's. Their spirits touched. Rachel repaired, picturing the tangles as strings to be tied off, sewing and smoothing. Time floated. Only the irregular pounding of their heart pumping Rachel's life into Dido.

I have to pull away. I'm losing myself. Rachel imagined herself coming out of a deep place, moving outwards to the skin layer. Physically she removed her hands from Dido's neck. They felt like giant sandbags hanging at the ends of her arms. Beyond exhausted, Rachel continued kneeling, head hanging.

Dido whined. She stretched out her front paws and heaved up. Her legs shook with effort. Adam kissed her. "I'm so sorry, girl." He smoothed the fur back on her face.

She's alive. That's good.

Rapid-fire shots erupted from near the road. Rachel squinted through blurry eyes. Everything in her vision was altered and distant, like she was watching a movie. Captain Lewis rolled around the ground with a rat. He thrust his knife through its belly and got to his feet. A huge tank sat in the middle of the road. *A tank?* A soldier, partially out of the hatch, sat behind a mounted machine gun.

The soldier climbed out, dropping to the ground, and another soldier followed. Both wore the black New Babylon military uniforms. After climbing down from the giant metal machine, they unstrapped their helmets. She was floating, locked in her own emergency.

"Hard core," whispered Adam, that familiar hero-worship written across his face.

As the one soldier surveyed the battlefield, the second had a bag in his hand. No more rats. Only red chunks splattered against the hillside. The second soldier picked up two chunks of rat and sealed them in the bag. Captain Lewis and the two soldiers walked over to where Rachel knelt.

"Sir," the first soldier said, "You're chasing down poor, helpless rats. You're quite the hero."

Captain Lewis laughed. "Yeah, didn't train for that at the Academy. But, I knew we were good when I heard the tank coming." He looked down at Rachel. "That's okay though, right, Rachel? Those weren't your good mutations."

Aware of being watched, Rachel put her left foot forward and pushed up to a standing position. She teetered, throwing her arms out for balance.

"Dido," he called. He frowned when he saw her fur. Holding her jaw he tipped her head back and forth. "Oh," he said. "This must be rat blood." He rubbed her ribs. "Rachel, these are my boys from New Babylon."

"We have to go," she said quietly through dry lips.

"What?" He leaned closer. "Why are you whispering?"

"There's black smoke everywhere. We have to go before the energy vultures come."

"Why? We'll kill them too."

One of the soldiers—the shorter—rubbed Caesar and scratched behind his ears. Caesar acted like a shameless dog, tongue lolling and wagging his tail.

Captain Lewis's easy manner disappeared; he was a commander once again. "Soldiers!"

Both men jumped to attention.

Captain Lewis said something, but Rachel didn't catch it.

Adam was examining the treads on the tank, running his hands over the machine in fascination.

The shorter of the two soldiers said, "So we helped put down the uprising in Baltimore, but the situation's unstable. Our first priority is the mutants. When we saw this pack we pursued, but lost them when they ran off the road. Luckily for you guys, we saw your signal last night. We were hoping to find you, and instead we found them." Barrel-chested, the shorter man had a twinkle in his eye and looked to be in his mid-forties. He rocked back and forth on his heels.

"Lucky for us, eh?" Captain Lewis's tone was dry, but Rachel thought she detected warmth toward this man. "We had it under control."

"Indeed, sir," the taller man spoke up. "We can see the carcasses near the fire circle."

"Did you also see the albino bastard jump me from the tree? Didn't know rats did that."

"Yes, sir," this was the shorter, older man who now had a definite twinkle in his eye. "But we didn't want to interfere as you had it under control."

Captain Lewis let out a short laugh and clapped the man on the arm. "Good man."

"Orders, sir?"

Rachel noted the deference these men were showing the archer. "Baltimore." She felt like she was going to pass out, but didn't want to show weakness before these men. "Is the city okay?"

The older soldier said, "Some idiots in the stadium started dumping bodies in the inner harbor. Same idiots thought it'd be bright to attack the hospital and stage a takeover, but couldn't hold it."

Rachel remembered the black cloud that she'd seen when deciding to head to the Bathhouse. She closed her eyes and said a prayerful "thank you" that she'd gone the right way.

He spat on the ground. "We had to string up the insurgents, and leave some of our personnel behind to set up security. Unless the captain here has new orders, we'll be reporting back to the City Consularis about both the Baltimore situation and the mutant rat extermination. I've got the specimen bag to bring back for analysis."

The younger said, "That's why all these towns need to be brought under New Babylon control." He spit to the side too.

The Captain jerked his chin toward the tank. "Alright men. Follow your previous orders."

"What about you, Captain?"

Captain Lewis raised his eyebrows at the younger soldier's question. The man's cheeks reddened. "Sorry, sir."

"I'll walk you to the tank." The captain's tone was ice.

Adam stood next to Rachel. He gave a long whistle. "Someone's in trouble. I'll roll up my blanket so we can leave." He scuffed his shoe in the dirt. "Thanks for saving Dido."

With a grinding noise the tank started up, the treads rolled toward New Babylon.

"You're welcome," Rachel whispered, or maybe she didn't. She meant to.

Captain Lewis walked back toward the fire circle and stopped in front of Rachel.

Her gaze rested on Captain Lewis's legs. *I think I'm going to puke on his boots.*

Distantly, she heard him say, "You and Adam were supposed to get to the ledge. I'm not expecting praise, but you could acknowledge that I saved your life."

Rachel collapsed.

FIFTY

Something cold and wet sniffed at her face. Rachel opened her eyes. "Hello, Caesar." The black wolf blinked great yellow eyes. His jaw opened in a canine grin.

"Hey, goat." Captain Lewis squatted down. "How you feeling?"

"Goat?" Rachel squinted against the dull sun as she propped up onto her elbows. They were in the middle of trees. Rachel recognized the needles of several cedar of Lebanon saplings, standing about her height. *We must be in The Weatherman's territory. Close to home. How'd I get here?*

"Yeah. It's what we call people who faint when they see blood or freak out during combat. Still," he said with a grin, "you did alright for your first encounter." He held up a finger. "Sorry, the moose. So, your second."

"Right." Her head pounded like a hangover. She didn't feel like explaining that she'd saved Dido by using an enormous amount of *etemmu*. He'd never believe her. "And you're not hurt?" He had scabs along his neck, but long sleeves covered any marks on his arms.

"Nah. Just something to add to my other scars." He shrugged as if it didn't mean anything. "I did a tour in the Middle East, caught frag from a landmine. Also tore my shoulder open during a training exercise. Now I've been attacked by angry lab rats."

Rachel looked around. Caesar stood by a tree to the right. "Where are Adam and Dido?"

"They went ahead."

Rachel struggled to her feet. "You let him go alone?"

"It's not far to your homestead and we weren't sure how long you'd be out." He tilted his head. "I carried you here. Figured we should leave before those—what did you call them?"

"Energy vultures." Muscles ached. Sweat broke out on her forehead. "They aren't bad, you know. They clean up the psychic debris. The *etemmu*."

He snorted, put his hands on his hips. "Ah, your 'good mutation' theory."

"Yes, Captain. Believe me that it wasn't an easy theory to accept." Rachel swallowed. Should she tell him how Adam died? He refused to believe her before, so what was the point? "Let's walk."

Caesar bounded ahead through the trees. Captain Lewis slowed his pace to match hers. Rachel felt better with each step, but so tired. *As soon as I get home I'm falling into bed for three days straight.*

"I'll listen."

"What?" Rachel turned to look at him in surprise.

"In a few minutes we'll never see each other again. Go ahead and lay your theory on me. I won't interrupt."

"My theory," she said. "The firestorm released a tremendous amount of energy. That energy can be harnessed in ways never imagined, or at least not by modern society, so it looks like magic. Instead of being curious, New Babylon dictates—black and white—that anything nonhuman is a mutation. And then wants to destroy it."

He shook his head. "That's not what New Babylon is about. We're building a successful civilization." He held up his hand and ticked off the list. "You need competition, science, the right to property, modern medicine, consumerism, and a dedicated work ethic."

She sighed. "Maybe that's what New Babylon thinks human society needs, but we aren't the only ones on Earth anymore. Ancient beings called Nephilim—half-gods—were here and now they're back. They manipulate *etemmu*. They're creating individual territories, forming a chessboard for war." Pieces of information spun in her mind as they walked, but Rachel needed time to think. She wanted to sit down with chalk and paper and sort it out until she could see the pattern.

Captain Lewis scoffed. "Come on. This isn't a religious thing. It's about the human race surviving a natural disaster."

"New Babylon is a military regime full of harsh judgments. The only thing I've seen is their leader's drive to get everyone exactly alike and kill anything or anyone that is different."

She watched his jaw clench. "And, since we're being honest, I know why you're walking me home. Why you're so grateful."

"I'm repaying—"

"Whatever." Rachel stopped walking and shook a finger in his face. "You're repaying the fact that your beloved Consularis Sharma would have killed you on sight if you'd shown up with that black-moose-mutation crap on your face. That's why you were so relieved to be healed. So you can go home, too."

"You're blaming me for being happy to be healed?"

Rachel's shoulders slumped in exasperation. "No. And I hope you're not blaming me for being happy that you killed the two-headed moose mutation. I'm not claiming all changes are good or all changes are bad because I've seen both since I left Hiraeth. What I am claiming is that the changes aren't random, just because we don't understand." Her stomach clenched. By her logic, the rats weren't random. Waking up to hoofbeats. The tank. The energy vultures. "Why did the rats attack us?"

"Because they're mutants." He made a face like he thought she was stupid.

"So, you acknowledge that something weird is going on?"

"Yes, there are mutations in plants and animals."

She pointed to his face. "This wasn't a virus, Captain Lewis. You know that."

The moment stretched. "Yes," he admitted.

"You became a mutation." Rachel pressed. "*Etemmu* is a real thing. Mr. Lee, that man with the whip, was collecting it. Did you see the blue lightning?"

"Yes." It was a whisper.

"I think the rats were sent to kill us for a very specific reason." Rachel swallowed. "The Consularis hates me. And you'd been infected with an imbalance of *etemmu*. And Adam, well, Adam is special. We were bait. All of us would die, the energy vultures would come." She swallowed. How would the rats collect their *etemmu*? Was Mr. Lee nearby?

Rachel faced Captain Lewis. "There weren't any jars. There didn't have to be. Because Ba'al was right there. That's what woke me up before the attack." Rachel ran a hand through her auburn hair. Yes, there had been a definite plan. She remembered Tamaki's story about the New Babylon soldiers who'd come to her hometown. How they'd responded to her refusal to join them by saying, "You'll be food for the Bull." She'd been thinking that Ba'al and New Babylon and Mr. Lee were all separate threats, but they weren't. Could Consularis Sharma really be that much of a hypocrite? To work for a god while denouncing mutations? Rachel shivered. She'd seen his true face at her table. He was a monster hiding in plain sight. "Other people know about Ba'al too. I'm not making this up." Rachel reached forward to tap his chest. "But here's the kicker. Your beloved consularis didn't care if you died."

Color rushed into Captain's Lewis's cheeks. "I'm the consularis' second. Hell, I'm engaged to his daughter."

Caesar stopped walking and pricked up his ears. Soon Rachel could hear it too. Something was running toward them. She reached for her knife.

"Hey guys," Adam said, bursting through the trees. He grinned. "You're taking forever." Dido stood by Adam's knee with her pink tongue hanging out. "Come on. There's this old guy waiting at our house. He says slugs could walk faster than you."

Rachel frowned. She only knew of only one old man in the area who talked like that. It wouldn't do to keep him waiting. "You heard my son. Let's go, Captain."

As they crossed the clearing, Rachel saw Scott's backpack hanging from a tree. "Tamaki?" Rachel said. She looked around as if she might see the Asian girl. "Go ahead," she said to the captain, "I'll be right there."

When he was farther up the path, Rachel unzipped the backpack and pulled out the letter stuffed in. Written on a torn out piece of Rachel's sketchbook was a message from Tamaki: *Something happened and I have to leave. Thank you for taking care of me. I owe you so much, but I need one more favor. Please take care of what's in here until we see each other again. WHATEVER YOU DO, DON'T TRUST NEW BABYLON.*

Tamaki had left. Sadness swept through Rachel and she leaned against Scott's tree. It felt like every time she started to make a home, it was disrupted. Rachel reached into the backpack and her hand touched something smooth. *What could make Tamaki leave Saki? And how long has the poor turtle-penguin been in here with no food?* She pulled the smooth object out. "Ohhh," Rachel breathed, realizing that what she'd thought was the turtle shell was an egg the size of a softball. "Saki's a mom." She cradled the egg close to her heart. Tamaki had taken Saki as a companion, but left the special egg for safekeeping.

"Are you coming?" Captain Lewis asked. He'd returned along the path and was tapping his foot.

"Yes." Rachel hid the egg back in the backpack and zipped it shut before slinging it over her shoulder.

They hurried up the worn, familiar path to the house, Rachel edging in front.

The front door swung open. The Weatherman stood there—finger pointing right at them. "Oh no. Not him."

FIFTY-ONE

The Weatherman looked past Rachel to Captain Lewis. Sunglasses shielded the old man's eyes, but silver and green swirled in his aura. *This isn't good.* He took off the sunglasses and his eyes glowed the same silver and green swirls. *Now it's worse.* When Rachel looked away from The Weatherman, she saw the outline of four other arms coming from his torso. It was disconcerting and explained why he hunched over. She tried closing one eye to see better.

He shook his finger and his voice lowered. "You. How dare you come back into my territory."

Adam skipped around the corner of the house, followed by Dido.

The Weatherman sucked on his teeth. "I should kill you now and send your body back to New Babylon."

Adam stepped forward. "You can't do that! Who do you think you are?"

"He's The Weatherman," Rachel said. "Also known as An, the god of this territory."

"Oh, from the radio." Adam seemed unfazed by the description. "Captain Lewis saved us from Mr. Lee and from the giant rats that attacked us. He's okay. He's a friend."

"He's not, Adam." The Weatherman shook his head. "He murdered Scott, put an arrow straight into him."

Adam looked at Captain Lewis with hero-worship dissolving in his eyes. "No, you didn't." He stepped forward toward the archer. "Tell him you didn't." Adam's voice cracked on the last word.

Captain Lewis raised his chin and pressed his lips together.

Adam took another step forward. "Why won't you say anything?"

Rachel felt the tightening that signals tears. Watching the dawning pain on her son's face, the realization. She was helpless during this last moment of his childhood.

Adam's fists clenched. He began to glow, his whole body shaking with emotion, his mouth open in a silent scream that mothers hate, a signal from children that real pain, real trauma has happened, the sound lagging behind.

Afraid of how the power inside Adam would manifest, Rachel sprinted across the yard.

"Enough. Stop it right now." She threw her arms around Adam's glowing body and felt the burn on her face, her neck, her arms, but she didn't let go. Abruptly the heat disappeared and Adam sagged against her, his head bent, his breath a harsh sucking sound. They crumpled to the ground, her arms still around him.

"He saw us safely back to Hiraeth." Rachel said to The Weatherman. "That was the deal."

"I didn't agree to any deal."

Adam's breathing returned to normal and Rachel removed her arms, staying on the ground next to him. There was no mark on her skin from his heat. She wondered again how much control Adam had. "I know you didn't, Weatherman." Rachel focused her eyes on the creature's aura. "But I also know that you aren't a murderer, that killing him won't bring Scott back."

The Weatherman laughed. "You don't know very much about gods, girl. This is my territory and I'll do what I want." He walked down the stairs from the porch, holding onto the rail with one of his many hands, his back hunched over and his white beard stuck out in all directions. He passed Rachel and stalked up to Captain Lewis.

Captain Lewis straightened his shoulders. "Be careful, old man. I don't want to hurt you. I'm a professional soldier."

"Oh, I'm so scared," The Weatherman shouted. "I'm quaking like a leaf, like a leaf in a tree being shaken by a gorilla in an earthquake." He switched to a falsetto voice, "Help. He's going to hurt me with his tiny little zinging toothpicks." With a grunt, The Weatherman seized Captain Lewis by the arm and by the shirt. Captain Lewis's feet left the ground.

The sky overhead turned dark gray. A yellow light shined through the cloud cover. Not sun. More like a giant helicopter searching for something on the ground. The rumbling came closer.

The Weatherman set Captain Lewis down. "Well. That complicates things, doesn't it? You're safe from me." The Weatherman grimaced. "For the moment."

But Adam, feeling the full force of betrayal, pulled himself from a heap on the ground and flew the remaining distance between himself and the captain. He pummeled the man with all the strength in his eleven-year-old fists, but there was no fire this time. Captain Lewis didn't fight back. Caesar stood nearby, ears pricked forward with what Rachel could swear was a quizzical look on his canine face.

Adam took a step back, breathing hard, one hand on his heart. "It wasn't right," he gasped out. "It wasn't right what you did to my friend."

Captain Lewis swallowed and straightened his shoulders, his gaze going over Adam's head as if he stood before a judge.

The whole house began to shake. Rachel's senses were heightened by the energy in whatever storm was coming so that she felt overwhelmed, drunk even. She placed the backpack with the penguin-turtle egg under the porch swing so her hands were free for whatever was about to happen.

"Are you making a storm?" Rachel looked up. "Because you're angry?"

"That's not me." The Weatherman shook his head. "We've got minutes at the most. No time to let the man run home."

"Minutes to what?" she asked as if she didn't know. As if by escaping the rats they'd escaped the bull.

The Weatherman looked up. "Ba'al. He and I will fight for this square. He's been stockpiling *etemmu*. Meanwhile, my two followers that I so graciously allowed to come into my territory and live here—that's you in case you don't understand—have defected, so I've got nothing. Needless to say, I'm starting on the defensive. Let him wear himself out and then I'll boot him."

"What can I do?"

"You humans are containers of *etemmu*. We draw on your belief, on your emotions. He will bring whichever humans he controls. If we lose, you will be consumed. Do not feed Ba'al. Understand?"

It was so loud. Rachel covered her ears, but it didn't stop the vibrations all around, like being trapped beside the speakers at a rock concert.

This was a battle between gods.

"Mom," Adam said. He turned his body back and forth, looking at the sky and into the forest. "I feel tingly."

The archer faced the woods and unslung his crossbow. "There's a mutation coming?" Both of the wolves looked up into the sky.

"Yeah," Rachel said. "You could say that." *Understatement of the year.*

Overhead, the clouds parted. Sickening yellow light poured down. The sound was overpowering, the vibrations pushing against her body, making the air so thick it was hard to breathe. The light pulsed stronger. And finally it arrived. The Golden Bull, Ba'al, charged through the sky and landed on the ground in front of Hiraeth.

In the sudden silence, Rachel drank in the sight of the monster. The bull was close to twenty feet high at his shoulder, completely golden with an aura that surged in sunbursts over its body. Two horns with sharpened tips, cloven hooves licked by fluctuating golden flames. There was no doubt that the bull was completely intact, a fertile animal worthy of being worshiped by an agrarian society.

Ba'al lowered his head, dug his front paw twice against the ground. Captain Lewis shot an arrow, but the bull raised his snout and snuffed, his breath burning the arrow to ash while still in the air.

The bull charged. Rachel leaped forward shielding Adam with her body while Captain Lewis loosed arrow after arrow. There was another sound, one that Rachel hadn't realized she'd heard until motorcycles crashed through the underbrush, bursting into the yard. Jeremiad and the motorcycle gang had arrived. Flamethrowers out. Only, Rachel noted, there were four gang members instead of three, circling the giant bull, distracting the creature.

"Here we go," Rachel said, her eyes on the bull, pulling her knife out.

Jeremiad drove up to the steps, pushed up his visor. "Rachel, my friend, we meet again."

"Yeah, um, last time I saw you was in a burning building," Rachel said, giddy with happiness to see him alive.

"Ha," Jeremiad laughed in his rich tone. "I'm hard to kill."

"Well, we found your Golden Bull. Question is, what do we do with him?"

Captain Lewis bounded over to the steps; his knife out. "My arrows aren't having an effect. Adam, you and your mom get in the house."

They both ignored him.

To Rachel, Jeremiad said, "We can't let him get away again, but Elijah needs time. Ba'al gets stronger the longer he feeds."

"I know—that's what The Weatherman said." Rachel gestured in front of the porch to where the old man stood, two hands on his hips. "Nammu said Ba'al wasn't very smart. Listen, you guys circle around him, keep him distracted so he can't pull on the *etemmu* from the river, until Elijah is ready."

"Like in an old Western?" Jeremiad chuckled, but then shrugged a shoulder. "Circle up," he called. Giving her a nod, Jeremiad reversed to join the riders.

Rachel locked gazes with Captain Lewis. "We're going to do our best impression of cowboys and corral Ba'al."

"You need to get inside," Captain Lewis said. "We'll handle this."

She shook her head. "Hiraeth is my refuge, my vision, and my home. I'm not hiding inside."

The riders on the motorcycles had slowed down, points on a compass with the bull in the middle. Rachel recognized Elijah's ride with the orange flames painted on black. He parked and knelt on the ground. The bull reared and charged, trying to break the circle. Captain Lewis and Rachel ran to join in. The bull ran against one of the gang members, difficult to tell who because he was still wearing a motorcycle helmet. The man aimed his flamethrower and pulled the trigger. Rachel hadn't known what to expect; it seemed to her that the Golden Bull was already on fire, but he reacted, backing away and tossing his head, bellowing in pain. *This isn't so bad*, Rachel thought. *Just stand in a circle until Elijah finishes up praying over there.*

Then the monkeymen came out of the forest. Like the zombie crabs, they must have felt or sensed the Golden Bull and come to help attack. Rachel recognized the poop-thrower in the lead. If anything, he looked even more like a primate than before. The couple who'd stolen her SUV were there too, as well as three of their friends.

"Hold the circle," Jeremiad called out. But the monkeymen attacked the fighters, pulling them away from their position.

"I need a tire iron." Rachel said out loud.

"You've got a knife," Adam said. He'd appeared at her elbow holding the fire poker.

"Don't even think about it, Adam. Remember what happened to Dido with the rats?"

"We're fighting for our lives. I'm not hiding."

Then one of the monkeys jumped from the porch rail onto Rachel's back. She spun around, shoving her back against the side of the house. It squealed in her ear at the impact.

"Uck," she said, "You are so gross."

Adam waved his poker, striking at a hissing monkeywoman, who retreated to a safe distance. Pride fought with fear as she watched her son.

She tightened her grip on the hilt of the knife. This close to the ley line in the river, Rachel's senses filled with the previous owner's fighting skill. She jerked the blade up and into the monkeyman's arm. It let go and Rachel spun around, plunging the knife into its middle. The creature collapsed, a puff of black smoke exhaled into the air. Rachel stared. She'd killed. These creatures were soulless, already belonged to Ba'al, but they'd been human once and that was different than killing the rats.

Adam gave her a thumb's up from his position next to her on the porch, perhaps already desensitized by the fight with the rats, maybe by the god's heart inside his chest. Either way, he was coping with the violence and taking care of himself. Across the yard, Captain Lewis slit the throat of a monkeyman. The body fell to the ground.

Rachel stepped forward and then the poop-thrower was right in front of her. He jabbed her in the stomach and she doubled over, dropping her knife. He leaped on her and knocked her to the ground, with him on top. She felt him pulling, scrabbling at her clothes. She beat at him with her fists, but it made no impression. Monkey stench filled her nostrils and his hands were on her breasts.

"Get off me!" she screamed. Rachel covered her face and bucked her hips as hard as she could. She felt the creature's weight shift off-center and she used the momentum to roll on top of him. Her knife lay off to the right and she stretched toward it, fingernails digging into the dirt to get closer. Her left hand pushed down on his chest as she felt him trying to wiggle away. Finally, she grasped the knife in her right hand. With one smooth motion she thrust the knife sideways into the monkeyman's ribs. She twisted. Blood spurted out of his nose and mouth. *His lung. I hit his lung.* He convulsed and his eyes rolled up into his head.

Rachel climbed to her feet, wiping the blade on her pants, and fingered the ragged edges of her shirt. She turned around in time to see Adam strike a monkeyman with the fire poker. There was no blood, but the poker glowed white hot. The metal had sliced right through the beast's shoulder down to his chest. Adam blew like he was making a birthday wish and the monkeyman exploded into white snowflakes.

"How?" Rachel cleared her throat. "What did you do?"

"I don't know," Adam said. He shook his head. "I felt this heat leaving my body and then the poker started glowing."

"Nice," called The Weatherman. "I like it." He was leaning against the porch like he was watching a movie.

"Hey, Switzerland," Rachel called. "Did you want to help us? Maybe 'boot' some of these invaders?"

The Weatherman's face darkened and Rachel wondered if she'd been too glib with a god.

"Please," she added, putting her hands together in a prayer position and batting her eyes.

He snickered and then he pulled on the brim of an imaginary hat. "Yes, ma'am." The Weatherman pointed a finger at the last monkeywoman hiding at the edge of the forest and the creature turned to ash. He blew on the tip of his finger as if it were a gun. "Boy, get over here and help me."

Adam dashed across the clearing to stand next to the wild-haired god. An showed Adam how to row his hands. Rachel didn't know how her son interpreted the movements, but she could see his fingers combing energy strings, gathering them for An's bundle.

"Thank you," she said. She turned her attention to the motorcycle gang and Ba'al.

Elijah was still on his knees and the motorcycle gang kept the Golden Bull encircled. Elijah stood up and put out his right hand. He spoke in a foreign language, sounding as if he were reading some type of command or a list. "El Shaddai. El-Elyon. Adonai. Yahweh. Jehovah-Nissi. Jehovah-Raah. Jehovah-Rapha."

The cloud cover above Hiraeth began to break up. For the first time since the firestorm rained down, blue sky showed through, beautiful and clean.

Elijah continued, "Jehovah-Shammah. Jehovah-Tsidkenu. Jehovah-Mekoddishkem. El Olam. Elohim."

The Weatherman cackled with mirth. "Didn't expect to see him, did you Ba'al? Picked the wrong side again, you stupid cow."

A red circle formed in the air around Ba'al. Elijah stood with his hands raised up, his eyes closed. His aura was a golden color flecked with myriad rainbow sparkles, unlike anything Rachel had ever seen, even at the Bathhouse.

The Golden Bull knelt down on his knees, lowered his head. The flames went out around his hocks; instead, black energy flowed like diseased blood, lightening to gray and then white as it moved across the yard to join the growing ball hovering in the air in front of An.

Rachel was so busy watching the energy flow that she almost missed Mr. Lee. He stood at the northwest edge of the forest, where the wild woods grew and the carnivorous fungi thrived.

"Master, a gift for you." He opened his coat and pulled out jars, ripping off the lids. Blue energy flickered across the clearing, moving through the red ring.

"No!" screamed Rachel. "He's feeding Ba'al the *etemmu* he's collected!"

No one in the circle seemed to hear her, intent on watching the god's death.

Ba'al inhaled the blue energy.

Captain Lewis shouted, "What's going on? Why is that thing getting up again?"

The Golden Bull climbed to his feet, gathering his hindquarters under him. Revitalized, he swung his heavy head toward Elijah, impaling the man through the stomach.

Gray clouds moved back to cover the sun.

Rachel stood in shock. Everything seemed to slow down as the Golden Bull shook his head: Elijah sliding off the horn, mouth opened in a silent scream like the Edvard Munch painting, falling to the ground, hands pressed to the giant hole ripped in his torso. Jeremiad's mouth hanging open. An holding a ball of energy that was being sucked back by Ba'al. Adam staring at the Golden Bull with fear on his face, realizing that he could be next.

Trembling, Rachel took a tiny step toward Adam. They had to get out of here. Without Elijah, they couldn't win. They'd all be sacrificed to Ba'al. Mr. Lee, she didn't have to be told, would make each death as painful as possible.

From across the clearing, An snapped, "Woman! This is your moment."

Rachel shook her head. She whispered, "I can't. I can't do it." She was exhausted, had used up everything on Dido after the rat attack, had failed the last time she'd tried to heal in front of an audience. She couldn't leave Adam to be murdered while she went into a healing trance. Elijah had a mortal wound. She couldn't do it.

"You're a god," she cried to An. "Can't you fix him? Fix this all?"

"I don't heal," An said through his teeth. He and Ba'al were psychically wrestling with the ball of *etemmu*. "That's what you do."

Rachel closed her eyes, afraid. She couldn't make herself step forward.

A flash of pain on her right wrist was the only warning she had before the whip wrapped around her left arm, squeezing like a tourniquet.

FIFTY-TWO

Mr. Lee's voice echoed inside her head. *You are so scared, but no one notices. Because you are of no consequence. You don't matter and you never have.*

It was true, so true. His words were inside her and she fell to her knees because she could not fight them. *You couldn't save your son. You couldn't save your marriage. You abandoned your life's dream.*

Mr. Lee's mocking laughter filled her mind.

Rachel curled into herself on the ground, pulled her knees to her chest.

Worship Ba'al, Mr. Lee whispered. *And you can have another chance. Go back to where you gave up your dreams and do it differently.*

She was at the hospital, sitting in a familiar hallway waiting for news about her parents after the car accident. *This is where you gave up your dreams,* Mr. Lee whispered. *Walk away from your burden of family. Walk away from all the planning, all the struggles, all the worry and you can draw all day long, more alive in your imagination than you ever were tending to everyone else. Walk away and you'll never experience failure again.*

Rachel felt part of her melt at the chance to go back in time to when nothing depended on her, but she shook her head. She would not turn into a monkeywoman, a mad shell of a human.

The hospital corridor melted, grew impossibly long. No doors. No turns. Buzzing fluorescent lights overhead. At the far end of the hallway, the lights flicked out. The darkness was coming. Rachel pushed against the white walls, but they wouldn't give. She began to run down the hallway, away from the dark.

"Hurry, Rachel." Mr. Lee stood at the end of the hallway. "I'll give you a new life as the artist you've always wanted to be." He snapped his fingers and Rachel, twenty-year-old Rachel stood beside him. Her hair was cut fashionably short, bangs swept to one side. A silver cuff on her right ear and a sketchpad under her arm. Shy smile and innocent eyes.

Rachel held her cramping side, slowing to a walk.

"Take my offer," Mr. Lee called. "You know you aren't strong enough. You certainly aren't smart enough. You are no use to anyone. You are not worthy of being loved. Your only use is being fodder for Ba'al."

He'd chosen her because she was the weak link in the team. Her pride stung, and Rachel gathered herself. *He cannot defeat me. Only I can defeat myself, by believing him.* Feeling as if she stood on the edge of a precipice. Rachel stood up straight and spread her arms to fly. A feeling of peace filled her. Whether she was able to heal Elijah or not, she chose to try. Her healing was an extension of who she was, a powerful extension.

Rachel clenched her fists and moved through her memories, grabbing onto the moments that she'd saved Scott from the fallen tree, carried Adam's body up to the Bathhouse, healed Captain Lewis. She was not a weak link. Rachel psychically reached for a connection with the nearby ley line in the river. "Yes, I wanted to be an artist, but I've become a warrior."

Surprise flickered across Mr. Lee's face.

She heard the darkness coming behind her, the snick of the lights trying to scare her.

"You're right that I'm not strong enough . . . alone. My family—birth, adopted, and found—they are my greatest strength."

Rachel put her hand on the walls meant to be a mental cage. She imagined lines of energy and plunged her hands into the space between the lines. The walls shimmered. Rachel yanked her hands apart, ripping a hole in the wall. She stepped through as the last light went out.

"Mom, open your eyes. Mom you're scaring me."

Adam. It was Adam.

"Mom, I need you. You said you'd fight for me. I'm fighting for you."

Adam leaned over her, cheeks blotchy and tears falling from his red-rimmed eyes. He wiped snot away with the back of his hand and wrapped his arms around her and Rachel held on.

I am loved, she thought. *Imperfect and messing up all the time, I am loved. And it is enough.*

"I'm sorry I scared you. I scared me too." With Adam's help, Rachel stood and unwrapped the whip from around her arm. She felt shaky, as if she'd been gone a long time. "But, it's over." And though she didn't yell, Rachel knew Mr. Lee heard because she saw the blood drain from his face.

"I don't think so," Mr. Lee said.

"I'll make it so." Captain Lewis said, striding toward the woods.

"How not very nice to see you again," Mr. Lee said as he walked forward, coiling the whip as he did.

"Indeed," said Captain Lewis. "Do you choose to submit and come with me as a prisoner of New Babylon?"

Mr. Lee scoffed. "I don't think so, archer." With a flick of his wrist, Mr. Lee sent the whip lashing out. Captain Lewis lunged forward and caught the whip in one hand, hacking at it with the knife in his other hand. The two men raced at each other, grappling and falling to the ground. Captain Lewis straddled the man and punched him in the face. Blood gushed from a broken nose. Mr. Lee tried to wrap the whip around Captain Lewis's neck, but couldn't reach.

"Help me to Elijah." Rachel turned away from the fighters at the northern woods and leaned on Adam to walk toward the clearing of Hiraeth. The motorcycle gang had gathered in an outward-facing circle around their friend, their flamethrowers pointed at the Golden Bull. The ball of *etemmu* hovered in the air. If he inhaled it, he would kill everyone. Ba'al leaped forward.

An's arms shook with effort.

"Chase the bull again," Rachel said, strangely calm. "Distract him now or he'll be too strong for us to fight."

Immediately Jeremiad surged forward with his flamethrower and Ba'al bellowed in surprise. Rachel straightened Elijah's body, feeling detached as she looked at the gaping wound. She closed her eyes and reached out to the energy in the clearing. She plunged her hands into the bloody mess, not using her own energy as she'd done with Dido, but becoming a vessel for the flood of *etemmu*. Rachel prayed to Elijah's god, El-Elyon, knowing he would answer for his prophet. Unlike the previous healings, Rachel had the sensation of trying to navigate a flood rather than being in control. She barely had time to pull her hands away as the flesh knit across his midsection, even his clothing stitching itself closed.

Rachel rocked back on her heels. Noise from the woods made her look.

Both Captain Lewis and Mr. Lee were on their feet, swaying from exhaustion. Mr. Lee's eye was swollen shut, his nose still bleeding. Captain Lewis had a mark around his neck like he'd been strangled with the whip. Lowering his shoulder, Mr. Lee charged into Captain Lewis, who grunted as he held onto the man, dragging them both to the ground.

Next to her, Elijah stood and began chanting again, full of renewed energy. The Golden Bull shook his massive head and let out a thunderous bellow, saliva dripping from its mouth. He took one step back, and then retreated another step. The motorcycle gang cheered.

The bull god gathered his massive haunches and pushed off the ground and into the sky.

"Hold him!" yelled An. "He's getting away."

"No!" Mr. Lee screamed. He scrambled to his feet and ran toward the charred spot where the bull had launched, ripping open his shirt to expose the burn scar on his chest. "I call upon the power of Ba'al. Take me with you."

"Ba'al's gone," Captain Lewis said. He'd put away his knife and nocked an arrow from his quiver. Assuming the readied stance, he pulled the string back to his ear. "Last chance to surrender."

"I call upon Marduk for deliverance," Mr. Lee searched the cloud-covered sky, his arms raised and fingers tensed so that tendons raised out from his arms.

"He's not allowed here." An opened his mouth and inhaled the giant ball of energy that had been hovering in front of him. He whipped off his sunglasses so that his otherworldy eyes glowed with silver and green swirls. Then, his body began to grow until he stood twenty feet tall, his six arms visible to all. "And neither are you."

An raised up his mountainous foot and stomped on Mr. Lee. When he removed his foot, there was only a pile of brown dust. He stepped back and raised his top two arms. Wind swept through like a dervish. Brown ashes rose in a mini-tornado and ascended toward the clouds.

An put his sunglasses back on and began to shrink back to human size. As he did, he opened his mouth and the white ball of energy came flying back out, hovering in the air.

"Rachel-girl, this *etemmu* is attracted to the ley lines and I can't hold it much longer. Quick, name your favorite fruits."

"Umm. Lemon? Strawberry? Apple?"

The ball of energy escaped An, speeding around the clearing like a released balloon trailing random strings of light. Rachel didn't know what everyone else saw, but for her, white energy strings wrapped the trees around Hiraeth and were absorbed into the vegetation, moving inside like a blood transfusion. The trees grew a foot, branches unfolded, leaves exploded from bare branches, suddenly vibrating with color. In other places the strings broke into small dots that flittered around the area evolving into what looked like lightning bugs.

An's six arms moved through the air, bouncing the strings back from the ley line. Rachel turned her head when Adam gasped. Their garden sprouted in a symphony of color. Yellow squash popped out from buds like popcorn. The smell of rich loam filled their nostrils. Green pumpkin vines climbed the wire cage. Wild red strawberries grew in a patch that looked like pampered specimens from a green house. As the *etemmu* soaked into the plants, Rachel felt the keenness of her senses begin to dull. She blinked in relief.

Then, one last particularly long string of *etemmu* seemed to plant itself at the corner of the house, growing into a glowing, three-dimensional tree trunk, expanding upwards into branches and a beautiful crown of glowing leaves. Round shapes descended. The glow faded and resolved into an ash-gray trunk, brilliant green leaves, and yellow lemons on the bottom branches. Small suns. Green apples with pink-red stripes grew on the middle branches and red apples grew on the upper branches. Citrus perfume wafted on a cleansing breeze.

FIFTY-THREE

The motorcycle gang, helmets off, clustered around Elijah. Captain Lewis cleaned his knife by the river, the two wolves panting at his feet.

Jeremiad waved her over. The dark-skinned warrior rolled his shoulders "So this is your modern day Garden of Eden, huh?"

"Garden of Hiraeth," Rachel corrected with a smile. Then she did a double take as she recognized the fourth rider. "You're the guy from Drossville. I thought you were dead!"

The youth, the one who'd warned her about the milk, nodded and moved closer to Jeremiad.

"Tyrez is one of us now," Jeremiad said.

"Complete with his own flamethrower," Rachel mused.

Levi and Jeremiad looked over her shoulder. Rachel turned around to see that Captain Lewis had joined their group. Dido and Caesar shoved in so that Rachel had to move to the side.

Dropping her hand down, Rachel rubbed along Caesar's back. "I can't believe I was afraid of this big baby."

Captain Lewis pointed at the charred spot on the ground. "Can someone tell me exactly what happened?"

Levi said, "The Golden Bull is also called Ba'al. He is a very strong and very old god."

"Nephilim," Rachel said. "In our stories, a cross between an angel and a mortal."

"Yes," Levi agreed.

"And . . . he got away." Captain Lewis's tone suggested that he wasn't sure.

Jeremiad gave out a war whoop. "He's hurt and he's on the run. Let the chase begin." Jeremiad revved his engine and the smell of gasoline filled the air.

They all grinned at his exuberance.

"Although," Levi said, "for a moment I was worried about you being turned." Levi reached out to touch Rachel. "I don't know what they promised, but I know you must have been very strong to walk away from it."

"It wasn't so much being strong as realizing the lie."

"Clever lies. That's their modus operandi."

Rachel laughed. "Shouldn't you be using a Hebrew phrase instead of Latin?"

He wrinkled his nose at her. "Equal opportunity linguist."

"Wait a minute," Captain Lewis interrupted. "You're saying that these mutations are gods and that there are more of them?"

Jeremiad nodded. "This is war, son."

Rachel put her hand over her mouth. She couldn't imagine anyone besides Jeremiad, or maybe Consularis Sharma, getting away with calling Captain Lewis 'son.'

"I have to report what's happened here with these gods and mutations." He stepped closer to the charred spot and nudged the burnt area with his foot. "And his prophet was Mr. Lee, the man with the whip and the bull scar across his chest." Captain Lewis looked like he was getting all of his notes in order. "Too bad we have nothing from either the bull or Mr. Lee to validate our information."

Jeremiad snickered. "I think I'd enjoy reading your report."

Captain Lewis's gaze dropped to Jeremiad's lower body and then flicked back up. He opened his mouth to say something, but seemed to change his mind as he looked at the charred spot on the ground. Rachel wondered if being on the same side as Jeremiad—a dreaded mutation—was challenging the captain's belief system.

"Do you really have to leave now or do you want to stay here overnight and rest?" Rachel looked at Jeremiad, but it was Elijah who decided.

Elijah spoke to Levi. The young man nodded. "I'm sorry. We appreciate the invitation, but we've got to roll. Darkness doesn't rest."

"Oh," Rachel looked around at the bountiful garden. "What can I send with you?"

"We're good. Ravens will bring us whatever we need." Levi winked at her and Rachel didn't know if he was joking or not.

Suddenly Elijah reached out a hand to Rachel. His flesh felt dry, like parchment. He looked into her eyes as he spoke. Levi translated. "You've been very brave and have a good heart. Go into your house and bring out a pitcher."

Surprised, Rachel walked into the cool darkness of her house. "A pitcher. . . ." she murmured as she wandered the rooms. The image in her head was a clay pot and she didn't have anything like that until she saw a decorative vase on an end table. It stood about two feet high and held several branches of dried pussy willows. Delicate white herons were in flight while koi fish swam in the ocean below. She'd bought it at a flea market years ago. Taking out the branches with her right hand, Rachel went back outside and handed the vase to Elijah.

Levi translated again. "Elijah would like to offer a gift as a symbol of ongoing friendship."

"Okay?" Not sure what was going on, Rachel shifted her gaze from Elijah to Levi. To the side Jeremiad revved with impatience again.

Elijah handed the vase back to her. Rachel almost dropped it because the container was so heavy.

"No way," she whispered. It couldn't be. She set it on the ground and cupped her hand into liquid which had not been there. The water tasted cool and clean, like one imagined water to be instead of the actual thing.

"That . . . never . . . gets old!" Rachel shook her head in amazement. And then, before he could answer, Rachel became aware that she had nothing to offer in return. Frantic to reciprocate, she held out the dried pussy willow branches that were still in her right hand. "Here," she blurted to Elijah. "These are for you."

Inside she was dying of embarrassment at her poor gift, but Elijah seemed to like them. He climbed onto his black motorcycle with the orange flames painted on each side and stuck the ends of the willow branches in the edge of his bedroll so that they stuck up like a flag. The branches began to expand, becoming more numerous, as Elijah put on his helmet. They grew high and then abruptly took a right turn, creating a canopy of shade for the rider. Elijah gave a wave and the gang rode in a circle around the clearing before cutting through the trees toward the road. The Weatherman waved from the garden. He was chewing on a giant red strawberry.

Rachel grinned and shook her head. "I wouldn't believe it if I hadn't seen it. Ha, I still don't think I believe it."

Captain Lewis looked into the vase. "What is it?"

"I believe this is a pitcher of water that will never run out."

Adam overheard as he walked over. "So cool. Those guys are awesome. Did they leave me a flamethrower?"

"Um. No." She reached out to ruffle his hair. Adam ducked away and went towards The Weatherman so that Rachel was alone with Captain Lewis.

Rachel said, "Did you see the water come from nothing and the dead willow branches grow and the Golden Bull and Mr. Lee?"

"I saw, Rachel." Captain Lewis cleared his throat. "And I saw you stick up for me in front of The Weatherman."

Rachel licked her lips and looked away. "Yeah. My version of Pocahontas, right?"

"What is with you and your son and these lame jokes? Be serious. This is my life we're talking about."

"Okay," Rachel said. "Here's serious. I don't know if I can forgive you for killing Scott. But I do know that letting you die doesn't make it right." Rachel bit her lip. "And I think you should consider not going back to New Babylon. You've changed. Not just your eyes."

"Thank you for the advice, but my life is back in New Babylon. I'll take your message with me. There are evil mutations like giant bulls and lab rats, but I also fought beside a man attached to his motorcycle and a woman who healed me."

"I thought you said 'the virus went away.'"

"I've reconsidered." His lips twitched. "You know, the first time I saw you I thought you were such an entitled housewife."

"Gee, thanks," she said. "I thought you were an arrogant frat boy."

"So we're both wrong."

She used petting Dido as an excuse not to answer, uncaring whether he understood or not.

"I'd like to say goodbye to Adam."

Rachel lifted one shoulder and let it fall, but together they walked over to where he stood by the porch steps. The Weatherman sat on the other end of the steps, not even pretending he wasn't listening.

"Adam." Captain Lewis licked his lips. "I'm a soldier. I make snap decisions and I obey the chain of command. I understand that the man— who did steal from us—intended to share with you and your mother."

"Scott was my friend!" Heat rose in Adam's cheeks. Dido whined and moved next to his leg.

Captain Lewis raised his voice. "I'm trying to apologize. Friendly fire is a bad way to go."

Adam rubbed his arm, deciding what to do. "What's friendly fire," he finally asked.

Captain Lewis said, "It's when you make a mistake and one of the good guys dies because of it."

Adam's lips pressed together.

Captain Lewis looked at Rachel.

What does he want me to do? I can't make Adam forgive him. She inclined her head in what she hoped was a gracious manner. "Thank you for seeing us home, Captain. It's time for you to go."

The archer whistled to the wolves. He was halfway across the homestead's yard when he realized Dido wasn't with him. Whistling again, Captain Lewis patted his leg. Impatient, he called, "Dido, let's go."

The white wolf pricked her triangular ears forward. She whined.

"Dido." He sounded frustrated. Caesar looked up at the captain and then across at Dido.

Captain Lewis set his jaw. "Looks like she's going to stay here for a bit." He met Adam's gaze. "Take good care of her."

"Can we?" Adam asked Rachel. "Please."

Rachel nodded. "Got to build up our family again."

Adam dropped his hand to Dido's scruff. He said, "I'll take care of her. I promise."

Captain Lewis disappeared into the forest.

With a sigh of exhaustion Rachel sank onto a step so that Adam was on one side of her and The Weatherman was on the other.

His flyaway white beard poofed out everywhere and he used two hands to smooth it down. Another hand scratched at his back and a fourth was rubbing his left knee. "Ack." He sat back down with a groan. "Getting ancient sucks."

Rachel sighed. "Did you have this many arms last time and I just couldn't see them?"

"Ha, stupid girl! Arms are quite handy." The Weatherman looked at Adam. "Like that one, did you? Quite *hand*-y."

Adam groaned.

Rachel looked at the backpack under the swing. "Tamaki left."

"I know everything that happens in my territory."

A feeling of sadness twinged inside Rachel for missing friends. "Right." She sniffed. "An, I probably don't want to know, but what if I'd dipped Adam's arm in our ley line?"

"What is it you humans say, 'It's about the journey, not the destination?'"

"You tried to get us killed for nothing!" Rachel raised her voice in disbelief.

"A joke." He held up four hands in surrender. "Adam was dying. That's not a DIY project. You could have plunked him in the river, but then he might've come out with a new tail and still died. I couldn't heal him, you couldn't heal him. You needed Nammu." He jabbed toward her wrist with a bony finger. "Besides, got yourself a shiny new mark, didn't you? That's an uh-oh."

"Yup, Nammu sends her regards." Rachel sniffed. "You could have warned me."

He scratched his nose, perhaps embarrassed. "Honestly? I didn't think you'd actually make it to the Bathhouse."

"Another joke?"

"No. I'm impressed. You and Adam are a hell of a team."

"Thank you." She was so tired. Gesturing to the scorch mark, she said, "So what happens now?"

One hand came down on her shoulder and gave a surprisingly gentle squeeze. "It's like that genius prophet John Lennon said, 'Strawberry Fields Forever.' That's all any of us can do."

Adam scrunched up his mouth. "That doesn't really make sense. And, why do you keep quoting music from before any of us were born?"

"I'm catching up. And, it's certainly better than—"

Rachel tuned out their bickering. Instead, she reached for the backpack and unzipped it, pulling the egg onto her lap. Stroking the smooth surface, she let her mind wander. Images flashed through of Scott. Tamaki. Adam opening his eyes in the Bathhouse. As if in response, she felt an electric tingle in her wrist, reminder that this moment of peace was finite. Rachel pushed the thought away, concentrating instead on the warmth of Adam's shoulder on her lower leg, the old god's scratchy, familiar voice, and the bright buds of fruit growing on the impossible apple-lemon tree.

ACKNOWLEDGMENTS

This book would not exist without Jennifer Azantian, agent extraordinaire. She's brilliant and kind, confident and considerate. She also surrounds herself with wonderful people. Thank you to Masha Gunic, for believing in this novel and giving excellent notes, and Ben Baxter, who not only correctly guessed where Adam is headed (that boy has ambitions!), but also helped with behind-the-scenes work.

This book would also not exist without Beth Canova, editor extraordinaire. I loved reading her comments every revision because she made the story stronger. And, because I wanted to make her laugh. And cry. You'll have to ask her if I succeeded. Thank you to Jeff Chapman who created the cover for this novel. He captured everything I wanted, but better. Thanks for the dragon!

My family is my strongest support. My sister Tammy had faith enough for both of us. My husband helped me shrug off the rejections, celebrate acceptances, and somehow, covered the household chaos so I could attend writing workshops and conferences. My son gave me insight into Adam and my younger daughters declared they are using their allowance to buy a copy. Even my teenager admitted that she's somewhat proud of me.

Many thanks to the Baltimore Critique Circle who listened as I brought in my work, 2,500 words at a time. And many thanks to the Almost Famous Critique Group (especially those who don't normally read fantasy) for reading in chunks of thirty-nine and a half pages. I'm grateful to the authors who agreed to read advance copies and to Wendy S. Delmater, editor of *Abyss & Apex* magazine for publishing my first "real" story and for reviewing this book.

There's another group of people, though, who must be thanked. During my daughter's treatment at Johns Hopkins, I was continuously humbled by the doctors, therapists, and nurses who worked on the pediatric oncology ward. Brilliant men and women who work so hard, often sacrificing family time to save the lives of every child who comes onto the floor. I could fill pages with stories about how Dr. Nico and Nurse Lauren aggressively cared about our family. How nurses Hatel and Kristen on the in-patient side saved my sanity by playing football with my little girl in the hallway so I could have ten minutes to cry by myself. There are so many grace-filled stories that I can't name everyone, but please know that you are in my heart . . . and maybe in the next books.

In the United States only 4 percent of federal government cancer research funding goes to study pediatric cancer. Please know that a portion my profits from every copy of *Walking through Fire* sold will be donated to the Johns Hopkins Children's Fund.

Love,
Sherri